HEIRS OF A BROKEN LAND
BOOK 3

SORCERESS
OF
SHADOWS

MARIE BILODEAU

Cover by Deranged Doctor Design

Editing by Jessica Torrance

Map by Kerri Elizabeth Gerow

To Kerri Elizabeth Gerow,
for being a kick-ass BFF and redhead.

(And for being chaotic neutral, which is kind of shadowy.)

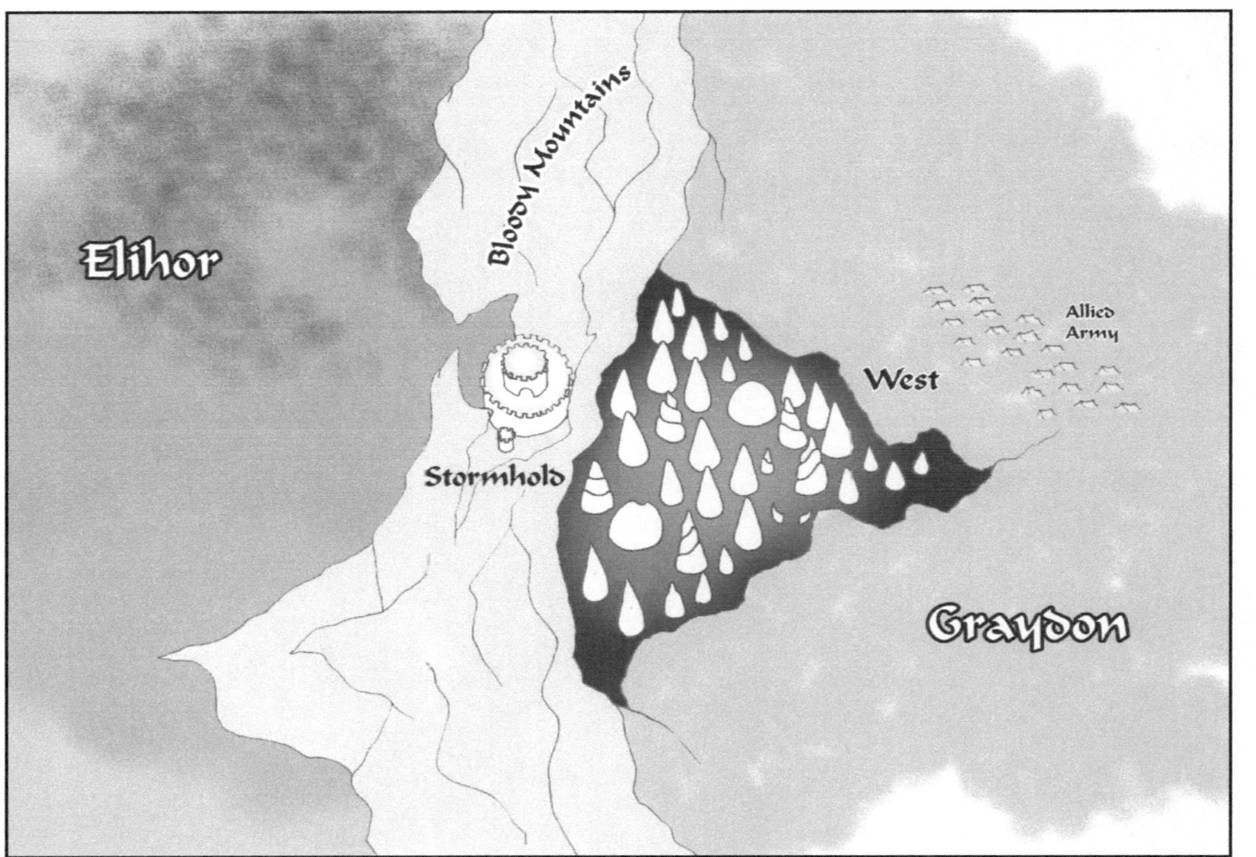

Elihor
Bloody Mountains
Stormhold
West
Allied Army
Graydon

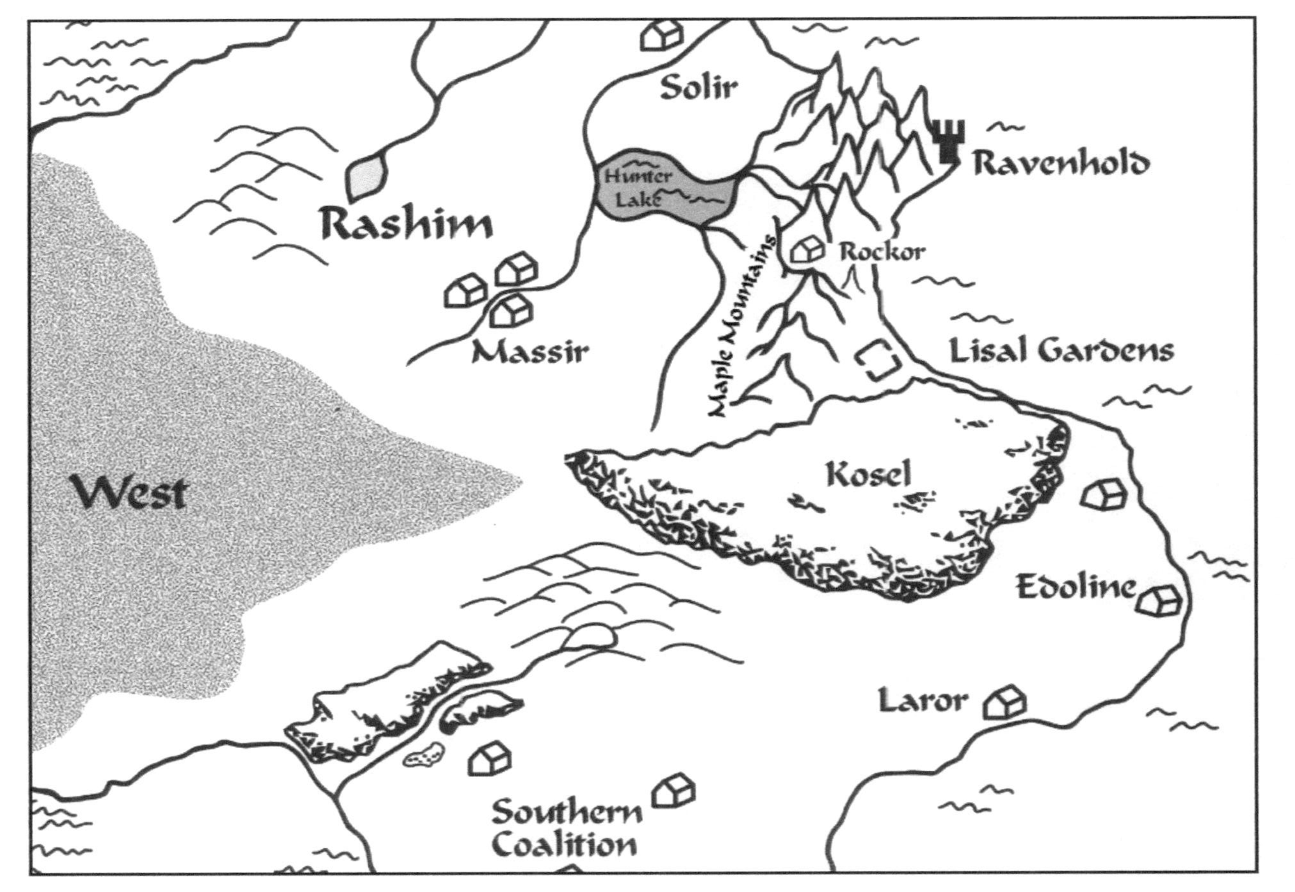
Solir
Ravenhold
Hunter Lake
Rashim
Rockor
Maple Mountains
Lisal Gardens
Massir
West
Kosel
Edoline
Laror
Southern Coalition

Ravenhold.

A thousand years ago, before the Wall of Loss was even formed, the keep was built to foster the magic of the land, a land whose unified name was now lost.

In all, three keeps were built.

Larkhold in the West, Ravenhold in the East, and Stormhold unifying them in the perfect center, nestled in a range of mountains.

Only a few years after their creation and the summoning of the first three Covenants, Graydon and Elihor, leaders of Ravenhold and Larkhold, failed each other and their magic by erecting the Wall of Loss.

No one in Circle history knew why, except that it involved the keeper of Stormhold, Siabala. Siabala, who had been convicted of crimes against magic so terrible that the Elders had banished him to a prison now known as Siabala's Rage.

With the rising of the Wall came the greatest loss of all: Ravenhold was cut off from the other two Covenants.

For years, and then centuries, the Circle attempted to make contact with the land now known as Elihor. But neither air, sea, land, nor the stars themselves could convey a message.

Until one day, a gifted Elder heard a simple message, telepathically passed through the weakening wall. It was more of an impression than words, but it was so strong that it had dictated Ravenhold's mission ever since.

Maintain the Wall of Loss, at all costs.

The darkness conveyed in what would happen should they fail proved so frightening that the Elder succumbed to her nightmares soon after receiving the vision.

Ever since, Ravenhold had vowed to maintain the Wall of Loss, sending magic into it when necessary, sacrificing the blood of adepts to cast stronger spells and, when their numbers began to dwindle, instituting harvests to gather those strong enough to uphold the sacred duty.

Shirina stood on the roof of the ancient keep, watching the Wall of Loss crumple in the distance. The backlash of magic traveling into Graydon was so strong, she could see it gathering towards her as an angry tide, and she wondered if all of their efforts had mattered at all.

Or if they had just led them to a more spectacular ending.

SHIRINA HAD NEVER FELT SO tired. Not even when first learning to wield the magic, forcing her mind to grasp invisible strings and her body to act as a conduit. Not even after draining the dark creatures of their magic to save Cassara and Avarielle, when she had thought they might make a difference in preserving the Wall of Loss.

She sighed and walked slowly down the softly lit halls of Ravenhold.

Sunlight filtered in through the windows, promising a warm and sunny day. The first day the lands of Elihor and Graydon stood once again united, as was their magic.

It should be raining, Shirina thought idly. She frowned. Her focus was off. She should be concerned with much more than the weather. The fate of the Circle, Ravenhold, and all of Graydon lay in the balance.

She took the stairs leading down, the clunking staff mimicking her steps. It was fast becoming a support not only for her magic, but for her body, as well.

She hated the dependence and wondered if she would ever be rid of her crutch. The magics of Elihor and Graydon were mixing and unsafe for any magic caster to wield spells.

The sproutlings she had saved would need to understand this. When they recovered from the teleportation spell and awoke again, she would explain it to them, and ensure they would not use their magic until it was safe to do so.

She reached the room with the great dead oak jutting in its center. Lights danced near its trunk, indicating where the old man now stood.

It was time to find out for whom Tangia had forfeited her freedom, and her life.

HE HAD CRAVED freedom for so long, his wish had turned into one for death. For it all to end, for sweet oblivion to claim him. For more than the constant darkness that had plagued Tangia's study for the past few months, the magic seal strong enough to keep even Ravenhold's magical lights at bay.

Yet, at the same time, he had wished for life more than ever. He hadn't wanted it to end that way: sealed in a dark room, no one ever knowing what had happened to him or why, his family left to grieve by an empty grave.

No, it wouldn't have been right. Not after the life he had led, one of adventure and boldness. He had crossed the Wall of Loss several times, through both straits and by Siabala's Rage itself. He had climbed the Bloody Mountains and even found Stormhold, long thought a myth. He had dared to confront Larkhold's Covenant when the Wall suffered attacks, and yet the Circle seemed to be doing nothing. Then his people began to vanish.

He stumbled forward, forcing his body to move as memories assaulted his mind. He squinted at the light, tears springing to his eyes, yet he refused to shade them with his hand. It was the light that stirred his past to life.

When he had crossed the Wall again, he had sought help for his people from Graydon's Covenant of Ravenhold. He had found a champion in Tangia, a powerful Elder. And her belief in his cause had cost her her life.

The old man took a deep breath, his chest inflating with pure air. He stood fully in the light now, and his skin tingled, even though it was not sunlight.

Crossing the threshold of Tangia's old study, finally freed from its sanctuary, he swore to find a way to repay her kindness and faith, by the blood of his ancestor, Elihor.

Kale Kolder stood before the great oak tree, now dead where it had brimmed with life when he had last seen light, and waited for the sorceress to return, knowing he could trust Tangia's pupil.

Still, he wished for nothing more than to be back home, growing old as he should, surrounded by his children and grandchildren, the breeze of the sea stroking his face with the soft caress of Elihor.

Perhaps there would be time for that yet.

PRIDE COURSED through the old man, his frame tall despite the thinning of his muscles. He stood before the oak tree, looking intently at it. The lights of Ravenhold danced beneath his feet, the tired magic muted but not silenced.

He seemed human enough from here, but his eyes told another story.

She walked towards him, the swishing of the loose robe about her ankles the only familiar sensation in these now-foreign halls. She longed for the ache of magic that usually coursed through the keep and not this sad cry that barely warranted an echo.

She examined the scene before her, fighting to remain cool and analytical. But her heart remembered how things had been the last time she'd traversed these halls: the tree full of leaves, a magical breeze shuffling them, the lights of Ravenhold dancing playfully around the students and teachers, the Elite and the Elders who frequented this place. Magic hushing softly, coursing at times like bees, at other times standing poised like a great cat.

She could feel none of these things now, the magic quiet, the lights mostly dead and the tree leafless and petrified.

She shifted her focus towards the old man, forcing her mind to break ties with the memories that assaulted her.

He turned to look at her, fully black eyes unflinching, shoulders squared despite his advanced years. She knew his kind, had heard Tangia speak of them, though she herself had never before met a resident of Elihor. Unless you counted Eloms in their mix.

Her voice was but an inquisitive whisper, too weary to summon forceful tones.

"Who are you?"

He examined her, only the light shifting in his eyes showing the flicker of his gaze. She held the staff more loosely. She would need sleep soon.

"I know you're from Elihor," she added, hoping to win his trust. "Tangia…" she swallowed hard. "Tangia spoke to me of your people."

The old man smiled, not hesitantly as she might have expected from someone having been in captivity so long. He had a quick, almost impish smile that lit the darkness of his eyes.

"You must be Shirina," he said, his voice cracking, unused to speech. "Tangia told me she had a gifted student she shared much with. And she told me that you would be the one to break the warding spell on her study." He coughed and gave a dry laugh. "Though your Circle claims no belief in foretelling, she was quite good at predicting the most likely outcome."

His features darkened. "What happened to the Elder Tangia?"

A fresh surge of adrenaline jolted Shirina awake. This man held some answers that she sought: knowledge of Tangia's final months.

She answered him, keeping a close eye on his reaction. "She was sent to Siabala's Rage a few months ago."

He closed his eyes and exhaled slowly. Shirina examined him, the slight drop of his shoulders, the crevasses etched in his face, the tear she thought she spotted trapped in his eyelashes, and she wondered how close he had been to Tangia. Although Elders were not forbidden from taking lovers, it was certainly discouraged as an unnecessary distraction.

Don't jump to conclusions she scolded herself. She decided to be direct. Not a usual Circle practice, but the Circle had changed now, and their practices needed to adapt.

"Why were you locked in Tangia's study, and what were you to her?"

He looked at her, his black eyes unblinking. "We were friends, and colleagues of a sort, you might say. We both believed in the same things and worked together to make them happen. I fear it cost her her life, Shirina, and I promise to do what I can to right that terrible wrong."

Before Shirina could ask another question, he asked: "Tell me, has the Wall finally fallen?"

"Finally?" Shirina had barely uttered the question when a large crack sounded throughout the keep, echoing down every hall and bouncing through every room. The entire structure seemed to exhale.

Silence followed.

A shiver ran down her spine and squeezed her stomach. Whatever battle Ravenhold had been fighting, it was losing. They needed to leave, now.

The old man stared at her, not afraid, simply curious. She spoke to him calmly, though fear beat wildly in her throat.

"There is an escape path at the back of the Elder's library. Do you know how to access it?"

She wasn't surprised when he nodded. If Tangia had felt this comfortable sharing a secret with him that only Elders and Elites knew, then he must have been of great importance. She had to make sure he stayed safe.

"I have to get the others. I'll join you. Wait for me there." He nodded again and headed off, shuffling as quickly as he could with muscles atrophied by inactivity.

Shirina turned around and ran back up the stairs, towards the roof where she had left the sproutlings and Grasky to recover from the shock of teleportation. She had not spent all of this magic only to lose them now.

2

*P*ushing past the fatigue of body and soul, Shirina used her staff like a third leg and moved as quickly as possible. The wood wore down her skin, her palm, long rendered numb by magic, now raw and blistered.

The lights of Ravenhold scurried before her, as though urging her to move faster, reminding her that time was almost up and would be unforgiving to the slow.

She rounded another corner and headed for the stairs that would lead her to the adepts. She picked up her speed as she planned her next steps. Ravenhold had to be saved. She had to find a way to keep it whole, not out of nostalgia, but out of sheer necessity. The history, science and magical wisdom of Graydon had been stored here since before the Wall had been erected. It could not be lost.

The people of Graydon would require a foothold in

this new world, and their past and cumulative knowledge would prove their salvation, she was certain.

She reached the top of the stairs, breaking into the dark, the magic lashing near her like lightning, thunder ripping the air.

The sproutlings stirred. Grasky, already fully awake despite his more advanced years, urged them to wake up faster. He hovered protectively around a few of them as the sky turned dark. The shields of Ravenhold were failing.

A gale struck them, winds of magic stealing their breath for a moment before being blocked by Ravenhold's magic. Yet the winds remained, howling as they lashed at the shields.

The keep cracked again and shook. Stones crumbled and crashed in the distance.

The keep was falling!

"We have to move, now," Shirina said with a calm she did not feel as she joined Grasky, looking up at the sky.

The adepts stumbled to their feet. They were strong, Shirina saw with pride. They would need to be strong for the Circle to survive.

"Let's go," she said, helping the last youth up. She counted quickly. Twenty-nine all together. It meant that the Circle now comprised thirty adepts, herself included.

There might be more hiding somewhere in Graydon. She vowed to find them as soon as the magic allowed her to do so.

"Follow me, quickly, and stay together." They did as

she commanded, Grasky bringing up the rear, concerned for the youth, uncaring that they held more power than him.

The keep cracked again. Shirina reached the bottom of the first stairway and ran down the hallway, the adepts close behind. It was rare to see an Elite or Elder move at anything more than a brisk walk, and she guessed that seeing her run pumped much-needed adrenaline into the adepts' tired bodies.

The second stairway. Another crack. The lights of Ravenhold grew frantic, dimming for a few seconds before growing strong again, pulsating and twirling around them at a speed that made Shirina dizzy.

The keep was dying, and with its last breath it shepherded its children to safety.

She was running down the second set of stairs when the stones of the keep groaned. The old tree, which they could now see as they descended, shivered. The ground shook.

"We're almost there!" she called back, each syllable like the beating of a war drum.

She reached the bottom and indicated for them to continue running towards the back. "The Library of Elders is open at the back. A friend is waiting for you there. I will join you shortly."

A few looked at her with gratitude, others with fear, and some with slight suspicion or curiosity. She noted those faces. They would be the first to reach Elite. If that remained a possibility.

With only a few minutes to spare, she took a great risk by delaying her departure.

But she needed more. She needed tools and knowledge to fight whatever was coming.

And she needed Ravenhold to survive, in one form or another, to win the day.

That was the only thing she was certain of, and, as an Elite of the Circle, she did not intend to choose fear or failure.

—

SHIRINA SKIRTED the tree and headed into Tangia's study. The footsteps of the running adepts vanished into the distance, and the keep became quiet, as though it held its breath. She did not fool herself into thinking she had time to waste. She crossed the threshold of the study and headed to the back of it, past stacks of books and ancient tomes, ignoring the knowledge that would be lost in them. Her heart ached as she headed towards the only goal she could target.

She climbed the three stairs that led to the desk, the walls around her lined to the ceiling with books. She ignored the smell of human waste and decay as she reached the desk. Its drawer was sealed with magic.

She reached down for it anyways, not having the time to examine it and cast counter-wards. Holding her breath, she made contact. The magic buzzed against her skin before vanishing. Shirina exhaled in relief as she pulled the drawer open. Her mentor had put an exception for her in the ward. Otherwise, she would probably be dead, or at the very least incapacitated, to perish with Ravenhold.

The drawer held a single notebook, its leather cover old and worn.

Shirina recognized it. She grabbed it and tucked it into her robes.

She left the room in a hurry, trying to pay no heed to the books she had once studied, hardening her heart against the loss.

The tree vibrated. Some of its branches snapped off to be caught by lower ones as others smashed through and hammered the ground. Shirina had barely cleared it when its great trunk cracked and came crashing down, it highest branches tearing her cloak, her robes caught in the torrent of its fall.

She ran faster, her staff supporting her as stones crumbled from the ceiling and crashed around her, the floor gasping with tremors.

She jumped into the library and ran to the back, books tumbling from shelves as the keep swayed. Shirina tried to grab some of the books, any book, to save them. Even one could change the course of Graydon's future. But before they hit the ground, they dissipated into a fine black dust. Ravenhold was taking its secrets with it.

"No!" she screamed, grabbing books off the shelf as they evaporated, vanishing into dust which remained suspended around her, caught in the currents of magic.

So much knowledge! All of Graydon's history, magic

and know-how lurked in these volumes, answers to questions thousands of years old, missives written by Graydon himself, truths that could never be rediscovered.

Don't take it all with you! Shirina pleaded as the books she held crumbled to ashes through her fingers. She fell to her knees, desperately trying to grasp some remaining knowledge—a page, a paragraph, a sentence that would otherwise be lost forever. Did the keep not understand that the Circle was nothing without its knowledge? Why would Ravenhold destroy them so? Couldn't it just take their lives instead, mere faded lights in the canopy of time compared to the wealth of these libraries?

Her hand came back empty, covered with the remains of the books, dark patches on her robes as she stood and stumbled forward. She couldn't give up. Other libraries remained, as well as the sproutlings. The Circle wasn't lost.

Not yet.

The youth waited for her, giving the old man from Elihor a wide berth. Grasky stood near him as they stared in awe at the black dust left behind by the destroyed books.

She hated them all. Didn't they understand what had been lost? Not just for the Circle, but for all of Graydon?

They didn't, and they might never, now.

Her eyes locked with Grasky's, his features etched with sorrow and understanding. She fought back a sob. He was worth saving. If nothing else remained of the Circle, let

Grasky remain, who understood as she did the loss Graydon suffered this day.

"Come near me, and do *not* use your magic," Shirina commanded, and they all obeyed, the keep threatening to collapse onto the cliffs below, pieces of it crashing into the turbulent sea.

Planting her feet firmly on the ground, she held up her staff and summoned her magic, the wood slicing the strands like a knife, feeding Shirina with only the purest magic.

She closed her eyes.

Keep of our Elders, please grant us escape from your grounds. No longer shall we be safe in your sanctuary.

Her heart clenched at the last words, and the magic of Ravenhold caressed her mind in an unfamiliar, soothing fashion. Pathways she didn't even know had existed within her opened up, and she could feel and see everything around her.

They were teleporting! Shirina knew it, and could feel everyone else with her. The magic of the keep supported her, guiding her magic, feeding her energy. The world spread out around her, and Ravenhold forced her to look towards the horizon, where the Wall of Loss was completely gone, and the magic of Elihor mixed with Graydon's.

There will be nothing left.

Shirina allowed herself to float in the keep's magic for some time, letting Ravenhold soothe her recent wounds and hold her in its weak glow. Grief weighed on her mind and she wanted to close her eyes and rest, but they remained open by a will not entirely her own.

Then she saw them.

Lights flickered in the distance. Lights she had failed to see during her last teleportation. Faint lights, but bright enough to alert her that other members of the Circle had survived, hiding in Graydon, guarding their magic as best they could. But they could never hide from Ravenhold and its Covenant. The keep knew they lived, and it ensured the knowledge passed on to Shirina.

Shirina followed the magic of Ravenhold, letting it fill her, and she called towards the lights.

Come.

She called more strongly, the word pulsating with the might of more than a thousand years of safeguarding Graydon. She screamed the word in her mind, the same word that legends claimed to be the final one shared between Graydon and Elihor. A call that Elihor herself had never managed to answer.

COME!

And she told her Covenant where to go. To follow the star in the distance, in the West, where she was certain the final battle would take place.

She instructed them to head toward the bright light which could only be a descendant of Graydon himself. Shirina was positive it was the young princess Cassara Edoline, her magic fully activated and now the most powerful in Graydon. Whether she realized it or not.

But the darkness creeping towards the princess grew

thicker yet, and she would need all the help she could get. For herself, and for Graydon.

The other Circle adepts began to shine, their wards falling as they answered the battle call, their glowing magic like stars beneath her.

Then the world shuddered and the ground rematerialized beneath her feet. Ravenhold's magic dissipated and abandoned them to a cold landscape.

She managed to remain standing as they reappeared by a forest. She did not need to see Ravenhold to know that it had fallen, and that only a cloud of dust and memories remained of her home. Of centuries of blood and sacrifice.

She looked towards the West, to focus on what could still be.

3

Avarielle's legs were cramped by the time she stood back up. She ignored Kryde's body. The earth would eventually claim it back, and his soul had already left. Her sword reflected the poor light, and she clung to it, letting its magic attack her.

Kryde had been turned against her, and now, so had Graysword. And her own body, assailed by the growth of a child she didn't want, had also become unpredictable.

What was there left for her to do?

Fight.

The word resonated in every fiber of her being. Fight, and claim vengeance, or die trying. Nothing else mattered now.

Nothing.

She stood and listened intently. She could only hear a steady drip somewhere on the horizon. Something was wrong.

She searched her recent memories for what had changed in her surroundings. She closed her fists as she remembered Siabala's laughter, the victory flashing in his eyes as she ran him through with Graysword, the feeling of her blade cutting Kryde down so easily…

The Wall! That's what was missing. The incessant buzzing of the Wall of Loss was gone. She had grown up with the sound, so minor and constant that she had never realized it was there until she had left for the East and lands so quiet you could hear the stars cry at night.

So, the Wall had fallen. She had been aware of it, but had been so engrossed in her own loss that she had failed to fully grasp its meaning.

Avarielle looked down, and from her peripheral vision she could see Kryde's unmoving foot. She swallowed hard, her heart as clenched as her fists.

"You say I took a blood oath with you, Siabala," she said, voice trembling with hatred. "Then know that I will satisfy it. Not by claiming Elihor's blood," she forced her hand not to go to her belly, "but instead by claiming yours. You've taken it all, and I *will* claim it all back in your death."

She could sense that he had heard her, and wondered if they shared a magical bond, forged by generations of her family spilling blood to activate a magic she now understood to be from the darkest source. Not that it mattered, really. She would continue to wield Graysword. She needed the sword's magic. Even if it killed her, she needed its powers.

And she needed more.

Avarielle was proud but she was not foolish. She knew that she needed help were she to claim vengeance. Walking over to the cooked remains of Delora, a look of surprise still etched on the witch's features, Avarielle grabbed the amulet from her dead hand and pulled. The hand came with the chain, torn off the body. Disgusted, Avarielle shook it off, sending it flying onto Delora. Her body and its shocked expression crumbled.

"What did you think would happen?" Avarielle mumbled, too tired to feel much victory over Delora's death. She tucked the amulet in her tunic. It would come in handy later, as long as Cassara had managed to survive this long without it. In the meantime, her own powers would have to suffice.

She looked at Kryde's foot again, and this time her hand did go to her belly.

The magic of Graysword wasn't after her own life, she knew.

Swallowing hard, she whispered, "I'm sorry."

She walked out without a single glance back.

THE AIR WAS thick with sulfur, a yellow hue clinging to every corner. Avarielle ignored the stinging of her eyes and burning of her lungs as she pushed back into Stormhold.

Siabala would be gone by now. After craving freedom

for so long, he would not tarry here. But she wasn't certain where to seek him out.

He had already destroyed most of Elihor, so Graydon would undoubtedly be his next target. Avarielle clenched her jaw. Or perhaps he had already claimed vengeance, or was just about to, and there was nothing she could do to stop him. Graydon might already be in ashes, like Elihor.

Her hands formed fists at her sides.

Had she really allowed herself to become a pawn so easily? Had generations of her family wielded Graysword unquestioningly? Or had they been like her—knowing, or at least suspecting, yet burying the truth deep within their psyche?

She crossed a threshold, lost in thought, when a hand shot out and grabbed her upper arm. She spun around and pulled Graysword free in one smooth motion.

A hoarse voice spoke. "Wait."

Avarielle narrowed her eyes but stayed her blade. The hand withdrew and a man stepped from the shadows, near the broken bars that had previously held him.

He had once been a man, but had been turned into a monster by Siabala's magic. His arms were too long, the bones protruding from his fingers forming partial claws, half-sharpened, half dull, and slick with blood. His skin was stretched and gray, riddled with dark veins, though not as much as full Eloms. A tinge of red still adorned the limbs, giving them a brownish color.

The broad shoulders betrayed Pack Nacker's identity. Kryde's oldest friend and trusted second-in-command stepped into the dim light, unafraid to approach her. Or uncaring.

Avarielle lowered Graysword.

Pack looked back from where she had come. She hardened her heart, wanting to detach herself completely from her words. Still, she only managed a whisper.

"Kryde is dead. I'm sorry."

Pack's shoulders fell and he looked down, showing as much grief as his new deformed body allowed him to.

Eyes fixed on him, her voice gained strength and kindness as she asked, "Should I end it for you, Pack?"

He kept his head down, shoulders rising and falling as he struggled to breathe. Graysword's frenzied magic danced through Avarielle's body.

Then his dark eyes looked at her unflinchingly. He shifted his gaze to the side and Avarielle followed his lead. A pile of discarded armor lay there. He headed for it and rummaged, his claws making it difficult to grab the correct pieces. Finding what he was looking for, he pulled out his breast plate, the metal dull and damaged. He tried to put it on, this last vestige of who he had been. And what he still intended to fight for.

Elihor.

Avarielle sheathed Graysword and walked over to help him fasten the clasps of his armor, his fingers incapable of pulling on them. She ignored the slight stench of rot and adjusted them as best she could on his deformed body, the armor sitting too high on his bent back and misshapen torso. He then walked over and grabbed his helmet, handing it to Avarielle.

He knelt before her and she adjusted it.

He stood up looking more like himself, though his arms, gray skin and claws betrayed what he now was. Or what he was becoming. His gaze lingered on a discarded broadsword, his claws flexing at his side as he came to terms with his inability to wield a blade into battle. Avarielle placed a hand on his arm, grieving for his loss and grateful for what he'd managed to retain.

"Are there more of you?"

He nodded and turned back into the shadows.

She followed him into their depths.

CASSARA WOKE up to the sound of hushed arguing. She lay in her tent, fully clothed. She sat up, dizziness blanketing her mind. She had no memory of getting there, or how long she'd been asleep. Her hands shook, and she knew she had overspent her magic.

And it had felt good. Even without her mother's amulet, she had managed to tap into her powers, in a greater way than ever before. She didn't need to step outside to know she had stopped the fires that would have consumed Graydon. She had felt them dissipating when faced with her magic. She had been the balm to a painful burn.

And she had not lost herself in her magic.

The arguing intensified, and Cassara shook the last cobwebs from her mind and stood up, pleased that she didn't sway. Her body would recover quickly. She was young, and she could take some overuse of magic, but she wondered how often she could afford to do so.

She took a deep breath to make sure she was steady, and then stepped outside the tent. The Westland warrior Trevon, her husband Dayshon, his captain of the guards Jiles, and Breck, the Westland leader, all stood nearby. Either keeping an eye on her tent, or waiting for her to wake up.

Their argument stopped the second they spotted her. Dayshon broke away and grabbed both of her shoulders, looking deep into her eyes.

"Are you alright?"

She nodded, but couldn't muster a smile. The air carried the smell of burning trees. He let go of her as she looked towards the Bloody Mountains, illuminated by the morning sun. The Wall no longer shimmered in the distance. The land, from the tip of the Bloody Mountains to about fifty feet from where she now stood, was scorched black. Nothing had been spared in the fire's path.

But it had been stopped.

"Whatever you're arguing about," Cassara said, not bothering to look back, "settle it quickly, so that we can begin planning our next steps."

"War," Trevon said. Cassara turned to look at him. The warrior shrugged. "Your husband and Breck are having a hard time deciding who will lead the combined army."

Breck looked unapologetic, and Dayshon set his jaw stubbornly.

Cassara sighed. "Can't you just cooperate and each lead your own men? Or is that too complex to fathom?"

"We will not ride under the banners of the East!" Breck spat.

Cassara focused on him as she spoke, hoping her own husband would prove more reasonable.

"Then keep your banners, Breck of the West. This enemy marches against all of Graydon, so the more banners we have from across the land, the better."

"We cannot follow one from the East." Breck crossed his arms across his chest, making it clear he would tolerate no argument. "It would be an insult to our forefathers."

Cassara put her hand on Breck's arm. He flinched slightly, but did not push her away, keeping his arms crossed and looking down at her.

Must all Westlanders be so tall?

"Follow yourselves, then. Follow the ideals of your forefathers. Follow what you feel is best, Breck, but at least walk alongside us in battle. Otherwise, we will lose the West, the East, and everyone within."

His eyes flickered towards Trevon, who just shrugged. Cassara kept her hand on Breck's arm for a moment longer before taking a step back.

"Will you fight in this battle?" Breck asked of Cassara, his voice losing some of its edge.

Cassara didn't look at Dayshon before answering. "I will be there until the end, Breck. That much I can promise you."

Breck weighed her answer for a few seconds before nodding. He turned to Dayshon.

"Then we are willing to walk alongside you, Heir of Rashim."

Cassara was worried for a moment that Dayshon would refuse and demand that they follow him, but the prince closed the distance and the two men shook hands. Trevon caught her eye and winked. She smiled.

She would be there until the end, that much she knew. But she wondered which end would come first—the war's, Graydon's, or her own.

Cold penetrated her skin and snaked around her bones, deepening the void left behind by Ravenhold's disappearance. She could feel it in the air around her, the spray of magic emanating from where the keep had once been, the strongest source of magic in Graydon.

The strongest source of light.

Using the Sight, she watched it dissipate as it mixed with the magic of Elihor, not in a great battle of light against darkness, but rather in a quiet, accepting embrace. Shadows filled the magical plain, Ravenhold's magic easily vanquished.

Shirina turned towards the other adepts. They stood together and waited, staring at her. Their magic flew wildly around them, but seemed fairly untouched.

"Contain your magic," Shirina said as she walked

amongst them, looking them in the eye. "Do not use it, and ward it within you. It is not safe to use, for now."

The Orange Circles did as she asked, not seeing what she saw, but accepting her words as wisdom. The Blue, Yellow and Green Circles did not yet have the skills to ward their own magic, and so she went to each separately and cast a simple spell of warding.

The precaution would not save them, in the long run. But it would buy them time.

"So," the Orange Circle Shala spoke up. The woman seemed a little bit less insolent than before, no doubt only temporarily tempered by fear. "Are we to never use our magic again?"

Shirina looked to each adept in turn. "You must decide." The words were strange and foreign in her mouth. She hadn't planned on saying that. She had planned nothing past this point, not certain they would even survive this far. She had anticipated that they could remain in Ravenhold, safe and growing their skill and knowledge while the storm passed.

Those plans were now as destroyed as Ravenhold.

"You must decide," she repeated, voice gaining strength, "whether you will stay in the Circle, first of all." She received looks of interest and fear. Some, mostly the younger girls, looked down. "The world has changed, and Ravenhold is gone. There are many left of the Circle, and they will join us in battle, and we could use you, all of you, no matter your abilities."

"You would just let us go?" a young voice asked, though she didn't see the speaker.

Shirina nodded. "Follow us to safety. After the battle, those who wish to remain, I will help you grow your abilities. But the magic is against us now, and we must first figure out how to safely use it. Those who wish to leave, I will not try and stop you. There are no guarantees that your families and homes remain, but you will always be welcomed back in the Covenant, if that is the case."

If we win the day. Many were young and not strong in magic yet, but that didn't matter. The battle ahead would require all their power, and she could not dismiss them beforehand. She took a deep breath, wishing she could let them all go, so as not to have so much blood on her hands.

"Who gave you authority to speak these words?" Pola, another Orange Circle, spoke up, goaded on by Shala.

Grasky stepped forward. "Shirina is the last Elite of the Circle." He glanced her way to see if her eyes would contradict him. She watched him passively, so he continued, "And a trusted adviser to many Elders in their day. Graydon's magic favors her. She has seen and experienced more than any of you have, and she needs not justify this further than these words. Should you not agree with this, I suggest you keep your opinions to yourselves and leave us as soon as the battle has ended. In the meantime, she is our best chance at safety, so I suggest you smarten up and follow."

Shirina hid a smile. She had never heard Grasky speak

so bitingly. But, then again, she had never questioned the system of authority enforced by the Circle.

"Shall we go?" he turned to her and asked when no objections were raised.

Shirina nodded and began the trek West, walking away from the sun rising slowly over Graydon.

RAVENHOLD HAD BROUGHT them close to the west. Two days walking should do, as long as everyone kept pace. The man from Elihor, Kale Kolder, walked up beside her. She had been worried he would not be able to keep up on his own and would need to be carried, but her fears had been unwarranted.

"Tangia would be proud of you, Shirina," he said. Shirina fought the urge to look at him. She wasn't certain Tangia would be proud or support her. Then again, she had never been fully certain of Tangia's motives— living in uncertainty is something Circle Elites were quickly trained to accept. Shirina knew what her mentor would say, however. She should have found a way to save the books, sacrificing everything else if necessary. Even the sproutlings.

Grasky walked nearby, his head lowered and lost in thought. She wondered if he would have agreed with her, and suspected he would. She used to believe the Keeper of Lisal to be simply a glorified innkeeper, but after dealing with him in the past few days, she had come to understand that he, too, guarded secrets. She hoped she would get to know more of them before fate claimed them.

As though reading her thoughts, Kale spoke up. "Tangia would have wanted to preserve the knowledge, too, Shirina, but not at the price you might have been willing to pay for it. No matter how obsolete it now seems, the Circle is more needed than ever. *All* of the Circle."

Shirina remained silent for a moment.

"Are there more of us left, Kale? In Elihor?"

Kale sighed. "The keeps were destroyed there too. Larkhold fell almost a year ago, and Stormhold, which kept Siabala in check, not long after. But some individuals from the Circle still survive, and there may be Elders left in Elihor."

She looked at him to gauge his reaction. "Are you one such Elder?"

He gave her a quick grin. "Tangia said you were quick. I wasn't an Elder, but I was in the Circle. I fell in love and left to raise a family. I never stopped loving the learning, but the Circle's fear of breaking its own boundaries proved too restrictive. I pursued the knowledge perhaps too relentlessly, crossing the Wall of Loss to find what remained of Graydon. That's how I found Tangia, and returned here to warn her of Larkhold's and Stormhold's collapse."

He sighed heavily. "But it was too late. Events were already in motion that would see to Ravenhold's downfall.

We worked to preserve what we could of the Circle, but events progressed much faster than anticipated." His voice turned to a whisper. "I just wish I could have saved Tangia."

Shirina allowed him a few moments to gather himself. "Why would they want the Circle to fall so badly?" she finally asked. "Not just fall, but be completely eradicated?"

Kale snorted. "To stop the Circle from stopping him, of course. The mingling of the magics is what Siabala truly wants, and the Circles, all three of them working together, could have filtered the magic. Just as you can with your staff."

Shirina nodded but didn't answer. She hated that he had so easily guessed the purpose of the staff. But then again, she imagined that, to the right eyes, it must have been pretty obvious.

She was about to question him further, to increase her knowledge of the situation and salve the wound of losing Ravenhold, when something cracked in the horizon.

They all stopped and Shirina looked up to where the Bloody Mountains loomed, clear in the crisp morning, no longer distorted by the shimmer of the Wall of Loss.

Another loud crack sounded, ripping the sky like thunder, and a cloud of dust burst from the Bloody Mountains.

"What's happening?" Shirina asked.

No one answered as they waited to see what would be revealed once the cloud had cleared.

5

The air buzzed like lightning, making Cassara's hair stand up at its roots. Then the sky cracked and the Bloody Mountains seemed to explode from within, firing a cloud of dust and stone into the sky.

"Not again," Gragor, her Edoline guard, muttered. She allowed herself a quick smile despite her racing heart. She doubted the Wall of Loss could be falling twice.

The Westland and Eastland troops both moved to the ready, stationing themselves between the camp and the mountains. Cassara took a deep breath and forced herself to walk towards the troops. Gragor and Loas, her other guard, whose loyalty had been won in her travels, followed her after only the slightest hesitation.

Dayshon nodded as she came up, looking at her inquisitively. She turned back to the mountains, took a deep breath, and tried to spot any magic that the soldiers wouldn't see. Even with squinted eyes, all she could see was dust and a clear sky beyond. She turned back to Dayshon and shook her head.

Trevon hovered near as well. They weren't telling her to stay back like they would have just a day ago. From the looks on their faces, she suddenly understood that they stayed near in case she needed protection, but they also expected her to save them all, too.

Cassara's throat dried up where her breath remained caught. Of course they would expect her to save them. She had already proved she had great power by stopping the Wall's onslaught.

She caught Gragor looking at her sideways, fear and wonder in his eyes. She turned away from him and focused in front of her, where the dust began to billow down from the mountains towards them, dissipating and turning to a fine gray mist.

"Stay at the ready," Jiles cried from up ahead. Dayshon passed by her and headed further up to be with the forward troops. Cassara lingered back, wishing she had the courage to move forward, too.

The earth trembled and cracked, sending most of the soldiers to the ground. Cassara managed to remain standing, thanks to Trevon's speed.

"We should leave, Lady Cassara," Trevon whispered in her ear as he kept his hand on her arm.

She shook her head as she looked forward, transfixed. A crack ran clear from the Bloody Mountains across the Westland desert, ending not far from where the troops rallied.

"We have to go," Trevon said more forcefully, grabbing her upper arm in an iron grip as he pulled her aside.

"Not without Dayshon!" Cassara hissed at him, trying her best to stand her ground, knowing full well the warrior could easily haul her off if he wanted to. He glared at her and let her go.

"Wait here," he ordered before walking towards where Dayshon and Breck were consulting, their differences quickly forgotten when faced with impending doom.

"Move it, you goats," Trevon shouted as he reached them in long strides. "It's obviously time for us to go, unless you know how to fight the ground itself!"

Dayshon cast a quick look Cassara's way and she forced herself to meet the question in his eyes.

Could she save them? Before she could answer, the earth cracked again, the ground surrounding the freshly formed crevice crumbling in. Tremors shook and the sand slithered out of sight. Clouds of dust covered everyone and everything.

Another loud crack and Cassara was jolted off her feet, falling on her side, clutching her head protectively as shards of rock flew around them. Then someone was on top of her, covering her. The earth shook a few more times, then grew silent. The tremors still vibrated in Cassara's bones when Gragor got off of her and helped her up.

She didn't even think to thank Gragor as she looked around, the dust stinging her eyes, senses tingling awake.

She walked forward quickly, heedless of potential

danger. The air smelled *wrong.* Like sulfur coated it. She had smelled that just one other time. When her aunt had opened a portal to Siabala's Rage, before Avarielle had been swallowed by it.

She forced the thoughts of the warrior deep within. Grief would slow her movements, and she would need to move quickly to meet whatever came their way.

THE ADEPTS SPOKE IN QUICK, hushed tones, having felt the quaking of the earth and seen the cloud of dust engulfing the Bloody Mountains and spreading over the West. Shirina stood aside, clutching her staff, letting the tremors of magic pulse into her arm. The magic coursed wildly through the earth, the beating of a great heartbeat that was not Graydon's.

"I've felt this before," Kale offered as he walked up to her, looking younger with each passing moment now that his skin had regained some color and his posture had straightened.

"In Siabala's Rage. I crossed it, once," he said softly, features set hard. Shirina stared at him. *Siabala's Rage.* She wanted to ask him about it, to understand fully, but her desire to remain ignorant proved too strong. And she hated how weak that made her feel.

"Siabala's attack has begun," Grasky said, looking remorsefully at the adepts.

"We're not through yet, old friend," Shirina said,

grounding herself back in the moment. She turned away from the Bloody Mountains to face both men.

"I will go ahead to reach them. I have to, Grasky," she added gently at his concerned look. "If Cassara falls now, I don't think we'll ever be able to fix this magic. You continue on, march to meet me. I can't sense any evil, so as far as I know, you'll be safe reaching us."

She knew she wasn't convincing either man. Or herself.

"I can't teleport you all," she added in a regretful whisper.

Grasky smiled at her. "We will be fine, Crimson Circle. You must remember that we are no longer the only ones from the Circle heading your way. We will all join up again…within a day?"

"Two days," Shirina said. "Very well. And you're right, Grasky, there are other adepts near, and they too are heading towards the West. But…" She let the thought linger, Grasky understanding her unspoken words.

That none of them could safely use their magic.

"I will be here, Shirina," Kale spoke up. "Perhaps my magic can help." Shirina doubted that whatever magic he had could help them, but she nodded nonetheless. She would need to leave them all behind. Had Ravenhold saved them all only for Shirina to abandon them so easily?

Then again, no Circle witch could afford to be dependent on another, especially not in these times.

She turned towards the adepts and faced the Orange Circles. "Shala," she called to their leader, the outspoken girl who had dared call a Harvest without Elder permission. She wasn't a perfect choice for leader, but the others would follow her without question, and speed alone might save them. "I must go west. You must follow me, and make sure to keep everyone safe. Grasky will be your guide," she added, giving the Keeper of Lisal what she hoped was some authority. He had already shown that he could handle the unruly youth.

Shala's eyes widened, a question forming on her lips. Shirina cut her off. "I don't feel the need to explain myself, adept. Just follow, and keep everyone together. Remember not to use your magic, and be prepared. Battle awaits."

Shala nodded slightly, no hint of victory flashing in her eyes. Only terror. Shirina had hoped the adept's desire for power would fuel her instead of fear. Greed was a safer emotion to rely on in these times.

Regardless, the Orange Circle would have to do.

Shirina turned to Kale. "We have much yet to speak of, Kale Kolder."

He lowered his head in acknowledgment. "I look forward to it."

She turned without further words and headed to the side to cast her spell. "May your steps be steady, Shirina," Grasky called after her.

She hesitated before answering. "May all of our steps be steady, and safe," she whispered, no bothering to see if he had heard. All of their thoughts would be heavy enough. And magic might not save them.

Planting the staff firmly into the tremulous earth,

Shirina called upon Graydon once more to bring her to the homeland of Avarielle Grayloft, to teleport her safely where she had not planned her path, straight into the heart of the battle.

THE MIDDLE SLOPE of the mountains collapsed into rubble, the rocks dancing as they shifted, a great crevasse leading from the flank of the mountain to the plain before them. The dust cleared to reveal the width of the crevasse. Cassara gasped, the ground having collapsed for at least a league, revealing stone formations below.

Not stones, Cassara thought as she squinted her eyes to see more clearly in the dissipating dust. *Buildings!*

She could make out a tower, half broken, leaning sideways onto another large structure, which resembled a manor. The soldiers surrounding her gasped as they too spotted the buildings spreading out before them. All the way to the Bloody Mountains, a city had emerged, some of it still encased in stone, other sections completely crumbled. But enough of it had survived to show it had once been splendid. Towers and parapets stood proudly and multi-storied buildings had withstood the trials of time in this forgotten, buried city, so large it rivaled Massir in size.

Her eyes lingered on the city before travelling up the mountain, easily visible despite being at least a day's walk away. It glowed red with swirling energy, yellow clouds billowing into the ancient city, snaking across forgotten roads and into collapsed buildings.

"Siabala's Rage," Trevon whispered beside her. A shiver traveled the length of her spine, but Cassara stood her ground, hands forming fists at her side, wishing the attack would just come already, while hoping it never would.

THE SECOND SHIRINA had cast her teleportation spell, her skin began to burn. Siabala's attack was coming, and he had full control over the battlefield.

Unable to break the spell, she summoned protective magic around her. Strands of magic lashed at her and whipped her, and she concentrated on maintaining her spell, unable to fight off the attack completely while still teleporting.

She looked around her, but there was no assailant in sight. In fact, she could see nothing. None of the lights of Graydon greeted her, the world covered in dark mist and red lightning. The staff pulsated with light, but no other magic of Graydon revealed itself.

Had they already lost? Was it already too late? If Graydon's magic was being devoured so quickly, there may be nothing left for even the staff to purify soon. And without magic...

Shirina pushed the thought deep within her and concentrated on finding her goal. Teleporting without first visiting the area was dangerous, but at least the West was large and mostly flat. If she could spot Cassara, she could simply home in on her. She squinted, looked around, but the princess' magic lay dormant.

She took a steadying breath and let herself hover for a time, a shadow in the battle of magic. The princess first had to use her magic for Shirina to spot her. With the red energies swirling in the distance, the sorceress doubted that would take long.

Her heart skipped a beat as she was hit repeatedly with wave after wave of dark energies. But she was strong, and a Crimson Circle Elite of Ravenhold. She did not intend to succumb.

She waited in the tempest for the real battle to start.

6

The city moaned. Not just its walls, nor its rubble-covered ancient streets. A cry of pain emanated from the whole of it, like the long cry of a dying seagull. Everyone stood silent, eyes riveted on the stone buildings.

Trevon pulled his sword free and stepped in front of Cassara. The princess struggled against the urge to reach for her amulet, even though she'd been without it for months, her hands uselessly flexing at her sides.

Horses whinnied and stomped their hooves, soldiers trying to keep the beasts calm as they fought their own fear.

Another moan, and the city shifted, as though its heart had begun to beat. One of the great buildings collapsed, a cloud of dust rippling from where it vanished. Another collapsed, closer, and the moaning doubled in intensity, emanating from the dust. And a third one, followed by more as the ground shifted again.

"Prepare for battle!" Dayshon cried out, both Eastlanders and Westlanders answering his call. He caught Cassara's eyes and nodded. She returned the gesture, suddenly missing the days she had to argue to come into battle. She took a deep breath and focused, Trevon's solid frame before her. She was not alone. And she could do this.

Before the dust had finished settling, a long, thin leg shot out of the nearest cloud, grabbing a leaning tower and crushing it. Another long leg jerked up toward the sky to fold back down, followed by another...until the entire creature revealed itself, a multi-legged beast shifting the rubble of the city. The long legs all connected to a spherical core as they engulfed a building and all of its tallest towers, easily five times the size of Edoline's manor, covering it completely. It pulsated and shifted, then it moved.

The building still stood, even more imposing than before.

Stone cracked as two more creatures appeared, covering two other buildings. The creatures stood at least as tall as the castle of Massir, and Cassara fought to keep her breathing steady, their size making her dizzy.

She glanced to Dayshon and Breck. Dayshon looked pale, but determined.

"Are they coming our way?" Dayshon asked.

"Not yet," Breck grunted.

"It looks like…" Cassara said, taking a step towards Trevon, who growled at her to stay back. She peered at the movements of the creatures, at the rocks crackling beneath them, and at the tower which now stood straighter on the first building. "I think they're repairing the city."

"Just as well," Breck said. "They can stay in that pit of death and leave us be." He shook his head and looked to Trevon. Cassara placed a gentle hand on the warrior's arm, understanding the longing in both their eyes. Their homeland had been splintered, and would probably never be the same again. It was a pain she understood all too well.

A knot grabbed hold of her stomach, twisting it, all of her senses coming to life. She cried out in warning, not certain why. A deep, guttural chant filled the skies, and the three creatures stopped.

For just a moment, they seemed frozen in place, monsters looming on the horizon. Trevon held Cassara's arm, as though to stop her from falling or running forward, and the troops looked from her to the creatures.

Suddenly, the creatures ran toward them, their multiple legs quickly carrying them across the rubble towards the awaiting army. Their legs shone in the light, like liquid silver falling from their perfectly spherical heads. Screams burst from the troops around her before they scrambled to take up position.

"All archers, fire!" Breck ordered and arrows flew, talking out some legs but hardly enough to matter. The creatures moved quickly toward them in one smooth motion, disturbingly quiet despite their speed. Dayshon ordered his cavalry to brace for the attack, the soldiers poorly suited to fight this enemy.

"Catapults!" Breck screamed, and the Westland warriors pulled up their few remaining catapults. They looked worn, probably a vestige from the Westland Wars, but they worked. A stone flew toward the creatures.

One of them stumbled and the army cheered, but it righted itself again, quickly gaining on them. Trevon pushed Cassara back toward her Edoline guards, Gragor and Loas, as rubble flew toward them. The two guards flanked her as she turned and focused on the beast, the familiar warmth of magic releasing the knot in her stomach and bubbling to the surface. She hurled her magic at the creature's legs. The ball of fire left her winded as it sped towards its target. The magic engulfed the creature and it shrieked as it fell down, taking several buildings with it.

Cassara didn't even have time to draw another breath before the second beast reached the cavalry, crushing some riders, spearing others through, and grabbing some to toss high into the air. Its legs formed an army numbering nearly as many as their soldiers, killing without mercy or pause, the earth shaking beneath its strikes. The horses whinnied in panic, collapsing on themselves and their riders in a bid to escape. The entire unit quickly lost any cohesion, despite Dayshon's attempts to keep them together.

Dayshon tried to jump on a horse to save his men, but Jiles tackled him and dragged him back. He moved him out of the way just in time for the third creature to crawl out of the city and onto the field, just a few feet from where Cassara stood. Fear fueled her magic and she threw a fireball at the legs, but her magic proved too weak to take the creature down.

Trevon leapt in front of her despite her screams, hacking at one of the nearby legs and slicing through it before being tossed aside by another. Loas and Gragor fired arrows beside her, but the weapons bounced off the legs harmlessly.

Just one more attack, please! Cassara took a deep breath and pushed out another fireball, screaming in rage as the fires barely scathed the beast. It turned and attacked the Westland troops.

She frantically tried to pull on her resources, but her fires only grew weaker. The Westland warriors cut legs down as quickly as they could, even as they were being slaughtered.

A warning scream sounded beside her and Gragor tackled her just as a leg swung for them, the creature having plowed through the cavalry. Loas screamed, his cry turning into a wet gurgle.

"Loas!" Cassara screamed. She needed her magic. It had saved him once, when she had thought things were just as hopeless. *She needed to save him again!*

She untangled herself from Gragor, unable to see Loas, Dayshon or Trevon, legs falling around her like a torrential downpour. Westland warriors ran between them as best they could as they hacked and were hacked down themselves.

"Dayshon! Trevon!" she screamed, knowing it was useless but unable to stop herself. She reached for her magic, dizzy and tired. Gragor stood beside her, eyes wide as he clutched his bow.

The creatures stood right over them, blocking out the sun with their legs, encircling them as though they were a building, sunlight slicing the battlefield as wildly as the legs. Cassara wished for light and sent flames up, the strands of her magic rivaling the number of legs, but still it did not cause enough damage. Warriors were cut down around her in the forest of legs as the beasts moved forward, uncaring of what they destroyed below them.

"We need to go!" Trevon screamed, suddenly beside her, a bloodied gash on the side of his face. He grabbed her arm and began dragging her away, Gragor keeping pace as he shot arrows into the fray.

"I have to stop them Trevon! I have to save the others!"

Trevon didn't bother answering as he dragged her along. "Trevon!" Cassara half screamed and sobbed in frustration.

A leg landed near them and Trevon avoided it, but three others blocked their path. Darkness swallowed them, and the warrior stood very still, uncertain where to go. Cassara held her breath and listened to the screams echoing off the dome of legs.

The air vibrated, a soft throbbing sound as the legs

pulsed with energy, the air around them thinning as it swallowed it up.

Like it must have done to the buildings. The air began to whoosh up, away from them, leaving them gasping.

Despite the noise, Cassara heard it. Chanting. Soft and swallowed by all the screams and vanishing air, she recognized it nonetheless. A Circle witch chanted near, and was about to attack. Cassara dared hope the Circle was attacking the creature and not them, but she doubted they'd be spared if the creature was killed. Should it fall, it would kill everyone here.

"Trevon, Gragor, get down with me and stay close," Cassara screamed over the din, closing her eyes. She concentrated on the men and women fighting around her, on their screams, on their tired breaths, on the stench of their fear and sweat. She touched the ground and sensed the energies of Graydon dancing just below her. The magic connected her to the life beat of every other living being on the battlefield, even the critically wounded, and those who hid, too frightened to fight, too ashamed to show their faces.

She found them all, one by one, including Dayshon and Breck. She swallowed hard, unable to find Loas. She tightened her spell around them as the chanting ended. The sky exploded in white fires above her and Cassara willed a protective barrier around each individual, soft like a lullaby on a tired mind, just enough to keep them safe from the Circle flames. She let her own shields be fed by the fires and absorb them, since both magics stemmed from Graydon.

The beast shrieked high above, and the legs around them dissipated in the consuming white flames, until only ashes and a fine layer of magic remained.

Cassara dropped her protective spell and stood. Others did the same, cautiously at first, and a few cheered weakly. They had lost many.

She glanced around, found the third beast, which had been downed by arrows and stones.

One by her. One by the Circle. One by the troops.

"That wasn't you, was it?" Trevon asked. Cassara shook her head and surveyed the landscape until she spotted a white-robed figure walking towards her, the ashes of the beasts she had just killed clinging to the bottom of her robes as she crossed the battlefield. She leaned heavily on a staff, crimson cloak billowing behind her.

"Trevon," Cassara whispered. "Point an arrow at her heart, and leave it there until I say otherwise or ask you to shoot."

Without hesitation he did as he was told, the witch not slowing her pace until she stood before Cassara.

Cassara studied the sorceress. Her features were drawn, more so than when they had left each other. Small cuts lined her skin, some trickling blood, others just red and angry. Regardless, she seemed to radiate more power, and Cassara knew it came from the staff. The energy dancing around it pulsated so brightly that Cassara couldn't look directly at it.

Cassara wanted to question the sorceress on her activities, on the Circle's involvement in the destruction of the Wall, on the city that had just appeared.

But the words all caught in her throat as all that she could think about was the dagger in her heart, still too embedded to be ignored. The dark, tired eyes looked back at her with no hint of remorse.

I killed for you, and you betrayed me.

7

"**W**ell met, Princess Cassara," Shirina said softly, lowering her head in greeting, ignoring the arrow aimed at her heart.

"I can't believe the pretty singer is a Circle witch," Trevon growled. "Did Avarielle not know?"

"Tell me why I shouldn't kill you?" Cassara asked coolly, though her blood boiled. She remembered Avarielle vanishing through the portal, after Shirina had cast the spell that had doomed her. She wished she could hear the warrior's laughter again. To feel that she had one ally she could fully count on, who didn't expect her to save her, and who could hold her own.

Shirina spoke up. "Because you aren't a killer at heart, or you could wield attack spells as easily as you wield complicated defense spells." She paused. "For what it's worth, I wish there had been another way to stop Delora."

"But not to save Avarielle?" Cassara's voice trembled.

Trevon's arm tightened, and Cassara hoped he wouldn't shoot until she ordered him to. Shirina might not be able to deflect the blow in her tired state, and she wasn't certain she wanted Shirina dead just yet.

The sorceress kept her gaze firm. "The Grayloft was not my responsibility, Cassara, no more than you were." She paused and looked down for a moment, either with regret or because she was trying to devise another approach.

When she spoke again, her voice was so soft Cassara could barely make out the words. "The Circle was my family, Cassara. I was doing what I ultimately thought would save it."

"Did it?" Cassara asked in a whisper, remembering the bloody end of her own home, wishing she could hear the sea and breathe its cool, salty air.

"It doesn't matter now, does it?" Shirina said. "All of Graydon is at stake, and I'm here to help end this."

Cassara studied her. She seemed tired, but not defeated. She hated to admit it, but seeing the sorceress again made her feel better. Shirina was powerful. And she was a piece of her past, someone linked to Edoline, who'd walked some of her journey with her.

"I wish you hadn't betrayed us, Shirina," Cassara said, meaning every word. If Avarielle had been with her these past months, so many things could have been different.

"I didn't," Shirina said, voice leveling. "I betrayed Delora, an Elder of the Circle, Cassara. Avarielle just got in the way."

Trevon growled, bowstring still taut.

Cassara kept her gaze fixed on the sorceress. She couldn't see any remorse, yet she couldn't see a lie, either. Then again, she was an Elite of the Circle, and she could probably convince her the stars didn't exist if she really wanted to.

Still, Shirina seemed…different. She was not standing defiantly before her, not even proudly. Trials had tempered her, but Cassara was uncertain that would prove to be an advantage.

Regardless, an ally was an ally, and with their troops beaten back so easily in the first battle, they needed all the help they could get. She would simply have to keep a close eye on her.

"Get some rest," Cassara said, nodding to Trevon. "Trevon will escort you to a tent. Trevon, make sure she stays there until I come for her."

Trevon cast her a dark look that clearly stated he wanted to finish the sorceress off. Cassara placed a hand on his arm and whispered, holding his eyes with hers.

"Look around us, Trevon." Cassara could hear the cries of the wounded and smell the stench of the dead and dying. "We need her help. We would all be dead already if not for her."

He looked away, his hand twitching where he still held his bow.

"Trust me, Trevon. If we need to take her out, I promise I will leave you the killing blow."

He seemed satisfied with that and roughly instructed

Shirina to follow him. The sorceress didn't hesitate, nor did she look at Cassara as she followed the warrior into what remained of the camp.

Cassara watched her leave before turning to help tend to the wounded.

Maybe Shirina was still just as proud after all. She just hoped she wouldn't regret trusting the sorceress again.

Avarielle would think I'm insane.

Thinking of what the warrior would say brought a slight smile to her lips, lending her strength to face the dying on the battlefield.

AVARIELLE HAD ALWAYS PRIDED herself on her ability to see in the dark, but this darkness was so thick and impenetrable that it proved impossible to navigate. Pack and the other survivors seemed to experience no such difficulty, which only frustrated her more. They made just enough noise around her so that Avarielle could navigate, praying that none were ducking or stepping over anything. The air grew thick with their stench. Not nearly as bad as full-out Eloms, but still definitely gag-inducing in the closed quarters. She gritted her teeth against the rolling nausea.

She lost track of time and tried to distract herself from the stench by gauging how long it would be until they reached Siabala's Rage. She wasn't sure how Stormhold connected to it so couldn't even guess, which frustrated her even more.

At least in Siabala's Rage the walls were lit with magic, its one good feature.

The whole mountain suddenly trembled around them.

The shuffling ceased and she stopped, losing the small noises she'd used to navigate. Now blind and deaf, her hands twitched for action at her side.

The mountain shook again, then cracked, so loudly it sounded like war drums.

Avarielle crouched and waited, the tension vibrating around her. She kept Graysword safely in its scabbard, afraid of accidentally taking out one of Pack's people.

Silence blanketed them for a few more moments before the mountain cracked again. Fresh air wafted in and the sound of rushing water surrounded them. Avarielle stood up and headed towards the source of the air, where some light peaked through.

It didn't take her long to reach the end of the corridor, which ended where the mountain had collapsed, the dust still clinging to the air. Avarielle squinted and looked sideways, mist cooling her skin.

She turned and looked at the settling dust, a city spreading long and far below her, a blemish on her beautiful sandy land. It was half destroyed, not one building fully spared the cataclysm that had buried the city. Despite it cutting through her home, Avarielle had to admit that it was still spectacular enough to tell of its glory days. Beside them, from another corridor, water rushed out, trapped long ago in the Bloody Mountains beyond the protective and impenetrable barrier of the Wall of Loss. It gushed into the city, finding its way down streets and into buildings.

More waterfalls breaking free, some large, some small, all rushing to freedom in the valley below. To Graydon. To what remained of the West.

Home.

"I say we follow the water's lead!" Avarielle screamed over the roaring water to Pack. "We can scale the mountain!" The fresh air lifted her annoyingly long hair from her neck. She wanted to close her eyes and allow herself to bathe in the waters, to let it wash away weeks and months of bad memories.

Instead, she analyzed the cliffside to select her route.

Pack brought up his hands, even more claw-like and barely usable. He cocked his head sideways, toward the sun.

Avarielle squinted at it, Pack taking a step back to remain outside of its few beams.

"Of course," she said softly, too low for him to hear. The Eloms didn't travel during the day, either. Pack couldn't follow her in the light, which she so desperately needed and craved. Time to work to both their strengths, then.

"You go ahead down through the corridors. Just be careful!" she shouted to him. "I'll head down the mountain and through the city. It's too dark in there for me to see anyways. We'll meet up at the other end of the city, in the desert!"

Pack hesitated a moment before nodding and walking back into the dark corridor.

Avarielle watched him vanish. Before darkness completely engulfed him, she could only see light reflected off his armor. For a moment, she could have mistaken him for the man she'd known.

Only for a moment.

She turned back to the task at hand. The cliff face was getting sprayed from the waterfall and would only grow more slippery the longer she waited. And she wasn't certain what demons waited for her in the city, though without Pack beside her, she could freely wield Graysword.

She stretched, warming up her muscles for the task ahead.

Exhaustion pounded every inch of her. She'd been pushed too hard lately, both physically and emotionally. But in the distance, past the ugly city, gleaming in the sunset, she could see the sands of her homeland.

And Eli's Blood, it looked welcoming.

8

Jayden Edoline looked out the window of his room as he fidgeted with the curtains. The fortified city of Sharrow spread out beneath him. It wasn't the biggest town in the Southern Coalition, but it now held the Council of the Southern Coalition, after bigger cities had proved impossible to protect against Elom attacks.

He would be meeting with the Council shortly, Colonel Simon Orliys had advised him. Jayden was inclined to trust the colonel, though he hoped his trust wasn't misplaced. The colonel had known his father, or so he said, and had not questioned him when he claimed to be his heir.

It was the closest thing to an ally he currently had. He tugged on the curtains a few more times and let his hand drop. He wished Avarielle was here to protect him. Or his sisters, to make him laugh. Or his father, to advise him. But he was gone.

He swallowed hard. He couldn't believe his father was gone. And Edoline.

And he had yet to learn of the fate of his sisters.

Or Avarielle, eyes wide as she was thrown from the boat…

A knock at the door. Jayden took another gulp of air and opened it.

"They will see you now, your Highness," the colonel said, his eyes kind. Jayden nodded. His father had taught him much, saying politics were like a game, or a great stage play. You had to be firm and confident, no matter what.

Jayden was only twelve, or perhaps thirteen now…he'd have to check. How long had he been in Siabala's Rage? How long in Elihor? It didn't matter, really. Either way, he knew he would have difficulty convincing the Council to take him seriously. He'd figure it out, somehow. He had to.

With the Wall of Loss gone, he felt he had a greater chance of making his case. *But what case?* What was he even going to ask the Council? He took a deep breath, letting his instincts guide him. His father had told him that, too: to trust opportunity and instinct.

He looked up at the colonel and stood tall.

"Lead the way, Colonel." The colonel nodded and walked ahead, Jayden following, trying to keep his head high when he wanted to do very little else but to hide his face in a pillow and wait for dreams to take him away from this waking nightmare.

KADEN, loyal guard to Edoline and its royal family, looked around him at the people wearing clothing as tattered as their spirits. Farmers, villagers and merchants lined the streets of Sharrow, too full to handle the influx of people who had been forced to take refuge in the walled city.

"Smells like a toilet," Carsyn mumbled beside him.

"I think it *is* a toilet," Emala added, holding a faded scarf to her nose.

"You should have stayed in Kosel, woman," Carsyn scowled at her.

"This place needs a woman's touch," she mumbled, looking around.

Carsyn gave a rough laugh. "It does make Kosel look like paradise, doesn't it?"

"Aside from Edoline, Kosel was paradise," Emala whispered.

Kaden ignored them. The trek from Kosel had gone well, only because they had met escaping merchants who had offered them a lift in their empty carts. Their purses had been full, however, so they must have made good money off misery. Of course, they had had to pay their way, too. Thank Graydon that Cassara had left them with so much money.

Foolish girl, Kaden thought as he remembered his ward and her warm laughter.

Be safe, Cassara.

"How do we get in to see Jayden?" Carsyn asked.

"Not bad," Kaden mumbled. "It's not even noon and you've already managed to ask an intelligent question."

Carsyn grunted.

"Let's get closer to the Council chamber," Kaden said, and the three shuffled forward, stepping over people and waste, careful to stay together in the throngs. Carsyn took the front and Kaden the rear, the two keeping Emala safely between them. Emala might not have needed their protection, but old habits were difficult to stop.

They heard a commotion up ahead as the great council hall, pride of the city, came into view. Sharrow had been a rich city-state before joining the Southern Coalition to acquire more riches, demonstrated by its chamber's stunning white marble palisade and complicated window iron works. Wrought iron also formed a tall fence leading to a gate, intricately designed with deadly sharpness at its top, blocking access to the silver and gold fixtures of the venerable building. Those, and an embarrassment of purple and gold-attired guards.

Two of those guards stood before the gates now, several more behind them, blocking a woman who trembled with either fear or rage and addressed them with an agitated voice.

"I am Princess Malir of the City of Sol of the Southern

Coalition. How dare you block me from accessing my own father!"

The guards replied something unkind, Kaden guessed, though he couldn't hear. He examined the woman. She was a mess, dirty and disheveled.

"That's a nice dress," Emala said admiringly from beside him.

"The dirty ripped one?" Carsyn asked, disinterested.

"Well, it was a nice dress," she said. "Obviously, she needs a better maid. But those are fine silks, a good dye job, and that sewing! I can tell from here it was made to fit her perfectly!"

"Really," Carsyn said, looking elsewhere. There were fewer people here, most having been routed toward the city's north, as far as Kaden could tell, with promises of shelter and food.

"Are you saying she might actually be a princess?" Kaden leaned in to ask Emala.

The question also piqued Carsyn's interest. He slowed down a bit to listen more closely.

Emala shrugged. "Posture is good, the sewing is personalized, she seems unaccustomed to being told no, so yes, I'd say she's a princess." She paused. "Not nearly as regal as our Princess Cassara, but a princess nonetheless."

"I tell you, lady," they were now near enough to hear the guard clearly. "You're not the first girl to make that claim to try and get in here. Almost lost my job on a much prettier looking thing than you." Princess Malir flushed bright red.

"See? Princess." Emala said from beside him. "Any other girl would have just punched him."

"Really?" Carsyn asked dubiously. "You would have punched him?"

"Care to try?" Emala answered drily. Kaden fought to suppress a grin as they approached.

"Follow my lead," he told them, the two snapping to attention. Kaden adjusted his weapons and clothing, hoping he looked remotely official. He straightened his back and took on his sternest air, usually reserved for Carsyn's particularly annoying moments.

"You will apologize at once to the Princess Malir, scoundrel," he growled as he walked up to the man, positioning himself slightly in front of the princess. Carsyn followed his lead and flanked her on the other side. Emala went to the princess and lowered her head respectfully as she curtsied.

Kaden had to hand it to Carsyn and Emala. Their minds were sharp and their feet quick.

The guard seemed flustered. "Who are you?"

Kaden took a step forward, nose to nose with the belligerent guard. "We are Princess Malir's retinue, or at least what remains of it after her journey." He turned and lowered his head respectfully. "Our apologies for getting separated, princess. We are all that remain." He hoped he wasn't contradicting anything the princess might have said. That would be their undoing and would probably get them killed.

Before the guard could regain his balance, Kaden

leaned in just a little bit more. "The princess has asked to see her father, leader of Sol. Will you not grant the princess her request?"

"And a room," Emala piped up. "You should be kind enough to offer her a room and a warm bath. And provide me with fabric to make her a new dress. Do you honestly think a princess is proud to be questioned by a simpleton such as yourself and made to remain in this condition before all of these people?"

Emala grew flushed with anger, taking a protective step towards Princess Malir, as she would have Cassara. Malir's stunned look would hopefully pass for one of great trial. Kaden hoped she would at least have the presence of mind to remain quiet.

The guards exchanged glances.

"This way, please. And our deepest apologies, your Highness." He gestured them toward the large door, the other guard scurrying to open it.

Princess Malir raised her head proudly and did not acknowledge the guard's apology, walking forward with purpose. The three from Edoline followed, hoping the princess would not reveal their ruse now and block them access to their rightful king.

***

Jayden stood outside the chamber, the Council members apparently intent on making him wait. It was a game they liked playing. He knew this, thanks to his father's stories. He stood, since no seat had been provided, his hands comfortably behind his back, struggling to remain calm and not betray his annoyance. He wanted to pace, but he knew he shouldn't do that, either.

The colonel kept watch nearby and, despite his claims of having known his father well, Jayden felt it wiser not to trust him too quickly. A lump formed in his throat. He wasn't sure he could trust anyone, anymore.

"I demand to see him now, not later!" a woman asked in shrill tones.

Jayden looked up with interest, as did the colonel, who took a step forward to block access to a woman who looked like she'd rolled in the mud. The only thing that shone on her were her eyes, which blazed with fury.

The colonel interjected, helping out the poor servant of the court who'd faced the woman's wrath. "Princess Malir, you must wait until the Council is no longer in session."

"I grew up with these politics, colonel, so you can't fool me into thinking that they're actually doing more than drinking in there!"

A few more people rounded the corner and joined the princess, a familiar voice speaking, "Would you not rather clean and change first, my Lady?"

Jayden's heart skipped a beat and he took a step forward. He recognized them as they recognized him: Kaden, Carsyn and Emala. Cassara's retinue was here.

"Prince Jayden!" Emala exclaimed, the three deserting the princess to join him. Emala gathered him in a fierce hug as she cried and mumbled, "They said you were alive, but I didn't believe those old coots! Oh, thank the stars, Jayden. I never thought we'd see you again."

He managed to disentangle himself, and Emala regained some composure, her face splotchy from tears.

"It is a pleasure to see you again, your Highness," Kaden said, bowing, an act that Carsyn mirrored.

Jayden swallowed hard. He wanted to jump in Kaden's arms and feel safe there, but the colonel was still watching. He did not intend to appear weak before the Southern Coalition.

"What of my sister?" he managed to ask in barely a whisper to keep his voice from cracking.

"She went ahead to Massir, Jayden, but we have no reason to believe she didn't make it." Kaden said. "She was with a powerful friend."

Jayden wanted to cry when he whispered the name. "Avarielle?"

Kaden's eyes grew wide. "How did you know?"

"I…met her. But she wasn't with Cassara anymore."

"Where?" Kaden asked sharply, worry edging his words. Jayden was grateful when the princess interrupted.

"Princess Cassara?" Princess Malir huffed, stepping up to them.

Jayden's head snapped up. "Yes. Princess Cassara is my sister."

Malir sighed. "Had I known you three were from Edoline, I would have left you back there." She waved her hand as though too fatigued to deal with the fate handed her. "But, you will hear this one way or the other, so you should know that your sister is now wed to Prince Dayshon, heir to the throne of Rashim." She swallowed hard after speaking the name. Emala's eyes filled with tears.

"She…" Malir's hardness seemed to melt away. "Dayshon and she are riding into battle towards the West. I'm here for that reason. To get at least one thousand men to help them stand against the invading dark creatures, which apparently come from Elihor. And now that the Wall has fallen…"

"From Elihor? But the Wall wouldn't let anything cross. Until now, anyway," the colonel asked, joining them and narrowing his eyes as though gauging the princess' sanity. She squared her shoulders as though ready for a fight, but Jayden stepped in.

"I did," he said softly, all five adults suddenly very focused on him. He looked at each in turn, settling on the colonel as he spoke. "I was there," he said, his voice surprisingly strong. "I was in Elihor, and I've come back."

"How did you…" Kaden began to ask, but stopped himself, as though he really didn't want to know. But Jayden needed the trust of the colonel. And the colonel studied him, gauging him now. No one else spoke, so the young heir of Edoline filled the silence.

"I was in Siabala's Rage," he said softly. Emala gasped. Jayden forced himself to speak the words. "I was kept there by a Circle witch." He would not get into all the details. Not now. "A friend of my sister's, Avarielle

Grayloft, saved me." Someone cursed. Maybe Carsyn. It didn't matter. All that mattered were the colonel's piercing eyes, analyzing his worth. All that mattered was getting Cassara the help she desperately needed. So that he wouldn't lose her, too.

"She couldn't get me to Graydon, so she brought me to Elihor. We stayed for a time, and then we crossed the straits to come back. I lost my friends in the strait," he added, as though not wanting to be called out for a lie. "I floated for a while, and then landed pretty much where we met, colonel."

A whistling sound had started in his ears. He felt numb, though he knew tears threatened to overcome him.

"This on Edoline I swear to be true," he added softly, then his words found strength. "I would wish this fate upon no one else, and whatever darkness is seeping into Graydon from Elihor must be stopped. I've seen what destruction can be wrought. I've smelled the ashes of that land, tasted the scent of death. We cannot, we must not, let that fate fall upon Graydon, as well." He took a step forward, closing the gap between him and the colonel.

"Colonel, without the Wall, the attacks will intensify. We need to stop them."

The colonel studied the young prince a moment more, then nodded. Jayden felt the pressure relieve from his chest at the colonel's trust.

"I see no reason to doubt you, Prince Jayden, for you have the same look in your eyes I've seen in seasoned veterans of the war. And," he added more gently, "as I've mentioned before, I knew your father. I have no reason to distrust his blood."

He placed his hands behind his back and Kaden spoke, surprising Jayden. He'd forgotten there were others in the room.

"So, you'll help?"

The colonel nodded. "I fear a thousand men will not prove enough, and I don't have that many left, either, that could move quickly. But the Coalition will not withstand another attack. Our city walls will collapse from the refugees of Solir and the countryside. Better to move now than to wait here digging our own graves."

"How do we convince the council?" Kaden asked, Jayden grateful for the guard's questions which allowed him time to catch his breath. To ground himself back in the here and now.

The colonel gave Kaden a slow, knowing smile. "Follow me," he said, turning on his heel toward the council chamber. Princess Malir followed him, holding her head high. Emala indicated she'd stay there, and Jayden had to look away from the tears in her eyes. Kaden placed a hand on his back, squeezed his shoulder, and nodded. "We will follow you, Prince Jayden."

He nodded and gathered himself, following the colonel and the princess, his loyal guards behind him.

The posted guards opened the doors of the Council of the Coalition, to be met with protests before the colonel quieted them with a stern look. The army had been keeping them safe, and Jayden could see from where he stood that they couldn't afford to anger its leader.

Princess Malir walked in next with purpose, shouts of joy resonating at her sight.

Jayden hesitated at the threshold. Kaden came to stand beside him.

"What of Edoline?" He thought he might be sick. Kaden placed a reassuring hand on his shoulder.

"I don't know, Jayden. But I do know that Edoline won't survive another attack from dark creatures."

Jayden nodded and took a deep breath. He wanted very little but to head back to the safety of his home. But first, he had to ensure that his kingdom would survive beyond whatever darkness Graydon had yet to face.

Holding his head high, with his two loyal guards behind him, Prince Jayden of Edoline crossed the threshold to address the Council of the Southern Coalition.

9

Shirina tried to sleep in the small tent, to no avail. Trevon stood outside at its entrance, apparently believing he could stop her.

She turned on her side, the sands of the West a harsher bed than the forest floors of Kosel. Her thoughts kept her awake even if her body neared exhaustion. Her direction was unclear now, and she knew no one but herself could forge the path, or even guide her.

Ravenhold was gone.

She closed her eyes and let the grief wash over her, still seeing the keep vanish into dark dust, taking its wealth of knowledge with it.

But it had saved them.

Why save us? Why not save the books, which can make an impact, and save so much more in the long run? Shirina wasn't certain of the keep's logic, if it was capable of any. Some

Circle Elders claimed it did, so infused with generations of magic and knowledge.

Shirina wished she could scream in frustration, but knew it would hardly help her situation. She felt helpless and unconvinced she could make a difference.

Other Circle adepts were on their way here, and she knew other Crimson Circles were amongst them, though she didn't know if any other Elites remained. If another Elite came, or perhaps even an Elder, though she doubted any had survived, then she could follow them.

Could I? The Covenant of Ravenhold was broken now. It had vanished before its keep and, even with one strong leader taking charge, it would never exist again. At least not for a long time.

If we can ever use our magic again. With Elihor's magic mixing with Graydon's, the magic proved too deadly for unprotected wielders to channel. Shirina was protected by the staff, but it was the only one, and could not be transferred to another adept. Or so Grasky had led her to believe. Should another Elite show up, she would still be the only one able to wield magic.

One witch with magic was not enough. She needed allies, too.

She sighed and sat up. She had been surprised to feel regret over the princess' lack of trust in her. Somehow, she had believed Cassara would have forgiven her, would have seen the necessity of her actions. She should have anticipated that the princess' attachment to the Grayloft would have left a deep wound.

But Shirina had chosen not to lie to her, and perhaps that would help to change Cassara's mind in time.

Usually she wouldn't have wielded truth, especially so clumsily and to such poor results, but the Circle's usual approach of hoarding secrets had brought all of Graydon to its knees before Siabala.

She lay back down, closing her eyes and steadying her breath. She needed sleep. She was exhausted, and this self-doubt helped nothing and no one.

She clutched the staff. She would simply have to find a way to make things work.

CASSARA TOILED all day with the wounded, bandaging wounds, speaking comforting words, holding their hands as they breathed their last. She had seen Dayshon only briefly, his eyes haunted, before he had left again to strategize with Breck. He had quickly told her that about half of their soldiers were gone.

Cassara had just nodded, not knowing what to answer. What could she say? Half of them dead, Loas among them. She had not cried for him yet. Not because she didn't grieve, but because her mind felt as numb as her body. Gragor had taken his death with great difficulty, the two having become quite close in their short time knowing each other.

She had left him to grieve alone, unable to comfort

him, not knowing which words to say anymore. Could words even help salve such wounds?

Cassara closed a Westland warrior's eyes and stood up, stretching her lower back. She looked towards the sky, away from the dead and wounded and from the mysterious city nearby.

Her magic had not been enough to save them, and words would not be enough to heal them. No matter what she'd said to Shirina and Trevon, they needed the Circle more than ever. The adepts could protect them where she might not be able to. Shirina had been right. Cassara didn't care for attack spells and was no good at them.

Just like she'd had a hard time killing Jesimae. She'd only been able to do so to save Shirina.

I only did what I felt was necessary, Shirina had said unapologetically. Just as Cassara had done in killing Jesimae. Maybe the two weren't so different, after all.

She missed the scent of the sea on the dry desert air, longed for the sounds of the surf.

No matter how she felt, it would prove difficult to convince the West of the Circle's good intentions. Twenty years ago, the wars, led by greedy Eastland leaders and fueled by the Circle, had ravaged the West. The wounds of its people were still etched on their land and actions.

Cassara suddenly had an idea and smiled.

Words could not heal the troops, but a song might cheer them up.

And she knew just the one to sing to help them all begin the long healing process.

TREVON BROUGHT the sorceress just as Cassara had asked. The sorceress said nothing, standing defiantly.

"It's time to make your loyalties clear, Shirina," Cassara whispered. "The wounds inflicted by the Circle in the West are deep, but we must begin healing them if they are to trust you."

Shirina nodded, uncertainty in her eyes. Cassara knew the sorceress hated being at a disadvantage, and so offered no other information. She also knew the sorceress still held loyalty for the Circle, no matter what she said. That was even fine with Cassara, but she needed the West to understand that the Circle was not all that Shirina believed in. That she believed in Graydon and its people, too. Cassara truly thought the sorceress did, or at least she fiercely hoped so.

Several fires had been built around the back edge of the camp, where warriors and soldiers had gathered to eat before the next battle, whenever it may come. Scouts had spread out in the city below, but none had yet returned. With a spread of kilometers, it might take them some time to return. If they returned at all.

Quite a few archers held their bows at the ready, eyes darting from sky to ground, from left to right, from shadow to light. The sound of popping firewood mixed gently with murmurs from the figures huddled around them.

To the east of the camp, where a beast had fallen and

ashes littered the ground, rocks had been piled to form an arrow pointing towards the West and the setting sun. Pointing the souls towards their eternal repose in the hands of Lady Fate, to join their ancestors and loved ones in the Afterfate.

Cassara stopped near it, the murmurs ending as she softly spoke, facing the direction of the arrow, and not of the warriors.

"For all the children of Graydon, in the East and in the West. Those who have passed now, and those who were lost years ago." Shirina stiffened, knowing no one would misunderstand her. For the Westland Wars, fueled by the Circle, had cost thousands their lives. Twenty years had hardly salved the wounds of invasion. She could sense the warriors shuffling, and spotted Trevon from the corner of her eye observing her.

Cassara kept her gaze towards the West, pulling out her flute. The wood, though dry, was still a comfort to her fingers. When Graydon had lost Elihor and raised the Wall, he had plunged into the sea, so that he and his love could be reunited through the waters. But what he had not realized then was that the wall had formed two straits on either side of the land, keeping the waters ever apart as well, the Straits of Grief and the Straits of Tears.

Cassara brought the flute to her mouth and spun out the first note, knowing that Shirina would immediately recognize the rarely played song. Of Graydon's soul attempting to reach his beloved even after death. Of his desire to have all magic freed, so that he could be reunited with her, and they could approach Lady Fate together. So that they would not be alone, where they might never find each other again in the vastness of the Afterfate.

High she brought the notes, not shy of playing them, not afraid of any repercussion, no more than she had been of learning the song when Avarielle had taught it to her. The Circle, who controlled the magic, had always felt the lyrics were against them, and the song had been banned. But in the West the song was the sweetest music, the greatest love song ever created. And one that no Circle adept would ever sing.

For at its end, the magic was let free once again, and the two lovers headed to the Afterfate together, reunited forever as one. The Keepers of Magic had failed in their duties. The Circle had fallen.

Shirina met the challenge fully and sang, though she did not utter the words as clearly as she would other songs. Cassara felt cruel for an instant, the song like a prediction of things that had now come to pass. The Circle had fallen.

When the notes formed the climax of the song, when the magic was freed and Graydon and Elihor stood before one another in the sea, when the Wall had crumbled and the straits vanished, Shirina's voice rose, without hesitation, breaking a bit at the high note, only to come down again, leading them gently to the Afterfate.

The song ended, with all souls reuniting and free in the Afterfate—free as the people who had been trapped in the eternal fear of magic. Cassara put her flute away, looking to the West, towards where legends said the Afterfate rested, with the setting sun. She wondered if, now that the Wall had fallen, Graydon and Elihor were truly one again.

She did not need to look at Shirina to know that her voice had not cracked due to thirst. She did not need to see the sorceress to know tears lined her high cheekbones and to know what she now felt.

The Circle had already fallen, but, unlike Graydon and Elihor's reunion, Shirina was still very much alone.

10

Night blanketed the land and Avarielle still had at least a full day's walk before clearing the strange city that had engulfed the flank of the Bloody Mountains and part of her beloved land. She had to be careful in her route, avoiding roads quickly turning into rivers. Thankfully the city wasn't level, and several deeper cracks engulfed the tumbling waters, clearing the way for her.

My brother died around here, she thought, knowing he had never been buried, left for the coyotes to pick apart. She fought a shiver. She could very well have died here, too.

She wondered how different the course of everything would have been if she had died here, at the hands of her own people. Would the Wall of Loss still be standing? Would the dark creatures have invaded? Would Siabala have given up before starting, knowing no heir of Grayloft could take another oath?

Why now? she pondered as she went, having lost interest in exploring the city, only wanting to reach home. *Why had Siabala chosen now to attack, to bring down the Wall?*

Something must have changed. Maybe it was because of her. Maybe since she was the last Grayloft to take up oath, he feared one of the pieces of the key would forever vanish.

Maybe. She wasn't sold on her theory. Surely, he would have come up with an alternative long ago. Something else must have triggered his movements. She hoped, she needed to believe, that something else made him move.

She gritted her teeth. The Circle had hastened Graydon's downfall by delivering her to Siabala. And, although it took time, he had eventually found a way to get her to summon Graysword.

The hairs at the back of her neck stood on end and she turned back, toward the Bloody Mountains. Her mind played tricks on her, she was pretty certain, but she felt as though Siabala observed her now. His voice rumbled somewhere deep in her mind, still, the admiration that he'd expressed with how she'd withstood days, maybe weeks, of torture.

Impressive.

That's what he'd said about her. Like he'd created her. Like he had a stake in her.

She narrowed her eyes and gazed back unflinchingly at the mountains. If he looked, let him see she wasn't afraid.

Let him see that she intended to fight him, still. To claim her revenge. Hands curled into fists at her side, she turned around and continued walking.

Maybe it doesn't matter why this happened now. What mattered was ending the curse on her family. The cursed oath her ancestor had sealed with Siabala, blood spent in every generation in need of the blade. The one she'd made to Siabala, not understanding the cost she would pay.

Not caring, in the throes of Graysword's magic.

That oath, she would make sure to break. By killing Siabala. By claiming revenge for turning Kryde into a soulless puppet, and for leaving her the duty of ending it for him.

Avarielle Grayloft had every intention of ending Siabala, no matter the price.

The anger burned away her remaining energy and the fatigue from the past few days caught up with her. She wanted to keep pushing forward to reach her people, but being stupid tired wouldn't help anyone.

It was time to get some much-needed sleep. She scouted the area around her briefly, headed for the buildings out of view of the mountains, just in case, and found a mostly standing home amongst the rubble. She looked for threats but spotted nothing. Her hand went to the comforting hilt of Graysword, but the magic stayed dormant. Still, she sat down in the darkest shadows to sleep at the ready, keeping Graysword loosely in her hand.

The magic swirled inside her long after she had drifted

off to sleep, where no dreams awaited her, cleanly plucked from her mind by the magic of her sword.

Avarielle woke up at dawn, feeling refreshed and healed. She jumped to her feet and sheathed her sword, glad no attack had come in the night. Getting a full night's sleep, a rare luxury this past year, was just what she had needed.

She felt slightly queasy but ignored the feeling as she pushed on, drinking the last of her water. The falls that had broken free from the mountains roared in the distant background. Their water had turned the deeper inset streets into swirling rivers, but most of the water had discovered other places to vanish underground. Avarielle didn't trust it. The water had been trapped by the Wall for so long, who knew what poisons lurked within it?

She stepped outside the building, squinting at the sun. If there was one thing she loved most about her land, it was the almost complete lack of rain. Of course, that meant she would require water faster, but she was certain she could reach her people and safe water sources before she succumbed to the heat or its illusions. She had, after all, grown up here.

A noise to the left caught her attention and she pulled a long knife free just as someone stepped out of a building.

"Pack," she greeted him. He looked uncomfortable in the full sun, shielding as much of his gray, taunt skin with his armor as possible. "I'm glad you made it all right," she added, pleased he had found his way and she had been able to find her own. She moved into the shadows of the building and he followed.

He tried to speak, the syllables all garbled. Avarielle could make one word as he pointed back towards the mountain. *Elom.*

"Siabala's mounting his attack, isn't he?" Avarielle asked, looking to where Pack had pointed. The warrior simply nodded.

"It's big, isn't it?" Another nod.

"Nightfall?" she asked, and he nodded again.

"Well, let's make as much headway as we can. We have to reach my people and get them organized first." *If any of them are left.*

The buildings near her seemed to be crawling with other half-Eloms, cowering from the light, some wearing partial armor, some none.

"There are a lot of you, aren't there?" she asked, looking around. Pack gave her a monstrous grin. She grinned in turn.

"I hate to say it Pack, but I'm looking forward to the battle tonight," she whispered and he nodded again, dark eyes like steel.

"We'll get our revenge, Pack," she whispered. "You have my word." He studied her for a few moments and then vanished back into the shadows. Avarielle continued alone in the light, hoping Siabala would make it easy for her and show up tonight.

No matter what else might come, she intended to be the one to finish him.

———

Avarielle could spot a few fires in the fading light, though the buildings made it difficult to see who had gathered there, and how many there were. Adrenaline pumped through her. She was excited to see her people again. To share stories and laughter. And to fight alongside them.

Not to be so alone.

Pack had exited the buildings in the fading light and walked near her, armor clanking slightly. She'd have to help him readjust it.

A scurrying sound caught her attention. Pack turned with her, toward the mountain. The streets turned to river shimmered in the moonlight. And the others…*moved*. Writhed. Spreading down from the mountain, quickly, toward them. It took her a moment to realize what she was looking at. In great streams, Eloms piled out of Siabala's Rage. There were more than Avarielle had ever seen.

"We need to reach high ground now! They're too fast. We let them pass, and we attack from behind while the others up ahead deal with them from their end!" Avarielle prayed that the fires weren't those of families or the elderly, hoping that warriors were amongst them.

She was too far to warn them. Her people weren't

idiots, and had survived the wars and the Eloms. They'd know to keep an eye out, especially with the strange city breaking out of the earth.

Pack moved quickly, leading the others up buildings, Avarielle following them over rubble. The last of them had just climbed up when the Eloms flooded the street below, moving faster than Avarielle had ever seen them move, a sea of misshapen darkness below her.

The Eloms ignored them, so intent on their goal up ahead. From their higher vantage point, Avarielle could now see that an army waited just beyond the edge of the city, warriors milling about, weapons reflecting the light of sunset. And she could see horses. Those were not her people, or at least not all of them.

A cold wind blew as the monsters continued streaming below, climbing over one another to reach the human flesh. These were the fiercest Eloms she had ever seen.

A few Eloms leapt towards her, missing the rooftop by a hair. Surprised, Avarielle stepped back. Leaping Eloms?

Pack stepped in front of her, as though to shield her. Then Avarielle understood. He was masking her scent with his own, which resembled that of Eloms more with each passing day. It seemed to work, as the Eloms passed them by, ignoring the would-be Eloms whose flesh did not promise the fresh blood they craved.

She heard shouts up ahead and she could make out the army moving in the fading sun. Then light exploded in the sky, and tinted the world in sickly yellow color. A Circle witch was there. Maybe more than just one.

Avarielle's hand clutched Graysword, but did not unsheathe it for fear of hurting Pack and his people. She would bide her time, and fight her way to the camp.

It seemed there were more than Eloms to hunt this night.

11

"*D*id you really think a simple song would convince me she isn't the enemy?" Trevon demanded the second he stood alone with Cassara, on the edge of the city.

"No," Cassara said as she surveyed the city in the fading light. "I don't expect much would, actually. But it might start to change things, maybe." She sighed and turned to face him. "Regardless, we need her, Trevon. We need the Circle. My magic isn't enough, and Shirina is very powerful."

Trevon spat on the ground. Cassara sighed, her own anger vanishing with her breath. Especially the anger she harbored toward Shirina. She had been angry for so long, but after speaking to the sorceress and hearing her side of the story, so factual and truthful…she didn't think she could afford to hang on to her feelings, no matter how justified they had seemed at the time. She needed the

Circle, and she needed Trevon to understand, since she also needed him.

"Trevon, I don't think Shirina attacked Avarielle, for what it's worth. I don't believe it anymore, anyways. I've been thinking about it all day." Her voice drifted over the city, away from them. "I hadn't allowed myself to really stop and think about it before, it was just easier being angry, I suppose. The truth is, she stopped Delora from gaining Graysword, and I'm not sure how she could have saved both Avarielle and the sword. I don't think she liked Avarielle, mind you, but I just don't think she attacked her, either."

Trevon's stared daggers at her. "You will not refer to her in the past tense," he said softly. "Until we find her corpse, we assume she still fights."

Cassara bit her lip and lowered her head. "You're right. She lived a few days ago, against all odds. She must have been the one to summon Graysword."

"You're accusing her of lowering the Wall of Loss?" Trevon growled.

"Not on purpose, no. She held out for so long, Trevon." The thought of Avarielle in Siabala's Rage for months slithered around Cassara's heart, leaving it hollow.

"Whatever she did," he said stubbornly, though some of his fire seemed to have vanished, "she did because she had to."

"I know," Cassara took a deep breath and pushed forward. "And so did Shirina."

Trevon crossed his arms in answer, looking stubbornly toward the mountains.

She cleared her throat. "I'm sorry Trevon. I wish there was an easier enemy to blame for Avarielle. I wish everything could be just…easier."

A shout sounded from the camp. "The city! It lives!"

Cassara and Trevon both looked down to the city, where the streets pulsated black. Buildings writhed and then vanished in the sea of darkness, as though something swallowed them whole. The princess squinted to see better, and she could just make out limbs. She gasped, took an involuntary step back, the shapes becoming clearer as the wave approached.

"Eloms!" she screamed. The word coursed through the troops like lightning. Soldiers scrambled up and donned their weapons as Breck and Dayshon shouted orders to prepare for battle, to form a front, to prepare to fire, for the catapults to be readied…it was chaos, the troops responding as quickly as they could in the newly fallen darkness, and with so many wounded.

"We need to back away," Trevon said, and Cassara nodded, following him deeper into camp. A crimson cloak and white robe caught her eye just to the east.

"Shirina!" she shouted, gaining a scowl from Trevon. "The troops will need light by which to fight!"

Shirina nodded and began chanting, a steady rhythm requiring neither pause nor breath. When Cassara could see the energies of the sorceress stabilizing, she knew the spell was ready to be unleashed.

"Cover your eyes!" she commanded the troops as the spell of light exploded above them. Thankfully, most acted quickly enough to avoid temporary blindness.

"Archers, fire! Catapults, fire!" Breck called back, the orders sounded off down the rows of soldiers. The city streets were thick with Eloms, crawling over one another to get to the awaiting soldiers, their gray skin cracking with dark veins, failing to reflect the light. Absorbing it to create more darkness below, a writhing river of monstrous bodies.

Cassara longed for the feel of a bow in her hands, to look down the shaft of the arrow at her enemy and let it fly, but she knew that she could be much more effective in magical combat.

She reached Shirina as the light spell ended, Trevon staying near with his hand on the pommel of his sword. "We need to help them," Cassara quickly told the sorceress. "There are too many."

Shirina nodded, clutching the staff as though it was a lifeline, the dark circles under her eyes accentuated by the mage light.

"I can attack the ones furthest from the troops, and you take those nearest. You have more control over your magical flames." Shirina focused on the princess. "Think of it like you're casting a fiery shield around them. Like in Rockor, when you protected Avarielle and the village from the Eloms with your flames. Don't think of it as an attack. You'll do better for it."

Cassara nodded, the sorceress' words helping her find

her confidence again. She'd saved seventy-two souls. She could save more, now. She had to.

"Let's stay together," Cassara whispered. She wanted to stay near Shirina to pull her out if she weakened too much. The sorceress was only useful alive, and there was no telling how much magic she could wield before she would collapse.

Also, she could keep a better eye on her this way. Just because Cassara had come to the realization that the witch hadn't attacked Avarielle directly, it hardly meant that she intended to trust her.

SHIRINA FOLLOWED Cassara to a small knoll, the Westland warrior right behind them, either unable or unwilling to trust her with the princess' life. Or because he intended to take her down if she turned on the troops. Either way, Shirina didn't care.

Right now, she firmly believed that Cassara, with her aura still pure with Graydon's light, could help save the Circle from the blended magic. But to find out how, she needed to ensure that the princess survived.

She planted the staff firmly in the ground, grasping it with both hands as she chanted pillars of fire to life in the midst of the Eloms. Far enough from the troops not to kill anyone, but close enough to offer them a reprieve.

The Eloms jumped up and Dayshon shouted for the cavalry to move forward, the Westland warriors putting away bows in favor of their swords. Then the great wave collided into them, the warriors fighting back as best they could.

Cassara summoned her magic, warming Shirina's cold skin like a wool blanket. The princess called her fires to surround the troops, killing the nearest beasts and slowing their progress enough for the warriors to down the rest of the first line of attack.

But still more Eloms poured into the street, a great tsunami swallowing all in its path. The catapults launched large stones into the oncoming hordes, taking out both Eloms and buildings.

She summoned more fires as Cassara did the same, but her mage light flickered and began to dwindle. She had used so much magic lately that her strength, even if amplified by the staff, rapidly failed her.

"You have to bring the light back!" Cassara said through gritted teeth, the princess also showing signs of fatigue, though her fires still shone brightly.

Shirina nodded and began chanting again when the light exploded above her, becoming much brighter than even her original spell. She scanned the horizon, using the Sight to see the source of the new spell. White-robed sorceresses entered the northern edge of the battlefield, riding horses into battle.

"More Circle," Trevon mumbled behind them.

"They can't use their magic," Shirina said, cold dread creeping into her limbs.

"I think they just did," Cassara said, out of breath from her latest spell.

"No, I mean they will die if they use their magic, Cassara. The magic is contaminated." Seeing the princess looking blankly at her, Shirina repeated, "They'll die, Cassara."

Cassara put a hand on the witch's arm, the princess' hand filled with the warmth of pure magic, stronger than that of Shirina's staff. It was so warm, Shirina had to fight not to hug the princess and try and steal all of that warmth, to feel that purest of magics for an instant, and not the constant ache of her infected throat.

"We'll *all* die if they don't use their magic," Cassara said, not apologizing for what was necessary, no more than Shirina had apologized for what she had done to Avarielle.

"I just…" Shirina whispered, then stopped. She wished she could save them. That the magic wasn't contaminated. That she could do *something*. But she couldn't, the ache of powerlessness spreading through her like ice.

"I'm sorry, Shirina," Cassara whispered before turning back towards the battle and unleashing her magic again. Shirina closed her eyes for an instant, looking around her with only her magical senses. The adepts were chanting battle spells, preparing for the fight.

The magic of Elihor was already within them, invading them like poison, traveling the length of their arteries and veins, propelled forward with each new word chanted and each heartbeat.

She couldn't save them.

She had told them to come, to gather here, only to helplessly watch them die, one by one.

THE WAVES of darkness just kept streaming below them, and Avarielle began to feel deep unease. She wanted to jump in and kill them all, but it would prove difficult enough not cutting down Pack and his people. She grounded her feet, forcing her heartbeat and breath to slow.

Fires raged in the battle up ahead, and Avarielle could feel something warm on her chest. She reached into her tunic and pulled out Cassara's amulet, which glowed brightly in the growing darkness. With each new pulse of fire up ahead, the amulet only grew warmer.

Cassara! The princess was up there, fighting for her life, somehow wielding her fires without her amulet.

But her amulet only became warmer, as though in a frenzy to reach the princess.

Maybe she needs this to be at her most powerful? she wondered as the wave of Eloms finally passed them by.

She tucked the amulet back into her tunic. "I'll get you to her," she promised, blood pumping in her veins.

"Pack, you and your men attack them from the sides. I'll come from behind. Whatever you do, give me and my sword a good distance. I don't want to have to deal with killing you, too!"

Pack nodded and she grinned and jumped down, pulling Graysword free as she ran after the Eloms. She caught the last few of the throng unawares, Graysword cutting through them with ease.

It felt good to feel the magic pumping through her, the blade swirling with power as she screamed and hacked the monsters around her, not worried about right or wrong or about the humans the Eloms had once been, or the pain around her middle, just focusing on this moment. On what needed to be done.

On the next kill.

THE ELOMS WERE TRYING to leap and scramble past them, drawn by all of Graydon and not just the flesh of the human army.

Cassara spread her fires to stop them from infiltrating Graydon and hunting down the remaining survivors, but still the creatures came, downing more and more troops. Cassara wished she could see Dayshon, but she had lost sight of him in the initial attack.

"Trevon!" she called back, the warrior appearing beside her immediately. Cassara glanced at Shirina, who still cast her flames, though she leaned heavily on her staff.

"Find my husband and protect him. I'll be safe here."

"Are you mad, woman?" he hissed.

"No, I'm worried for my husband. Please, Trevon.

We're stronger with him here, and I can take care of myself."

Trevon turned to Shirina, annoyed. Then, apparently deciding the weary witch wasn't a threat, he ran down towards the fray, sword drawn, where last they had seen Dayshon. Cassara watched him down two Eloms and knew that he was more in his element than he was babysitting magic casters.

The other adepts had taken position not far from them, still on horseback, casting flames at a rapid pace. Shirina looked at them once in a while, and Cassara knew what she saw, for she too was gifted with the Sight.

The dark magic clung to them a little bit more with each spell cast, and Cassara doubted they would survive much longer. The princess looked at Shirina, but saw that her energies still seemed clean. The sorceress drew power from the staff, which glowed brightly with magic.

Shirina ended a chant, and Cassara saw something she had failed to spot before. A dark patch of magic laced around Shirina's throat like a lasso. She looked away. So Shirina was infected, too.

Uncertain how she felt about that, Cassara focused on the battle. The troops were managing to hold their ground, the West and the East working as one efficient unit. Cassara focused her magic on the ones trying to get by them, to stop them from moving further inland.

Some of the Eloms grew increasingly erratic in their quest to get past the troops, a few of them now heading towards the adepts. They were easily dispatched, but in the effort, one of the orange-cloaked adepts fell. He did not stand again.

Cassara forced herself to concentrate on the battle, hoping Shirina could manage to do the same. Her hands shook with fatigue, and she wished she could sit down, but there was no time. More Eloms headed toward the Circle witches, but Cassara burned them to ashes, hoping to help the tired adepts.

Shirina offered her a thin smile. Then the sorceress looked up, toward the city. Surprise lit her features and she seemed to find energy to stand straight again.

"That's a magic I never thought I would see again," she said, pointing towards the back of the army of Eloms, trailing to just outside the line of buildings where white fires exploded in the growing darkness.

Cassara's heart raced as she squinted to see better, not needing to see the wielder to recognize the flames of Graysword and the graceful movements of Avarielle.

She cried out in joy, her heart missing a few beats in its relief, when a cold chant echoed over the battle.

More Eloms broke free of the main troops to stream toward them. Cassara was trying to identify the origin of the growing chant as a few neared, Shirina dispatching the incoming creatures.

"What is that?" she screamed to Shirina over the chant. "It sounds like Circle magic."

Shirina didn't answer, looking up at the white mist now spreading along the foot of the mountains like a veil. Cassara looked away to beat back the growing number of

Eloms, trying to ignore the scream of one of the adepts as she vanished in black flames.

She thought of Avarielle, coming toward them despite all odds, and allowed herself to believe that they could still win the day.

AVARIELLE EASILY DOWNED the monsters around her, so frenzied in their lust for blood that few even turned to face her. She knew she was barely making a dent in their numbers, but she didn't care. It felt good to wield Graysword again. How she had missed its strength and power.

Pack was nearby, far enough away that she would not hurt him, and he was doing well, growing accustomed to using his claws as weapons. She wondered how he must feel, cutting down his own people with claws so like theirs, and imagined he was trying not to think of it. A warrior simply doing what needed to be done to win the day.

Just like her, ignoring the magic tumbling in her abdomen, ignoring the rising nausea and the pain.

Cassara's amulet practically burned her chest now. Avarielle glanced up between blows. The princess' magic had weakened on the horizon, the fires not as strong nor as bright as before. Her strength was failing, but the amulet might be able to save her.

Avarielle cried a battle cry and doubled her attacks to

get through. Everything slowed for a moment as a song drowned out every battle noise. Avarielle didn't need to look back to know that kealers had been let loose. She looked at Pack with concern.

"Tell your men to back out! If you're injured, they'll kill you trying to heal you!"

Pack jumped back, and she could clearly see a gash running down the side of his face, his helmet sliced right through. Her heart sank.

The kealers would come and take the remaining survivors of Elihor away. Unless she found a way to stop them.

12

____

he white mists were almost upon Avarielle.
Cassara stopped casting her fires, Shirina
quickly picking up the princess' defenses.

"What are you doing! You'll get us killed!" Shirina
hissed, but Cassara barely heard her. She was being drawn
towards the Westland warrior, could taste her fear, her
heart beating like war drums in the distance.

Her skin felt warm and no longer hers. Dizziness
wrapped around her mind, and she stood elsewhere, away
from the mill and Shirina, by Avarielle.

Avarielle! Cassara's head spun and she gasped, forced
herself to stand upright, back on the hill. She thrust her
magic forward, but it only sent her back onto the
battlefield below, in the city.

Not her. Just her spirit? Her mind, maybe? Terror
froze her.

Had she died? Had Avarielle come to take her home?

No. Part of her felt the magic supporting her, still. But was Avarielle really back? Had she really fought herself free of Siabala? She glanced at the graceful movements of the warrior, choppier than before. More intense. More broken. At the new scars, and hard-set features. Cassara stood near her, unseen, untouchable, unable to beg her magic to bring her back to her body.

Her heart thundered and the world slowed. Avarielle turned around, away from the Eloms, and leapt towards another Elom-like figure, one wearing armor. She protected him from an attack, screaming at him to take cover.

What are you doing! She wanted to scream, but couldn't. Her heart fluttered and she panicked and looked back, spotting herself standing on the knoll, so far away. Eloms attacked from all sides, Shirina desperately trying to keep them at bay.

What's happening? Then she felt it, tugging at her like a string.

My amulet! Her mother's amulet. Avarielle had it, and it called to her. It demanded her attention, and her focus.

Avarielle jumped sideways, the mists upon her. But Cassara saw that it wasn't mist at all, but rather ghosts. *They* were the ghosts. Not her, nor the warrior. And they were what Avarielle feared, not for herself, but for the strange Eloms. She stood against one, Graysword's magic dancing around her but simply passing through the apparition, leaving it unscathed.

Avarielle swore. Cassara smiled. It was still her. No

matter what else had changed, that was Avarielle fighting before her.

And she was losing the battle.

Avarielle tried to attack another ghost, but to no avail, Graysword uselessly slicing through the air. She screamed at the quasi-Eloms to run away, to turn back, to leave now, but they stood their ground, trapped between the ghosts and the all-too-real monsters. One of the ghosts took hold of one of them, and it screamed before falling over, dead.

All sound dropped away save for Avarielle's voice, frantic in her need to save them, the amulet throbbing on her chest. Responding to the needs of Cassara. And of the warrior.

The princess reached for her amulet, willing its powers to life. They enthusiastically obeyed her, as though having waited for her for too long. Avarielle jumped in surprise as flames leapt from the amulet around her neck and surrounded her and her armored friends. Cassara willed her magic to protect them, the spell so strong it looked like glass to the naked eye. The ghosts tried to pass through, but just harmlessly bounced off, continuing on their path towards the armies of Graydon.

Avarielle gulped hard as she looked from the glowing amulet to the protective glass. She turned back and made sure her strange friends were all protected, and then she turned to the East, where Cassara stood on the knoll, though she didn't think Avarielle could see her. The warrior smiled and whispered, "Thanks, Cassara."

Pain ripped through Cassara's side and she was thrown back into her body. She gasped awake to find herself pierced through by an Elom, Shirina fighting it off with her staff.

Cassara spat blood and summoned fire, throwing it into the Elom. She fell to her knees as two of the other adepts reached them, summoning protective fires. Shirina knelt beside her.

"I don't have the power to heal you," she whispered.

Upon hearing the regret in her voice, Cassara was suddenly glad that Shirina was here, with her, at the end of it all.

SHIRINA WATCHED HELPLESSLY as Cassara spat up blood and closed her eyes. The princess' magic was stronger than ever and it spread across the entire battlefield, from here to Avarielle, in a feat of magic Shirina could not even begin to understand. And her energies remained stable, even though she was clearly dying.

It seemed that her magic didn't even need her mortal shell to burn, as though it had grown greater than mere flesh and blood. Shirina held the princess as the white mists reached them. Shirina had no more magic to summon, so she stayed kneeling, the princess' blood spreading on her white dress.

Shirina looked at these new creatures only to see ghostly faces looking back at her.

Not just any ghosts. She let out a gasp, and so did the other Circle witches.

Adepts! Those were adepts from the Circle, some of whom Shirina had once considered friends. One hovered near and entered Cassara, making Shirina cry out. But the princess seemed to grow stronger for it, the Circle magic mixing with hers, casting a strong healing spell.

The ghost was healing her! Another one came and bonded with Cassara, lending her its strength, too.

But then it disappeared. As Cassara's energies grew, so did the Circle adept's magic wane, a final sigh escaping its ethereal lips before completely vanishing.

Cassara's eyes flew open.

"Stay here," Shirina told her as Cassara gulped in fresh air. The princess looked around with wide eyes, but she didn't seem intent on getting up right away. Shirina left her on the ground and stood to better survey the attack. There were hundreds of Circle ghosts, enough to count for most of Ravenhold and its outposts in Graydon. All of the missing adepts had not been killed, as she had believed, but rather turned into monsters.

They hovered over the fields, infiltrating Eloms and killing them, or fading over the wounded soldiers and saving them. But they avoided Shirina and the other adepts, most of them unmoving on the ground, their magic so warped it glowed a sickly gray, a color Shirina could now only associate with death.

A ghost stopped before her, deep-set eyes and wild hair still recognizable even as mist.

"Tangia," Shirina whispered, reaching out to touch her old mentor, her hand simply cutting through her. She was as cold as winter.

Shirina had so many questions she wanted to ask her, too many to count or to voice. What had happened to the Circle? Had she seen what would happen and sent Shirina away for her own good? Had she ever cared for her more than as a student? What was she supposed to do now, with so little left? How was she supposed to go on without her guidance?

Tangia stayed before her for an instant and smiled in a way she never had in life, pride beaming from her as she pointed at the staff. Shirina had never felt closer to her mentor. They couldn't communicate, but for the first time, Shirina felt truly seen by her mentor. And her mentor let her pupil see her true emotions.

Probably because she's not Tangia at all. Shirina pushed the treacherous thought deep, unable to bask in the glory of that smile as she analyzed what her mentor had become, unable to enjoy Tangia's presence due to her own training. Tangia frowned, looking at Shirina's throat. Shirina's hand went up instinctively, the scarf unable to hide the dark magic from her mentor's ghostly eyes. Before Shirina could ask anything or move, the Elder threw herself into Shirina, who gasped at the shock of magic in her throat. She choked as she felt Tangia being cut apart by the dark magic residing there.

And she was gone, the dark magic still clenched on

Shirina's throat, her mentor's attempts at saving her having failed.

Tears streamed down her face as Shirina finally allowed herself to grieve the woman who had turned her into Shirina, the tears intensifying as she also grieved the girl she had been before meeting Tangia.

13

assara held the adept in her arms, Shirina standing near, her face still glistening with tears in the moonlight, the mage light long gone with the passing of the other adepts. Of the six adepts that had ridden to their rescue, two Crimson Circles and four Orange Circles, only one of the Crimson Circles still breathed, her face contorted in agony as she choked on the magic that had invaded her. A great shadow covered her magic, a darkness that now lay beneath the surface.

The princess glanced at Shirina, the sorceress not speaking. She sighed and looked down, seeing the dark magic mixing in the adept, the magic of light, of Graydon, losing to the darkness. Well, not *losing*, exactly, but rather blending, changing, to something that could not sustain life in the body.

"It'll be all right," Cassara said, the words feeling hollow in her own ears. Grasping what she could of her own magic, feeling rejuvenated by the ghost, Cassara slowly fed light into the woman's throat, one drip at a time, as though feeding someone dying of thirst. Greedily the woman tried to inhale what Cassara offered her, but the magic fell to the darkness as soon as Cassara released it.

The adept shook and choked, then her body went limp before vanishing into gray dust, spreading on the ground in the windless night. Cassara stood up slowly, fighting the urge to throw up as the dust clung to her. She closed her eyes and took a deep breath.

Shirina studied her closely when she opened her eyes.

"What was that?" Cassara whispered.

"Death," Shirina said simply before walking away. Cassara let her go, not feeling particularly talkative herself. She looked down towards the crumbling city to try and spot Avarielle. In the darkness it proved impossible, but she knew the warrior would make her way here.

Avarielle. She'd survived, though something was different about her. Could she have been sent as a trap? Infected to infect others?

No. To fall prey to every fear this battlefield imposed on her weary mind would mean losing all hope and the courage to fight. She couldn't afford that. Once Avarielle had arrived, they'd figure it out.

She hesitated for a moment longer before walking towards what remained of the battlefield to find her husband and to see how many soldiers had survived to fight the next onslaught.

An onslaught she desperately hoped wouldn't come this very night.

Shirina walked to clear her head and gain some perspective. The Westland warrior followed her, and she wasn't convinced he wouldn't just finish her off without Cassara's intervention. And Avarielle was back, so that alone might prove her downfall. She doubted the warrior would be very forgiving after spending months in Siabala's Rage because of her.

Good. End it all, so I don't have to linger in indecision.

She had hoped Cassara could make a difference and save the Circle, save Graydon. Cassara's magic was powerful, that was undeniable, but she had failed to purify the magic of the Crimson Circle.

Shirina had known her. *Persephone.* The woman had been in her class. She had gained Crimson Circle at the same time as Shirina, though she had failed to make Elite.

She hailed from a village not far from hers. They were from the same Harvest, and Shirina thought that maybe the two had even been friends before the Circle, but she couldn't quite recall.

Shirina was annoyed that she couldn't remember Persephone's birth name. She had had a name too, before the Circle, just like Shirina. But she couldn't remember it, or her smile, or anything else about her. Only that they had made Green Circle together, and every other Circle at the same time, except for Elite.

Why did her memory favor accomplishment over happy moments? She was proud to make higher Circle standing, but not happy. There had been happiness before the Circle. But…that was gone now.

Just like Persephone was gone. And Shirina had been unable to comfort her in her final moments, already crushed by grief.

Shirina stared at the staff, bound to her wrist so she wouldn't easily be separated from it. It was a lifeline. To let go of it meant that, were she forced to use more magic, she would die. And she knew without a doubt that she would be forced to use more magic before this battle had ended.

She brought her other hand up to the tie. Maybe if she channeled magic, she could see how to purify it herself. She was an Elite of the Circle, after all. She had training, power and knowledge that few in Graydon ever dreamed of, much less achieved. Cassara did not benefit from those, even if her magic was stronger.

*Perhaps I can…*her hand dropped, knowing she was fooling herself. If she could filter the darkness out, she would have figured out how to by now.

Killing herself would hardly solve any of her problems, or any of the Circle's, or Graydon's. But living could make a difference.

For whom?

She wished the Westland warrior would just go away. That he would stop so obviously keeping an eye on her, that he would let her be with her dark thoughts and moods. But no, he stayed near her, making no secret of the fact that he followed her.

"Avarielle is back, you know," she said casually. He looked up in surprise. "She's coming towards camp now."

"If you lie…" he growled as he took a threatening step forward.

"If I lie, you can come back and kill me. As it stands, I believe it's more likely your infuriating leader will do that herself."

"Probably," he said, and leaned against a tree, but stared at the encampment more frequently. Shirina sighed. She had hoped he would leave.

Maybe *she* could just leave, instead. Just leave it all here, where there could be no victory. Drop the staff and walk away, change clothing, never mention she was from the failed Covenant, find a corner of the world in which to hide.

Until Siabala found her and killed her. She shook her head. That would be no escape either. She couldn't run away from an enemy that was everywhere.

"Since you're here," Shirina said, tired of her own thoughts. Trevon looked up. "Where would you go, if you could go anywhere in the world?"

He looked at her as though she were mad. "Why would I want to go anywhere? This is my home." Then he added gruffly, "Is this a Circle trick?"

Shirina gave a bitter laugh.

"No, Trevon. Having a home is certainly not a Circle trick."

He was wise enough to let the matter rest, but still he did not leave her side, even when shouts of joy sounded from the camp below.

Avarielle Grayloft had finally made it home.

AVARIELLE CAME ALONE, her companions wisely staying away for now, until she could properly warn the troops. She looked the same, yet different. Her hair was still as unkempt but longer now, falling to her shoulders. She wore different clothing, but that was no surprise as her clothing had been mostly ripped tatters the last time Cassara had seen her.

And there was a darkness around her that made the princess pause. It didn't blend as in the adepts, and it wasn't a shadow. It was just pure blackness, even Graysword pulsating with it. Cassara pulled her coat tightly against the new chill, watching as Westland warriors greeted their lost leader with unreserved joy, patting her back, hugging her, clasping her hands.

Avarielle returned each gesture just as enthusiastically, speaking words of greeting and comfort, making jokes, and gracefully making her way through the throng.

Then Avarielle spotted her and an even wider grin broke out on her face. Cassara forgot all her reservations as she let go of Dayshon's hand and went to greet her, gathering the woman up in a hug. Avarielle returned the gesture, crushing Cassara.

"Thank you," the warrior whispered in her ear before letting her go. Cassara didn't bother wiping the tears from her eyes. They were tears of joy, and it had been a long time since she had felt those.

She gave a quick laugh, the world dropping away as though all that remained was Cassara and Avarielle, and they were back in the orchard of Edoline, talking about possible darkness, and not standing in the middle of it. Cassara kept her hands in Avarielle's, the warrior's callused grip comforting. Grounding her as she looked at her friend, trying to discern what had changed. Bruises and cuts lined her body, and her energies had been tempered. Avarielle met her gaze, unflinching, and offered no explanation.

What happened to you? Cassara didn't dare ask, the words unable to escape her lips. She didn't think the warrior would answer, anyway. Not until she was ready to, if ever.

Instead, Cassara smiled, relief flooding her as the hands tightened around her own.

"Welcome back, Avarielle."

14

Avarielle felt better for having seen Cassara, and her people, again. They'd taken some hard blows, but they were not defeated. Not by a long shot. Neither was Cassara, having married the prince and raised an army to come to her people's aid.

She shook her head and grinned. Cassara Edoline was not to be trifled with. Any friend who had your back when the world ended was definitely worth fighting for.

"Lady Avarielle Grayloft," Breck said as he stepped in her path. She'd been wondering when he'd approach her, having spotted his bulky frame in the back of the crowd. She'd hoped he'd wait until later to annoy her. She really wanted to see Trevon, having missed him terribly. And she knew what Breck was after and hated the formalities.

"Cut the 'Lady' crap, Breck," she growled. "Keep leadership here. I'm not interested." Even if leadership was her family's birthright, she knew without a doubt that

Breck was a steadier choice, and the people would follow him. He was a good man and had been in the West for the past year, while she had been tramping around the East. He had one loyalty: to the West and its people. Hers were divided, which could prove dangerous. Avarielle loved her people enough to let them go. She'd done it before, after all, and she would do it as often as necessary.

"I hate these wasted formalities," she added, piercing him with her gaze. A slow smile spread across Breck's lips.

"It'll be good to fight at your side once more, Avarielle Grayloft." He nodded respectfully and vanished into the shadows, his steps silent on the desert sand.

Avarielle smiled and took a deep breath of dry desert air. It felt good to be home. Her people were tired, but not beaten. Her land was broken, but not gone. And even though ashes clung to the air, it was just as dry as ever, despite the water still gushing from the mountains, too far away to see from here.

She watched the moonlight coat the landscape in radiant beams, shadows creeping between sand dunes, and she allowed herself to feel how much she'd missed this place. Her hand automatically wrapped around the pommel of Graysword. She remembered, long ago, running along those dunes, before monsters had stalked her land.

Now a different kind of monster stalked it. And it would eventually drive her away from her beloved land again, she was certain. By her own choice, to claim revenge wherever Siabala had run to.

But first, there was someone much closer she intended to deal with.

<hr>

"TREVON, you old goat, I told you we'd meet again!" Avarielle clasped wrists with her old friend and sword teacher, pleased to see he was still mostly in one piece. A few more scars, but those were only signs of an active life.

"You're always as good as your word, Avarielle," Trevon laughed, then his eyes turned to steel as he looked sideways toward the growing darkness. Avarielle nodded to him. She knew who stood there. She turned from him, having no doubt he would stay near.

"Did you think I wouldn't find you, Shirina?" she hissed, walking warily towards the sorceress. Her back was turned, the crimson cloak torn at its edges, ashes muting some of its vibrant color.

"Turn around and let me see your treacherous face," Avarielle demanded, mostly to ensure the sorceress wasn't chanting a spell. Although immune to some of the magic of Graydon, such as sleep spells, a full-on fireball would quickly see her dead. She hadn't come this far simply to die at the witch's hands.

Shirina turned around without a word. Her face was drawn, the dark circles under her eyes reaching her high cheekbones. Small scars covered her skin, and she leaned heavily upon a staff, though Avarielle could tell the sorceress was trying not to let it show as she stared back coldly at her.

"You look like crap," Avarielle said, hand still on the pommel of Graysword. "You need a walking stick now? Is your conscience too heavy to bear?"

Shirina sighed. "Small talk with you is always so enjoyably juvenile, Avarielle."

From the corner of her eye, Avarielle saw movement, not needing to turn sideways to recognize the blond hair of the princess. She also didn't need to turn around to know that Trevon would keep Cassara out of the way, if necessary. These were Westland matters now, and although Avarielle respected her, the princess had no right to interfere.

"I hope you don't expect an apology from me," Shirina said, grip tightening around her staff. Avarielle raised an eyebrow.

"Are you goading me on, Elite?" Avarielle took a step forward, making herself taller. "Do you want me to finish you? To put you out of all of our miseries?"

To her credit, Shirina did not back down. But she didn't meet the warrior's eyes, either. And her grip on the staff loosened, as though preparing for the blow.

"I have dreamt of killing you, you know," Avarielle said, resuming a casual stand.

"I know," Shirina whispered back, this time meeting her eyes. Defiant, but also tired. And, something Avarielle had never seen before in the eyes of the sorceress, in the months of her hunting her across the East: accepting.

Avarielle crossed her arms, disappointed in herself. Her blood no longer longed for the death of Shirina. All of her vengeance was targeted at Siabala. And Shirina just looked so...pathetic. Already defeated. Why would she finish her when letting her live would prove greater punishment?

Shirina sighed. "Just finish it, Avarielle. I'm too weary for your tiresome blather."

Avarielle gave a quick laugh, unable to help herself. Eli, she hated the woman, but at least she had wit and guts.

"You're not worth it," Avarielle bit off every word for full impact. "The Shirina that sent me to Siabala's Rage is already defeated and gone."

Shirina scoffed. Avarielle cut it short, striking Shirina hard across the chin, sending the sorceress flying to the ground, staff still tied to her wrist.

"Eli that felt good!" she exclaimed as Cassara rushed to the sorceress' side. "I've been wanting to do that forever!"

"Feeling better?" Trevon asked, arms crossed as though trying to stop himself from finishing the sorceress himself. He wouldn't, though, and Avarielle knew it. Not without her say so. She stepped back to join him, squeezing his arm and forcing him to meet her gaze. He glanced at her, his eyes softening at what he saw.

That she did feel better. The hatred against Shirina that had curled in her stomach for months had dissipated. Even she had only so much capacity for hate, and she had bigger worries than a broken sorceress. She hadn't even punched her full out, afraid of finishing her in her weakened state.

Trevon nodded and looked back toward Shirina, arms still crossed.

"Hope I didn't get any of her cursed blood on my gauntlet," Avarielle mumbled with concern as she analyzed her armor, in a bid to distract Trevon. A slight grin began to split Trevon's lips. She'd missed that sight.

"Let's get out of here," Avarielle said softly to Trevon, the two turning around to join their people. She punched Trevon playfully on the shoulder, feeling more and more like herself.

"Avarielle!" Cassara called after her.

Avarielle turned around and raised an eyebrow.

"Can we meet after I deal with this? I have questions regarding what else might come down that mountain."

"I'll be around." Avarielle winked at her. Cassara returned the smile as Shirina tried to push her away, though the sorceress could barely sit after Avarielle's blow.

"I'll come find you two."

Avarielle nodded and walked off in silence with Trevon, blood rushing to her ears, heart beating for the chance to claim the revenge every fiber of her being desperately craved. She hoped destroying Siabala would lead to much greater satisfaction than hitting Shirina had.

SHIRINA WAS angry at Avarielle and herself, and the care of the princess did not help matters. Cassara sighed and sat back as Shirina pushed her off, finally managing to sit up on her own. Her jaw hurt, but it was not broken, leading her to believe the wretched warrior had held back her strength. That added insult to injury.

The princess was observing her. Shirina wished she would just go away.

"What will you do now, Shirina?" Cassara asked. "It seems that using Avarielle as your easy exit strategy isn't going to work. Do you have another plan? Or will you simply throw yourself in the path of some other homicidal maniac?"

Shirina cast an angry look her way, a gaze that would send even Crimson Circles running for cover. But the princess just sat there, looking at her, eyes piercing. How could she read Shirina so easily? Was she using magic on her?

No. She was just becoming obvious. She was directionless, and therefore had no set behavioral rules to follow. Had she truly let the Circle rule so much of her life that she couldn't even act without their guidance?

Pathetic.

"Avarielle was right," she slurred, wincing at the pain of her jaw. "The Shirina she knew is dead. She died with the Circle."

She felt so small and tired. So useless and used. The Circle would just keep dying around her until nothing remained. And so much of it was already gone. She just wanted to crawl into the land of dreams and live out her days in the library of Ravenhold, learning and teaching and hiding from the world and its woes.

But there was nowhere left to hide.

"That's true," Cassara said softly. "So what is this new Shirina going to fight for? Or is she just going to wait for death to claim her?"

When Shirina didn't answer, Cassara sighed loudly, annoyed. "Look, I understand that losing the Circle is a blow to you, and it will take some time, perhaps even forever, to get over it. But we are in the middle of a war, and we need you. We need the Circle. And, unless my eyes deceived me, those were Circle adepts who died back there. And I'm willing to bet there are probably more survivors, and they will need a leader."

Shirina scoffed. "I couldn't save them and neither could you."

"Yes, but we've never dealt with Elihor and its magic. But Avarielle has." Shirina stared openly at Cassara. The princess continued. "I'm not saying that Avarielle knows more than us, but you saw her magic, didn't you? The same darkness clings to her, though it doesn't seem to be hurting her. It's not blending with her magic."

Shirina shook her head. She hadn't thought to use the Sight on the warrior.

There had been no need. She had never intended to fight her.

She felt foolish. Cassara was right to be discouraged by her. She was acting like a grumpy child. She was certain

Cassara wasn't happy with the situation either, married to a man she barely knew, fighting a war far from her kingdom. Yet she still had the guts to fight.

Of course, Shirina thought bitterly, *she still has Edoline to fight for.*

But Cassara had been right. There were other adepts. And perhaps Avarielle, or at least her magic, could reveal answers they needed to fight back this black death that was killing the few remaining adepts of Ravenhold.

"I'll come with you," Shirina said, refusing Cassara's hand as she struggled to get up alone. She would need a good night's sleep after this encounter.

"I don't know, Shirina," Cassara said as Shirina finally stood up. "I think you're just as stubborn as before."

Shirina could have hugged the princess for saying that but feeling more and more like herself, simply walked past her to find the warrior.

She heard Cassara sigh and allowed herself a slight smile, cursing at the pain in her jaw, dreaming of the day she would use her staff across the Westlander's face and pay her back the favor.

15

*E*mala had truly believed she would one day get to enjoy a good bed and perhaps even a full night's sleep. But three short hours after the Council meeting had ended, the colonel had announced his troops would be ready to leave by morning. *Early* morning. Dawn breaking in the East type of morning.

Emala sighed as she poured bath water for the princess. To top it all, Princess Malir had seemed fond of the idea of her as a maid, and had asked Emala to help her bathe and change. Of course, Emala didn't need to ride out with the army tomorrow. That had been made clear to her. She could stay here, to tend to the princess.

Throwing some lavender in the warm water, Emala found herself torn. Cassara was married now, a grown woman in her own right. She was certain she would welcome Emala with open arms, but how would the maid's skills stand up in court? Massir was reputed to be so big that Emala feared it. In truth, if she was truly honest with herself, no matter what she had told Cassara in what felt like a lifetime ago, she wanted to be back in Edoline, perhaps tending to the Lady Altessa instead, or being a cook. She was good in a kitchen, too.

She stirred the water with her arm, enjoying the warmth. She loved Cassara, and even the two old guards. But was her place really at the side of the woman who would become queen of the largest kingdom in Graydon? Would she not be better off elsewhere, tending to something smaller, that needed her more?

Lost in thought, she did not hear the princess walk in. Malir cleared her throat and Emala jumped, spilling water. She curtsied. "My apologies princess. I did not hear you."

"Don't worry," Malir said, still wearing her dirty clothing, looking quite disheveled. "Would you help me, please?" She spoke softly, and Emala was surprised to hear her ask politely.

"Of course," Emala said, deftly starting to work on the small buttons at the back of the dress. There were many, all encrusted with dirt. This would take some time.

"This is a beautiful dress, my lady," Emala said, hoping to strike up a conversation.

"Thank you," the princess said. "My last maid sewed it. She passed away recently."

Emala slowed her work. "While coming here?"

Malir lowered her head, hair cascading forward.

"It's all right, you're safe now, princess," Emala cooed

as she undid the last button and pulled off the dress. Malir took off her underclothing and stepped into the bath.

Emala began scrubbing the layers of grime from her back.

"I love him, you know," the princess whispered.

"Love who?" Emala asked as she continued scrubbing.

"Dayshon. Your princess' husband." Emala forced herself to keep the rhythm steady.

"I'm sorry," she whispered in turn.

"Me too," Malir said, letting the maid scrub her raw in silence. Emala tried to envision Cassara so torn up over a man, or anyone for that matter. Emala knew her princess would persevere no matter what, and she would be proud to see her grow, even from afar. Cassara had always done what she felt needed to be done. And Emala intended to do no less.

There would be room for Emala here, tending to Malir's broken heart and spirit. Although Emala still hoped to make a perfect blue dress for Cassara.

There might be time for that yet.

Or perhaps it was a dream for another life.

"I CAN'T BELIEVE you're not coming," Carsyn mumbled the next day as Emala bid them farewell.

"You're heading into battle. I have no place there. My place is here, by a princess' side."

"But what about Cassara?" Carsyn exploded. "She'll be heartbroken!"

"Now don't go starting a fuss, old man," Emala scolded him. "Cassara is a grown woman now, with an entire court to tend to her needs. And what would I do there, Carsyn? I'm useless in battle. My place is here, at least for now."

"You're not useless, where did you get a stupid idea like that!" Carsyn exclaimed.

"I'll miss you too, Carsyn," Emala gave him a quick kiss on the cheek and he mumbled something. She smiled.

"Best to you, Emala," Kaden said, kissing her on the cheek.

"And to you, Kaden," she whispered, swallowing hard. "You'll take care of the princess?" she added, knowing it was unnecessary, but needing to hear the answer. Kaden smiled at her.

"Do you really think we've pursued her halfway across the world just to watch her get herself into trouble? We're getting well involved this time, Emala."

"And you'll take care of yourself? And Carsyn? And Jayden!"

Kaden grabbed hold of both of her shoulders and looked her straight in the eye. "We'll take care of each other. And when this is all over, we'll call for you, and accept whatever you choose."

Emala looked down and forced a smile before looking up again, though the tremor in her voice betrayed her growing emotions. "Thank you, Kaden."

"We'll see you soon." He squeezed her hands and let go of her. Carsyn was still mumbling as the two walked away to join Jayden, the young prince so nervous that he had forgotten to wish her goodbye.

Which was just as well.

She was really no good at goodbyes.

***

Jayden was terrified, more so than he could even understand. Since he had been in Siabala's Rage, his fear had been kept at bay by a thin veil of uncaring he had crafted for himself out of sheer need, and by the sickness that had invaded him. But finding Emala, Carsyn and Kaden again had efficiently shattered the veil, leaving him scared and exposed.

He should be heading back to Edoline. He should go there and begin his reign. Walk the orchards. Except that he didn't know if the orchards, or his people, still existed. Or Edoline, for that matter.

Still, he shouldn't be heading into the heat of battle, not after everything he'd seen.

I've survived worse than this, he reminded himself, remembering his time in Siabala's Rage, and what he could of Elihor, when his memory was spotty from the sickness. Except he hadn't been heading into battle, there. His aunt had locked him away, but he'd been essentially left alone. And Avarielle had protected him in Elihor, and even made sure he got home safely. Something she failed to do for herself.

He took a deep breath. This would lead nowhere. He couldn't afford to spiral into fear, or question his own strength. What mattered was that, against all odds, he'd survived all of that.

And he would survive this, too. With Kaden and Carsyn by his side, he felt safer. They wouldn't abandon him.

Colonel Orliys led the procession, having cut through Southern Coalition politics quickly and efficiently.

"What do you think of the colonel, Kaden?" Jayden asked in a whisper. "He says he knew my father."

Kaden nodded. "Lots of people knew your father, Jayden. The colonel is old enough to have been in active duty at the time of the Westland Wars. He probably knew him then. You father was quite the legend, for stopping the war."

Jayden smiled. He was proud of his father, and certainly didn't want to let his good name down by being afraid. He took deep breaths and focused on what could be.

Kaden continued. "From what I heard of the colonel, he's very driven and loyal, but only to leaders he respects. Rumor has it that he's been discontented with the Coalition of late. Too much bickering amongst the politicians."

Jayden nodded, and Kaden let the matter rest. If the colonel was unhappy where he was and he proved a good man, perhaps Jayden could win him over. His kingdom, after all, would need a leader for its army, which he intended to keep in Edoline.

Never again would his kingdom be caught so unprepared. At least not as long as he was king.

16

"Avarielle, you're being unreasonable," Cassara exclaimed.

"I let her live, that was plenty reasonable." Avarielle stood defiantly before her, arms crossed. She looked directly at Cassara when she answered, ignoring the sorceress. "I'm not about to let her poke around me with her magic too. You can't expect that much of me, Cassara."

"I just need to touch your magic, Avarielle," the sorceress said. "I hardly want to do anything else with you. And it's just to see if we can understand more of what's happening."

"You mean what's happening to the Circle," Avarielle turned to Shirina, eyes like steel, "which I don't care about anyway?"

"Maybe just a bit of cooperation on both your ends would be helpful here," Cassara said, exasperated.

"An angry bull would prove more cooperative than Avarielle," Shirina stated flatly.

"Eloms!" The shout came from the camp. Avarielle turned on her heel and ran off without another word.

Cassara followed quickly, leaving the sorceress to trail her. She hoped she could withstand another attack. That she would have the strength to make a difference. Watching the warrior run before her, she felt more confident than she had for a while, despite her successes. Avarielle reached the front before anyone else, where archers were pulling their bowstrings taut. She gasped as she threw herself past them and held up her hands.

"Hold your fire! HOLD YOUR FIRE!" The Westlanders lowered their bows, the Eastland troops hesitating.

"Dayshon, please do as she says," Cassara said as she walked up. Dayshon gave her a skeptical look, but ordered his men to lower their weapons regardless.

Avarielle grimaced at Breck. "I have allies here. I meant to mention it earlier, but the opportunity never arose. I was too busy beating on Shirina."

Shirina ignored the warrior.

Avarielle took a step forward, addressing the gathered soldiers, standing tall before the Eloms behind her. Making it clear that she would protect them, even from her own.

"This is Pack Nacker, and his people are from Elihor," she shouted, loud enough for the troops to hear. "They bravely fought Siabala until they were cursed by him, but they retain their humanity!" A threat laced her voice. "If any of you dare attack them, I will consider it an attack against me and react accordingly."

A few grunts and shuffling feet could be heard from the line, but no one questioned her.

Avarielle examined them all for a moment, daring them to defy her, then she stepped forward. She motioned to an armor wearing Elom to follow her, which he did without hesitation.

"Pack, these are my allies," Avarielle said, walking up to Cassara. "This is Princess Cassara Edoline. She saved you from the kealers."

Pack nodded at her, a long lowering of the head that could be bowing. Cassara returned the gesture out of fear and respect. She fought not to gag at their stench. Not as strong as Eloms, but still unmistakable. But any friend of Avarielle's deserved her courtesy.

"Thank you for being here," she said, uncertain how to address the half-Eloms. "To you and your pack."

"The Pack," Avarielle grinned at her and Pack Nacker. "I like that." She then turned and pointed to Dayshon and Breck, who had joined them. Dayshon stood protectively beside Cassara, but didn't step in her way. "That is Prince Dayshon, her husband and leader in the East. That is Breck. He is a leader in the West."

Cassara noted that Avarielle omitted herself as a leader. Perhaps they already knew. Or, more likely, Avarielle didn't plan on staying long. Her breath caught in her throat and she pushed her worries down, focusing on the moment. And on hiding her surprise at Avarielle's next introduction.

"And this," Avarielle said, motioning vaguely, "is Shirina. She is from Ravenhold's Circle."

Pack lowered his head again towards Shirina.

"Why are you here?" Avarielle faced him. "I thought you would stay safe in the city. I don't mean to chide you, Pack, but you do look like the enemy right now."

Pack motioned towards the back of the city. "Others are coming?" Avarielle asked. He nodded.

"Friend, or foe?" Pack pointed to Shirina, to the Circle above her heart. "Undecided then," Avarielle said coldly. "What if they decide to attack?" she asked Cassara and Shirina.

"I doubt they came all this way simply to attack," Shirina said.

Avarielle ignored her and turned back to Pack. "How long before they're here?"

He pointed high in the sky.

"Well, it looks like we still have time for some rest, then. Breck, send a few scouts, but give them a wide berth. From what I know of the other Circles, they're a bit friendlier, but be wary nonetheless. A witch is a witch."

Breck didn't argue, nodding and heading off to his troops. Dayshon whispered in Cassara's ear, "I'll make sure we keep an eye out."

He broke away from them and headed to their camp.

Avarielle stretched and bid Pack goodnight, keeping an eye on him and the others that were still assembled. Even then, she waited quite a few moments after the Eloms had all vanished into the ancient city before she turned around. She cast a look of warning at Shirina and, without another word, walked back into camp and vanished into a tent.

Cassara watched her go and hesitated a moment before following.

AVARIELLE HAD to admit she was glad Pack had showed up. If nothing else, the sorceress now had another creature from Elihor to contend with, which meant she would give up her incessant quest to read Avarielle's dark energies. If she let them analyze her and her magic too closely, she feared they might detect the growing child within her. At least six weeks pregnant already, her body was already shifting, her armor snugger than it should be.

She guessed the change in magic Cassara had seen was due to Kryde's inheritance. And she couldn't afford to let them know. Not that she was pregnant. Nor who the father was. Or the child.

The last heir of Elihor.

It might be wise of her to stay out of battle. To make sure the child lived and the bloodline survived. But then she'd rob them of Graysword, and her magic would make a difference. Especially with the Circle witches unable to wield theirs.

She didn't care to ask anyone's opinion. Her life, her choice.

She was removing weaponry, readying for a quick nap when she heard scraping outside. She sighed.

"Come on in, Cassara."

The princess stuck her head in and knelt inside the tent, near the entryway. "I'm sorry, I know you want some sleep," Cassara said.

"You don't look so great yourself," Avarielle said.

"What other monsters can we expect?" Cassara asked.

Avarielle shrugged. "That's pretty much all I saw in Elihor. Those winged stone things, those might come too, but they're less strong than the ones we fought by Hunter Lake." *A lifetime ago.*

"You *did* make it to Elihor," Cassara said, eyes searching hers out. Wanting to know what Avarielle had suffered at the hands of Siabala. How long she'd been tortured. What she'd done in Elihor. Why she'd summoned Graysword, in the end. All the questions lit up the princess' eyes, her hands fists on her lap as she forced herself not to ask them. To let the warrior tell her what she chose.

Avarielle was grateful for the princess' patience. She would wait for a long time, perhaps forever. Still, the silence stretched too long and she really needed some sleep. As did Cassara. She threw her a bone.

"Your aunt is dead."

Cassara's face hardened. Avarielle reached inside her tunic.

"But I did get this back for you," she whispered, handing the amulet to Cassara.

The princess hesitated for a moment before taking hold of it.

"It's…different," she looked at it intently, puzzled. "It has some of the same energy as you now. Maybe it absorbed some of your magic?" Cassara asked skeptically.

Avarielle shrugged. "Maybe." She wasn't about to tell her it was Kryde's energy, trapped by Cassara's aunt, and that Avarielle's energies were the same because of the child growing within her.

A shadow passed by, familiar staff in hand.

Though Avarielle couldn't help but hope that Shirina would fall on her face, the sorceress proved skilled at using her new staff as a walking stick. The sorceress headed towards the other edge of camp, which was just as well. Avarielle wanted to sleep well, without that witch near.

"What's that staff for, anyways?" Avarielle asked, curious how this new weapon was a crutch to the sorceress. She didn't care for Shirina's well-being, but figured knowing her weaknesses might come in handy. The staff had been tied to her wrist, like she couldn't afford to be separated from it. That alone was worth exploring.

Cassara whispered, "It filters the magic of Elihor from Graydon's, allowing her to use her magic."

"That makes sense," Avarielle said. "It's like in Elihor, the magic attacked Jayden since he was one of Graydon's descendants." The second she said it, seeing Cassara's eyes grow wide, she wished she hadn't.

"Jayden lives," the princess stated, as though she had known all along. Or hoped so strongly for it that no room remained for doubt.

Avarielle sighed. "He did, Cassara. We escaped Siabala's Rage together and headed to Elihor." She took a deep breath. She hadn't been looking forward to this part of the reunion. "But I lost him, Cassara, in the Straits of Tears. I don't know if he made it."

Her heart ached far too much, rendering it numb. She was swept back to that day, tumbling on the Straits, the monster attacking, Jayden floating away, holding Kryde well into the night, trying to forget her woes with him.

"I think he did," Cassara said stubbornly, clutching the amulet in her hand so tightly Avarielle feared she'd cut herself. "If he's survived so much, I'm certain he survived that, too."

Cassara didn't meet Avarielle's eyes, as though afraid of seeing pity in them. She wouldn't have, Avarielle respecting the need for hope. Still, without another word, she excused herself and stepped out, not asking any further questions, as though knowing less would make it easier to convince herself that his survival was fact.

17

Cassara stepped back out into the fresh night air, wishing the warrior would have trusted her with more, but accepting that Avarielle had chosen to keep her own counsel and dark thoughts. Her heart still tumbled at her relief and worry for Jayden.

Avarielle had saved him. And lost him. But he had lived, and she had to believe he still did. Anything else proved too difficult to bear.

She looked towards the edge of the city, where a few of the armored Eloms gathered. She hadn't asked Avarielle the question that burned within her, though she already knew the answer from what Avarielle had said.

Eloms had been humans, the people of Elihor, turned into monsters by Siabala. She was sorry for so much, but mostly for the fact that the Eloms weren't just faceless monsters anymore. That her family had been destroyed by people. That she had taken so many lives.

Was she any better than the monsters invading the land? Than the people turned into monsters to destroy her land? Could they be saved, and not just slaughtered?

She spotted Dayshon off to the side, setting fire to the large pyre that would take the fallen to the Afterfate.

Loas. He had been unquestioningly faithful since Rockor, since the first time Cassara had truly used her magic, to save him and his people. She had wanted to save them all back then, refusing to let Avarielle and Shirina leave anyone behind.

But she had been helpless to save him, in the end.

In the end, will we save anyone?

Jayden lives. She clung to that hope. If Jayden lived, she knew that she would be willing to kill many more of Elihor's people. As long as he survived, as long as Edoline still stood, she would do everything in her power to make sure the attacks would never reach them again.

She joined her husband and held his hand as they watched the dead turn to ashes.

* * *

SHIRINA STOOD ALONE by a small fire, the warriors and soldiers of the camp too suspicious of her to share warmth with her. That was fine with her. She craved peace and solitude.

She held her mentor's journal in her hand, wishing she had never gone back for it. The one piece of knowledge she had managed to save from Ravenhold was the one that could undo them all.

She had read Tangia's notes, riddled with scribbles captured as new information came to light, some circled with giant question marks. So many questions remained, and would probably never be answered. But it had been clear that her mentor had known where Eloms came from.

Avarielle had been right all along, even though Shirina herself had not known. The Circle of Stormhold had created the Eloms accidentally, trying to send emissaries across the Wall of Loss, to warn Ravenhold of Siabala's activities. The people of Elihor, however, did not fare well crossing the Wall, mutated by its magic. Siabala had then found the Eloms, the result of Stormhold's failed attempts at crossing the Wall, and replicated the experiment on a wider scale with any living being from Elihor he could capture.

Ravenhold had received pieces of messages and knew something was happening. But the message was still unclear. And so they needed more Eloms, to see if some had retained enough memories and thoughts to divulge more information. As Siabala's Eloms grew in strength and number, it became impossible to tell Stormhold's adepts from Siabala's monsters without deep study, which took time. A commodity growing more precious by the day.

Before Shirina had been ordered to hunt down the last Grayloft, her mission had been to find Eloms and bring them back to the Covenant. *They were people, too,* she was told.

She gazed deep into the fire, watching the logs burn. Just as she had burned so many.

Twenty years ago, the West was being invaded by the first Eloms and its people started fighting back. The Graylofts led the battle with their magic, and the Circle had needed to stop the warriors. The Elders needed to gather the Eloms and not have them killed, the message lost in their ashes. But negotiations and covert tactics had failed. The Eloms were dying at the hands of Westland warriors, taking with them the message of Elihor.

A message the Circle had decided it needed, no matter the cost.

And so the Westland Wars had begun. The Circle thinking it was saving the Eloms, the West believing it was being annihilated, and the East joining in to gain rumored treasures from the mountains. Rumors fueled by the Circle.

Shirina was not proud of the history, but she understood the necessity of it. The Elders had done what they thought was best, but they hadn't realized at the time that they were playing right into Siabala's hand.

Shirina clutched the small journal. It was all that remained of her mentor.

The Circle had tried to stop the Graylofts. Or Graysword, at least. For the first time in Circle history, they created a special military unit to deal with the Graylofts, one they could easily deny as theirs. But the special units failed and killed the wife of Grayloft by accident. The woman she came to know as Avarielle's mother.

And the monsters kept coming, long after the Circle had left to lick its wounds, the message still incomplete, no matter how many Eloms they studied. If any of Stormhold's messengers remained, they had been slaughtered by the West or turned into one of Siabala's flesh-starved creatures.

All that Tangia had recorded of the message was: *Wall falling. Need magic unite.*

But no instructions. No way to stop it. And no details on how to unite the magic. Details that could now save her few remaining brothers and sisters.

Perhaps the Circle of Elihor would know. She would find out soon enough, when they arrived.

She wondered how much of Graydon's history they knew. She guessed they didn't know what had happened to their emissaries. They might not even know that Siabala had created Eloms.

No one must know, she knew without a doubt. To know the Circle's role in the Westland Wars, to understand its role in keeping Eloms alive, in trying to save them, even, would be Ravenhold's final undoing.

Shirina ran a finger slowly over the leather cover of Tangia's journal, the old, wrinkled book small but heavy with knowledge. Knowledge that she should have left to die with Ravenhold, that she wished she didn't know herself.

Taking a deep breath, she tossed the book into the flames and watched it be consumed, slowly turning to ashes, joining the rest of the Circle's knowledge in obscurity.

AVARIELLE STAYED IN THE SHADOWS, watching the sorceress burn something in the flames.

No doubt something incriminating, she thought bitterly, fists forming at her sides. She took a deep breath and loosened her hands again. She needed a favor from Shirina, so she didn't intend to question her on whatever she'd just burned.

Not yet, anyway.

She checked around again to make sure she wasn't being followed. The last thing she needed was Trevon to overhear anything. She had pondered asking Cassara at first, but she wasn't certain the princess would know how to help her, and she didn't need Cassara asking questions. Besides, even if Shirina knew the whole sordid story, she wouldn't care, and right now that would be an advantage.

She stepped out of the shadows, the sorceress so deep in thought as she stood by the fire that she didn't notice her at first. She was obviously startled when Avarielle stepped around her and sat on the other side of the fire. Shirina hesitated for a moment before sitting down as well, looking suspiciously at the warrior.

Avarielle wasn't interested in chitchat, and so cut to

the chase. She needed to make sure she would be safe meeting Elihor's Circle tomorrow. If they learned that she was bearing the last heir of Elihor…she didn't even want to have to think about dealing with so many witches.

"Can you hide my energy?"

Shirina narrowed her eyes and then nodded.

"Can you do it now? And if you try anything else…" Avarielle let the threat linger. Shirina gave a thin laugh.

"Cassara can see your energy has changed, but she lacks the knowledge with which to interpret that change." Shirina paused, then added more softly. "I can help you with that, too, if you'd like."

Avarielle clenched her jaw, annoyed at the soft tones. So, the sorceress knew she was pregnant. Not too surprising, given the witch was annoyingly perceptive. *She could help her?* By removing the child, Avarielle didn't doubt. She hesitated for a moment. That would simplify things. But did she truly trust Shirina with such a delicate spell? One that could easily rob Avarielle of life as well?

And was she ready to let go of Kryde's final legacy? Shirina observed her, a thousand questions dancing in her eyes. Just like in Cassara's. Well, let her wonder, too. Avarielle owed her nothing.

"Just hide my aura," she said wearily. "And if you promise to keep my secret, I promise not to question you on what you just burned."

The witch's eyes grew wide before narrowing again. She pursed her lips and nodded.

Shirina chanted softly, a strange tingling forming around Avarielle's abdomen, and then the witch stopped.

"That's it?"

Shirina shrugged. "Simple warding spell. It will hold as long as I live."

Avarielle gave a slight smile. The witch was no fool. The warrior got up without thanking her and walked back into the darkness, wondering when the opportunity would come to discover what Shirina had been burning.

18

"Is that them?" Breck asked casually as he adjusted his weapons. Avarielle was glad he was in charge. He was a good man, if a bit thick-headed. But then, so was every good Westlander.

"Yes, that's them," she answered, watching the witches walk through the rubble, some wearing black robes, others gray ones. They waited for them on solid ground overlooking the shattered city, lit by the breaking dawn. From a place of advantage, where they could see any incoming treachery.

"The black-robed ones are from Larkhold, that much I know," Avarielle said, remembering the crazy old Elder Tan who had sacrificed herself to save her and Jayden. "The gray ones from Stormhold, I assume." She looked to Pack, who nodded.

Avarielle surveyed the battlefield, by the edge of an ancient city that had yet to reveal its purpose or history, and grinned at the oddity of the warriors. Fully armored Eastland soldiers on horseback, at least those who still had horses. Westland warriors donning leather armor, bows and swords. A few old broken catapults at least twenty years old. And Eloms, some wearing armor, some not.

I'd think twice about picking on us, she thought, still counting a fair number in their ranks. Less than a thousand, but well-led, this army could take on many more than their number.

Too bad the land is working against us right now. There was nowhere on the landscape to ambush incomers, and the mysterious city could not be trusted. At least none of her people's villages remained this close to the eastern border. She hoped none had been destroyed when the vast crevasse had torn the land asunder. A worry for another time.

Shirina came and stood beside her. Avarielle cast her an annoyed look.

"Their magic is still whole," she whispered, "but if they use it, they'll also get infected and die."

Avarielle bit back a reply when she heard a cry resembling birds from the mountain.

Srocks!

"Enemies approaching, from the air!" she warned, loud enough for the Eastlanders to hear.

"Archers forward! Cavalry back!" Dayshon and Breck shouted orders seamlessly. Avarielle ran to the nearest horseman.

"I need to borrow this," she said, and before he could argue, she grabbed the reins, jumped up and pushed him down, a satisfying clatter of armor as he tried to hang on.

Shirina appeared beside her. "I'm coming with you."

"In your worst nightmares you are," Avarielle growled.

"Hop on with me," Cassara said, riding up on her white steed, extending her hand to Shirina. The warrior scowled.

"We can stop the attack before it hits the army and the adepts," the princess replied coolly as Shirina accepted the offered hand. "We need as many people to survive as possible, Avarielle." Without another word, Cassara kicked her steed's flank, sending it into a run, Shirina sitting perched on the back as though serenely enjoying tea.

Eli I hate that witch! Avarielle thought as she kicked her own horse into a run, focusing on staying balanced and comfortable.

Up ahead, the sky grew dark with srocks.

***

SHIRINA CONCENTRATED on the incoming adepts. They were not using their magic, despite the obvious imminent attack, so they must have been aware of their current limitation.

Good. They would serve no purpose dead, and Shirina needed all the help she could get.

Cassara deftly guided the horse over rubble and onto

the safest paths, Avarielle following her lead. But the srocks were closer to the adepts than they were. She held up her staff and began chanting, coordinating her movements to the horse's so that she would not fall.

She summoned protective fires around the adepts, not nearly as good as what Cassara could pull off, but she doubted the princess could both steer and cast at the same time. The flames danced around the adepts and they stayed put.

Good Circle training, she thought, pleased that the standards seemed as elevated for the other two Covenants. If not higher.

Her fires would not hold back the srocks for long. If Avarielle had spoken truth, these would not be as strong as the two they had originally faced, the ones that had contaminated Shirina's magic.

They must not be from the same nest. She wondered if they would encounter the stronger ones again. She doubted she could safely absorb their energy this time.

The first srock landed near Shirina's fires, crushing what remained of a building before jumping out of it, shaking off the dust from its great wings. The creature stared at the fire and approached, only to jump back again, flapping its wings in distress.

Definitely not as strong.

An arrow flew by them, missing Shirina by a few inches. It struck the srock in the eye, the creature shrieking and tumbling back as red energy began to bleed from its open wound.

"That's the magic of Siabala," Shirina hissed, avoiding sudden movements in case the crazed warrior decided to fire another arrow.

Shadows danced on them from the rising sun, the srocks above them thick enough to slice the light. They crashed loudly around them, the ground trembling with their weight. Cassara reined the horse back as one landed before them. Avarielle's arrow quickly dispatched it.

Shirina jumped off the horse to join the Circle adepts. Cassara followed her and cast protective magic around them, the sky covered as though by glass. The creatures bounced off harmlessly.

"Good, but kind of ruins the fun, don't you think?" Avarielle said as she came to stand by Cassara.

Shirina ignored them both as she approached the adepts. There were maybe thirty in all, almost half of which were men. That was unheard of in Ravenhold.

"I am Shirina, Crimson Circle Elite of Ravenhold," she introduced herself without flourish. "Who is your leader?"

A black-robed man stepped forward, his long dark hair braided, his eyes only reflecting twilight. "I am Rolje, Crimson Circle of Larkhold, and I am leading this expedition."

Shirina nodded. A Crimson Circle, not of Elite rank, was the highest surviving rank of Elihor. She hoped he had hoarded more knowledge and secrets than she had managed to.

"Shirina, they're going to reach our troops!" Cassara cried back.

"Do not use your magic. Stay with us and trust us," Shirina ordered and Rolje nodded, ordering his adepts to do the same.

"Let's move them towards the troops," Avarielle said. Cassara nodded and began walking, her shields staying close to them, keeping the srocks at bay.

"Can you maintain the shield?" Avarielle asked.

"They're not using fires, so it's actually quite easy," Cassara shrugged, though a hint of pride infiltrated her voice.

"Good. Stay here with them. Shirina and I will go help the troops and we'll be back for you."

Cassara opened her mouth to say something but closed it, simply nodding. Shirina wanted to argue, wanting to question the adepts of Elihor right away, but knew she would not win. Cassara would keep them safe, and they needed to save as many warriors as they could.

"Let's go Shirina," Avarielle said, jumping up on the horse and extending her hand to help the sorceress up. Shirina grudgingly took it.

"Hang on!" Avarielle said, kicking the horse into a mad dash through the city to reach the troops, srocks raining around them from the sky.

***

AVARIELLE CONCENTRATED on keeping the horse on track, whispering soothing words near its ear as its nostrils flared in fear. She was glad for the horse's eye guards, sparing the poor beast the sight of monsters falling beside them, although the tremors of the ground terrified it.

Shirina chanted continuously, casting precise fire spells that exploded right in the creatures' eyes, shattering the red glass that imprisoned their magic and life force. She could take out many at once, but so many more kept coming that Avarielle wasn't convinced they were making much of an impact.

She spotted Pack and his men running into the city, battling with the srocks, piercing eyes with their long claws. But if they weren't quick enough to get out of the way, they were either crushed by the stone monsters, or the escaping fires consumed them. The entire city stank of dust and death.

A volley of arrows flew up, towards the North and South instead of directly at them. Breck avoided shooting in the city, where so many of his allies currently battled.

A srock suddenly landed right in front of them. Before Avarielle could pull on the reins, the horse smashed into it, snapping its neck. Avarielle had just enough time to cover her head with her arms before striking the stone monster full force. The srock tossed her aside, the great arm hitting her side, pain robbing her of breath. She turned sideways to avoid a direct hit to her belly, instincts kicking in as the beast moved in for the kill. She landed awkwardly and pushed herself back, pulling a knife free from her belt. She sent it flying, striking the creature in the eye. It fell and Avarielle jumped sideways to avoid its thrashing.

She bent forward and held her side, wincing at the pain and catching her breath.

"Are you alright?" Shirina asked as she finished a few nearby srocks.

"What do you care?" Avarielle hissed, wishing she'd brought Cassara instead and let the sorceress figure out her own Circle crap.

The sorceress shrugged. "The blow wasn't fatal, if you care."

Meaning the child was still alive. Unexpected relief washed over Avarielle. She steadied her breath and her heartbeat and gingerly stood up, testing her side. Nothing seemed broken, though she'd have bruises for days. She unsheathed Graysword and positioned herself with her back to Shirina. Around them the demons kept falling and crashing into stones and buildings, leaving a shower of dust and shards in their wake.

Avarielle slashed with her summoned fires, threw what knives she had left and parried more blows than she could count. Shirina's fires erupted constantly behind her, small targeted spells that killed instantly.

"They're not attacking the troops," Shirina remarked calmly.

"Well, that's good," Avarielle said as she parried a blow. Her muscles screamed for a break.

"They're destroying the city," Shirina continued and Avarielle ignored her, concentrating on landing the next blow. If the sorceress wanted to chitchat while fighting, she could do so alone.

By the time the battle ended, the ancient city lay in ruins, destroyed by the srocks and the magical fires.

Avarielle sheathed Graysword, the last few srocks struck down by the army's archers.

"I'm surprised they didn't run out of arrows," she mumbled as she stretched, wincing at the pain in her side, wondering which demons Siabala would send after them next as she watched Cassara and Elihor's adepts make their way to them.

19

Shirina greeted the adepts and walked in silence with them to the camp of Graydon. Cassara and Avarielle followed behind, also silent. The warriors were exhausted but in good humor. They had lost relatively few in this battle, only a few scouts. Thankfully, Avarielle had already warned them on how to dispatch the srocks.

She turned to Rolje, the Crimson Circle from Larkhold. "Tell me," she said, and he came closer to her, "we faced some of the flying monsters a few months ago, and they seemed much stronger…" Shirina fought the urge to touch her throat, where their dark magic slithered.

"Did they have Siabala's magic, or Elihor's?" Rolje asked. Shirina narrowed her eyes.

"I believe Elihor's, but I'm not sure, to be honest." She'd absorbed their life essence in a desperate bid to stop them.

Infecting herself, and still failing to stop Siabala from gaining what he needed to lower the Wall of Loss.

"Siabala copied the guardians of Larkhold, after capturing them when the keep fell," Rolje said. "Poorer imitations, but still powerful." He offered her a tentative grin, an odd sight on a Circle adept. "Without you, however, we would have been doomed."

Shirina nodded and focused inward, the adept sensing it and moving away from her. It made sense, that there were different nests. Siabala had copied Stormhold's accidental Eloms, after all, so he must have been using whatever resources were available to him in his Rage. Including replicating stone monsters that could help bring him people who would turn into his armies against Graydon.

Still, Shirina was disturbed. This had been too easy. Why would Siabala send such puny adversaries against them? Did he not intend to annihilate them? How did he expect to do so with such weak and spread-out attacks?

Unless they weren't the main target. A shiver clutched Shirina's spine. What would his target be? Something in the city? She slowed her pace down, to join Avarielle and Cassara.

"Something's wrong," Shirina whispered.

"You're choosing our company over your own, so yes, I'd have to agree," the warrior said, but she too looked around at their surroundings with questioning eyes.

"What is it?" Cassara asked, the princess having been lost in thought.

"He wasn't targeting us, or the army," Avarielle offered. Cassara looked at the destruction around them with wide eyes.

Shirina continued. "Siabala must be trying to achieve something else. He is just trying to distract us. Or downright ignore us. What could he want?" She focused on Avarielle.

The warrior growled a reply. "I don't have any insight, if that's what you're hoping for, Shirina."

"The only thing all of those monsters have in common," Cassara said, placing a calming hand on the warrior's arm, "is that they entered this city. Not one of them made it any further."

"And not one of them was very strong," Shirina added. "Even the Eloms were stopped by those kealers, which we can only assume Siabala let loose."

"Or someone else," Avarielle suggested.

"Well, the one thing we know for sure," Cassara sighed, "is that the strongest demons haven't shown up yet. Not the deadly srocks from Hunter's Lake, nor the intelligent Eloms. We're dealing with the scraps, and we don't know why."

"Eli, I'm tired of these games. Can't we just have one nice big final battle and call it a day?" Avarielle exclaimed. "Maybe your little friends will have answers?" She nodded towards the adepts.

"They don't seem to have any surviving Elders either," Shirina said. "But I'll find out what they know."

"They did have a few Larkhold Elders left," Avarielle

said, then shrugged. "They might be dead by now, but a couple were mentioned to me."

"Care to share more?" Shirina asked, wanting to throttle it out of the warrior. Elders could make all the difference in this war.

Avarielle pierced her with the steel in her eyes, but before Shirina could say anything else, Cassara spoke up.

"Those aren't our troops." Both Avarielle and Shirina's heads snapped up.

Flying proud over the battlefield just past the city, the flags of the Southern Coalition flapped in the wind.

***

As soon as Cassara had reached the camp, Gragor came running up to greet her.

"You have to come quick, Lady Cassara," he was out of breath and obviously excited, running back before waiting for a reply. Cassara followed him quickly, Avarielle on her heels, while Shirina chose to stay behind with the adepts. The princess navigated the excited crowd of soldiers with difficulty, until Avarielle came beside her and elbowed their way through.

Then she stopped dead in her tracks as a soldier turned to greet her. His face beamed the second he saw her. She closed the gap and hugged him fiercely.

"Kaden!" She was too happy to see him to ask any questions just yet. She just wanted to feel safe in his arms.

"No hug for me?" Carsyn beamed from the side.

Cassara broke the embrace with Kaden and hugged him as well. He then turned to shake hands with Avarielle, who grinned at him.

"We'd heard things hadn't gone so well for you," he said softly. Avarielle blinked and turned slowly, looking past them.

"Cassara," she said softly. The princess followed the warrior's eyes to Dayshon, deep in conversation with two men. A man and a boy, more to the point. She swallowed hard and started walking toward them, Avarielle staying with the guards.

Cassara choked out his name.

"Jayden?"

Her brother turned to her. He looked the same, but so different. His eyes were sunken in, and he had lost weight. He was taller, and his hair tumbled around his face in waves. But when he saw her and broke out in a smile, she saw her little brother again. She ran to hug him, no longer needing to crouch down as he was now her height.

She didn't say anything as she cried, not caring that she was surrounded by warriors.

She had finally found her little brother, and Cassara Edoline intended to lose herself in this moment, to commit it to her memories, so that its light could warm her on even the darkest days.

By nightfall, Grasky, Kale Kolder and the remaining Circle adepts from the Lisal Gardens had joined them. Shirina clasped hands with Grasky and welcomed the adepts, but she had to focus her attention on their next steps.

"Are there really no Elders left amongst you?" Shirina asked Rolje as they stood aside from the other adepts. Kale was in deep discussion with the younger adepts, no doubt telling them stories to cheer them up.

Shala glanced her way a few times, but did not seem interested in joining them. She supposed the Orange Circle was already thinking of leaving the Covenant when the opportunity arose.

So be it.

"None that we know of, and we looked," Rolje said. "But without the ability to use our magic…" He looked at the staff Shirina held.

"It filters the magic of Graydon, and answers only to me," she said by way of explanation. He nodded. She glanced to a gray-robed Crimson Circle. "Can the adepts of Stormhold wield the blended magic?"

The tall woman shook her head. "We can wield magics from Graydon and Elihor, but not the blended strands." She seemed content staying on the sidelines, and left the Crimson Circles from the other two Covenants to debate next steps.

Shirina pursed her lips and turned to Rolje, nodding to her staff. "Do you have such items that would help you wield your magic?"

He shook his head. "None that I know of. Anyone who might have those answers is long gone."

"That man is from Elihor and seems knowledgeable in such things," Shirina said, pointing Kale out with a quick movement of the head. He spotted it and walked toward her.

"There is no need to involve commoners," Rolje said, annoying Shirina, even though it was a perfectly reasonable Circle response.

"There is no one *not* involved in this," she bit back, and the black-robed sorcerer nodded slowly. Kale joined them, a slight smile playing on his lips. "Kale, do you know of any items such as this staff that would allow Rolje to use his powers?" Rolje's eyes grew wide.

"Kale Kolder?" He practically spat out the word. Kale seemed amused by the Crimson Circle's reaction.

Shirina looked from him to Kale. "You know him?"

Rolje turned to Shirina. "He is a descendant of Elihor, and practically brought down Larkhold years ago, stealing some of our precious knowledge."

Shirina raised an eyebrow and looked at Kale. The old man shrugged.

"Well, that doesn't answer my question," Shirina pushed on. That hardly seemed important right now. "Is there such an item, Kale?"

"Did you not hear me, woman?" Rolje asked, and Shirina turned on him.

"You will refer to me as Elite, Crimson Circle." All of the other adepts hushed up and looked at them, as did the nearby soldiers. But that did not stop her. "And you will be grateful for whatever allies and knowledge the Circle yet retains. That Kale stole some of it only means that it is still accessible, unless you've managed to retain more from your libraries then we did of Ravenhold." Rolje narrowed his eyes and shook his head.

"I did not think so," Shirina said. She glared at him for a moment longer and turned to face Kale. "I'm not condoning your actions, old man, but right now I'm glad for them. Now please answer the question. Is there an item that will allow them to use their magic?"

Kale shook his head, a slight smile clinging to his eyes.

"Then is there an item that will allow us to cleanse the magic once again? So that we may all safely use it in defense against whatever attack will come next?"

"I fear not, Shirina. But there might be a way, by combining magic users from Graydon and Elihor, casting the same spell at once. It may direct the energies into the right wielder, instead of them blending to create the new magic. But it will be risky, and not guaranteed."

"That's not a bad idea, Kale," Shirina said, pondering the possibility. "What do you think, Rolje?"

Having thankfully quickly recovered, Rolje merely nodded. "It sounds like a plausible theory, but the magic users would have to time the ebb and flow of the magic exactly."

Shirina nodded. It might work. It might not, and it could claim the rest of the adepts' lives. But more would be coming from Graydon soon, and she hoped from

Elihor, as well. Perhaps even Elders, if Avarielle spoke truth, which she probably did. If enough of them could pull this off, if enough were paired off well, they might be able to make a difference, after all.

KALE BROKE AWAY from Shirina to leave her and Rolje to their planning. He liked her, Tangia's pupil. She didn't crave power, though she thought she did, and she cared for people more than most adepts ever did, which she also didn't realize. She would be good to lead the new unified Circle, if she survived that long.

Of course, if anyone else stood in her way, she would simply snap their heads off. He chuckled as he walked towards the old city, curious to explore it a bit.

"You shouldn't venture too far, old man," a red-headed warrior said as she walked toward it herself. She hauled scraps of meat in a large cloth bag, the blood seeping through.

"You're taking your meat for a walk?" he asked casually, and she grinned at him.

"Going to feed a few allies. Not a whole lot of food to go around I fear," she said, as though apologizing for not offering him any.

"Don't worry," he said, raising his hands, "I already had my fill of old raw meat today." She grinned, then grew serious.

"I'm sorry about your land," she spoke softly. "I was

well greeted there, when I became trapped in Elihor. I'm sure it must have been beautiful in its prime."

Kale swallowed hard, looking at the woman as though seeing her for the first time. She'd crossed to Elihor, too. He was wondering what treacherous path had led her there, when a man broke free from the shadows of a building, or what once had been a man. Although Kale no longer recognized the man, he certainly recognized the armor.

He felt ill as he walked towards the misshapen creature. The warrior shot him a look that clearly questioned his intentions as she dropped the meat, hand lowering to her weapon protectively. The man ignored her and looked to the misshapen creature. And he saw in those eyes the same recognition that lurked in his. The man lowered his head.

Kale took hold of both of the man's shoulders, feeling the strength beneath the armor, and choked as he spoke the name.

"Pack Nacker." It wasn't a question, just a statement. They had turned his grandson's best friend into a monster. He fought to keep the tears in check. He was getting too old for such sorrow.

"What of my grandson, Pack? What of Kryde?" Pack turned toward the warrior, eyes wide and lined with recognition. And sorrow.

Kale turned to her and pleaded with her.

"Do you know what happened to Kryde?"

"Who are you?" she whispered, though he thought she already knew the answer.

"I'm Kale Kolder, his grandfather. Please tell me what has happened to him," he begged, remembering the young face filled with wonder as he brought him to the Wall of Loss, and as he told him stories of his insane adventures. Kryde would follow in his footsteps one day, of that he was certain. The wanderlust and magic were strong in his blood, no matter what Kryde thought or what duties he felt he owed Elihor.

The woman shook her head, as though trying to break free from a nightmare. He closed the gap and took hold of her shoulders, forcing her to meet his eyes. Her face flashed with anger for a moment, giving her the edge she needed to be able to speak the words he dreaded.

"I'm so sorry," she said, voice trembling, "your grandson fell by Siabala's hand."

He let go of her, shaking his head, and took a few steps back before falling to his knees, a sorrow escaping from so deep within him he thought it would choke him. Then the woman was beside him, holding him in her strong arms and sharing his tears. Pack knelt near them, a monster unable to show grief for the man who had once been his best friend.

It was dark before Kale could move again, letting the warrior escort him to a tent and remove his boots for him, knowing no sleep save death would ever be deep enough for him to escape this pain.

20

"Where's Kale?" Shirina inquired the second Avarielle stepped out of her tent. She'd heard they were seen together, and she wanted to chat with him about his potential knowledge.

"What business is it of yours?" Avarielle snapped.

The sorceress shrugged. "I just wanted to make sure he hadn't wandered off and that he was all right, that's all."

Avarielle gave a bitter laugh. "I doubt he's all right. I just told him his grandson was dead."

"How do you…" Seeing the obvious answer in the angry, grieving eyes of Avarielle, Shirina dropped the question. "I'm sorry, Avarielle."

She was surprised that she meant it, and even more surprised that the warrior didn't turn on her. Instead, she just pointed at her tent. "He's in there, resting."

"You can take my tent, if you'd like," Shirina whispered.

"Don't push your luck," Avarielle growled and walked off into the night, to find somewhere else to sleep.

Shirina hesitated, wondering if she should check on Kale. She decided against it. With any luck, he would be sleeping.

She sighed. Cassara was busy rejoicing at the reappearance of her younger brother, and Avarielle was busy grieving a man she had once loved. She had hoped to discuss possible scenarios with them, but that would have to wait until morning now.

Shirina stepped towards the city, sitting in the moonlight to enjoy a moment of peace away from the other adepts. They didn't seem to have any more useful knowledge than she did, so her interest in them had waned.

She needed to figure out her next steps, which proved difficult without knowing Siabala's full plan. Still, if the Circle was to be unified now, she needed to focus. Should they all reform under one Covenant, or were all three still necessary, despite the falling of the Wall?

Shirina lacked so much knowledge it infuriated her. She had been spoon-fed history and politics, magical theories and spells, but none of them seemed connected and, after reading Tangia's journal, she wasn't certain that she could trust any of it.

What if most of it was just a carefully crafted lie, to further the ambitions of the original Circle? She wasn't certain what to think anymore, and with no Elders left to question, she didn't know where to get the much-needed answers.

"May I join you?" Rolje asked from behind her. Shirina was careful to hide her surprise. She had been so deep in thought that she hadn't heard him approach.

She nodded and he sat down beside her, looking at the ancient city cast in deep shadows.

"Do you know anything of this city?" Shirina asked, not surprised when he shook his head.

"It might cross to Elihor, I supposed, but the land didn't crack, there. It's huge, or it was, anyway, in its prime. I wonder how much of it still lies hidden?"

Shirina looked up, snapping to attention. That was it. Siabala was after something still hidden. Something he hoped srocks falling from the skies, marauding Eloms and spells casters would unearth for him. She looked closer, and noticed that more of the city could be seen, the battle revealing new layers where buildings had been destroyed.

She forced her eyes to pierce the darkness. To look at the magical currents. Magic pulsing with Siabala's energies slithered below. Strands stuck straight out of the earth, reaching up like tentacles.

There was something deeper, below the city. That's what Siabala wanted, and he couldn't get it himself, not without them first destroying what covered it.

Shirina stood abruptly. "I have to go." He stood up quickly and grabbed her arm.

"Wait!"

She turned and gave him a look that would make most

adepts cry. To his credit, he didn't back down. "I want to try casting a spell with you. You're protected by the staff, and I think we have a connection. We could pull it off, and spare the life of other adepts by testing it ourselves. Failing would only cost one life—mine."

Shirina shook her head. "No. We're not certain it will work. I might not even draw from the same strand of magic if I only draw on Graydon's. It's too risky."

"We're all dead if we don't wield our magic, Shirina," he said. "And this might be the only way for the Circle to survive."

She sighed. "Yes, perhaps, but I'm not certain this is the way. Let us wait a bit longer. I believe other answers will reveal themselves."

He leaned in on her. "Would you sacrifice it all to save the Circle?"

She kept her eyes fixed on his, the answer easily rolling off her tongue. "No."

He let go of her arm and nodded, obviously disappointed.

Shirina left him there and walked off to find Cassara or Avarielle, annoyed that now that she was reunited with other Circle adepts, the warrior and the princess still seemed her strongest allies.

Siabala was enjoying the show. He had been annoyed when his flash fire had been halted by Graydon's magic, but after stumbling upon a final gift from Elihor and Graydon, he had been glad that the descendants of Graydon had been spared.

He paced and jumped around the Bloody Mountains, wondering what he could send next. He had kept his best for last, but he didn't want to exhaust the poor humans completely before they had done one final task for him.

Using his powerful muscles, he leapt to the highest peak and took a deep breath of mixed magic. This was how it was supposed to be! Not those washed-up magics Elihor and Graydon had created. His brothers might disagree, but the three could argue at length once they'd been freed. And, hopefully, they'd now understand their folly at making deals with humans, so long ago.

He wondered where the so-called Lost Lovers were. Were they truly dead? He couldn't escape still, trapped on the Bloody Mountains, though now able to roam further than just his old castle, his Rage.

The two pests must have left something else to keep him here. Did they not yet know this was his land, and their children needed to die so that his people could rise again, the earth seeded with their blood?

Siabala jumped down and landed on top of Stormhold, cracking the great structure.

"What a satisfying sound," he rumbled, wishing he had never welcomed humans on his land, them and their silly superstitions. He wasn't certain what he would do once he was rid of them. Once he had freed his brothers, they could bring their people back. Samala and Pashal had betrayed him, but they were still his blood. And few things spoke louder than blood.

The Grayloft would learn that, should she live long enough. He would need a commander for his armies, and she would be perfect, once under his control.

But first, he needed his finest army, trapped too long in his brothers' accursed city.

He needed them to find and destroy the final key that would set him free.

21

They formed an intimate circle around a campfire, away from the troops and prying eyes. Cassara huddled in her coat, glad for the comforting feel of her amulet under her shirt. After hearing Shirina's plan, she could use whatever little comfort she could find.

"Are you suggesting we just leave them?" the princess whispered. "You do realize we're the only magical defense they have."

"I'm well aware of that," Shirina said. "But there's more at stake." She put up a hand to stop the objection forming on Cassara's lips. "And I don't mean the Circle, but all of Graydon and Elihor. Siabala wants something from us, and I believe it's below this city."

"Say it is," Cassara said. "Why would we go to it? Isn't that playing into his hands?"

"I wish I knew," Shirina said, staring at the flames as she answered. "We have a choice: to wait here until the monsters come and destroy us or until we're manipulated into doing his bidding, or to head off now and try to beat him at his own game."

"So," Avarielle said, leaning back against a crumbled wall jutting from the sand, "you think there might be something below the city that Siabala wants, and we need to go to it even though it may play into his hands."

Shirina cocked her head. "Maybe, yes."

"We need more reassurance than that, Shirina," Cassara said. "We need to know we're leaving everyone for a good reason."

Avarielle leaned forward, eyes ablaze. "Could Cassara stay here?" She continued before the princess could object. "Don't get me wrong, you'd be very useful, but you actually have family here." She shrugged and looked at Shirina. "It's more than either of us can claim."

Cassara flushed with anger. "Which is why I should be involved. I'm going to fight harder than both of you combined to see them safe."

"Besides that," Shirina said, sounding unconvinced by the princess' claim, "we need the magic of Graydon and Elihor, as pure as we can get them."

Avarielle shot her a nasty look, which Cassara did not miss. "What do you mean? What magic of Elihor?"

"She means," Avarielle said, emphasizing every word. "That I've been infected by dark magic, obviously. By Elihor herself." Cassara remembered the dark energy surrounding the warrior, though she could no longer detect it. But, if she focused her eyes just right, she could see the shimmer of a warding spell on her. Which meant she'd asked Shirina to disguise her energy. Cassara had vowed she would respect Avarielle's privacy, but couldn't help but feel hurt that she hadn't trusted her, instead. She'd trusted the Circle above her, of all things!

Avarielle turned to the witch. "But why would you come, Shirina?" Cassara felt small for it, but the words made her feel better.

Shirina shrugged. "I'm an Elite of the Circle. I hold knowledge the two of you simply don't. And I still have power to spare, even if weakened."

"Still," Cassara sighed, "I'm just not convinced this journey is even necessary. How do we know that we're not just heading on some wild goose chase?"

Avarielle perked up. "We ask Kale. He knows more history of this world than anyone else. He might be able to help."

"The old man from Elihor?" Cassara asked, glancing from one woman to the next, hoping someone would provide an answer as to who he was.

For a second, Avarielle's jaw tightened, as though intent on brushing aside any question. Then she sighed and relented, the sorceress keeping her gaze fixed on the fire before her.

"He is…was the grandfather of someone I met in Elihor," Avarielle said softly, turning her own eyes toward the flames. Cassara kept hers riveted on Avarielle. "He meant a lot to me."

The warrior seemed like she might say something else

as Cassara held her breath, her heart aching for the obvious grief her friend still struggled with. She thought she might say something else and held space for Avarielle's words, but instead the warrior suddenly stood up.

"I'll go speak to him," she said, then added in a whisper, "alone." She vanished before they could protest. Cassara sighed, hoping this man would tell them the journey was unnecessary and that she could stay here with her brother and husband and face the end of days with them.

KALE SAT ALONE NEAR A FIRE, the morning sun peeking over the horizon. He felt old. His body and his heart ached. He had not realized the depth of Elihor's falling. The Larkhold adepts, once over their dislike of him, had told him of the vast destruction, mostly out of respect for his bloodline. A flash fire, burning bodies, children eating children to survive, Circle outposts destroyed one by one, survivors mercilessly hunted and turned into monsters.

And meanwhile, he'd lain trapped in Tangia's study, waiting for answers, for rescue, hoping it would come from his grandson.

He pulled the blanket closer to him. Someone moved on the other side of the fire and sat down. It was the warrior from the day before. She looked at him and then at the fire, glancing up at him once in a while. The silence stretched for a few minutes, then she spoke.

"My name is Avarielle Grayloft. I was with Kryde when he died," she whispered, struggling to form the words. "We met," she hesitated, and he looked at her encouragingly. "We met on this side. But we didn't really meet until I was in Elihor."

"He made it to Graydon," Kryde said with a smile. He'd always known he would. He looked at the woman, at the grief heavy on her shoulders. "Did you ride a horse together?"

She gave him a half smile, eyes sparking with momentary joy. He laughed. He could see what Kryde had seen in her.

"How did he die?" he asked, ready for the answer. It seemed easier facing the death now, in the morning light.

She hesitated, as though struggling for the right words. He waited for her to speak, slowing his heart, bracing for whatever he was about to hear. When she spoke, her words were so soft he strained to hear. "He died protecting me, Kale. Using his magic to save me, but not himself."

Kale swallowed hard and gave her a sad smile. "That was the curse of Elihor, you know." Avarielle looked at him, eyes shining in the firelight. "That her descendants could not use the magic to protect themselves. Only those they truly loved."

"Why?" the warrior asked bitterly. "What's the point of magic if it can't save you?" Kale poked at the fire.

"I wondered that for a long time too. There were many wonderful stories my mother used to tell me. About how it had been a test set out by Graydon, and Elihor had failed it, failing to save him in the last moment since she didn't truly love him. Or that it was a curse from Siabala, who had loved her and wanted her to reveal whoever she loved most by saving them, so that he could kill them in turn. All wonderful stories, but in truth, Avarielle, I just don't know."

"I wish it wasn't so," Avarielle whispered.

Kale nodded slowly. "Me too."

A few moments passed in comfortable silence, as both dealt with their grief as best they could. Then she broke the silence again. "Do you know, Kale, if anything lies beneath the city? If Siabala would be trying to uncover something?"

Kale searched his memories, which were still as sharp as when he was a boy. "I don't know much about the city. I read a legend once about a large central city, oldest in the world, where magic worked as a single unit. Ancient gods lived within it, or so the story goes. And that it had vanished overnight and the Bloody Mountains stood in its place. That much seems accurate, though the city seems little more than rubble now."

"We think Siabala is trying to get at something underneath it."

Kale shook his head. "Maybe. I don't know. There might be something under Siabala's Rage. Or in Stormhold. If Siabala himself hasn't trekked down the mountains yet after gaining his freedom, we can only assume he's still trapped."

Avarielle's head shot up, steel in her eyes. "I was wondering where he was hiding. Never did I think he would still be there. I would never have left, had I known!"

She stood up and Kale followed her lead.

"Avarielle." He gently took hold of her arm to stop her. She didn't resist, but he could feel her muscles tensing. "Siabala is very powerful. He was different from Elihor and Graydon. Some say he was an ancient god, others a creation of magic itself," he finished, making his point clear. "He's more powerful than you."

Avarielle's hands curled into fists at her sides. "I know. And I don't care. I will find a way to avenge Kryde, this I swear."

Kale sighed, and then chuckled. "Of that I have no doubt. Ah, to be young again. I will tell you this, granddaughter," he used the title affectionately and she softened visibly. "Graydon and Elihor were separated. Their magics were kept apart, by the Wall of Loss. They contained Siabala, but they could not destroy him. If they had had the chance to unite their powers, the two strongest sources in the land, they might have succeeded."

"Are you suggesting they're not the ones who erected the Wall of Loss?"

Kale shrugged. "I don't know. But ask yourself: why would they separate themselves? It contained Siabala, but it kept him safe from them, too. They're dead now, and he's almost free. They must have set a safety net for when the Wall failed. To give their descendants time to accomplish what they couldn't."

Avarielle looked pensive for a few moments. "Why not just kill them all then?"

Kale's eyes beamed. He felt young again, his mind dancing with possibilities. "Because he still needs something from them. Either to drop the safety net, or to activate something. He is no fool, he laid down his own measures, playing off of Elihor and Graydon, and their close friends, I'm sure."

He removed his hand from her arm, speaking carefully. "And I know of the story of the Graylofts and their magical sword." She looked at him, standing still. He pushed on, in case her family no longer remembered. "The blood-bonded assassins of Siabala, gifted with a sword activated by the blood magic of Siabala, that could kill Elihor herself."

Avarielle looked at him with surprise, then set her jaw firm. So, she'd known. He gently patted her arm, and she didn't move away or stop him.

"It's another story, Avarielle. I don't know the truth. I do know that your ancestor, the first one to wield the blade, did not kill Elihor. So he made a choice. Just like you will have to choose your allegiances."

She nodded, then added gently. "I'll be leaving soon. Please tell no one. When I return, I'll find you. We have much to share still, Kale Kolder."

Kale was starting to feel old again. He didn't want her to leave. He felt kinship to her in a way he felt with no one else here, probably because of their shared bond with Kryde. "You might need me," he said, unconvinced. "I am a descendant of Elihor. You will probably need my powers."

Avarielle placed a hand on his shoulder. "We will find a way, Kale. Stay here and be safe. I will come and find you. I promise, grandfather."

He smiled at the word and watched her turn around and walk away, wondering if he would ever see her again, the descendant of a cursed family.

And the closest thing to family he had left.

CASSARA SAT on the ground near Jayden and Dayshon, waiting for Avarielle to return. The two had been exchanging stories as they shared the morning meal. They had set up out of view of the battlefield and city, Dayshon saying the smell of death was turning his stomach. She was pretty sure he'd said that to spare her and Jayden, and she appreciated him all the more for it. Her husband seemed to enjoy the company of Jayden, taking him under his wing and listening intently to his advice.

She smiled and laughed at their jokes, glad the two were getting along, wishing she could fully enjoy the moment. But she only half listened, impatient for news of Avarielle.

Shirina stood off to the side with other newly arrived adepts, discussing the theory of using magic as a pair, dissecting possibilities and fail-safes.

Well over thirty adepts from Ravenhold had joined

them, an impressive number considering Ravenhold had fallen. Plus, there were the adepts from Larkhold and Stormhold.

She watched as the Westlanders cast wary glances their way, and then the Eastlanders' way. She didn't blame them. They were outnumbered almost three to one now, in their own land. Not a comforting thought. Nearby, Carsyn and Kaden stood watch. The sight of them made her feel safer, and sadder, too. They should not have had to follow her to this battlefield.

"Cassara, do you remember?" Jayden asked, looking to his sister.

Cassara turned to him. "I'm sorry Jayden, remember what?"

"If your sister ever slept," Dayshon teased, "she might be able to follow a simple conversation."

"Oh, she never slept," Jayden said, looking exasperated. "She used to sneak out at night all the time!"

"Jayden!" Cassara warned, making him break out into laughter. Dayshon looked at her inquisitively.

"I used to play music in the village, that's all," she offered by way of explanation.

Dayshon smiled. "Your flute playing is beautiful, Cassara." She blushed, pleased with the compliment. She had barely had the chance to breathe, much less practice, so it was nice to know she didn't sound too rusty.

Cassara spotted Avarielle from the corner of her eye, the warrior walking up, grinning as she joined them.

"I can't tell you how happy I am to see you again," she

said, sitting beside Jayden. Her brother immediately hugged her and she wrapped her arms around him. They stayed that way for a few moments, then broke apart, smiling at each other. Everything they'd needed to say had been shared in that moment.

"You know," Jayden turned toward Dayshon, looking very proud of himself, "in Elihor, Avarielle and I are married." Avarielle broke out laughing. Cassara raised an eyebrow.

"I hope you don't take this too personally, Jayden," she said as he grinned, "but I think I favored another."

Jayden's grin faltered for a moment. "Did Kryde…"

"He saved me," Avarielle said, swallowing hard. "And he fought hard for his people. He'd be glad you're okay, Jayden."

He looked down, staring at the fire as he struggled with his own grief. Avarielle let him be for a few seconds before gently elbowing him, making him grin as he looked up at her. She reached over and ruffled his hair. He looked very insulted, every inch the kid trying to be king.

"My apologies, your Highness," Avarielle said somberly, making Jayden laugh and breaking the dark mood that had settled over him.

"Cassara, when you have a moment, can we chat?" Avarielle said. "I think Shirina wants to go on about some theory of magic or another." She rolled her eyes theatrically, winning another grin from Jayden.

Cassara smiled. "Well, my brother was just trying to embarrass me in front of my husband, so I think I'm available now!" She quickly stuck her tongue out at Jayden. Dayshon stood up with her.

"Is everything all right?" He gathered her hands in his.

Cassara smiled and leaned in for a kiss. "As all right as we could expect things to be, Dayshon," she said.

He nodded. "Well, Jayden, I have to make the rounds to make sure everything is in order. Care to join me, future king of Edoline?"

Jayden stood up and very seriously accepted. Cassara mouthed the words "thank you" to Dayshon before heading off, following Avarielle away from her family.

***

"So that's it?" Cassara asked, leaning against a tree as Shirina and Avarielle stood nearby, infuriatingly calm. "The old man says something is probably down there, so we're just going to go?"

"He's right, Cassara," Avarielle said. "Siabala would have come down if he could. We have to stop him completely while he's still trapped."

"Can't we just let him remain trapped?"

"He can still attack, Cassara," Avarielle answered, her voice kind. "So far, they've only been minor attacks, but it still cost us more than half the army. That's half the army of most of Graydon. The last army remaining, Cassara. If they fall, no one is left to protect the people to the East of here, including Edoline."

"I know," Cassara said, wishing she didn't sound so

tired. And afraid. "But we don't know where we're going, we don't know what we're looking for, and we suspect Siabala wants something from us, too. It feels a bit like suicide. We could just be making things worse."

"The Circle waited things out too, Cassara," Shirina said in a whisper. "And look at what happened to us."

Cassara swallowed hard. It was hard to imagine leaving Jayden and Dayshon. Her heart had not felt this entangled since leaving Edoline. But she couldn't risk all of their lives, either. Avarielle waited her out patiently, leaning against the tree and looking elsewhere.

"You're right," Cassara said softly. "I'm sorry. I just...I know I said I'd come. But..."

"I'd think you were insane if you were eager to leave your family again, Cassara," Avarielle said gently.

"When do we head out?" Cassara asked, not feeling so alone anymore.

"As soon as it's dark enough for us to vanish into the city," Avarielle answered.

"We're just going to sneak off?" Cassara was horrified at the thought.

Avarielle shook her head. "Not necessarily, but we need the cover of darkness so that Siabala won't see us. Shirina will hide our magical trail." She looked at the sorceress, who nodded.

"But let's not tell everyone. It's better if fewer know," Shirina intoned. "They will be more confident for the next attack."

Cassara's stomach fell. More confident, believing the three were still there with their magic to protect them.

"The Circle will protect them," Shirina said, reading the look of fear on Cassara's face. "We think there's a way to use the magic safely. There are no guarantees, but there's a fairly good chance of success."

"Besides," Avarielle added, "once Siabala figures out we're no longer here, if he truly needs us for something, he'll probably send his monsters after us, instead."

"Comforting," Cassara mumbled. Despite her protest, she did feel strangely comforted by that. She'd face armies of demons if it meant sparing her brother any further pain.

"Then it's settled," she said, crossing her arms. "We leave at dark."

2 2

Indecision tore through Cassara. She wanted to tell Dayshon and Jayden, but she didn't want to see the look in their eyes, lest it stop her from leaving. She sat in her tent and sighed. Making it easier on herself didn't make it better for everyone else.

She fidgeted with the letter she had just written to Dayshon. Telling him what she knew of his father, that he lay dying following Circle treachery. That he might in fact already be dead, and Dayshon needed to survive to take over the throne of Rashim. And that he should marry again should she not return. Rashim would need an heir, and she could hardly bear him one dead.

She hadn't decided if she would tell him that she was leaving, or simply leave the letter. She could only deal with so much before heading into battle herself.

As for Jayden, she would wait until tonight. There was

no reason to ruin the boy's day just yet, not when he was enjoying himself playing king with Dayshon.

At least they'll take care of each other.

She felt comforted by the thought and stepped back out into the evening chill. It was a perfect night for a bit of music, before she would head into the darkness, where she would only hear the sound of her own fear.

"WE CAN'T TRUST all of those Eastlanders," Trevon exclaimed the second he spotted Avarielle.

"Oh, and how do you suggest we break it to them?" Avarielle held up her hand to silence his response. He was fuming, which she had rarely seen Trevon do. Of course, the contingent of Circle witches nearby probably fed his discomfort and anger.

"I'm leaving tonight, Trevon," she whispered. His eyes grew wide.

"You would leave now? When Siabala attacks?"

Avarielle's blood pumped at the implication of desertion and she quickly closed the gap between them, close enough to feel his breath as she spoke. "I am leaving *because* Siabala attacks. He needs something below the city, and I intend to get to it first."

"Are you going alone?" he growled after a few moments.

"Cassara and Shirina are coming with me."

"You would trust that witch with your life again?" he

sounded exasperated. "How well did it serve you the first time, Avarielle? Can you learn nothing!"

"Keep your voice down, Trevon. I'm only telling you because I have a favor to ask." Trevon might not understand all of her decisions, but he would support her, no matter what. She would bet her life on it, and had time and time again. He looked at her with narrowed eyes, like he still questioned her sanity. Then he deflated and shook his head.

"You're going to do this no matter what I say, aren't you?" He sounded so discouraged that Avarielle couldn't help but smile.

"I am. I've never listened to you, Trevon. Why would I start now?"

He gave her a rough smile. Avarielle counted her favored stars for having an ally like him. "I need you to keep an eye on Cassara's family. Her brother and her husband."

Trevon sighed. "I hate when you ask me dull things like that."

Avarielle grinned. "It'll be the heat of battle. Trust me, those two won't stay out of it, so you'll be in the thick of it with them." He crossed his arms, but he eventually nodded. He wasn't pleased with her.

"And Trevon," she added, "play nice with the Eastlanders. Whether we like it or not, we need them right now."

"You ask a lot, Avarielle," he grumbled. She clasped his shoulder.

"I do, and I have one more thing to ask." He looked about ready to protest but she cut him off. "Stay safe, Trevon. The West would not be home without you, old friend."

He nodded, a slight smile appearing on his lips before disappearing just as quickly. "Meaning you intend to return?"

Her hands fell from his shoulder.

"Take care, my friend," she said and turned away from his piercing eyes.

She never once looked back.

CASSARA SAT on a stone and pulled out her flute. The sun was dipping below the horizon, signaling the end of a thankfully quiet day. She was far from the troops and she didn't care. She played for herself tonight.

She brought the flute to her lips and gently blew into it, stringing one note into the other, not playing a song but letting the music create its own melody. She closed her eyes and played note after note, softly, as though she didn't want to awaken the darkness.

And then she played the Travelers' Song, her mother's favorite song, the last one she had taught Cassara before dying.

Before I killed her.

Cassara didn't miss a note as she played, the pain not as acute as it had been not long ago. She had been scared and a child, and if she couldn't forgive herself, then no one could.

She strung the notes together, letting them fly in the wind, and ended the song, feeling at peace. She opened her eyes when she heard her brother ask, "You're leaving tonight, aren't you?"

Cassara forced a smile. "Why do you say that?"

"Because you always get lost in thought before you head off at night," he said quickly, as though annoyed by the stupidity of her question. She let the smile drop. Now was as good a time as any to tell him.

"I am leaving tonight, Jayden. And I'm sorry for it."

"I want to come with you," he demanded, stepping right up to her, grabbing her arm as though never intending to let her go, wide eyes filled with fear.

"Jayden," she said softly over the lump in her throat. "I have to go. I need to do something, to stop Siabala. You have to stay here with Dayshon. He'll need you."

Jayden still clung to her, eyes filling with tears. "What if I never see you again?"

Cassara jumped up and gathered him in a hug.

"We'll always meet again, Jayden. You're my brother. You, me and Altessa, we'll always be linked in a way few ever are."

Jayden clung to her. "Do you think Altessa is all right?"

"Of course she is. She's waiting for us in Edoline." She broke free of his embrace and looked him in the eye. "And we'll go meet her there, together." Jayden closed his eyes and smiled, and she imagined the sound of the surf, the wind in the orchard, the smell of the sea.

She kissed Jayden on the forehead, hoping dearly that if she didn't return, her younger brother would make it home safely, where he could see the orchard blooming when spring returned.

But first, she had to make sure spring would return.

"If the pairing doesn't work," Shirina told the adepts, having tried to teach them too much in one day. "If you feel the wrong magic infiltrate your own, pinch your partner and both stop at the same time. Keep your timing identical so one doesn't take more of a hit than the other."

The adepts nodded, some looking intrigued, others eager. Most just looked terrified. There weren't enough adepts from the keeps to pair everyone up, so the youngest from Ravenhold had been spared having to fight. For now.

Shirina looked to the Crimson Circle of Stormhold, an older woman named Liza. "You cannot use the shadow magic at all?" The sorceress was disappointed. The gray robes certainly suggested Stormhold worked with the shadow magic. The woman shook her head.

"I wish, Crimson Circle Shirina. We can wield the magic of Graydon or Elihor separately, but not as one. And we cannot separate them ourselves."

Shirina nodded. "That is unfortunate for all of us. You

and your adepts stand back as the adepts of Larkhold and Ravenhold pair. Their pairing seems more instinctive."

"We will be here if needed," Liza said, lowering her head respectfully. Shirina invited Rolje to join her. She expected him, as the only Crimson Circle from Larkhold, to take charge once she had left. The Stormhold Circle understood. They would not be joining them on the battlefield.

"If I cannot give you orders, then listen to Rolje," Shirina instructed everyone. The adepts nodded, as did Rolje. He looked scared too, his shoulders drooping just a bit. "Go and have some supper," she told them, the adepts quickly dispersing. Only a few rays of sunset remained on the horizon.

"Care to take a walk with me?" Shirina asked, beginning to walk before he answered. He followed her casually.

When they were far enough away, Shirina turned to face him, keeping her voice soft. "You must not let them see your fear, Rolje. They count on you to be more than a just an adept."

Rolje gave her a shy grin. "Is it that obvious?"

She nodded. "To me it was. To them, it will be. Keep your shoulders proud. We will find a way to vanquish this evil, and to wield the new magic."

"What if we're wrong? What if the merging won't work?"

"Then try something else," Shirina said, not including

herself in the sentence. If Rolje noticed, he chose not to point it out.

He gave a short laugh. "I joined the Circle because I didn't want to be a farmer and I was a quick study," he said, grinning at her. "I never imagined I'd live through its darkest hour."

"I don't think any of us did."

"Why did you join the Circle?" he asked, a simple question. Shirina did not disguise the truth. Darkness had engulfed the land. She would soon have to get ready.

"Those in Graydon do not join the Circle, they are chosen to join at a young age, taken from their family, and grow up in the Covenant."

"Oh."

Shirina sighed. "I promised the adepts that they could leave if they wanted, once this was all over. That they could return to their families."

Rolje was quiet for moment. "What about you? Will you stay in the Circle?"

Shirina wanted to tell him that of course she would. That she had nowhere else to be. Instead, she turned towards the dark shadows of the Bloody Mountains in the distance as she answered.

"We'll see."

CASSARA KISSED Dayshon as he slept, exhausted from battle and worry. He muttered and moved, smiling in his sleep. She leaned in and whispered in his ear.

"I have to go, but I promise you I'll return, if I can." He muttered something else and she fluttered another kiss on his lips. She could have loved him, easily.

She left the letter on her pillow, where he would find it in the morning. Still fully clothed, she pulled her boots on, grabbed her small pack and headed outside. Trevon had seen to it that he was on guard duty tonight, and he nodded as she walked past, pointing to the tent where her husband slept and then to the one where Jayden lay. He then brought his fist to his heart.

She went to him and clutched the fist and looked at him, conveying her gratitude. He would keep them safe. He *had* to keep them safe.

She swallowed hard and let him go, crouching as she ran along the side of the camp. The watch, focused outwards on possible incoming assailants and not on the camp itself, was easy to avoid. She carefully made her way down to the crevasse and the city, then entered a half-destroyed house to get out of sight of the guards.

Avarielle and Shirina were already there, eyes shining with determination in the night.

Pack Nacker stood near.

"They've found an underground passage that leads…" She looked at Pack, who had no words to provide her. She shrugged. "He'll see us to it," Avarielle whispered, and Cassara nodded. The warrior handed the princess a bow and a quiver of arrows. Cassara took it gratefully, quickly fastening the quiver on her back.

The three followed Pack into the ancient city, below the Bloody Mountains.

Cassara's heart hammered in her chest. She felt like the young girl leaving Edoline all over again.

Except this time, she was leaving of her own accord.

2 3

Shadows licked every corner and darkness crowded every building around them. Shirina invoked the Sight to gaze deeper into the velvet night, trying to foresee any threat. The three women moved effortlessly over rubble and cracks, slithering into the city as the warriors from Elihor kept watch on them.

Two hours had passed since they had left and she hoped they neared the underground passage. Or whatever Pack led them to. The Bloody Mountains loomed before them, quiet and still, a dark shadow blocking the stars on the horizon. A hint of winter clung to the air. Shirina pulled her cloak closer, partly to hide the white of her cotton robe, partly to ward off the cold.

With autumn having gripped the land as early as spring this year, no doubt due to Siabala's dark energies, it was no surprise that winter seemed to already be on its way.

With the poor summer, droughts and Elom attacks, she doubted enough food remained in Graydon to feed everyone through the winter. Their salvation might come from the many deaths. Fewer mouths to feed.

But add further attacks to the ordeal, and come next spring, should the season of life ever return anew, there would be even fewer survivors.

Avarielle turned into a large building, ducking under the slab of stone half blocking the entryway. The princess and Shirina followed. It was pitch black inside, but the sorceress could see well enough with the Sight. Avarielle seemed to travel with enough ease, and Cassara barely hesitated. Shirina remembered the first cave they had ever entered together, below Edoline, when Cassara had barely been able to keep one foot in front of the other in the dark. But, then again, that was before Cassara had developed the Sight.

The warriors from Elihor ran past them, their presence betrayed by the slight tainting of the air on their passage, like a corpse just beginning to rot. Shirina was unclear if all of them were trailing along, or if some remained with the troops. She was certain of one thing—that they would not follow them all the way to Siabala. The Grayloft might be proud and impulsive, but she was no fool in battle.

To bring so many would be like lighting a flare warning Siabala of their arrival.

They crossed a doorway and ended up in a corridor.

The darkness here was impenetrable to human eyes, and Shirina watched in amusement as the warrior obviously struggled to keep pace, one hand outstretched to feel for walls. She was disappointed to see no obstructions in her way.

Avarielle was silent, though Shirina imagined she cursed internally. One of the warrior's hands was placed protectively on her belly until she seemed to realize it and quickly lowered it, as though trying to convince herself she wasn't pregnant.

If she didn't want the child, she should just have taken Shirina up on her offer to get rid of it. It was already almost viable on its own, so strong was the child. Or, blessed with the magic of Elihor, it simply grew faster in her womb. If she wanted to get rid of it without physical consequence, now was the time. At first, Shirina had feared the pregnancy had been the result of torture, but it was clearly the child of someone she'd cared deeply for. One of Elihor's bloodline, to top it all.

Kryde Kolder.

She shook her head. The warrior was a fool. To get herself pregnant in these times only highlighted the fact. If she wanted to run after Siabala with a body unbalanced by child, she was welcome to do so. It would ease Shirina's decisions following the fall of Siabala. Leaving the Circle and admitting defeat would be much easier without the Grayloft around to witness it.

They turned a corner, the warrior barely faltering,

annoying Shirina even more. A faint yellow tinge infiltrated the hallway from the next doorway, barely revealing the outline of the walls.

Pack Nacker led them faster towards the breach. Avarielle quickened her pace and Cassara did as well, though not as much. She glanced back to look at Shirina, undoubtedly to make sure the sorceress could keep up in her weakened condition.

If the princess keeps trying to coddle me, Shirina mused, *she's going to be the first one I hit with this staff, instead of the warrior.*

Avarielle reached the end of the hallway and vanished. Shirina quickened her steps, curiosity winning over her fatigue. The yellow light was probably a Circle spell, bearing the same hue as her own light spells.

She crossed the threshold and squinted in the growing light. The princess gasped beside her.

Below them spread a city. Another city, not like the one above them, this one untouched by the passage of time and war. No corners graced any of the structures, each one smooth and rounded, some bigger at the top than at the bottom. Some structures seemed to grow out of the ground itself, like a garden waiting to be plucked, or a shoreline smoothed out by waves.

Clusters of these strange buildings formed the city, each wall grazing the next building, with just enough space for the yellow light to infiltrate and cast shadows. It gave the illusion that the buildings were in constant motion, like dancers bowing to each other before one more dance. A great stone dome spread over it, lit by the same light, keeping the cities above and below separated.

An underground lake shimmered in the distance, the water vast and smelling fresh even from here. *Hunter Lake.* The waterways of Graydon had been vanishing. Shirina guessed they had been drawn here, through underground channels reopened as Siabala's powers grew. But still, he himself had not been able to reach this place, or so they hoped.

Streets zigzagged between the buildings, reminding Shirina of the rivers of Solir, which cut the land in much the same pattern. The yellow light emanated from globes lining those streets.

Shirina could see the strands of magic well contained within the globes.

She had been mistaken. It wasn't Circle magic, though it resembled it greatly. But it was different enough to send a shiver down her spine. The magic was the same, but deeper. *Older.* Like a wizened aunt of the magic she courted, with more layers and wisdom than its younger counterpart.

What was this magic? Who had built this?

The princess stared in awe at the city, very still. But Avarielle turned to look at the sorceress, hand on the pommel of her sword, eyebrow raised. She met her gaze and shrugged. Avarielle sighed and turned back to the dark corridor, where she clasped Pack Nacker's hand.

"Be careful," she whispered. "And, thank you. I will not fail in my promise, Pack Nacker." His eyes held hers for a few more moments before he vanished back the way they'd come, a great shadow engulfed by the night.

"We should move," Avarielle said softly. Cassara barely nodded, still lost in awe at the sight before her. "Let's get out of sight," the warrior said, gently prodding the princess to move. The Pack had found a pathway for them, but they had to scale down a hefty slope to reach the streets of the city below. And, until they reached solid ground, they'd be uncomfortably exposed.

Avarielle took the lead and set as brisk a pace as possible without losing their footing on the wet ground, earth covering stone and shifting uncomfortably beneath their feet.

Shirina took a deep breath and tried to use the Sight, but found herself forced to focus on her steps, instead. To keep up with the Grayloft, lest she be left behind.

<hr>

Cassara guessed it neared noon by the time they stopped, hidden by two buildings. If she was correct, they had walked the city for at least six hours. She looked around as she chewed slowly on some dried meat.

The constant yellow light projected up to the ceiling without fading, outlining the smooth rock that sheltered the city. The walls were also smooth, as though artisans had spent relentless hours perfecting their domed cage.

The buildings showed no signs of breakage, of chinks or of dirt.

They had entered a few out of curiosity, but found nothing. No furniture remained, no people, and no sign that either had ever existed.

Cassara started when Avarielle broke the silence by whispering to Shirina.

"Do you know where we are?"

Shirina finished chewing before answering. "Some of our most ancient books tell of an ancient people, here long before our ancestors ever landed on these shores. They had great powers and their cities were unlike anything ever before seen. The books often referred to them as gods." She shrugged. "But then again, those books spoke of anyone with magic as gods. Superstition, at best."

"Our ancestors came from another land?" Avarielle asked incredulously. "Which one? No one has ever discovered another land."

Shirina shrugged. "I'm not sure. It might just be stories. But it's the only reference to beings with strange architectural skills I can think of." She hesitated for an instant. "Some of those stories link Siabala to those god-like creatures."

"Didn't think that was important to mention before, did you?" Avarielle scowled.

Shirina's eyes narrowed as she flushed red. "I didn't even think of that story until we entered this city. The city above hardly made me think of anything vastly different. It just looked like an old, battered city."

Cassara stepped in before Avarielle could muster another angry reply. "I have to agree. Strip the paint, brocades and people from Massir, destroy half of it, and it would look very much like the city above."

"So we're assuming the city above wasn't built by whoever, or whatever, built this city?" Avarielle said, still looking at Shirina.

"It seems the logical conclusion. I assume the city above was built to keep the city below hidden."

"Or they didn't even know this was here," Cassara offered.

Shirina nodded. "Regardless, the city above was built long enough ago to have been hidden by the Bloody Mountains and then forgotten by history."

"So before the Wall was created," Avarielle said, leaning back against the building, taking another bite of stale bread.

"Why would Siabala want this city uncovered?" Cassara asked. "If that is indeed what he's using his creatures for, to try and weaken the city's dome until it collapses."

Avarielle raised an eyebrow at Shirina. The sorceress seemed to ponder her answer for a few moments before giving it.

"He either needs something to get in here, or he needs something freed from here."

"Very enlightening, thanks," Avarielle mumbled.

"Regardless," Shirina said, ignoring Avarielle, "we need

to figure out what he's after and stop him from acquiring it."

The two seemed content to finish their meal in silence. Cassara forced food down her throat, finding it impossible to convince herself they had done the right thing by leaving the troops above, with very little protection or hope.

2 4

*Y*our father is possibly already dead, fallen by Delora's treachery...

Your mother wanted to keep it secret, so that you would not falter in battle...

If I should not return, remarry. Please. See to it that Graydon rises from the ashes of this calamity.

I'm sorry.

The letter ended with those words. *I'm sorry.* Not *I love you,* or *Stay safe,* or even *See you soon.* Just *I'm sorry.*

Dayshon had read and re-read it so often the paper already showed wear. At first, he had believed his dreams had woven this reality, until he had come to accept that those were indeed Cassara's words.

And she was gone.

He threw the covers off, stood and began dressing. The day was already bitingly cold, and his breath fogged with each exhale.

His heart wanted him to sit down and take the time to grieve, his head wanted time to think. He could afford neither.

The fact would remain that Cassara was gone, and she had been the glue that kept the Eastland and Westland forces together. Without her and her magic, he feared Breck would choose to branch off on his own. They needed to work together, were they to stand a chance.

Dayshon folded Cassara's letter and slipped it into his tunic, near his heart. He couldn't afford to have anyone else find it. If word that his father may be dead escaped, it could tip the balance of power. And he wasn't clear how Jiles would react. His captain might very well drug him and ship him back to Massir.

Dayshon grinned slightly at the thought as he stepped out of the tent. Jiles stood on guard, and he nodded to him. The Westland warrior, Trevon, also lingered nearby. Dayshon wasn't fooled.

Cassara had asked him to keep him safe.

He walked towards him. Why had she been so worried about him? She was the one foolishly heading into Siabala's Rage!

He took a deep breath and focused. Cassara had made her choice. He hoped she would survive, but she was beyond his help now, and he had other matters to pursue.

He addressed Trevon. "I would like to speak to you and Breck." The Westland warrior nodded, his eyes not lined with the suspicion the Westlanders had greeted the Eastlanders with upon their first meeting.

But, then again, over the last few battles, Dayshon and the Westland leader seemed to have grudgingly won each other's respect. Which was why Dayshon needed to be the one to break the news to Breck.

It could seal the trust further, and without his remaining allies, Dayshon feared there could be no victory for Graydon.

***

JAYDEN STOOD to the side of the camp, not wanting to mingle with the soldiers, who frightened him a little. They looked mean and disheveled. Most of them sported scars or bloodied bandages. Their eyes were either rough or broken, and even those who chatted and laughed seemed distant, as though the only way to deal with the next wave of attack was to separate themselves from the here and now.

He stayed nearest to the Southern Coalition's troops, which were not yet battle worn. Colonel Orliys stood near, and Jayden knew Dayshon would soon be calling for the two of them. He must have read Cassara's note by now.

He forced himself not to fidget or, even worse, cry. He would give anything for Cassara to still be here. She had been like a warm fire on a cold night.

But she's gone, now.

He took a deep breath. They would need to figure out

what to do next. He tried to concentrate on what they now had, not on what they might have had.

The Circle adepts were aloof, and he wasn't certain they could use magic. His sister had warned him they might not be able to make a difference, and to keep that in mind. The Southern Coalition's forces were the freshest, but also the least tested in battle. The only man Jayden believed had actual fighting experience was the colonel, who had proven solid and true to his word so far.

The Westland warriors and Rashim's forces had suffered the strongest blows, at least half of their men already destroyed by Siabala's attacks. That had seemed to help them bond, Dayshon and Breck having formed a tentative truce based on mutual respect.

And he had Cassara's amulet. Jayden could feel the cold metal on his skin. Cassara could filter magic through it, she had said. But he couldn't feel a thing, not the warmth she had spoken of, nor their mother's spirit.

Maybe it was because he was the youngest and had barely known their mother. Maybe he didn't share the link with Alayna that her other children had. Or then again, maybe it was because he was a boy. He remembered his history lessons, from when Edoline was a monarchy. Maybe that was why.

So that the women, who could wield the magic, could rule more efficiently.

Jayden looked across the warriors and the broken city to the Bloody Mountains. Somewhere below them his sister now journeyed, searching for Siabala, in a desperate bid to stop him.

The amulet could have helped her, he was certain. Though she seemed confident that she could deal the final blow without it.

"Your Highness." He recognized Trevon's voice and grinned. He liked the Westland warrior, who reminded him so much of Avarielle. Avarielle, who was also gone.

"Dayshon and Breck would like a word with you," Trevon said, grinning back at the prince.

He nodded and turned towards the colonel, who had come closer. "Colonel, if you'd care to join me." Colonel Orliys nodded and followed quietly. Jayden needed the colonel's loyalty, and didn't intend to exclude him from any discussions.

He would need him in the long run, he strongly suspected. Even beyond the current battlefield and into the orchards of Edoline.

FROM THE LOOK on the young prince's face, Dayshon had no doubt that he already knew his sister was gone. Of course, Cassara would never have dreamed of leaving without first reassuring her little brother. Especially after searching for him for so long.

"You're aware of your sister's disappearance?" Breck said gruffly. Jayden nodded and, to his credit, did not turn to look at Dayshon.

"She didn't disappear," Jayden said. "She went to defeat Siabala."

Breck grunted. "I suppose if anyone can, it's your sister and Avarielle." Then he added, mumbling, "Still a bother, though."

Dayshon intervened. "I'd love for nothing more than to pretend we don't need them, but truth be told, we need their magic more than ever. If we're going to win the day, we're going to have to work like one unit."

Breck grunted again, though he didn't contradict Dayshon.

"Our troops are ready for battle, though they number less than a thousand," Colonel Orliys said. "And they do not have your experience in battle," he stated, nodding towards Breck. The Westland warrior seemed both surprised and proud of the statement.

"What of the Circle?" Trevon asked. "Can we count on them to help?"

Dayshon curled his hands into fists. Cassara's flowery script flashed before his eyes. *Your father is possibly already dead, fallen by Delora's treachery...*Delora. A Circle Elder.

Could they trust any of the Circle?

Jayden was the one to answer. "I don't know that we have much of a choice."

Dayshon looked at the men nodding around him, taking this young boy's word. Treating him like one of their own. The heir of Rashim was amazed by Jayden's calm and rational thoughts. He had heard stories of Alexavier Edoline, had grown up on them, and now understood why his father had affected such change in Graydon. By watching his son unknowingly and easily win others' loyalty, as Cassara had also done, he understood Alexavier's strength had not been in battle, but rather in forging alliances.

Dayshon was glad Jayden was his ally.

"I think we're about to find out," Trevon suddenly said and the men looked up, towards the sky, which was growing dark despite the early afternoon hour.

"Is that…"

"Srocks! Get the troops ready!"

Dayshon broke from the Westland troops, heading for his own, wondering how exactly he was supposed to get his troops ready for monsters they could barely defeat without the help of magic.

The three women had just resumed their journey when the ceiling erupted in thunder.

"What is that?" Avarielle asked as she pulled Graysword free. Shirina wondered if Cassara noticed the warrior's wince before setting her jaw stubbornly. From the wide-eyed look of the princess, she doubted she had. Graysword reacted to the dark magic above, and to the child of Elihor growing quickly within her. The warrior truly was a fool.

"Another attack above, I assume," Shirina said, clutching her staff.

Another thunderclap and the stones cracked.

"Is there a chance the ceiling will fall?" Cassara asked, her voice choked by fear.

"Let's find cover," Avarielle said, running ahead as the others followed.

"This way!" Shirina cried as she turned down a street,

towards a large structure composed of one dome. Magic danced around it strongly, as though protecting it. With its large size and thick stone base, plus the extra magic firmly covering it, it seemed sturdier than anything else nearby.

"Move it!" Avarielle screamed as the ceiling shook and showered stones around them. Small pebbles struck Shirina but she ignored them. There could be much worse than these stones.

"Where's the door?" Cassara gasped as they reached the structure. Shirina began running the length of it as the ceiling cracked above them.

"The door, Shirina!" Avarielle screamed. The sorceress ignored them as she ran, using the Sight to try and detect something out of the ordinary that would show them the door. A crack, a change in paint, a magical glow... *Anything!*

"WHAT ARE THEY DOING?" Dayshon asked, watching the srocks fall from the sky, plummeting against the city below. Some would simply fall, others would tip down and strike it headfirst, all of their speed behind them.

Some would rise again and start over, others would stay fallen, too broken for even Siabala's magic to mend.

"This is insulting," Breck exclaimed from beside him. "Does Siabala know nothing of combat, and relies only on tricks and magic?"

"They're trying to reveal something from beneath the ruins," a Circle adept spoke up from beside them. Dayshon quickly placed himself between him and Breck.

"What is below?"

The adept, a man from Larkhold named Rolje, shook his head. "I do not know. Crimson Circle Elite Shirina is gone to find out, but unfortunately we still lack the knowledge."

Dayshon's eyes grew wide at the realization. "You mean Shirina, Cassara and Avarielle are below?"

The man looked darkly at them and nodded.

"We have to stop them," Dayshon turned around to Breck. The Westland warrior shook his head.

"I'm all for suicide missions, but how do we stop those monsters? They're not even after us. It seems that Avarielle and the others have a better chance at survival with their magic."

"Not if the city falls on them." Dayshon looked back towards the Circle adept. "Is there anything you can do?"

Rolje bit his lower lip, worrying Dayshon. This was not a usual Circle action, showing fear and worry. In a Crimson Circle, he expected more reserved behavior. Was Larkhold's Circle not as powerful as Ravenhold's, or were its adepts simply more human?

"We might be able to stop some, but I doubt all." He seemed to make up his mind as he looked Dayshon in the eye. "We'll try it. We'll attack and try to stop Siabala from gaining what he seeks."

"Good luck," Dayshon cried out after him as the

Crimson Circle ran back towards the other adepts, white, black and gray robes mingling together, different colored cloaks, if any at all, covering their shoulders. Running was also very different behavior than Ravenhold's adepts. He hoped their powers would at least prove comparable.

"Look over there," Breck called out, pointing to the edge of the ruins, where fewer srocks attacked. He saw shadows moving and squinted to see clearer.

"What are those?" he asked, seeing a srock go down and not get back up. In fact, none of the falling srocks in that region were rising again. The shadows seemed to swallow them whole.

"Pack Nacker's men, if I'm not mistaken," Breck said, his hand on his sword.

"The Circle is about to unleash its magic on that battlefield," Dayshon said, not clear what to do. Were these Eloms, the so-called Pack, truly friend or foe?

"We could use their help later on, I'm certain," Breck said, spitting on the ground.

"I agree, but how do we warn them, without getting ourselves killed in the process?"

Breck spat again and looked down at the ground, as though too embarrassed to declare his lack of ability to save their allies.

Dayshon itched to jump on a horse, ride like lightning and warn them himself.

But then his kingdom would be left without a king.

This was not the time for heroics.

He stood rooted in place.

Unlike Breck, however, he forced himself to look at the carnage below.

KALE KOLDER WATCHED the adepts prepare to attack, so young and so nervous it made his heart ache. Their plan might not work. It probably wouldn't work, truth be told. Shirina had known as much as he did that, unless the blended magic changed, all of the adepts were doomed regardless.

But Graydon would fall more quickly unless the Circle stepped up to protect it.

He looked at the battle raging on, Pack's men trying to make a difference where they thought they could. They were making one, but such a minimal one that Kale's heart also ached for the boy he had once known.

A few adepts began chanting in perfect unison. He hoped they would survive. He hoped they would find a way to use their magic and save them all, without sacrificing themselves.

He looked towards Pack and his warriors again. What might be the last survivors of Elihor. He closed his eyes, remembering Kryde and Pack playing as children, running down the endless fields, wrestling and tumbling, laughing as boys should, without worry of death or fear of repercussion.

The adepts increased their tempo, their spell almost set. He could feel the air around him congeal with Elihor's magic, with his blood. The magic was much clearer now that the adepts called upon it, succeeding in breaking the strands, at least temporarily. Kale knew this. This was *his* heritage. And his power to protect others.

He grasped at the dark strands, pulling them away from the adepts of Graydon as best he could, hoarding the magic and wishing it elsewhere.

He noticed Orange Circle Shala looking at him intently, but concentrated instead on pulling Elihor's might within him. And repaying Tangia's kindness by saving her own.

PACK NACKER STRUCK with his claw, the limb feeling so natural now that his mind no longer contested the lack of dexterity or fingers. He lusted to see the demons fall. He wished to see their final breath escape, to see the magic of Siabala erupt from their broken stone, to see them collapse and become an empty shell.

Empty. He struck again, grunting, wishing he could scream at the top of his lungs. But all he could do now was grunt. And he understood that this too would eventually be taken away.

His claws were sharp. Not dull as even just a few days ago. He could feel them slice through the stone, reaching the frail membrane between this world and Siabala's magic, and cutting through it.

He wished he could see the red magic escaping, but his

eyes failed him in the light. He could only see shadows, colors forever stolen from him. He understood that in another day or two, his transformation would rob him of his remaining day sight. Then he would truly be a creature of darkness.

The sky erupted in fire, so bright he had to look away, a scream locked deep within him.

Is this it? he wondered, fear and relief pumping in his blood. Warmth invaded him. The warmth of Elihor. Like a soothing blanket it coated him, hushing him to be quiet, to let the magic hold him until he slept in its arms.

He let it, remembering his boyhood days of running wild with his best friend, of planning to join the sports and becoming champions, of fighting a completely different kind of battle.

Never had he dreamed he would become a monster lusting to kill. Never would he have believed it possible.

As Elihor's magic cradled him, he let himself be lulled and wondered how long his humanity would remain.

"Shirina, where is this bloody door! We need to take cover, now!" Avarielle screamed over the battle sounds raging from above. Strike after strike could be heard, rocks tumbling down around them as they sheltered close to the building.

"I don't know!" Shirina screamed back, still looking ahead. "It has to be here somewhere…"

"There!" Cassara exclaimed, pointing at a section Shirina had missed on her first pass. The magical signature was so subtle it was nearly impossible to detect.

Shirina ran towards it, staff in hand, launching her magic into it, to try and key it open. This building could hold. It had to hold.

"I just need a moment," she said, concentrating on the door. If she could break Tangia's locks, surely she could break this one as well.

"Hurry up!" Avarielle ordered through clenched teeth.

A large chunk of ceiling collapsed, taking out three of the nearby houses, sending shards of stone over the three of them. Cassara stepped back as she covered her face, the princess still looking bewildered.

Shirina supposed none of them expected death by crushing had been an option when they had set out on their quest.

Rolje could feel the magic of Graydon like a chain around his throat, despite his timed casting with the Ravenhold witch. Gritting his teeth, he kept casting, standing atop a sandy knoll, surrounded by soldiers ready to protect their last magical defenses.

If only they knew.

Rolje knew. He understood their plan had failed, and he could see that the seven other adepts casting knew it as well.

Yet none of them stopped or paused. They continued as though success was assured, black and white robes united. Sweat streamed down his back under his black robes, the sun having vanquished the morning chill. Even the breeze failed to beat the heat, his crimson cloak billowing to his left and wrapping around him

Reminding him of his place. *Crimson Circle*. And how proud he'd been to get that title.

He squeezed the witch's hand and they released the spell at once. And every other sorceress and sorcerer followed suit, soldiers gasping as they pointed up toward the sky, where balls of fires erupted among the monsters. Their combined energy formed like a star, making the day even brighter.

He allowed a smile with his partner, and they nodded, beginning the next spell, the noose around his neck growing tighter. Srocks rained from the skies where they'd been destroyed, but many more remained. They could not rest, the words tumbling from his mouth in a practiced, rhythmic cadence.

He wondered how different casting this spell would have been had Shirina been the one casting alongside him. As his Ravenhold partner crumpled, choking on her own blood, he wondered if, had Shirina been here clasping hands with him, he would have lived to see another sunrise.

He pushed through, ignoring the pain, the taste of iron, and managed to complete the spell, as did the few remaining adepts. The sky above them exploded in an arc of light, engulfing the city below, srocks shrieking. He crumpled to his knees in that light, his final thought for his family and the peace of the farm. How different his life would have been had he chosen another path but the one leading to the Circle.

THE SKY ERUPTED in flames as Dayshon and Breck madly screamed for the troops to get back. The earth shuddered and Dayshon dragged Jayden to safety as the land cracked and quaked all around them.

The heat of the flames stroked Jayden's face even from there. Fires meant to kill all in its path.

"Everyone fall back!" Dayshon screamed over and over again as the troops ran, only the Circle adepts and the old man from Elihor staying put. But most of the adepts had collapsed, the soldiers forming a protective barrier around them nonetheless, in the hopes that they may stand again.

Beneath, the city cracked, dust exploding up as the land shook, glittering in the fading Circle light. Jayden clutched the amulet, the metal just as cold as when Cassara had given it to him.

Graydon's blood might run in his veins, but he was beginning to think that his magic never would.

FIRES LICKED the top of the ceiling, cracks forming where large stones came crashing down, deafening Shirina as she worked to get the door open.

Another building was crushed nearby but the sorceress ignored it. Her spell was taking effect, and the illusion magic faded. A direct blow wouldn't work. She feared she would take out more than just the door and weaken the structure, leaving the building compromised when it would undoubtedly take a hit.

The magic grew frantic, as though urging them to move faster, until the illusion finally fell away. A door had been carved in the rock, but with no means to open it. No handle, or hinge, or even a keyhole.

Magic. This whole building was magic, which reinforced Shirina's belief that they'd be safe within. If they could get in.

"I just need to open this door," Shirina said, beginning to cast another spell.

"What is that?" Avarielle said, and Shirina cast a sideways glance. Red rivers seemed to shimmer out of the back of the city, far enough away that it must originate from below Siabala's Rage itself.

"Blood?" Cassara asked.

"No, some kind of monster." Avarielle pushed the princess closer to Shirina. The sorceress redoubled her concentration, before the red tides could find them.

Shirina grunted as a stone fell on her shoulder, knocking the staff from her hand. She would have dropped it completely had she not secured it to her wrist. The instant the staff left her hand in the middle of her spell, she began choking on the magic around her throat.

Blood gurgled through and she spat it out, trying to remain calm, trying to focus, intent on not choking on her own blood.

The falling rocks seemed a more fitting death.

Shirina spat blood, grasping her staff and trying to focus on her breathing, her hand against the wall the only reason she hadn't fallen to her knees.

Too stubborn to, Avarielle thought, though her stomach churned. Without the sorceress, they suddenly had a lot less protection. Avarielle unsheathed Graysword and positioned herself between the others and the quickly moving tide of red, ready for battle.

She analyzed the monsters as Cassara tried to help Shirina. The yellow light bounced among them, reflected by shining black weapons and polished red armor. Avarielle was certain they weren't human, moving much faster, and too low to the ground. Her grip loosened around Graysword and she took a deep breath of stale air. There were too many to fight, and she didn't even know if Graysword's magic would work against them.

Blood pumped in her veins as she analyzed their rhythm and movement, preparing herself to parry and strike the strange long limbs. They'd already crossed what would easily take the three of them another half day to travel.

If they lived. The monster soldiers' speed alone could be their undoing.

The ceiling cracked and dust showered down on them as a great piece separated from the center, yellow lights dancing frantically. The piece of ceiling crushed a section of the city, Shirina finally collapsing to her knees at the tremor. Avarielle managed to remain standing, but her bones still shook with the ground.

For a second, the warrior hoped the monsters would be stopped, but they easily leapt over the chunk of ceiling, at least two stories tall itself.

"Shirina, please," Cassara urged the sorceress. Avarielle glanced back, catching the eyes of the sorceress. Dark and defeated, her own blood covering the front of her dress.

"She can't, Cassara," Avarielle said. "She's given up." Fury sparked in the sorceress' eyes.

She turned around, the monsters now only a few blocks from them.

"Grab her and get out of here," she instructed the princess. "I'll buy you as much time as I can!"

"I'm not leaving you behind," Cassara said, suddenly standing beside her. Avarielle grabbed Cassara's arm and forced her to meet her eyes.

"It's *my* job to protect *you*, Cassara. Not the other way around. Now grab that useless sorceress lump and get out here. Now!"

Cassara set her mouth stubbornly and Avarielle pushed her back, willing her to grab Shirina and run. She turned around to meet the incoming enemies. They drew near, so silent Avarielle couldn't hear them, their faces hidden by masks.

A shiver ran down her spine at their speed and stealth.

She positioned her feet, focusing away from Cassara, preparing to meet them in battle.

Fires broke through the ceiling, licking the edges of

the stone as they cracked, stone crumpling down. Avarielle loosened her knees to absorb the fresh impact of stone on ground, finding some comfort in the creatures' faltering. So, they could be affected.

Sunlight streamed in along with a gush of fresh air. The fires travelled along the ceiling, trailing down toward the city, to be stopped by the yellow light. It formed a dome where the ceiling had vanished, stopping more buildings from the upper city from collapsing in.

"Those are Ravenhold's fires," Shirina whispered behind them.

"Run!" Avarielle shouted, meeting the first creature with her sword, almost shouting in relief as Graysword's powers answered her call, slicing it in two. She'd been expecting more resistance and almost slipped sideways at the strength of her own blow, drawing the energy into spinning around and striking the next two. They collapsed as silently as they ran, but there were too many.

Avarielle took down three more, biting back a scream as a sharp blade cut her arm.

"Let's go!" Cassara grabbed hold of Avarielle. The warrior swore.

What was she thinking?

And then, the world vanished in blinding light as the teleportation spell took them away from the incoming enemies. Avarielle called back Graysword's magic, even though the spell had started before her magic had been recalled. Shirina had warned her before about not using her magic while her spell was active...but this wasn't Shirina's spell.

Avarielle turned around to see the princess's eyes glowing unnaturally blue. Shirina looked up at her with narrowed eyes.

"Cassara?" Avarielle asked as the teleportation spell ended. Cassara collapsed, and Avarielle just managed to catch her before she hit the ground.

They were plunged into darkness.

27

Shirina shivered and gathered her cloak closer.

"Shirina," Avarielle hissed, her voice lost in the vastness of the space. "Can you give us light?"

Shirina coughed and closed her eyes to concentrate, despite the smothering darkness. She managed to utter the few needed syllables and a weak light spell barely illuminated the room. It proved so vast that the light vanished before striking much more than the ground directly beneath them. It looked like the same sandstone as the rest of the city.

Cassara's eyes flew open. Avarielle indicated to her to be quiet as she stood and pulled out Graysword. Shirina watched, feeling detached. Her breath grew steady again, but her throat felt lacerated and she could still taste and smell blood. Just one second without her staff, and it had almost cost her her life.

She clutched the staff more tightly as the ground

shook beneath them and the building swayed. Another crack and the building trembled again, a chunk of its roof collapsing on the other side, thundering through the ceiling. Light poured in.

Shirina looked up toward that light. It wasn't that of the sun, but of the Circle. The fires of Ravenhold shone brightly, then dimmed and were extinguished, leaving behind only sunlight, which seemed dull and washed out in comparison.

The ground stopped trembling, as did the sky above them.

"Is it over?" Cassara whispered.

Avarielle sheathed Graysword. "For now, I suppose it is." She gave a thoughtful look to Cassara. "That was your spell, wasn't it?"

Cassara nodded, frowning. "I just…I needed to get us out of there. I thought about coming in here, made sure I had both of you, and," she shrugged. "I don't really remember much immediately after that."

Avarielle glanced toward Shirina, but the sorceress was too tired to answer.

She wanted to warn Cassara about the dangers of overusing her magic. Her magic had increased in leaps and bounds since the Wall's collapse. And how dangerous it could prove to be. Not to mention the stupidity of using a teleportation spell without first investigating where you'd end up.

But the thought of pushing all those words past her lacerated throat silenced her. Avarielle helped Cassara up.

"I guess the army must have moved on," Avarielle said, not sounding pleased. "I hope the others are ready for them."

"You think they're heading to the camp?" Cassara asked.

Shirina struggled to her feet, grateful the warrior didn't see fit to start helping her now. She leaned heavily on the staff. Avarielle just shrugged at the princess' question, knowing full well the creatures would more than likely be heading there. The words didn't need to be spoken.

"What do you think this place is?" Avarielle asked instead, looking down to the room now flooded with sunlight from far above. Row upon row of seats led down to a central stage. The sunlight danced on the walls, as though it couldn't stand still in this space.

Cassara kept an eye on Shirina, but did not move to help her. The sorceress looked around, trying not to wonder who had cast the spells her eyes could discern, streaks of dark and light magic slowly dancing together, but not becoming one like the treacherous shadows above. Had the casters of this city survived? Or had the magic merged for them, too, and killed them with its shadows?

*Just one second...*Just one second without the staff had almost finished her. She was already infected, so another adept would take longer to fall. *Long enough to cast a fire spell.*

Shirina forced herself to take small steps and help the

others explore the large building. It seemed to only consist of this one room.

Cassara looked back at her from time to time, but wisely kept her counsel.

"Shouldn't there be some dust?" Avarielle asked from where she stood, near more debris. Huge slabs of stone had been knocked down, but still not one mote of dust in the air.

"Is it some form of magic?" Cassara asked, looking back towards Shirina.

The sorceress took a tentative gulp of water, the pain in her throat dissipating as she clutched her staff. She shrugged, her voice cracking when she whispered. "The rules of magic are changing, and I'm not sure what's possible anymore. Although if whomever used to live here bothered wasting magic on dust-repelling spells, then it's safe to assume they had a lot of magic, and still might." Shirina crossed another row of chairs and took a bit more water.

They were in an amphitheater, that much was clear. Something on the center stage was covered by a thick blanket the color of earth, just like the walls and chairs.

"If the magic is still functional after all this time," Shirina added, "it's also advisable to assume that someone is still alive to maintain these spells. Or they're from a whole other caliber than the Circle."

"You mean better?" Avarielle asked from nearby.

"I mean more powerful or tapped into a different..." Shirina fought back against a cough.

"If they were that much more powerful," Cassara asked, buying Shirina time to catch her breath, "then what exactly could have destroyed them?"

"A good question," Shirina said as the three stepped onto the stage.

Avarielle cocked her head at Cassara. "Wanna take a bet as to what's under this thing?"

The blanket before them was huge enough to be a tent. Whatever was underneath it was crooked, and Shirina feared she might know what it was already. She cast a sideways look at Cassara.

"Avarielle and I can uncover it, if you want to keep an eye out," she told the princess. Cassara's eyes widened. Then she stubbornly set her jaw.

"Go ahead and uncover it," she ordered. Shirina sighed. *Well, at least I tried.* She supposed by now the princess had seen enough bodies to be desensitized.

Avarielle and Shirina tugged the blanket sideways at the same time, to reveal not a body, but a monster.

The creature could have almost passed for human, but the horns of a ram stuck out of its forehead, and its legs resembled those of a praying mantis. If the creature stood, it would tower over them. Its skin was gray, its torso muscular. It lay on its side, arms folded against its chest.

Avarielle slowly unsheathed Graysword, her voice a rumble. "Is it dead?"

Cassara looked to Shirina for confirmation. The sorceress nodded. "It certainly looks like it."

"What is it?" Avarielle asked.

"I have no idea," Shirina said. "For all we know, it was once human and died in transformation. Like Eloms."

Avarielle grunted, not agreeing or disagreeing.

"Did they watch it die?" Cassara whispered, her arms crossed before her. "Did they sit in those seats and watch it die for sport?"

"I don't know that, either," Shirina answered, feeling more and more out of her element. She didn't have the knowledge to help these two, after all. Nothing in Circle history or training had prepared her for what she had seen of late.

She needed to look to what she knew. They were still in Graydon, and it was still their land. The rules couldn't be that different.

Shirina focused on the strands of magic around her. She spotted Graydon's magic first, then Elihor's, and then the blended shadows formed by both magics. She let her eyes rest on that combination and watched its patterns, following its movement. Magic was more like water than wind. Channels and dams could control its flow.

She allowed her eyes to follow the energy to its core, to see where it ebbed.

It led straight to the creature.

"That thing is absorbing the magic of Elihor," Shirina said.

"Oh? Is that good or bad?" Avarielle asked, placing Graysword's blade against the creature's skin. "My sword's not reacting at all."

"I don't know."

"Big surprise."

"If it's absorbing the magic," Cassara asked, "then does that mean it still lives?"

Shirina was about to answer when the warrior spoke up. "She doesn't know, Cassara. She doesn't know anything."

"Well, if it's absorbing the magic and trapped down here," Cassara continued, "then does it mean it's a creature from before the time of Graydon and Elihor?"

Shirina spoke before the warrior could cut her off. "It might. Nothing in the records indicates as much. I'm just not sure." Shirina was frustrated at her own lack of knowledge.

"Could this thing come back to life with the magic it's absorbing?" Avarielle asked after a moment.

"At this point, I feel it's safe to say that anything's possible."

"In other words," Avarielle said softly, "you still don't know."

"I still owe you for that hit, Grayloft. Stop pushing me."

Avarielle ignored her as she circled the creature. She stood by its head, Graysword held loosely in her hand.

"What are you going to do?" Cassara asked, alarmed.

"I'm going to make sure it doesn't come back to life," Avarielle said, eyes like steel. "You might want to turn around for this."

"You can't just lop its head off," Shirina hissed, stepping in. "It's unlikely it'll come back to life, it might not be our enemy, and it's a body probably older than Elihor herself. Have you no respect?"

Avarielle pierced Shirina with her eyes. "Can you guarantee that it won't come back to life and it's not an enemy? From what I can tell, at best I save us the trouble of fighting something bigger and more powerful than us, at worse I decapitate a thousand-year-old corpse. Either way, I'm not losing sleep over it."

Avarielle raised an eyebrow. "Well? Any guarantees you'd like to give me before I take care of this?"

Shirina clutched the staff more tightly. She could blast Avarielle. A good wind spell would send her flying backwards. But the warrior would recover quickly and take down both the creature and Shirina. And Avarielle did have a point, though Shirina feared losing the opportunity of gaining invaluable insight from this ancient creature.

"I think Avarielle is right, Shirina," Cassara said in a voice so soft the vastness of this space absorbed it. "All of Graydon stands in the balance. Can we really afford the chance of having to fight this thing or, worse, of having it attack the troops? It's absorbing magic, so it must have a purpose."

"Would you behead it?" Shirina asked the princess. Cassara flushed red, but she didn't look down.

"No need to ask her that," Avarielle said, "I'm more than happy to do it."

Shirina looked at the creature once more. Lying there, part man, part goat, part insect, a vestige from a world they no longer remembered and probably would never understand. She wondered what wisdom it had died protecting. And what magic it had known in its time.

"At least give us the time to go outside, first," Shirina asked. Seeing the protest on the warrior's eyes, she cut her off. "Don't worry. We'll make sure none of that army stuck around. They seemed more interested in reaching their destination than dealing with us, anyway."

Avarielle considered Shirina's words for a few moments and then nodded. The princess didn't argue and began climbing back up to the exit, one row of seats at a time.

Before Shirina could follow, Avarielle caught her by the arm.

"Are you getting soft or scared, Shirina?" she whispered. "Because both those traits are useless to us, right now."

She let the sorceress go and turned her attention to the creature.

Before she could think better of it, Shirina whispered back, "There is no more Circle." As though it excused her actions, or inaction. It sounded weak, and she hoped Avarielle hadn't heard her.

But the warrior had, turning to look at her. "No, there isn't, and I'm ecstatic, even if I'm still stuck with you. But you're still there, Shirina. I don't like you, and you don't like me, but at least do us all the favor of waking up and fighting, or of going to sleep and letting us take care of what needs to be done."

Shirina wanted to reply with something piercing. Something cunning and painful. But her throat was sore and bleeding, her limbs were numb, and she was too tired to even hate Avarielle. She looked at the creature one last time and remembered the books of Ravenhold vanishing into black dust.

She doubted the warrior would understand her grief.

AVARIELLE WAITED until Cassara and Shirina finally managed to open the door and it was well shut again behind them. She looked down at the dormant creature, imagining its power. She could almost feel the strength flowing from it, a warrior's calm that resonated through the ages. He had never been human, she was certain. She had rarely felt small and insignificant in her days, but standing beside his body now, she felt like an ant beside a human.

And she didn't like it.

Neither did she like having to down him like this. He would make a worthy foe, and she held no illusions that she could easily best him. Still, killing him as he slept... *snap out of it, foolish girl. He's probably already dead.*

If he did in fact have Elihor's magic running through him, Graysword should be able to cut through him easily.

More importantly, she wanted him dead because his size, color and even his torso reminded her of another monster.

Siabala.

The others had never seen him and so hadn't linked the two, but Avarielle had. She'd been up close and personal. She'd been hurt by him, so bad she'd wanted to die. And she'd run him through with Graysword. This creature reminded her of him, and it terrified and angered her. Blood pumped into her sword hand, willing her to strike a killing blow.

Avarielle stood still, Graysword held before her. She'd never thought she'd behead something dormant or dead. But the time to hesitate had vanished with Kryde's death.

She lifted her sword for the final blow.

SIABALA FELT the blade as though it pierced his own skin. Searing and sharp, it struck without hesitation, severing bones, ligaments and aorta, stopping the slight but precious flow of blood that kept the body alive.

He let the pain wash over him and then allowed nothingness to take a hold of him, clutching his stomach and wrenching it, twisting the tender skin until raw.

No heartbeat. No breath. Nothing.

He could no longer feel his brother, the connection severed by the sword he had fashioned. *By his own magic!*

Never would he have believed it possible for humans to make it into his ancient realm, and to catch one of his brethren so unaware as to slay him. But he supposed he had made it easy, by leaving them so exposed.

Not all of them, he thought, though some he suspected were long dead from lack of magic. Graydon and Elihor's seal had been powerful, even though human-cast.

Still, the Grayloft was there now, and she might not be alone. He couldn't see into his home, for finally the sun had reached it. Once the moonlight would strike, then the city would come back to life, and he hoped the Grayloft would be destroyed. If not, he'd deal with her once she'd reached his home.

He would have enjoyed playing with her some more, but he couldn't afford any chances that she would get further.

His soul was too high a price to pay for some amusement.

2 8

Cassara sat in the sunlight, amongst the rubble of the city. She felt dwarfed by the layers of city and the broken dome rising around her, the sunlight just a reminder of how deep they now were. Surrounded by mountains on all sides, with little hope of escape. Around her, buildings had been destroyed by the rock that had once shielded the city, chunks so big they stood taller than the houses they had crushed.

"Did Siabala get what he wanted?" she mused aloud, wondering if bringing down the dome of the city had been part of his plan, as they had originally suspected. If so, what did it mean? Was it a ploy to free his army? Or to grant him access to this place?

She was surprised when Shirina bit back. "I wish you would stop asking me these things. I don't know, Cassara. I have no clue what he wants."

Cassara turned to look at the sorceress, who stood

nearby, refusing to sit down even though she leaned heavily on her staff.

"It was more of a rhetorical question, Shirina." She sighed and leaned back, missing Dayshon more each time she had to deal with Shirina and Avarielle. He was much more reasonable than those two combined.

"I don't think Avarielle should behead the creature," Shirina said, as though by way of an apology.

"It's probably already dead, so no harm done, really," Cassara said, failing to convince herself. Shirina clearly didn't buy it either.

"You saw as well as I did, princess. It was absorbing energy. Something lives within it yet."

Cassara wrapped her arms around her knees and looked up to the blue sky, the sun dipping to the horizon. Even here, in this old, ruined city, the sky of Graydon was beautiful.

"We don't know what it would have done, Shirina. It looked menacing."

Shirina gave a harsh laugh. "Yes, it did. And if we kill everything that looks menacing, just in case it should ever rise up against us, than I can think of quite a few people who'd have to go, including Avarielle."

Cassara's face flushed. "Not humans, Shirina. But monsters, more than likely doing Siabala's bidding." What was wrong with the sorceress? Did she not want Graydon to win the day?

"Right. So, we should kill Pack Nacker and his people as soon as we get back."

Cassara bit her lower lip. Shirina was right, but still…"I'm just trying to protect my home, Shirina."

The sorceress didn't relent. "So am I, Cassara."

Avarielle appeared in the doorway, Graysword sheathed and an expression on her face as chilly as the grip of winter in the air around them.

She cast Cassara a questioning look. The princess met it as she stood up but said nothing.

"Where did the army go?" she asked softly, looking back toward where they'd come. The ramp they'd used had been crushed by pieces of falling dome. Which meant the army hadn't gone that way. And their escape route had been cut off.

The three shared a look, Cassara feeling her hands grow numb. Would the army turn back and attack them? Or would they find another place to escape? Maybe somewhere far from Jayden and Dayshon. But, then, they'd get access to the East.

She took a deep breath and tried to find comfort in the eyes of the warrior. Avarielle met her glance and held it for a few moments before turning back towards the heart of the Bloody Mountains.

"Let go find Siabala already," she said. "This place makes me sick."

SHIRINA WAS DISGUSTED by the warrior, the princess, Siabala, the Circle, and all of Graydon. Most of all, she was disgusted with herself. She had read Tangia's journal, outlining the Circle's quest for knowledge. They had killed Elom after Elom, knowing they were the citizens of Elihor, in order to gain knowledge.

They had not tried to heal them, nor ease their pain, nor stop Elihor's trials all together. So obsessed were they with finding out the contents of that message, with acquiring the lost knowledge, that Graydon had paid a terrible price for their carelessness.

And she had wanted to do the same. To keep that creature, in case it should come back to life, to question it. To gain knowledge, and begin replacing all that Ravenhold had lost. She was no better than the Elders.

I'm just like them. A few months ago, that would have pleased her.

Now it disgusted her. She still believed Avarielle had gone to unnecessary extremes, but she hardly had a noble goal in mind in wanting the creature to be allowed to live.

Shirina stepped over stones as she looked at the back of Cassara's head. Her magic was still so pure it made Shirina's heart ache. Her own magic felt so heavy beside the princess' that she could barely carry it.

How can I use that to my advantage? She couldn't figure out how to cleanse the magics or separate them, using Cassara's magic. Perhaps Cassara and the unborn child could do it, but the child's magic was still locked away and mixed in with his mother's magic. And she strongly doubted Avarielle would let her look closely at the child that still slumbered within her womb.

Avarielle was many things, but cooperative was rarely one of them.

They walked for hours, until the sun set and the eerie glow of the city's witch fire and the faint rays of the moon took over for the sun.

Lost in thought, Shirina did not notice when the ground near her trembled and a long leg began to pierce through.

29

King Darmir struggled with his breath, each exhale desperate to escape and each inhale reluctant to return. He walked lazily around his private gardens, trying to enjoy the bit of sun the day still offered, despite his discomfort and pain.

He could hear the hustle of the court and knew it was nearby, but it seemed far away to him now. He felt disconnected and struggled not to show it. He did not need uprisings in court, not while his son was away.

To war.

He sighed. He had been to war, too, in his day. The Westland Wars were by far the most vicious he had ever witnessed, with more civilian deaths than had allowed him to sleep well at night afterward. And all on the Westlanders' side.

Then King Alexavier of little-known Edoline had stepped in, winning the Council one by one, himself included, and stopping the Circle's wretched invasion. No proof of the riches in the Bloody Mountains had ever been found.

Alexavier. They might have been friends, had time and circumstance been different, and had Darmir allowed himself to make friends. He had respected the king and his courage, which is why he was pleased with his son's chosen bride. Had he chosen that whiny creature Malir, he would have had to arrange for a disappearance.

His left leg trembled, making it difficult for him to continue walking. He sat on a nearby bench and leaned back, looking around him. His gardens were beautiful, and he mostly kept them this way for his wife, who preferred solitude over politics.

A smile crossed his lips. Not that she wouldn't be good at keeping those vultures at bay while awaiting Dayshon's return. She would surprise them all with her wit and cunning, since they all thought her weak. But for Darmir, Traina had proved to be his greatest ally and confidant.

He hoped Dayshon would find that in Cassara. He would need it in the years to come.

He closed his eyes for a moment, willing the pain of his failing body to pass, when suddenly the alarm bells rang clearly across the crisp air. He stood, adrenaline pumping through his blood, and headed toward his generals.

Perhaps war was not done with him, yet.

QUEEN TRAINA WAS TRYING to make small talk with some refugee politician from Solir, a difficult feat as he proved more concerned with the quality of his new jacket than the wellbeing of his people.

She kept an indulgent smile on her face as she formulated a careful and non-insulting reason to leave. Her husband was declining rapidly and, although she knew matters of the court had to be maintained, she wished to spend as much time with him as possible.

She had settled on telling the man that she was required at another meeting when the warning bells rang clear across the castle. First one, then two, then three and more as nearby bells echoed the sound, leading down toward the town surrounding the castle.

"What is that?" the man asked.

Traina ignored him and stood, quickly leaving to find her husband.

She turned down the hallway which led to their room and saw him struggling towards her. She reached him in a few steps and took his arm, to make it look like they were simply showing affection. When he leaned on her, she needed all of her strength to keep him standing. He was growing weaker.

She cast a sideways look at him and he caught it, giving her a slight smile with his eyes. He was in agony, she could tell. She fought to keep her tears in check. She was getting good at hiding her own pain, to help disguise her husband's.

The bells sounded all around them as they walked

towards the ramparts. Soldiers took up their stations at parapets and murder holes, protecting corridors and rooms, bows and arrows distributed freely, pausing only to let the king and queen pass.

"What is happening?" Darmir demanded, his voice ringing clear with only the faintest of tremors.

"A large army is moving our way, quickly, your Highness," General Samich said, bowing his head. The general had been in Darmir's service since the beginning of his reign, and her husband trusted him.

Darmir nodded.

"Have we evacuated the city below?"

Samich sighed in frustration. "We are trying, but the citizens are frightened and move slowly. And the invading army is moving fast."

He nodded towards the northwest, past the city below, where shouts of fear could be heard as people ran, pushing each other to get within the castle's ramparts. The city used to be walled, but generations of growth had seen them converted and mostly useless, lining markets instead of stopping invaders. With the refugees from all over the land, thousands upon thousands of people either struggled to get into the one access to the castle, or decide to bunker down in place and hope the danger would leave them be.

Beyond the chaos below, Traina spotted a growing shadow on the horizon. She sucked in breath. Not just a shadow, but a quickly moving army, like a red wave engulfing the land.

"Get them in, General," Darmir whispered, and the general nodded, though even Traina could tell they would not be able to bring them all in, not now, not with the speed of the army.

They weren't human.

The realization crackled through her and she protectively stood closer to Darmir. Within minutes, the army reached the city walls. Traina held her breath as the army broke apart and entered the city from its sides, soldiers quickly cut down, as though no resistance had been given.

"Archers, fire!" Samich ordered.

There are still people down there! She clutched her husband's arm and leaned on him as much as he on her now. He brought up his hand and covered hers. He still had strength to lend her, too.

"General, close the main gates!" Darmir ordered, and she heard the slight tremor in his voice. The general looked quickly at his king before nodding and shouting the order. Screams could be heard from below. So many of their people were still trapped on the other side of the ramparts.

So many would be lost! The soldiers lowered the heavy iron gates and she heard screams of pain and fear, cries for mercy. She feared she would be sick. She focused on the enemy, her heart racing. They were large, and quick, and carried weapons unlike any she had ever seen. The strange weapons fired arrow-like projectiles and they picked off their archers easily.

Darmir moved back, out of sight of the enemy, dragging her with him.

"Are those Eloms?" she heard her husband ask, too numb to voice the question herself.

Samich shook his head before shouting for his archers to take cover. "No. These are bigger, quicker and hold weapons unlike any other. I don't know what they are, your majesties." He paused and looked back, awaiting his orders.

"Send your fastest messenger to my son," Darmir said, his voice soft. Traina closed her eyes. The message would not be for him to come rescue them, but to hold his ground. The king had foreseen this possibility, intent on saving Graydon, even if it cost his own kingdom.

The general nodded, a pyre lit to the right. The messenger waited far outside the city already, to reach them more quickly.

"I thought we'd have more time," he whispered to Traina. She squeezed his hand to lend him strength. He turned back to Samich, his voice steady as he spoke, telling the general what he already intended to do, but absolving him of responsibility by making them a command.

"Close the secondary gates, general."

The general turned and moved closer to the ramparts, calling for soldiers to gather near the gates. The monsters streamed below, the screams of citizens so guttural Traina wanted to cry, but fear stopped her tears. Then, a few of the invaders jumped clear over the ramparts, slicing their soldiers.

"You should go," Darmir told her, though he still held on to her arm, to keep from falling. She managed to smile at him and focused on his eyes, where he concealed the emotions reserved only for her.

"My place is by your side," she whispered and saw the love, the pride and fear all mix in his eyes. She found herself grateful.

That she would not have to live with his death, nor he with hers.

30

Moonlight bathed the land, the partial sphere rising steadily on the horizon. Avarielle led her companions steadily towards the heart of the Bloody Mountains. She was hungry, and angry, and hated everything about this place which had taken over most of her beloved West.

She wondered if the West was a desert because of this city, hidden underneath it. Then again, she didn't care. Desert or not, it was her home, and following the Westland Wars and the constant invasion by Eloms, it deserved a break from calamity. The people of the West deserved the time to rebuild, raise their families and re-solidify their roots.

She realized her hand hovered on her belly again, and sighed. It was impulsive, and she had never been one to control her impulses. The child was kicking now, and taking up space, though thankfully she hid it well with her height and muscles. It seemed to be growing faster than it should be. Then again, she wasn't sure how babies from Elihor grew, especially ones fed by magic.

She was tired, her back hurt, and she felt so hungry she had stolen half of Shirina's lunch. She planned on stealing half of her supper, too.

The nights were falling earlier now and snow would soon follow. With the way the seasons had gripped the land this year it was hard to predict exactly when, but it would come soon enough, and they weren't equipped to deal with it.

All I need is to find Siabala, and kill him. I don't need to make my way back anyway. She stubbornly set her jaw.

She felt a slight tremor. At first she feared it was her rumbling stomach, before realizing it was coming from below.

She stopped and cocked her head sideways. Her companions stopped as well and listened intently. Avarielle pulled Graysword free. Every fiber of her being screamed at her that danger was imminent.

"Let's go, quickly and quietly," she whispered to the other two, running in a crouch between two buildings. The others followed, so quiet that Avarielle had to peer back from time to time to make sure that at least the princess still followed.

Another slight rumble. Then a house fell in the distance. Avarielle stopped and looked towards where there should have been a cloud of dust, and was blinded.

The yellow spheres suddenly flared brilliant white

before washing the walls around them with colors, vibrant and festive, bright reds and blues and greens, covering the buildings generously. Flowers sprouted from street corners, blooming where there hadn't even been earth moments before. The air grew thick with a gentle breeze, as though it carried an ancient melody.

Avarielle let her eyes adjust and looked up. The sky was still dark, and she could see the stars perfectly, even though day now seemed to rule down here. "What magic is this?" she hissed.

"Old. I can't even see it," Shirina replied.

Cassara bit her lower lip. "It's … strange. I can't see it, but I can feel it." She looked far away, her blue eyes unnaturally lit.

"Cassara, be careful," Shirina said, placing her hand on the princess' arm. She jumped. "Close your eyes for a few moments to center yourself." The princess was about to protest, but then followed the sorceress' instructions.

Shirina turned to Avarielle and gave her a look that implied they needed to keep an eye on Cassara. Avarielle nodded, and then the ground rumbled again.

"What is that?" she asked as a giant leg shot out from a nearby square, followed by several more, until Avarielle had lost count.

Cassara looked up as the beast pulled itself clear of the ground. "It's one of those monsters from the city above!" she exclaimed. Avarielle didn't have the time to ask for elaboration before every door in the city flew open and people stepped out.

Or what looked like people, except taller, and not quite right. They swayed in a breeze that didn't exist. They wore long robes and broad-brimmed hats, hiding their features.

Avarielle stood before one as it came near. It didn't attack, and so neither did she. Beheading dead monsters was one thing, but she wasn't sure yet what these people were. If they were people at all.

Avarielle turned around to see that Shirina had vanished. An illusion spell, or some such Circle trickery.

"Can you do that?" Avarielle asked Cassara, who shook her head. The warrior cursed the sorceress for not taking the princess with her.

The strange tall people surrounded them, swaying in unison around them. "I wish you'd do something," Avarielle mumbled. "You're making me dizzy."

"I think they're looking at Graysword," Cassara whispered. Avarielle shifted Graysword, and all of the broad-brimmed hats followed suit. She swung slowly the other way, and they followed again.

"Is that good or bad?" she asked Cassara as she went around the princess, the creatures, or whatever they were, swaying with the passage of the blade.

"I'm not sure," Cassara said. "Try putting it away. We'll see what happens."

"Won't it be like taking a toy away from a toddler?"

"Maybe. I don't know."

"You're starting to sound like Shirina."

"Avarielle, please."

Avarielle consented and slowly sheathed Graysword, careful not to alarm the creatures. Beyond them, the giant spider-like creature worked with its hundreds of legs to clean out the mess of the fallen rocks. Three others lurked in the distance.

As soon as Graysword was fully covered, some of the creatures stepped aside, forming a path.

"I guess they want us to go that way," Avarielle said.

"Is that a good idea?" Cassara asked, staying close to the warrior.

Avarielle shrugged. "You're the one who wanted me to put my sword away. We might as well follow this through, at least for now."

Cassara nodded and followed Avarielle. The warrior wrinkled her nose. Despite the blooming flowers, the freshly painted buildings and the walls of creatures forming a corridor, all that she could smell on the air was dust and decay.

SHIRINA WATCHED their interaction with the creatures from within the shadows she had concealed herself in. They seemed incapable of deciphering her illusion spell, at least so far.

The creatures were strange, more of a vague memory than actual independent entities. Theirs was not a magic she could see either, and she wished that she could borrow Cassara's powers for just a few moments, to tap into Graydon's purest energies. But she couldn't, and would have to make peace with what she had.

The warrior and the princess were on the move, led by a path of creatures. Shirina followed from far enough, careful not to be spotted and diligent to keep out of the giant silver-legged creatures' paths. She watched one of them for a moment. It wrapped its legs around a piece of rubble at least three-stories tall, and took it within its body, disintegrating it. They were cleaners. Maybe they were the reason no dust existed in this city.

Yet she could read no magic from it. Maybe they weren't magic at all. Maybe they were something else completely, beyond the realm of her understanding. And she wanted to understand. She craved the knowledge of this ancient realm. Briefly she wondered if an ancient and still-stocked library existed in this city, before setting aside the idea.

She had to follow Avarielle and Cassara first and worry about Ravenhold later, if at all. Whether a Circle remained, and whether she chose to stay within it hardly mattered right now.

She trailed them for some time, the warrior and princess following the creatures complacently. Shirina was not fooled. From what she could see, Avarielle's relaxed muscles were ready for battle.

She could sense the princess tense even from this distance, her energy lashing out at Graydon's magic. Shirina looked up.

Before them loomed another amphitheater, and the

creatures were leading them straight for it. The magic light danced strongly around it, covering it completely, Elihor's magic gently dancing with some strands. As Cassara approached it, her own aura grew, surrounding her until Shirina could no longer see the princess for the light.

She wondered what monster lurked there, and doubted it would also be dead. And Avarielle and Cassara were headed to meet it, with the stench of its brethren's blood still clinging to the warrior's blade.

31

Trevon didn't know who to trust anymore. He liked the Eastlanders well enough, and had vowed to Cassara to take care of her husband. The wars were long gone and he had seen worse evil since.

He hated the Circle like every sane person should, but eight of their adepts had sacrificed themselves to try and buy time for Avarielle and her friends, though he wasn't certain that throwing the city on top of them had been the smartest move.

And he disliked all of the people from Elihor with their dark unreadable eyes, yet Avarielle had vouched for them.

There was no one left to distrust in their troops, he thought, which bored him a little. The only enemies were the ones Siabala sent after them, but the attacks were now few and far between. And Trevon was starting to suspect that they weren't even targeting the army, but rather the army was just a pest standing in the way of success.

That proved annoying too.

Still, he wandered the perimeter for something to do, making sure everything was well set up and none of the Eastlanders had screwed up.

He was halfway through camp when he spotted a horse riding in from the north. They hadn't seen anyone since the Southern Coalition's arrival.

Maybe a scout to tell us more help is coming?

Trevon watched the cloud of dust coming towards them, until it stopped abruptly. He stared a moment longer, before realizing that the horse had fallen, and probably wasn't getting up again.

Trevon took a swig of water and began running towards the fallen rider. Anyone willing to ride into the Westland desert and push their horse until it was dead was probably not bearing good news.

He hoped he could reach the messenger before the desert claimed him, as well.

Eight Circle adepts had perished, and twelve more from Ravenhold had shown up, no one ranking higher than Orange Circle.

Not that it matters since none of them know how to use their magic! Dayshon was frustrated. The adepts were young, inexperienced for the most part, and they had no idea how to safely use their magic. He tried to convince them to leave, to just go back home. What use were they here?

They would just get themselves killed, one at a time, trying to fight a war that could probably not be won.

Not here, anyway, Dayshon corrected himself. Cassara might make a difference wherever she was. He hoped she was safe and that she hadn't been destroyed by the falling city. He closed his eyes and took a deep breath.

What were any of them doing, now? Their armies were useless, barely keeping at bay the attacks that just happened to come their way.

To protect Graydon, he reminded himself. To keep all of the innocent survivors beyond this point alive and well, until Siabala was safely put away once more.

And perhaps even killed.

"Trevon says he has urgent news," Jayden said as he popped up beside him.

"Let's go," Dayshon said, following Jayden towards the edge of camp, near the adepts. Breck, Trevon and the Southern Coalition colonel had already gathered, quieting the second he approached.

"What is it?" Dayshon said, not bothering to hide his temper. Westland tempers were so fiery it hardly mattered if he allowed himself to lose his once in a while. He would simply fit in better.

"We have news from Massir," Trevon said, a hint of regret in his voice.

"What news?" Dayshon asked, his voice sounding strange in his own ears.

"A messenger came," Trevon continued. "He died giving me the message." He paused, and Dayshon was about to rattle the answer out of him when he continued. "Massir has fallen."

Dayshon could barely mouth the question. "How? They should be safe! They're beyond our line, and no attack made it through!"

Massir has fallen. The words danced around his battle-weary mind. *Your father is dying, possibly dead...*

Breck took over. "There must have been another force which headed north instead of crossing through the city. They cut right through Massir, plowing it to the ground as they went."

Trevon continued. "But the enemy continued on its way. Massir is not occupied."

"That's hardly a comfort," the colonel muttered, and no one dared look at Dayshon, save Jayden, who studied him intently. The youth's eyes were filled with tears, and Dayshon felt better for it. He wasn't alone in understanding what it felt like to lose a home. *Then again,* he thought as he looked around, *I suppose most people understand what that's like here.*

"I would never tell a man not to return home to his family in times of war," Breck suddenly spoke up, staring at Dayshon.

The prince met his gaze. "And I would never desert a man on the battlefield," he answered. Breck nodded slowly. The two clasped arms, and Dayshon was grateful for the strength of the leader of the West, and his humanity.

Jayden suddenly piped up. "If they were simply passing

through Massir, then where were they heading?"

"Circle Keep?" Breck asked, looking disgusted at the very mention of it.

"The keep is gone." A Ravenhold adept with short brown hair walked up to them, orange cloak billowing in the wind. "My name is Shala, and I apologize, but I could not help but overhear." Breck snorted. She ignored him.

"Ravenhold has vanished, taking its knowledge with it. I doubt that is what they seek. Siabala must be aware of the keep's fall, as I am certain he had something to do with it."

She seemed proud of her deduction, looking annoyed when no one else seemed impressed by it.

Breck mumbled, "Obviously."

"Was Ravenhold not the seal?" the old man from Elihor asked as he joined them as well.

Dayshon looked around and opened his arms, shouting, "Would anyone else like to join now, or are we good?"

A few people looked up, some embarrassed for eavesdropping, others confused as to the prince's strange behavior. He turned back to catch Jayden hiding a smile and Breck chuckling, his wild red hair bouncing on his shoulders. Dayshon took a deep breath. He'd be more like a Westland warrior than an Eastland prince, following this journey. He fought back against the treacherous thought that it no longer mattered.

He pushed down the worry threatening to overwhelm

him and focused on the old man. "What seal do you speak of?"

"The seals of Siabala. Larkhold and Stormhold were the other two, keeping his soul tied down. If one of the seals is not yet broken, that would explain why he himself has not climbed down the mountains."

"I know of no seal," Shala said, then relented. "But I am still training." Dayshon waved over the Crimson Circle of Stormhold, the highest ranking remaining adept. She was a fairly big and intimidating woman, older, and with hair the color of a wheat field. She loomed over even the Westland warriors.

"Crimson Circle," he began.

"Liza," she told him. "Call me Liza." Her voice was deep, but she sounded friendly enough. He quickly explained the seal to her, Kale providing her with the few details he knew.

She shook her head. "I know of no seal in Ravenhold, though our stories may not coincide." She paused and pondered for a moment, her eyes shining with intelligence. "I have seen a map of your world, however. Would this seal need not be on the eastern and western most points of the land?"

Kale nodded slowly. "Ravenhold is not the easternmost point of Graydon."

Dayshon turned slowly to Jayden, who had turned white.

"It's Edoline," he whispered. "They're heading for Edoline, aren't they?"

3 2

$\mathcal{C}$assara felt strange. Not sick, but not right, either. She suspected it had something to do with her magic. Ever since the magic of the city had been activated by the moonlight, she walked as though in a dream.

A fine mist had settled between her and the world and she seemed unable to cross it. She followed Avarielle, careful to keep the warrior close. The strange creatures contributed to the mist, she was certain. They seemed made of it themselves, ghostly apparitions in white robes and dark-brimmed hats, covering their faces in shadows.

She didn't feel threatened by them, but her connection with reality was tenuous at the moment, so she doubted she had the best judgment.

Focus! her mind would scream, and then forget the word immediately. She suddenly noticed they were entering an amphitheater, like the one from earlier in the day.

Or was this a memory too? Avarielle came to her side, whispering something Cassara couldn't hear. The warrior pinched her and the pain helped her focus.

She saw everything clearly for only a second before drifting away again.

She was in Edoline. She smiled as she stood in the orchard by the sea, the waves striking the rocks. The flowers bloomed and petals flew all around her, white and pink, swirling as she twirled with them…

Darkness. She gasped and almost fell, feeling someone grab her and hold her up. The blooms were gone and night had fallen. Even the sea was quiet. She could only smell rotting flesh.

She sobbed.

"I'm going to have to hit you," she heard Avarielle mumble, but unable to respond, she withdrew back into herself and relived the death of her home.

Avarielle held Cassara up, the princess' feet still moving, but her eyes glazed over, tears streaming down her cheeks. Avarielle was convinced the princess would either walk into a wall or fall on her face if she didn't support her.

What's wrong with her? Avarielle wracked her memory, trying to identify anything that might have contributed to this. Since coming to the old city, the princess had been a bit aloof, but none of them had been too keen on talking.

Had she been aloof or getting lost? The warrior had no doubt that this was magic-induced. The only other time she had seen Cassara so distant was when she had overused her magic in Rockor, trying to save villagers she didn't even know. Her magic had engulfed her then, which had frightened both the warrior and the sorceress.

Shirina. She might be able to help. But the sorceress had vanished into shadows.

If she doesn't follow us, I'll throttle her, Avarielle thought as she helped Cassara into the amphitheater. The creatures filed in after them, streaming into the rows of seats. With the magic now activated, the amphitheater was cast in warm colors, and the seats looked plush and comfortable. Red carpet cushioned their steps as they walked down the stairs. Avarielle cast wary glances around to ensure Cassara wouldn't stumble down the stairs. She didn't like this at all. She considered trying to leave, but feared resistance. She could hardly fight with the princess in such a useless state.

Cassara cried out and sobbed. Avarielle debated hitting her, as Shirina had done in Rockor to bring her back. But she'd probably just knock her out, and then she'd have to carry her. She'd keep that as a last resort.

"Come on, Cassara," Avarielle urged her, trying to will the princess back to her.

The creatures filed behind and beside them to guide

their path, making sure they went down the stairs and onto the main stage.

"Great," she mumbled. Cassara broke away from her and walked to the right, sitting down on a chair in the front row. She reached into her small bag and pulled free her flute.

"What are you doing?" Avarielle asked as she moved toward her. Cassara didn't respond as she brought the flute to her lips, blowing the first few notes of the Traveler's Song.

"Cassara…" Avarielle didn't finish her sentence. The middle of the stage suddenly collapsed, an altar rising from it with a gentle whoosh. A creature stood on it, not unlike the one she had beheaded earlier. Except this one looked more human, though even bigger. He reeked of fish and his back sported a bent fin. He knelt, his back slumped, face in his hands as though grieving. A lump formed in Avarielle's throat and she swallowed hard. She couldn't help but respond to the majesty of the creature, its vast size curbed by its slumped shoulders and covered face.

The creature did not move. Avarielle approached it warily, hand on Graysword but not unsheathing it just yet. As Cassara ended the song, the creature took a deep, sharp breath, its fin now straightening. He stood up, head and shoulders much above Avarielle, muscular chest glistening in the light. Avarielle suddenly realized that all of the lights in the theater had gone dark. Except for those on the stage and the first row.

Wonderful.

She approached it just as its eyes opened. They darted back and forth, moist and glistening, and so round they resembled those of a fish.

"Welcome!" he shouted in a great booming voice. The audience cheered.

Avarielle had had enough.

"Who are you and what do you want?" she said, her hand itching to pull Graysword free and strike him down, wishing she had done so while the creature's head had still been lowered.

"I am Samala." He looked down at her, insulted. "Do you not know me, mortal? No matter. You will know me now…"

He paused as he looked towards the seats, his eyes piercing the darkness.

They became even rounder and he gasped.

"They are but memory!" he exclaimed. "Mist and illusion!"

He howled, falling back to his knees, his hands clutching his head as he wept. His cries echoed up into the dark, empty dome.

"How long have I slept?" he demanded, raising his head, looking deeply at Avarielle. "How long!"

"I have no idea," the warrior said, hand resting on Graysword as she calmly stood before him.

He turned around and looked at Cassara, who still sat on the chair, hands limp in her lap, eyes emotionless as she stared ahead.

"How long, child of Graydon!" He leapt towards her and Avarielle swore as she pulled Graysword free, screaming at Cassara to move as she tried to intercept, knowing full well she would be too slow to reach the princess in time.

***

Shirina observed from the shadows, only stepping out when the creature leapt for the princess. She stood in front of Cassara, holding her staff protectively up in front of her and raising her other hand. "Hold, Samala."

The creature stopped, seeming more confused than frightened. He narrowed his eyes at her. Avarielle ran up beside Shirina, her sword at the ready. Shirina was surprised that Avarielle didn't simply strike.

"You are from the Circle?" Samala asked as he stood straight again.

Shirina nodded. "I am Crimson Circle Elite Shirina of Ravenhold." Samala seemed to relax at those words, and he sat down cross-legged before them. Shirina watched him carefully. She could guess who and what he was.

Whereas the last creature they had met was absorbing the magic of Elihor, this one absorbed Graydon's magic. Shirina could not feel the effect, as she had carefully guarded her gates of magic. Cassara, however, was unable to do so, her strong connection to Graydon linking her directly to this creature, the magic ebbing and flowing from one to the other. She was trapped in its spell, like a puppet.

"Greetings, Great One." Shirina lowered her head respectfully.

Samala seemed pleased. "Graydon promised he would find a way to heal us and return. Is it time now? We've waited so long." He paused and sniffed the air. "Pashal is dead, isn't he?"

Shirina nodded, assuming it referred to the creature Avarielle had killed.

Samala looked at Graysword, then to Avarielle. "Did Siabala send you to kill us? Why would he do that?"

Shirina stepped in front of the warrior, earning a curse in the process. She assumed the warrior would see she was trying to help and refrain from running her through, though that was always debatable with the Grayloft.

"Not at all. We are here as friends." She held up one hand, palm up and open to show no trickery and only friendship.

"Have you slept since Graydon's time?" Shirina asked.

He nodded. "Yes. Graydon was to bring back the balance of magic. So that we could live again." He took a deep breath. "He forgot about us, didn't he?"

"I don't know, Samala. But Graydon has been dead for a long time." He looked up with interest. Shirina continued. "For one thousand years."

Samala chuckled, the sound trapped in his great chest reverberating like a deep drum. "A thousand years is not that long for us, mortal. Tell me, why does the child of Graydon awaken me now? Why does she play my song?"

"She is under your spell, Samala," Shirina said. "She knows not what she does."

He looked surprised. "Can she not control her magic?"

"To some extent."

"She is not with the Circle?" Shirina shook her head.

The great beast looked pensive. "Siabala is dangerous, you know. He needs the magics to mix to be more powerful than ever. He craves freedom, revenge, the rebirth of his people."

"His people?" Shirina quickly interjected, only to be dismissed by the wave of a giant hand.

"Crimson Circle, he must be stopped. You have a staff filled with Graydon's might, therefore my powers, and it will aid you. You must go and stop him."

Shirina took a step forward. "Can the magics be untangled?"

He cocked his head sideways again. "The magics were always untangled and tangled. You cannot separate them any more than you can stop the rain from infiltrating the earth. What you need to learn, or relearn, I suppose, is how to create better barrels with which to capture the water."

"Very helpful," Avarielle said, sheathing Graysword. "Can you please release your hold on Cassara?"

He waved towards the princess. Her eyes closed and she fell forward. Avarielle quickly closed the gap between them and caught her before she hit the ground. Her eyes flew open.

"What? Avarielle?"

Cassara's eyes were wide at the sight of the creature, shrinking into the warrior as she helped her up. She stared at the flute and ran her fingers gently along it, moving absentmindedly to mimic a melody. She gazed up at Samala, giving him a half-smile as she put the flute away in her bag.

"That was my mother's favorite song, and mine as well," Cassara said, taking a step towards the creature.

"And it will be for each of your family members. It's my song of awakening. I suppose Graydon kept it locked within him." Samala smiled. "He did intend to come back for me, after all."

His look quickly turned grim again. "You must be careful with the magic of Graydon. It is powerful, but it can consume you easily, as well. It was never meant to remain in your bloodline like this. I would have released Graydon of it had he returned, but…" He trailed off.

"How do we defeat Siabala?" Avarielle asked, taking a step forward.

He raised his eyebrow at her. "*You*, who carries Graysword, would kill Siabala?"

Shirina looked with interest at the warrior, not certain what Samala meant. From the determined stance of the warrior and the defiance in her eyes, it seemed that Avarielle at least understood.

"So you would," Samala said softly. His voice gained

strength. "You ensure his soul and his body do not reunite. Two of the seals have been broken. If the third is broken, he will become powerful enough to escape the Bloody Mountains." He cocked his head sideways. "He is near it, now. His armies will take the third seal and free his soul. You must destroy his body first, and then his soul, or all is lost."

"But how?" Shirina asked before Avarielle could. There was so much else she wanted to know. So much else she *needed* to know. The Circle could live on the knowledge of this creature alone!

Samala peered closely at Avarielle and Cassara. "You have everything you need here to form the dams and barrels that will keep Siabala's powers at bay. Without the shadows, he has no soul."

"What in Eli's Blood does that even mean?" Avarielle asked, fingers tightening around the pommel of her sword.

Samala chuckled. "It's the best I can do for you. I can only dumb down my understanding of magic so much. Now, I wish for you to leave. I grow tired."

Shirina was about to protest when his eyes met hers and silenced her. "All but the Crimson Circle. Stay a moment longer, Elite of Ravenhold."

Avarielle cast a wary glance at Shirina. The sorceress was uncertain if the warrior feared she would betray them, or if she simply didn't trust her alone with the powerful creature. After lingering a moment longer, the warrior nodded reluctantly. Taking the princess with her, the two stepped through the darkness and out into the magically lit night.

Shirina stood before the creature, admiring his strength. Not the physical, which was certainly impressive, but rather his magical strength. He breathed and absorbed the magic of Graydon like air.

His magic, she corrected herself. This was the creature who had granted Graydon such might, making him the most powerful sorcerer in all of his land. And Elihor had probably gained the magic from the other creature, the one Avarielle had so cruelly beheaded.

"Times change, Elite," he said, his voice rumbling through the room. Shirina waited, feeling it was not her place to question or interrupt. Like she stood before the greatest Elder of the Circle.

"Has your Covenant fallen?" he asked, as though making small talk.

Shirina chose her words carefully. "It is…wounded. But it may recover, in time."

"Siabala would like Graydon's and Elihor's Covenants destroyed. He was always angry we had given our powers to humans. That's in the past now."

He supported his head with his hands, elbows on the ground. He looked ready to nap.

"It's not that bad if you fail, you know," he said through a yawn. "The world will continue, just in a different shade than it is now. Maybe there will be no humans left, but that's not so bad. You won't miss yourselves once you're gone."

He paused and looked towards the ghostly figures in the audience. "Those are all my memories. All gone, our people. Long ago…" He gazed at them for a moment longer. "I didn't want them to die either, you know, so I understand why you choose to fight. I didn't. I thought everything would be all right."

He gave her a sad smile. "It's over for me now, too. You must do me one final favor, Elite. End it for me. I cannot do it myself, I will only fall into deep rest. But I will awaken alone again, with no one to bear witness."

Shirina stiffened. "That is a silly reason to want to die and I will not kill you."

He raised an eyebrow. "Is it? You still have witnesses. With no one to witness our lives and deeds, we are nothing. I am nothing, now. And, it is to your own benefit. Kill me and my soul will be freed. With my brother's dark magic now freed from his weary body as well, you will have more power to save yourselves. Though know that Siabala can feed off both our souls to create his own by blending them. But you already know that, don't you?"

He looked at her throat, still carefully covered by a scarf. His eyes were not fooled by the poor disguise.

Shirina looked down towards the base of her staff, the wood sturdy against her palm. Real. She faced him again.

"There is so much I wish to know still," she whispered, feeling like a sproutling again, wanting nothing more than to climb the ranks of the Circle and learn everything.

She could see Samala's magic lessen. As he released his powers, Elihor's dark strands danced with them as equal partners, fighting back some of the darkness, other strands just becoming blended.

Shadows.

He was already doing it, slowly, stopping the breath of his power. He just needed her to sever it completely. She could do it, she knew, like warding another witch from using their power.

"Your knowledge will be useless without a Covenant to share it with, and your Covenant will not resurrect as long as Siabala lives. Knowledge is eternal, Crimson Circle. Time, however, is fleeting. Especially yours."

He rolled over onto his back and looked up towards the ceiling. Apparently, he didn't intend to die standing. "It is survival or knowledge, Crimson Circle. Choose."

"But can the Circle survive without the understanding of its own magic?" Despair laced her words, and she didn't care. "Is that not why we are dying now?"

Samala sighed, as though annoyed at a pest interrupting his nap. "You are dying because you forgot the knowledge that you once had. You should instead learn to acquire it yourselves." He let his breath escape him as he whispered, "It's a better skill, in the long run."

Shirina nodded slowly and clutched her staff before her. Samala had almost severed his connection to the magic. His features seemed old, the human side of him gaining years as the magic escaped into the air around him.

Without witnesses, we are nothing. She wasn't convinced by his words, but it was his desire to die now. Did she have the right to deny him? She could refuse him. But the battle ahead would need equal grounds for both the light and the dark, which could not be achieved with Samala anchoring his magic.

Shirina owed it to Graydon and Ravenhold to give the light a fighting chance. She held her own breath as she cast her spell and watched the eyes close and a smile curl the lips before the features went slack.

SIABALA FELT HIS BROTHER DIE, and he threw up. He would weep if he could, but he did not yet have his soul back. He was just a body.

A shell.

His Circle had pretended to understand when he had contacted them again. Stormhold had been his, but its adepts had been turned against him. As had Elihor's, though that hadn't been a surprise. He had killed as many as he could find. Graydon had been a surprise. Cut off from the other two, the Keep had lost much knowledge, and it was ruled mostly by fear, and therefore easier to control.

He had killed those who had not followed him.

Samala. His brother had known this, and he was hurt by it. His magic of light was feared and hated by the children of Graydon. And he had chosen to set it free.

Which could make Siabala stronger, or make him fall harder. He needed the third seal to break now. He longed to feel his soul enter him, for his powers to throb in his veins, for the ability to properly grieve his brothers.

And he had taken steps to ensure the children of Graydon would live to witness his reign. He would help the Circle of Ravenhold grow, so that he would not be left alone in freedom, as his brothers had been.

33

*J*ayden's hands formed useless fists at his sides. Edoline was about to be attacked, and he was too far away to do anything about it.

Edoline. Where his eldest sister, Altessa, waited for him still. And where he was king, or would be upon his return.

"What is Edoline? Is it a kingdom?" Kale asked, looking at Dayshon. But it was Jayden who answered.

"It's my home." His voice gained strength as he continued. "I am its king. Or will be, when I return to it." Kale nodded, conveying sympathy and respect.

"Why would the seal be placed there and not in Ravenhold?" Shala demanded. The Crimson Circle gave her a look that left little doubt the Orange Circle should listen, and not speak. Regardless of their different Covenants, Liza outranked her.

Dayshon answered this time. "The Edolines are descendants of Graydon."

Kale's eyebrows shot up at that. A smile broke across his lips and he took Jayden's hand and firmly shook it, the prince taken by surprise. "As I am a descendant of Elihor. Our bloodlines are connected, King of Edoline." A shadow crossed his face. "So, the third seal was hidden from Siabala, though now he has found it."

"Your Eastland ways are strange," Breck mumbled, making Trevon smile.

Liza spoke up, her voice warm and soothing. "Graydon would not have hidden a seal and then left it without defense. That makes no sense."

Her words pierced Jayden like an arrow. He reached within his tunic and pulled the amulet free, the silver and gold shining in the fading sunlight. Its metal remained cold and indifferent to Jayden's touch.

"Elihor's amulet," Kale whispered. "Elihor gave Graydon her amulet, to help protect the final seal."

"But it's here, and not in Edoline," Jayden said, looking at the powerful item. "It's no good to us here."

"Can you use it?" Liza asked, the woman kneeling before Jayden, more to face him than to show respect, he was certain.

"Cassara could, but I can't." He was embarrassed at the confession.

Liza smiled at him, a kind, warm smile that showed she understood what he was thinking. "If this is indeed Elihor's amulet, then it is meant to be wielded by a woman, Jayden. No power on earth could help you wield that which is not meant for you."

Jayden nodded, trying to hide his relief. He had started seeing his lack of mastery over the amulet as a personal failure. At a time when he needed to become much more than he was, he could hardly bear the thought of failing so miserably.

"Is Cassara the only female left of your line?"

Jayden shook his head. "The eldest is Altessa, and she is in Edoline now."

Liza smiled and stood. "That is good. But we must get her the amulet so that she may use it in the battle to come. Even it may not be enough to defeat Siabala's army. If Massir fell so easily," she cast a sympathetic look to Dayshon, "then we can only assume they are very strong and dangerous."

"How do we get the amulet to her in time, adept? Do you know?" Breck said, with a hint of respect in his voice. Jayden had to admit the adept from Stormhold was much friendlier than the ones from Ravenhold. Shala seemed aware of it, too, shuffling impatiently behind them.

"We teleport it, with a note warning her of the danger." She turned to Jayden. "Written by you, of course. There will be comfort and familiarity in your words."

Jayden nodded.

"Why not simply tell her and not waste more time?" Breck said, and Jayden felt so small and useless when he saw the Crimson Circle's sad smile.

"Because although I can get it to her, I can only do so by exposing myself to the blended magic, and I very much doubt I will survive long beyond my teleportation."

Breck stared at her, as though sizing her up. Then he lowered his head and crossed his arms.

"Let's get this done," Dayshon said. "At the rate they move…"

Jayden was already composing the note in his head, his words carefully selected like wards against his fear for Altessa, and against his grief for the woman he'd just met who looked at him with kind eyes.

KALE WALKED UP to Pack Nacker and lowered himself down slowly to sit before him. Pack looked more and more like the demon Siabala had tried to forge. Kale looked deep into his eyes to try and see the boy he had once known. He was still in there, of that he was certain.

But for how long?

Kale knew Pack no longer required sleep, and could move much more quickly than they could. He knew that he and the people of Elihor could make a difference, were they still willing.

"Pack, there is a boy who needs your help."

Pack cocked his head sideways. Kale smiled. "He reminds me of Kryde when he was that age." His smile faltered a bit. "His home is going to be under attack, much like Elihor was. Siabala wants to destroy it." At the mention of Elihor and Siabala, Pack perked up, his shoulders straighter.

"Listen to me, Pack. You need not become a monster. If

anyone can best Siabala, it's you. And I'll help. I'll stay here and question every adept from every keep until we figure out how to bring you back."

Pack stayed still for a few moments. Then he nodded slowly. Kale doubted he had fooled him. There was no cure for this, at least none that could be discovered without at least one Elder.

But at least this way, Pack would have the chance to die in battle, fighting against Siabala, and not for him.

It was the least Kale could do for his grandson's best friend, who had proved loyal until the last.

LIZA KNELT on the ground and faced the heir of Graydon. He had beautiful eyes, and she imagined that, had her own son lived beyond his birth, he would look much the same. The boy was scared, she could tell. Only the two of them remained, now.

She had told all of the other men to leave. She needed to concentrate to cast her spell. They had wished her good luck, but she knew they were terrified. She was the highest-ranking Circle member here, and without a Crimson Circle, it greatly limited the attack potential of the remaining adepts. But so be it. Only Crimson Circles and Elders could teleport, and the choice seemed obvious. Should the third seal fail, should Siabala's soul be freed, then he himself would come down the mountain, and no magic, from the Circle or otherwise, would be capable of stopping him.

Jayden fidgeted with the rolled-up parchment. She grabbed both his hands in hers and took the parchment gently before it was destroyed. He looked embarrassed and she gave a short laugh.

"I promise I'll get this to your sister, Jayden." He nodded and pulled the amulet free from his tunic.

"I promised Cassara I would keep this safe."

"Then I will take that promise by extension. I promise I will only give it to your sister." *With my last breath.*

"I told Altessa I would come quickly. Kale says the Pack can go fast and carry me." He started fidgeting with the bottom of his shirt. "Maybe if we get there fast enough, maybe we'll find a way to help you."

She smiled at him. "I'll wait for you then," she said, and she could see he wanted to believe her, but didn't. She had never been good at lying, which was why she had never made Elite.

But she had made peace with that long ago. Her humanity had always been more important to her than magic.

"Jayden, think of your sister with all of your heart," she said softly, ignoring the fear rumbling deep within her. "Think of your home, and a safe place for me to arrive."

"Like a courtyard?"

"That would be perfect. Think of it, of its scents, of the feeling it evokes in you, of its plants and lifeforms, its stones and shapes. Close your eyes and think of it all, so that I can feel it too," she ended in a whisper. "Guide me safely to your home, Jayden."

He nodded, hesitated for a moment and then hugged her. Deeply, without reservation. Taken by surprise, it took her a moment to hug him back, her fear turning to calm resolve. He whispered "Thank you," and broke free of the hug.

"Thank you, young king," she said, keeping her voice low so that it would not tremble.

He looked up to the stars as though getting his bearings, smiled, and closed his eyes as he concentrated on his home.

Liza stared at the boy and his energy, of his memories taking on the shape of the courtyard. She could find it, she was certain.

She closed her eyes and focused all of her magic on this one leap. She did not summon it until she was certain of where the place was. It was far, this she had known, and even without the magic of Graydon attacking her, she doubted she would have survived such a long leap.

She found comfort in that as she clutched the amulet and opened the floodgates of magic.

She vanished in a halo of gray light.

ALTESSA SAT in the Courtyard of Stars, waiting for the sun to vanish. The moon would be low on the horizon this night, winter's clutches gripping the land. It would be a perfect night to gaze at the constellations, which she had done so rarely of late.

Bestian was long dead, finally released from his painful shell a few days after Delora's final visit.

Gragor had never sent help, and so she assumed he was dead, which saddened her deeply. Cassara and Jayden had both vanished, and were probably gone as well. She had no one left to turn to.

At least the guards had lessened their hold of late. She had overheard that Delora had not contacted them in some time, that they lacked direction. They now let her wander the halls of her ancient home as well as its courtyards, with some peace. But that was as far as she could go.

The villagers dropped by for visits once in a while, which the guards allowed as well, as long as they could eavesdrop. They brought her supplies for embroidering, and gossip from the few villagers. No one had received any news from other lands in a long time, and Edoline felt even more isolated than before. Like a great bubble had been blown over the tiny kingdom.

No merchants or traders came, no Circle witches, no Southern Coalition, none of Bestian's family to inquire about him and, thankfully, no Eloms. Only the guards, Altessa, and the villagers remained. And her husband, father, and mother, sleeping in their tombs, whom she spoke to more than was probably healthy.

Stars began to pepper the night sky, and Altessa stood on the stone marking the spot with the best view the first constellation. The Leaping Gazelle, Jayden's favorite.

Someday, I'll leap just as high and go on as many adventures, he had declared to visitors viewing the constellation.

She swallowed hard as she gazed through the viewing port, one of fifteen. She would watch them all rise this night, and end on the Lost Lovers, the most celebrated constellation. Some stories even claimed Edoline was founded here for the visibility of the constellation, and the stone that marked the constellation had been set in this earth on the day of Graydon's death. Those were nice stories, but they hardly comforted Altessa.

She needed to reconnect with her roots, with something that marked who she was, and the porthole of stars seemed like a good start. The scent of cedar washed over her as a breeze played through the courtyard, carrying the salty sea air with it.

She was moving to the second stone in the dark of night when the hairs on her arms all stood at attention and a shiver gripped her spine. The air stopped dancing, the scent of cedar vanished, and all noise simply ceased.

A light began to grow on the stone marking the constellation of the Leaping Gazelle, where she had stood but moments before.

It was a strange light, not white so much as gray. Altessa knew she should be frightened, yet she could not pull away.

The light grew until it was bigger than Altessa. The

guards ran in, hands on their weapons, uncertain whether to draw them or leave them be.

Altessa ignored them and concentrated on the growing light. It began to dissipate, vanishing in a fine mist, and a woman stood before her. She was tall and wide-shouldered, and her hair was almost the color of gold in this light. She was from the Circle, though Altessa had never seen this particular robe. Two Crimson Circles were linked over her heart on the gray garment. And unlike all the other adepts Altessa had ever met, her eyes were kind. The woman smiled.

"Altessa?" She choked on the word, spitting blood before falling to her knees. Altessa knelt before her and held her shoulders, which shook as she coughed. The woman toppled sideways, closing her eyes as tears streamed down her face, unable to breathe as a black patch spread over her throat.

"From...Jayden..." she managed to gasp and lifted her hand slightly.

Altessa's heart hammered in her chest as she took the note and the amulet.

Mother's amulet.

Before she could process what it meant, the woman shuddered in her arms and Altessa looked back into her kind eyes.

"Thank you," she whispered to the woman whose name she did not know.

The Crimson Circle smiled as death claimed her.

34

"You don't have to do this, Jayden," Dayshon said, standing before him.

"I need to do this," Jayden repeated patiently, which annoyed Dayshon even more. He forced himself to remain calm. The youth had been through Siabala's Rage and Elihor and made it back alive. He was either very good or very lucky. Either of those, or preferably both, would serve him in the days to come.

Jayden locked eyes with his. They were so much older than they should be at times that Dayshon found it unnerving. "If you could rush out to save Massir, would you?"

Dayshon bit back harsh words and took a deep breath before replying. "You're right. I would rush out, on the back of Eloms too, if necessary. But you're my brother now, and I can't help but worry." Jayden smiled at that. He liked having a brother, and so did Dayshon. He just wished his little brother wasn't quite so stubborn. But he could also understand it.

Dayshon laughed suddenly. "You remind me of your sister!"

Jayden grimaced, making Dayshon laugh even more.

He sobered up quickly. Night was midway to dawn, and they needed to go. The other army had struck Massir and so would need to go around or through Kosel, which would take longer. There was a chance to catch them, still. But only if they moved now.

"Here," he said, pulling free one of Cassara's handkerchiefs, which the maids of Massir had insisted she take, despite Cassara's protests. Jayden looked at him quizzically.

"To mask the scent. Cover your nose with it as you travel. It'll cut back some of the stench, at least. In this case, every little bit counts."

Jayden nodded and took the piece of fabric. He extended his hand to Dayshon, and shook it warmly. Dayshon gathered him in a hug. Jayden held him back, nodding as they parted, as though fearful another word would break his determination.

Dayshon watched him go toward the waiting Eloms, feeling a familiar presence beside him. "I feel old this night, Jiles."

The captain grunted in response.

With the king of Rashim's security in his hands in the middle of a battlefield, he guessed his captain felt very old this night as well.

KADEN STEPPED out of the light of the camp and walked amongst the Pack. He was a guard of Edoline, had fought in this very land during the Westland Wars, and fostered an illegal but deadly magic. He was not intimidated by these men, rather he felt sorry for them. Loyal to the last, Carsyn followed him, his hand on the pommel of his sword to hide the tremors that now beset it regularly.

His left arm had never quite healed following the attack in Kosel. But, to his credit, Carsyn didn't seem to hold a grudge against these Eloms. He too felt sorry for their stolen lives.

Some of the Pack eyed them curiously, others slept, and some just sat there, looking into the distance, as though no longer certain if they were human or beast. These were the ones that worried Kaden most.

He walked until he found the man he was looking for. He stood taller than most, fighting the twisting of his leg bones by forcing himself to remain tall. His armor was distinguished and mostly complete, unlike that of the others. He seemed more human, somehow. He focused on Kaden as he walked up to him.

Kaden struggled not to show his disgust at the stench, impressed that Carsyn had not retched. The old guard must have been terrified of being left behind if he was on such good behavior. Or he wanted to leave this dark land of memories and return home to Edoline.

Home. The last time he had been in the West, wielding

green fires and killing innocents, a pawn in the Circle's games, he had not believed he would ever find a home again. And then Alexavier Edoline had come along.

He intended to see that Jayden had a longer rule than his father, and he still planned to retire by the sea.

Another man joined them, and Kaden turned enough to recognize the youngest guard of Edoline, Gragor.

"I promised Queen Altessa I would bring help, Lieutenant. I'm coming with you." It was so simply stated that Kaden could do little else but nod. They could use the help, he was certain.

The three remaining guards of Edoline reached the leader of the Pack. "Pack Nacker. My name is Kaden, and this is Carsyn and Gragor. We are Royal Protectors of Edoline. The last guards of Edoline." The Elom seemed to size them up. They didn't look like much, he knew. The starlight simply outlined the creases of time on the older guards' faces, the bags under their eyes and their lean frames.

"I'm certain," Kaden said, "that you would not judge another man by appearance alone."

Pack's dark eyes narrowed. Kaden feared he might have gone too far, but they couldn't afford to be left behind. The Elom's claws could easily cut them all in two before they could utter a cry of protest.

Kaden continued. "We only wish to protect our king. All that we ask is that you bring us with you. We will not be a burden."

He rested his case. He could say no more, really. The

Pack could easily leave them here. They owed him nothing.

Yet Pack Nacker motioned to three of his men, big burly Eloms that still had some of their armor. The Eloms nodded to them. The guards returned the gesture.

If they managed to survive the journey, it seemed that they would soon be in Edoline once again.

JAYDEN CLUNG to Pack Nacker's back, the trees of Kosel a dark impenetrable mass in the distance towards the north. To the south there were only farmlands, and he thought that if he squinted hard enough, he would see all the way to the sea. They were moving fast and would reach Edoline the next night, to hopefully beat Siabala's army, which traveled a much less direct route.

They would rest during the day, the Pack's eyes no longer able to tolerate light. And hoped the other army would need rest, as well.

The repetitive movement of the Elom made him both tired and nauseous. The stench was thankfully whisked away, but he could still hear the grunts of the creatures despite the wind whistling in his ears. He looked back to spot the old guards, glad they were with him, and he watched the Eloms running behind him. There were at least a hundred of Pack's people, maybe even more. He had known that, but seeing them now, running at a speed defying any other living creature, some running on all fours, others still on two legs, some jumping over obstacles, others plowing through them…it was terrifying.

He had to turn around. The moon cast large shadows on the land, his eyes tearing in the wind until he couldn't tell what anything was. He tried to see Edoline in the distance, but every time he convinced himself it was home, it turned out to be just another patch of trees, a deserted farmhouse or worse, a pyre left to burn itself out.

His heart began racing at the sight. He remembered the Eloms coming for him the night of Edoline's fall. He remembered them breaking down the door, killing the guard, the blood, the stench of death, being carried away to his awaiting aunt. He imagined the incoming attack, with Eloms running towards Edoline, ready to destroy what remained of his beloved home.

Altessa. She was all that he had left there, the sister that was more like a mother. He clutched Pack's armor, trying to ignore the feel of the cold flesh, trying to block away the memories of losing his home, and a piece of himself.

Promise you'll take me on one of your adventures someday, Cassara?

His old self seemed like a displaced memory. He didn't understand himself anymore, the pre-attack Jayden. He didn't want the adventures anymore, he just wanted home. And his family.

He clung to the Elom and tried not to think of death.

PACK COULD TASTE the boy's fear, could feel it in the air around him, in the beating of his heart, in the small noises he undoubtedly thought the wind would whisk away.

Pack could feel and hear all of it. And he craved tasting it.

He wanted the boy's blood. And he knew he wasn't the only one. His people ran faster, stayed closer, some running on all fours now, more monster than human.

The old guards weren't of interest, their blood not as appealing. Theirs didn't court the magic of Graydon as the boy's did. They weren't fresh fodder and heir to the Fallen One.

But the boy…Pack caught himself salivating. He bit hard into his own flesh, forcing bitter black blood down his throat, the taste of rotten, diseased corpses.

He was running out of time before the madness consumed what remained of his mind, and he was terribly aware of it.

35

Cassara sat with her back to the wall of the amphitheater, wishing the magical lights would dim or that sunshine would warm her skin. But the night chill still clung to everything, and no matter how tightly she wrapped her coat around herself, she could not keep warm.

Avarielle paced nearby, casting wary glances at the doorway, and then at Cassara.

"Are you all right?"

"For the tenth time, Avarielle, I'm fine. Just a bit groggy." *And suffering from a splitting headache.* Cassara remembered everything that had happened to her, but the memory was nested comfortably in her mind, like a dream.

The warrior resumed her pacing.

Cassara was terrified by how easily her magic had been manipulated, rendering her little more than a puppet. And not due to a recent spell, either, but an old one, probably cast by Graydon himself, to keep a promise he himself could not fulfill.

She closed her eyes and leaned her head back. It felt stuffed with wheat. What had Samala said? That he had granted his power and song of awakening to Graydon? How did this all fit into the puzzle? Would she ever know?

Cassara opened her eyes just as Shirina stepped out of the amphitheater.

Avarielle stopped pacing. Shirina faced them and formed her words slowly. "It seems that now, both the magic of Graydon and Elihor are on equal footing. When the opportunity comes, we should be able to separate them once more, which in turn should rob Siabala's soul of his power."

"His soul? How can his body exist without his soul? Do they mean soul as in magic?" Avarielle demanded to know, crossing her arms.

"I believe their souls are their magic, and their magic their souls." She lifted a hand to stop Avarielle from inquiring further. "That explanation will have to suffice for now." The warrior looked annoyed, but held her peace.

Shirina turned towards the princess. "Do you understand what this means, Cassara?" she asked in uncharacteristically gentle tones.

Cassara shook her head, immediately wishing she hadn't as pain exploded in her skull.

Shirina looked at the princess. "If I understand this correctly," she cast a quick glance at Avarielle, waiting for the sarcastic comment. Avarielle didn't bite, and so Shirina continued. "The magic of Graydon will increase in the air around us. If you look with the Sight, you can see it growing now."

Cassara forced her tired eyes to focus on the strands of magic, to see beyond the veil of the physical world. She gasped at what the Sight revealed. Ribbons of light danced with dark ones, some merging into shadows, others lashing out at each other like snakes. There were so many that Cassara could barely see her companions anymore. The strands shifted and moved so quickly around her that it made her dizzy.

She closed her eyes and took a deep breath. "What does this mean, Shirina?"

"That you need to be careful with your magic, Cassara. I don't quite understand your link with the magic yet, but it's strong and you don't control it. Absorbing too much of it could easily be your downfall."

Cassara opened her eyes, the strands of magic now just whispers on the wind. She could control some of it, but Shirina was right, most of it was based on gut reactions. She had no idea if any other triggers existed within her. Her magic felt alien to her, not the boon she had first imagined it to be.

"How do I control it?" Her own voice sounded weak in her ears.

Shirina sighed. "You spend years in the Circle studying and refining your skills. But since we don't have that luxury, let's see what we can do to at least allow you control over intake of magic. That alone could be enough to save you."

Cassara nodded and turned to Avarielle. "Where are we setting up for the night?"

The warrior looked around in disgust. "Some night. Let's at least find some shelter. I'll keep watch while you two chat, and then we'll rotate the watch. It's going to be a short night, so take advantage of it while you can."

<hr>

SHIRINA SAT cross-legged in the entryway, her staff across her lap. She listened to the silence as she reviewed the princess' progress. Cassara was a quick study and had already mastered so much of her magic that it had proved fairly easy teaching her the basics of closing the floodgates.

A few more lessons and she would master that, too. Shirina remembered being a Green Circle and having to learn to pry open the floodgates of magic. She had never met an adept that didn't need to learn that skill, and not the other way around.

Of course, Cassara isn't an adept. It was a shame, really. The princess was gifted with magic in a way that few were or could ever be. Cassara would prove an asset to the Covenant, especially with her knowledge of diplomacy and trade.

Of course, she would also need to learn to control her emotions. Which Shirina knew would prove impossible.

That's why adepts were selected at a young age. Children were easier to mold.

Her grip on her staff tightened. But that would change, too. The Circle would no longer harvest children, and so adepts could become Green Circles at any age. And that could include Cassara, or even her older sister, Altessa, who must also be courted by the magic of Graydon.

"How is she doing?" Shirina started as Avarielle walked up beside her.

The sorceress scowled. "Shouldn't you be sleeping?"

She shrugged. "Not tired. How's Cassara doing?"

Shirina didn't look at the warrior as she answered. "Fine. She's learning quickly, and should master the intake of magic soon." Then she added, looking at the warrior this time, "She would make a fine addition to the Circle."

The warrior looked at her pensively. "Are you going to maintain the Circle, Shirina?"

Even a few weeks ago, the sorceress would have scoffed at the question. But now it felt like a valid one. She didn't feel the need to lie as she whispered.

"I don't know, Avarielle. I guess I'll concentrate on this battle first, and then I'll decide what to do next."

Avarielle stood silent, letting seconds slip into minutes before speaking again. "I think you should." Shirina looked up, surprised. The warrior's jaw was set and she didn't meet Shirina's eyes as she continued. "In a different way, of course. No Harvests, no wars, no secrets and haughty attitudes. But the teaching of magic is important.

I mean, Cassara would probably kill herself with her magic if not for your teachings."

Avarielle then turned back into the house without another word. Shirina watched her go, wondering if the warrior would feel the same way if she had any intention of surviving the battle with Siabala.

AVARIELLE SHIFTED TO HER SIDE, unable to fall asleep on the hard floor, especially with the fake bright lights. She listened to the princess' soft breath and envied her clear conscience.

She sighed and resigned herself to being on her side. Having loosened her armor a bit for the night, the child found more room to play and enjoyed kicking.

A dancer, like me.

Avarielle hardened her heart against the thought, surprised at the tears welling into her eyes. This pregnancy was annoying for more reasons than Avarielle cared to count.

But she realized that, at some point in the journey to the West and then Elihor, she had come to think of the unborn child as not only Kryde's heir, but as her own, as well.

If I don't return from battle with Siabala, she prayed in her heart to her family eagerly waiting to welcome her in the Land of Beyond, *then please at least spare the child. Let at least one descendant of Grayloft wield Graysword without the blood oath to Siabala.*

Avarielle would accept that as her greatest victory. Even more so than claiming revenge.

THE MAGICAL LIGHTS of the city faded with the sunrise, leaving it more somber than during the night. Cassara pulled her coat closed, breath misting before her eyes.

"We should reach the Bloody Mountains by midday," Avarielle said as she tightened her armor, the warrior's eyes deeply lined with dark circles. "Once there, we may not be able to rest again, so I vote we get closer and prepare for battle before heading in." She paused, her voice soft as she continued. "Siabala's Rage awaits us."

Shirina nodded as she followed, but Cassara did not acknowledge the words, too preoccupied by the sight of Avarielle's instinctive placement of her hand on her belly at the mention of Siabala's Rage.

Orange Circle Shala found sleep elusive that night, as on most nights since Ravenhold's fall. She quietly exited the tent, which was occupied by four other adepts, and stretched in the fresh dawn air. Wrapping her orange cloak closer, she walked to the edge of camp.

Shirina's words haunted her still, and she hated the Crimson Circle for it. They were free to leave the Circle, any time after the battle. It would become a choice, suddenly.

But why would anyone choose any differently than to belong to the strongest organization in Graydon? *Or so it used to be.*

Ravenhold was gone, and should the Covenant meet again, it would be under that blasted Crimson Circle Elite, the highest-ranking remaining adept, as far as anyone could tell. Shala would never rise to become much more under her reign, especially if she was too soft to even hold a Harvest, when one was clearly of the utmost importance.

At least now, with all remaining Crimson Circles gone, I am one of the highest-ranking.

A commotion drew her attention. Guards moved up and screamed back, torches were lit, archers mobilized. Curious, she approached.

Prince Dayshon was arguing with the Westland leader, though their tones were hushed and she could make out no words. It was obvious that the prince was not succeeding in convincing his ally.

Shala looked further still, where cloaks caught her attention. White robes and cloaks that looked black in this light. *Could it be?*

She increased her speed, careful not to let her eagerness show. She began recognizing faces. One Elder. Six Crimson Circles. All from Ravenhold's Covenant.

Relief washed over her as she reached them, lowering her head in respect. They returned the gesture, welcoming her as one of their own.

Shala was home again. Ravenhold's Circle would live yet.

"We can't send them away, Breck!" Dayshon argued, keeping his voice low so that others would not hear. There were many stray ears in this camp.

"They can't stay. Circle youths, I'll accept, but full-blown Elders and Elites are another matter."

"You allowed Shirina to stay, and she was an Elite too!"

"Avarielle seemed to trust her, or she wouldn't have allowed her to live. That speaks highly enough to me."

Dayshon opened his arms in supplication. "Look, we can't just send them away. They wouldn't survive out there. They can't use their magic, remember?"

Breck grunted. "If you're so fond of your Covenant, then answer me this: Why did they just arrive from the side of the Bloody Mountains and not from Ravenhold?"

Dayshon looked back towards them, other Circle adepts now joining them. They were so bloody hard to read, and with Delora's betrayal still fresh, and his father's life compromised by her…his hands turned to fists.

"I don't know, Breck, but let's find out right now."

"If I don't like their answer, I'm finishing them."

Dayshon sighed. "All right, but let's at least hear them out first. Whether we like them or not, they're still powerful allies. But," he added, "it's your land, so do as you will. I'll not interfere there."

Breck grunted again, a satisfied guttural sound, making Dayshon smile. He truly liked and respected the man.

He vowed that should they win the day, the East and the West would never fight again. At least, not as long as he was king. Should he live long enough to wear his crown.

THE PRINCE and the Westland leader made their way to them. At the flick of a wrist, Westland archers surrounded the Circle newcomers. Shala was indignant, but was careful to hide it.

"Greetings, Prince Dayshon of Massir," Elder Mott said, a wizened old man who would look like anyone's grandfather were it not for the ice in his eyes.

"Elder," Dayshon said, nodding to the man. "This is Breck, and he is leader here." Shala noted that Dayshon did not limit Breck's title by calling him 'leader of the West,' making it clear to the Elder that he would need to prove their worth to him.

And it was made doubly clear they would need to do so, with archers pointing deadly arrows at their hearts.

Prove their worth. Shala couldn't believe it. Only a few months ago, an Elder of the Circle would be greeted with awe and reverence, as it should be, not with superstition and fear.

Elder Mott nodded respectfully to the Westland leader.

"Leader Breck, a pleasure to make your acquaintance." Shala was proud of the way the Elders and Crimson Circles presented themselves. They stood proud, unapologetic and ignoring the arrows. *This* was the Circle she belonged to. Not the one that would be diluted by Shirina.

She fought the urge to smile. Shirina would

undoubtedly be punished for her promises of freedom to the other Circle adepts.

"Where do you come from?" Breck asked gruffly, not ordering his men to lower their weapons.

"We are from Ravenhold's Covenant," Elder Mott said with cold laughter in his eyes. It sent a shiver down Shala's spine. "But I believe you are asking why we are coming from the ancient city. We were on a mission to stop the Wall of Loss from vanishing, but we failed, as you can see."

He lowered his head in grief. Tears of pride and loss rose to Shala's eyes. The Circle would win many other battles, of this she was certain.

"Wall's not that far," Breck said, looking unimpressed.

The Elder's smile did not reach his eyes. "We were exploring the ancient ruins. Such a fascinating vestige of our history, wouldn't you say?"

"Funny you didn't fall in when most of it collapsed."

Shala looked to Prince Dayshon. Would he really allow an Elder of Ravenhold's Covenant to be treated in such a manner by this animal? But the prince simply stood back, analyzing the Elder.

"We were thankfully on the edge, taking refuge from the flying creatures." The Elder clenched his teeth. "We are, after all, currently unable to use magic."

"So I hear." Breck turned towards Dayshon.

The prince stepped forward. "What of the Elder Delora?"

Even in the twilight, Elder Mott's face darkened. "She

made deals with forces the Circle was formed to oppose. She is no longer welcome amongst us."

Shala was surprised by his fury. The Elder composed himself quickly, but his hand still trembled.

"Did you know of Elder Mott's scouting mission?" Dayshon asked, facing Shala. The Orange Circle fought to keep her head high and show the Elites and Elders she was one of them.

"I did not. But I am not privy to the dealings of the Elders, either." Short, concise, factual without giving away too much.

The prince studied her for a moment before nodding. She felt elated.

Except that when the Wall had collapsed, the Elder who had rescued them all from Ravenhold had said she was the last Elder of the Covenant. Shala cast a sideways glance to the newcomers. Either Elder Crimanon had been mistaken, or these were imposters.

She would need to keep a sharp eye out to see, and then decide if a stronger Ravenhold was worth the sacrifice of Graydon.

37

Altessa walked the length of the front courtyard, followed by ten guards, all of whom she managed to ignore. Captain Emran had refused to take the note seriously. Altessa had pleaded with him to at least warn the villagers, who were still fairly unprotected despite their newly built walls.

But he had refused that, as well.

Altessa held the note in her hand, not needing to read it again to visualize it. It was Jayden's handwriting, she was certain, though it seemed more confident, and yet also more hesitant than before. The hesitation lay in his forming of the letters, as though he had not practiced his penmanship of late. And his confidence laced every word.

Monsters coming...

Destroyed Massir...

Protect Edoline with the amulet...I'm coming to you...

His sentences had been full, eloquent ones, yet those

were the passages that jumped back into her mind constantly. The amulet rested around her neck, but she had no idea how to use it. She'd analyzed every piece of it, frowning at a memory tugging at the back of her mind. And remembering her sister.

Cassara. Jayden and she had obviously met again, but his letter did not give news on her welfare. She wondered where she was, and if she was queen of Massir now. Or if she was just another casualty of this war, like their father and her husband.

She grieved the former, but not the latter. She grieved the child her womb had rejected more than she grieved her late husband. He had shown his weakness in the end, and left Edoline in dire straits.

She continued walking to the edge of the courtyard. Dawn had just cracked the sky and she could barely see, but she craved the fresh air. She needed to get out of the manor, if just for a moment. With no one to speak to and nothing to do, Altessa feared she would go mad with boredom. And worry. That Cassara would not find Jayden. That Jayden was dead. That Cassara was dead.

Fear of the monsters destroying Edoline was secondary.

She thought she spotted something on the horizon. She peered closer, focusing on the shadows. Something *had* moved.

But what was it? An animal?

It came closer and she saw it, or rather, *them.* She

wasn't certain what they were, but there were at least five of them, running towards her at breakneck speed.

Someone tugged her back, and she turned and began running back through the courtyard, some guards ahead of her, a few brave ones behind her.

She heard one of them scream but kept moving as another guard pulled his bow free and turned to fire, only to fall beside her as something jumped on him.

Something large tackled her legs and threw her to the ground, rolling heavily on her before skidding to a stop near her head, long toenails jutting from dark feet. Above them, red armor. Altessa pushed herself back to her knees as a guard attacked it from behind, his sword bouncing uselessly off the armor as the red assailant turned around and cut the man in two with a curved blade.

Altessa was on her feet and running again, the amulet warm on her chest and pulsating with light.

Protect Edoline with the amulet...

Altessa snagged the amulet free of her dress, clutched it with her hand and turned around. She faced the monster still chasing her and blasted it with white fire. The force of the magic sent her stumbling back. She struggled to remain standing as she sent the white flames rippling into the other monsters, their screams accompanied by the stench of burning flesh, only their armor remaining.

Altessa lowered her trembling hand, breathing hard. She knew this magic, had always known it lived in the amulet.

She had seen it before, on the day that her mother had died, when Cassara had summoned the cursed fires that had taken her life away.

Altessa took a deep breath as the surrounding guards recovered and more poured out of the castle to join them. She found Captain Emran and looked him straight in the eyes.

"There were only five of them, so I assume they were a scouting party. It's safe to assume more will come, either this day or tonight. Warn the villagers, captain. And prepare your men for combat."

He examined her closely and she straightened herself to be every bit as regal as her father ever was. He lowered his head slightly.

"As you command, your Majesty."

As he walked towards his men, barking orders, Altessa did not feel relief. She would not allow herself to feel that way until she was certain that Edoline was safe.

38

Kale watched the Circle Elders join the other adepts, to be greeted by reserved but evident enthusiasm. He remained hidden on a nearby sand dune.

"Ravenhold is saved," he overheard more than a few of the Green Circles say as they eagerly walked towards the Elders. The Larkhold and Stormhold adepts were definitely more reserved in their approach. None of their Elders or Crimson Circles remained, having sacrificed themselves to the greater cause.

They stayed back, wary. Kale watched them, proud of the youth of his land who did not regard this arrival as happy coincidence. They greeted them politely, but with suspicion.

Which was just as well.

He pulled his blanket closer to ward off the chill of night. He felt ill, as though the magic of Graydon was growing weary of him and had decided to attack his soul. Or his age and the many sleepless nights were catching up with him. It was difficult to tell.

But he knew one thing that definitely contributed to his fatigue, and that was his worry, which gnawed at him. Because he had never trusted coincidences. Just as he didn't now, the Elders and Crimson Circles of Ravenhold conveniently appearing when no other Crimson Circle remained.

Crimson Circle being the level the Sight was acquired at, which could uncover magical deception.

But of course, he doubted they'd expect an old man and Circle deserter would know how to use the Sight. Kale was not only gifted with the powers of Elihor, but he was also a quick study and had never given up the learning, even long after leaving the halls of Larkhold. He had in fact taken some of it with him, eliciting their ire. With the stolen knowledge, he had taught himself the Sight.

He had practiced it with Tangia, too, in her study, when not reading ancient tomes or discussing magical theory and debating history. Her green eyes, infused with light, would shine in the candlelight as they huddled close, whispering of things forbidden and forgotten. He would see the fear behind those steady eyes when she shared her suspicions of fallen Circle Elders. Before she too had vanished, and he had been powerless to help her.

He looked at the Elders now, their energies wild and infused with darkness and shadows, the very air crackling with the competing strands of magic, fighting for both the wielder and its soul.

Siabala had finally sent the attack that could doom them, and Kale knew the Circle could not stop them alone.

DAYSHON WALKED the length of the camp, greeting warriors and soldiers as he went, sharing a joke or a respectful nod, checking their defenses and trying to get an accurate count of how many fighters and horses they had left. He took reports from each squadron leader, shook their hands, named replacements where necessary, dismissed men who were too broken to continue fighting. But he could only send them to the back of the camp.

He walked that section too, where the Westland and Eastland healers had set up tents. Too many had been wounded in the first few attacks, and men were lying outside as well, exposed to the harsh sun and the bitter nights.

At least it doesn't rain much here.

The camp smelled of death, and the cold wasn't helping. Some of the Westlanders were weaving blankets as quickly as possible, but most of their supplies had been destroyed. A few nearby villagers had brought what they could, but it still wasn't enough. The injured would freeze soon, if they couldn't find a way to keep them warm.

He watched their breath fogging in the frigid air, some

coming quickly, others slowly, some no longer. Greeting the healers, he thanked them for a job well done. He could see the questions in their eyes. Could they have more supplies? When could they leave? Would another attack come?

But they didn't voice the questions, and so he didn't have to pretend he had answers.

He didn't know much of anything, anymore. Their army had seemed useless, winning mostly through magic, or out of luck. None of the attacks that they had faced actually seemed destined for them. Dayshon felt like they were simply in the way of the rest of Graydon and the blood of its people, which Siabala's creatures lusted for.

That's reason enough to stay, Dayshon told himself. Except he wasn't convinced. Massir had been destroyed. He didn't know the extent of the destruction, or if his mother at least lived yet. But he knew he shouldn't count on a hero's welcome when he returned. He should be prepared for the worst, and ready to help his people rebuild their homes and spirits.

I could have done nothing to save them, he told himself over and over again, imagining never having left, greeting the attacking army in Massir, stopping them and protecting his home.

He sighed. Silly boyhood fantasy. He was needed here, and no amount of daydreaming would change that fact.

And he needed a working army.

Jiles followed him closely, a second shadow who understood his need for silence and time to reflect.

Some of their cavalry remained, though less than two hundred horses, and maybe three hundred capable riders. The Westland warriors numbered around the same, and the Southern Coalition troops numbered about eight hundred. He feared that Colonel Orliys would soon take some of his troops to Edoline, to help preserve the seal. He was intent on his belief that stopping the rebirth of Siabala was the only road to success. Even if Dayshon argued that Pack Nacker and his men would reach the small kingdom first and any outcome would be long decided by the time the colonel and his troops would arrive.

Edoline. That was where it had all started for him. When he had met Princess Cassara and asked for her hand in marriage, he had set in motion the events that had brought him here, to this battlefield, away from the one in Massir.

It might have saved my life, too. He allowed himself a slight smile as he thought of his vanished bride. She would not indulge his worries, he was certain, although she would be kind about it.

He looked towards the fallen city, lit by a strange glow in the night which vanished as the sun rose. He needed to get some sleep, if only for a few hours.

He turned around as the camp sprang to life, only to come face to face with Kale Kolder, his dark eyes impenetrable, yet the creases at their corners betraying his worry.

"Do you have a moment, your Highness?"

Dayshon nodded. Sleep would have to wait.

———

THE ADEPTS of Ravenhold gathered in the evening upon Elder Mott's request. They moved some distance from the camp, Westland warriors staying close.

Larkhold's and Stormhold's adepts were still in camp, respecting the request of Graydon's Covenant for a moment of reflection as one. But the gray and black-robed witches had acquiesced with suspicion in their eyes. Shala couldn't blame them. She, too, found the proceedings suspicious. Why wouldn't all three Covenants join?

They formed a giant circle, Elder Mott sitting to the west. The Crimson Circles, who seemed incapable of speech, spread amongst the other ranks. Shala counted thirty-six adepts of Ravenhold remaining.

Thirty-seven if you count that treacherous Crimson Circle Shirina.

Shala wouldn't, until she was certain the rogue witch had survived and would be allowed to remain in the Circle. Still, it was a painfully low number. Almost ten times that number had been part of Shala's Harvest year alone.

She remembered the day of the Harvest, feeling both terrified and proud. She had hated her previous life as a merchant's daughter. If she had stayed on that path, she would have never amounted to more than a merchant's wife. Then the Crimson Circle had come and told her she would become more, and she had believed her. The small ceremonial sum had been paid to her parents and they had let her go, either too afraid or too uncaring to utter a word of protest. She had not taken the adept's hand when she left, simply walking alongside her, admiring her long raven hair, her high cheekbones and dark, determined eyes…she'd wanted to be her, and had been thrilled when her new name began and ended in the same manner.

Shala.

Shirina.

Which had made the betrayal all the more intense when Shirina had told them there would be no more Harvests, and that they could leave if they so desired. It was like her hero had given up on the life she had promised the young Shala, long ago, in a town near Solir.

And then, she had just left. With the adepts dying to protect Graydon, with the historic reuniting of the three Covenants, Shirina had simply vanished into the night, without a word of explanation to anyone.

She imagined the fierce eyes of the Crimson Circle Elite telling her that she didn't need to inform her of any of her plans or passages. Shala swallowed the bitterness in her mouth, wishing Shirina would have trusted her, amongst all the others, and given her the chance to prove herself.

"My children," Elder Mott began speaking. Shala snapped out of her reverie and scolded herself for the childish indulgence.

"We are at a crossroads—at a time when our Covenant is threatened not only by a magic that has turned against us and by the fall of Ravenhold," he paused and looked at each in turn, "but also by our failing numbers. Our Covenant will not survive this day unless our numbers grow. For the survival of Graydon, we must ensure the survival of our Covenant."

He looked at each in turn.

"Which is why we must have a Harvest."

Most of the adepts looked uncomfortable and shifted where they sat. But none voiced Shirina's words. That there would be no further Harvests. That they would be free to leave.

Shala felt terrible for them.

How dare Shirina give them hope, and then allow it to be ripped away? Why was she not here to protect the sproutlings, whose flame of hope was lit and then doused so easily?

Shala fumed but fought to hide it. The Elder continued, oblivious to or uncaring about the worried expressions around him.

"We have uncovered a way to use magic." The excitement and curiosity in the Circle became palpable.

"The Crimson Circles will take you, one by one, and show you how to use it safely. It will only work for our Covenant, I fear, but we can help the other Covenants by keeping them safe until later. The Crimson Circles will also gift you with the Sight, so that you may head out into the world tomorrow morning and begin the Harvest immediately. We have precious little time left."

He had everyone's rapt attention. Shala was disgusted by his words. *Gifted?* That meant implanting the spell into the owner, and not teaching the caster to grow it. It was a dangerous and ridiculous tactic.

Although, she conceded, *these are desperate times.*

But Shala intended to surprise them. She had meant to impress Shirina with her advanced techniques, but she and the Crimson Circle had started on bad footing. All of Shala's efforts to impress her, from leading a Harvest to providing her with a fresh robe, had only led to the sorceress' distrust of her.

This, however, was different. She could win favor from the Elder and the Crimson Circles. All of the countless hours meditating and reading on theory had forced her eyes and her mind to seek deeper answers. She had learned that the Sight could be summoned from within, not dependent on the cursed magic and therefore not dangerous to wield. At least not yet.

Shala practiced now, to impress them later. It was still difficult for her to conjure, not instantaneous like the Crimson Circles, who benefited from years of practice. She was no Crimson Circle and didn't pretend to be, but she *was* a very advanced Orange Circle.

She let her eyes focus differently, taking deep breaths and concentrating on the Elder's aura. His would be easiest to pick up, so much more in tune with the magic of Graydon than anyone else. After a few moments the strands of his magic appeared.

Graydon's magic was a bit wild around him, especially for an Elder, but the magic was different, now.

She allowed herself a slight smile. She could see it fully. Then she saw something else, too. Strands of black were mixed in with the magic. Red, as well, forming a deeper aura around the Elder.

She looked around slowly, careful to hide her surprise and fear. The Crimson Circles shone with the same energy. She focused on Trit. His aura was pure white, restrained as he had not used magic in some time to protect himself. No other sources of magic spoiled his aura.

What were they planning to do to the other adepts?

Shala blinked a few times, the energies remaining the same. Then she allowed her eyes to relax and saw only the adepts, the magic dissipated. But she knew full well they were not what they seemed, and heralded the end of the Covenant, not its rebirth.

"We'll begin with the Orange Circles," Elder Mott said.

Shala felt ill as she stood and followed a Crimson Circle further away, watching Pola and Trit do the same. She wondered what Shirina would have done in the days when she had cared enough for the Circle to fight for its survival.

39

Shirina placed her hand on the stone wall that effectively marked the end of the old city.

"I guess it would make sense that we can't reach Siabala's Rage from here," Cassara said. "I mean, if he was trying to break in using his srocks, obviously there would be no passage to his realm…" Avarielle crossed her arms and the princess stopped at the annoyed look on the warrior's face.

"I can't find a magical seal," Shirina said, turning to face them. "No door."

"This is ridiculous," Avarielle growled. "There must be a way in there. Are we supposed to walk around until we just find somewhere to gain access?" She threw her hands up in disgust. "That could take weeks! We're in a giant fishbowl of a city, underground, with who knows how many other weird magical creatures just begging us to kill them!"

"There are streams of magic heading through the wall," Shirina said, ignoring the warrior's tantrum. "So one assumes it would be safe for us to teleport through."

Shirina looked to Cassara. "How did you know where to reappear, inside the structure?"

Cassara bit her lower lip. "I'm not sure. I just...I needed to save you."

Shirina nodded, having expected as much. The princess was great at protective magic, and not great at attack magic. Entering Siabala would put them in danger, so Cassara would probably have a hard time activating her magic, no matter how much they tried to convince her otherwise. Unless she believed she could save her friends. And going into Siabala's Rage hardly seemed like it would help save them. She'd probably somehow just teleport them all back to Edoline, which would prove rather useless.

"So, what, we can't get in there?" Avarielle said, the warrior looking like she was considering pulling out Graysword and using it on the wall.

Shirina sighed and turned to the warrior. "There is another way." The warrior's sharp eyes immediately connected with hers. "It's not something I'm fond of doing, but I can tap into a memory to teleport." She didn't offer further explanation, but Avarielle narrowed her eyes and studied her.

"What do you mean?" Cassara asked, stepping forward. "You can look into Avarielle's mind and just...bring us there?"

Shirina nodded. Cassara held her breath, the air thick with tension. The sorceress was surprised the warrior even considered it. She must have been even more desperate for revenge than Shirina believed. That did not necessarily bode well, but they were also running out of options.

Moments trickled by with Shirina and Avarielle staring at each other, until finally Avarielle spoke, voice low. "What do you need me to do?"

Shirina tried to keep the surprise out of her voice. She'd expected a lot more resistance, which worried her even more. "I need you to focus on one place in the Rage. Just one area. Focus on all the sights, scents and memories you have of that place. I'll tap into it and teleport us there."

Avarielle's voice was a whisper. "I don't remember a lot, Shirina. I'm not sure how far this place is."

"I can handle it," Shirina said, and almost added, *if you can handle going back there.*

A few moments passed. "Only that memory," Avarielle said. "You'll only see that memory."

Shirina nodded. She didn't have the power to force the Grayloft's mind to open, even if she'd wanted to. She also wasn't sure she could get them all there, if the location proved too distant. But she was convinced Siabala's Rage couldn't be too far. She could handle this.

The warrior nodded, eyes shining and jaw clenched shut.

"Get closer, Cassara," Shirina whispered. "And, no

matter what, don't activate your magic while I'm teleporting us."

Cassara looked like she wanted to comfort the tense warrior but decided against it, standing a breath away from the two women.

"Only that memory," Avarielle repeated.

Shirina gave her a crooked smile. "Believe me, Avarielle. I don't want to be in your head any more than you want me there."

The warrior returned a slight smile, some of her tension easing. But then, clearly coming right back as she focused on the memory. Shirina looked into it, casting her teleportation spell, trying not to cry out at the pain inflicted on her body. Her left arm felt broken a hundred times over, her insides shredded, her entire body on fire.

She gasped, forcing herself to stay with Avarielle in the memory.

It's just memory. Not even mine.

Free me, the warrior's words rang in her ears. Just speaking the words felt like fire, her own white flames surrounding the three women as the teleportation spell triggered. She locked eyes with the warrior, eyes as hard as the stone around them, and gritted her teeth as she brought them to Siabala's Rage.

AVARIELLE'S STOMACH turned as soon as she smelled the sulfur. Shirina's spell vanished, the circular room forming around them, dry blood, *her* blood, on the ground. The ropes that Kryde had cut beneath her feet.

The sorceress tipped slightly as the spell left her drained. Avarielle reached out and held her up, their eyes meeting. Avarielle had shown her an intimate memory. One where she'd been weak. Hurt. Afraid. And then she'd shown her Kryde. She felt raw, and vulnerable, and she hated it.

Shirina met her gaze and did not look at her with terror, or sympathy. Not even understanding. The sorceress didn't care.

And that made Avarielle feel better. She swallowed hard and let go of the sorceress's arm, her staff now stable at her side.

The princess observed them both, and the ground around them, her eyes falling on the ropes. She hadn't seen Avarielle's scars, left behind even after the kealer's spell. Avarielle didn't intend to share.

"Let's go," Avarielle said softly, hand on Graysword. At least she was properly armed this time.

She motioned for her companions to follow her. Silence blanketed the Rage. The last time she had been here, screams had resonated throughout the prison. Siabala had secured those by casting prisoners down shafts, and through torture and death. She had fallen, too. But she'd gotten up again.

"Eli, this place still reeks," Avarielle muttered. The princess put a comforting hand on her arm, though she looked distressingly pale. Avarielle assumed she was thinking of her brother being trapped here.

"Jayden was kept safe by your aunt," Avarielle whispered. "He suffered imprisonment, but not torture."

The princess glanced at her and nodded, absorbing the information.

"And you?" she asked softly.

Avarielle turned away from her and focused on finding her way. She rounded another corner, getting her bearings.

Movement at the end of a hallway sent her leaping back. She glanced at Shirina. The sorceress nodded as she held her staff at the ready.

Avarielle quickly turned the corner, pulled Graysword free and ran low towards where the movement had been. Turning the next corner, to come face to face with an old woman.

Avarielle did not lower her blade.

Especially after spotting the black Circle above the woman's heart.

SHIRINA KEPT her features in check, betraying nothing as she stepped beside Avarielle and nodded respectfully. The warrior hadn't struck her down immediately, but the slightest reason would secure a blow, Shirina was certain.

"Elder Tally, what an unexpected surprise."

The woman nodded back. "I have managed to escape

my cell, but I fear I cannot find my way out."

Shirina examined the old woman closely. She knew Elder Tally, but not very well. Like most Circle Elders, she was aloof and mostly kept to herself. Her mentor Tangia had seemed to think that Tally was a waste of space, and had made cruel jokes at her expense on occasion. That was all Shirina knew of her.

"Elite Shirina, is it now?" she asked, smiling slightly. Shirina nodded. "Tangia's pupil. I remember now. Tangia expects great things of you."

She smiled again. Shirina was surprised—Circle Elders rarely smiled, much less paid compliments. But, then again, Tangia had said she was different.

"Would you like to see the others?" Tally asked suddenly.

"Others?" Avarielle asked before Shirina could.

Tally ignored Avarielle and concentrated on Shirina. *Well, at least she acts like an Elder in that respect.*

"The other adepts. There are a few left, not yet turned into those, those monsters." Her eyes shone with fury. "We're all looking for a way out, before Siabala turns us into his deadly ghosts."

Shirina nodded. The Elder turned around, black cloak swirling around her robes as she began walking down the corridor.

Shirina cast a sideways glance at the warrior, who effectively conveyed a threat. The warrior would follow along to stop Siabala from forming more monsters, but she didn't trust the Elder.

And neither did Shirina.

ELDER TALLY WALKED BACK towards the antechamber where her companions waited. They knew she was coming, of course. They also knew their role consisted of killing the Grayloft and the descendant of Graydon, who grew too powerful for Siabala's liking.

Tally knew that Siabala did not really want to kill the Grayloft. He had conveyed that much in his hesitation. He liked the family, and had hoped they would take his side in the new order. But it was unlikely now, not after Siabala had toyed with her lover.

If he had had a soul, he would have known better, Tally thought as she walked ahead of them, not bothering to look back to see if they still followed her.

But all that would be fixed soon. He would have a soul once more. And he would have the Grayloft still, to win her over. She wielded his magic, after all, and so shared a bond with him. It should be fairly easy to bring her over to his side. Tally would personally see to it, as a gift to her master.

And the Crimson Circle Elite would help. Tangia did not mentor fools, and Shirina would soon be given the chance to become an Elder in the new Circle.

It was the Circle's bidding, and therefore her will.

AVARIELLE FOLLOWED THE BLACK CLOAK, clutching Graysword. Saving adepts was worth it, if for no other reason than to stop Siabala from creating more kealers, which could take down Pack and his people.

And she wanted to trust Shirina. She'd shown her more of herself than anyone else, leaving her raw. The sorceress had seemed willing to let go of the Circle but, with an Elder still around, that would no longer be an option.

Would the sorceress realign with her own? Would she try to solidify her shaky footing to win the Elder's trust?

It would have been easier if the Circle witch hadn't shown up. But she should have expected others to be here. She'd heard their screams, after all. And Siabala wasn't done creating monsters.

Eli's blood, it would always be easier if the Circle didn't show up!

She followed the black and crimson cloaks, staying close to the princess. They entered a large chamber, the walls glowing red. It took Avarielle a second to recognize chanting. Her blade was freed in an instant, focusing on the Elder before her without hesitation. She struck down, but coils of air gripped her arms and legs. She grunted, tried to fight against them, but they crushed her limbs as they tightened, forcing her to the ground. Graysword fell from her grasp with a clang.

She heard the princess swear as she too went down, and Avarielle smiled grimly.

It was nice to know she had an influence on Cassara after all.

SHIRINA WOULDN'T BE able to get a spell out in time, of this she was certain. Her two companions had easily been immobilized. There were no more adepts here, but two other Elders, instead.

Five Elders had been sent to Siabala's Rage at the same time as Tangia, and six still remained in the Circle at the time of its fall. She simply needed to figure out for whom these Elders fought.

Avarielle tried to break free, but even the Grayloft couldn't break the bonds. And Cassara's magic seemed to be warded. Shirina didn't even bother trying to cast a counter spell. These were Elders, after all, not amateurs. They could outspell her any day of the week.

The sorceress examined them. The two other Elders who stood by Tally were slightly younger. Shirina recognized them.

"Elders," she said, cocking her head.

"I swear I'll gut you if you betray us, Shirina!" Avarielle threatened through clenched teeth.

Shirina ignored her, focusing on the new enemies.

"Elder Tangia was sent here," Shirina said, not a question but more of a statement. She was a Crimson Circle Elite, after all, and not expected to play politics with Elders.

"Tangia," Tally practically spit out the name, "was a traitor to the Circle. And so, she paid the price." She narrowed her eyes. "But you were away at the time, hunting the Grayloft. Were you aware of this?"

"I was not." She tightened her grip on the staff, biting back the next words that might otherwise come out. *And if I had, I would probably have helped her regardless.*

"Elite Shirina, a new day is dawning for the Circle," Tally continued, satisfied. "We must find fresh footing in this world in order to be true to ourselves and our own. Will you join us in this cause?"

Shirina turned her head slightly towards the warrior and the princess. "What of these two?"

"The princess, I fear, must be killed. The Grayloft may be gifted to Siabala."

"That doesn't seem like much of a gift," Shirina said, to annoy the warrior and buy herself time.

Avarielle took the bait.

"Let me loose and I'll show you a gift, you cowardly Circle witch!"

Elder Tally opened her palm towards the warrior. Avarielle grunted as the bonds tightened.

"Careful not to kill her," one of the other Elders said.

"She'll live," Tally said. "Siabala already tested her, and she's survived much worse."

Weak. They were all weak, and Shirina hated them for it. Their magic was all over the place, filled with light, darkness, red like this Rage...they had sold their souls to Siabala. And doomed Ravenhold in the process.

"Was it worth it?" Shirina whispered. "Selling your soul. Was it worth it?" Elder Tally smiled a cold smile, her eyes turning to steel.

"It was. And all those who wish to remain in the Circle will also know that glory. Even the adepts you've kindly gathered for us in the West."

Shirina's head snapped up. "What are you planning to do with them?"

"Harvest them for this new Circle, of course. One soul at a time."

Shirina glanced at Avarielle, who struggled to remain conscious as the bonds cut the air from her lungs. Cassara looked back at her, her face determined, but Shirina could see that the bonds still warded the princess' magic.

I could never cast quickly enough to stop them. The Elders were faster casters.

But even the fastest casters needed time to set their spell.

Shirina took a deep breath and pulled herself to her full height. "You should have never betrayed Ravenhold."

Tally flashed her teeth. "So, you've made your decision."

Shirina nodded and, before the Elder could begin chanting, Shirina stepped forward, the end of her staff striking the sorceress across the face, sending her reeling back as blood flew from her mouth. Shirina turned to the second Elder, who had also begun casting, and struck him with the bottom of her staff. Screaming, she turned and raised her staff, striking the last Elder on the top of the head before she could utter the last line of her attack spell.

The Elder's skull collapsed and she lay dead, her energies freed. The other two were rising and casting again. Shirina was about to turn and strike when magic slammed into her, sending her flying back. She would have hit the stone wall hard, had Avarielle not caught her.

The warrior dropped the sorceress to the ground and whipped out a long knife, plunging it deep within the nearest Elder's chest.

Elder Tally hissed and vanished in a teleportation spell.

Cassara helped Shirina up. "Are you all right?" she asked, her eyes wide as she focused on the eyes of the sorceress. Shirina nodded, her stomach turning at the strong stench of iron mixing with sulfur.

Avarielle walked up as she cleaned her hunting knife and picked up Graysword.

"One of them got away," she said, "and hopefully that won't come back to haunt us. We should move fast. Siabala is next."

Cassara cast one more look at Shirina before following the warrior.

Shirina stood with her head lowered for a moment before following them, the staff feeling foreign in her hand as she clutched it, still caught in the sensation of the skull crushing under the blow. She now understood that the Circle would never have started or participated in any war, had they killed with more intimate means than magic.

4 0

Altessa stood in the front courtyard of Edoline. Once a beautiful orchard, it was now a graveyard of tree stumps, trampled grass and broken branches. The villagers and farmers of Edoline had pulled through that day, erecting a wall with the trunks and a ditch with what little time daylight provided.

She glanced at the beams of moonlight exposing the holes in the wall, soldiers positioning themselves around its perimeter with bows and arrows. She wished she could convince herself they stood a chance.

It would be a quick battle for the enemy, Altessa knew. She hoped the villagers would be safe, at least, hidden in the basement of her home.

Altessa took a deep breath as she peered into the descending darkness. She had never seen Massir, but knew it was huge and well-fortified. That it had fallen so easily did not bode well for Edoline.

At least they would not be taken by surprise as Massir had been.

Captain Emran stood nearby, fidgeting with his weapons. She doubted he had ever seen combat, and guessed he was more used to giving a good show. But still, he had stayed with his men. She suspected it was not out of loyalty to her or Edoline, but rather out of a fear of disobeying Delora's orders.

Cowards, Altessa couldn't help but think. She wanted all of them to leave. She would protect Edoline all by herself, if necessary. But still they came, armored and ready for battle, to defend a kingdom they held no allegiance to.

She hoped they would at least give them a fighting chance.

She pulled out the amulet and ran a long finger along its smooth edges. The gold disk and silver crescent seemed to shine more deeply, not with the light of the moon, but from a light that came from within.

It's ready for battle as well, she thought.

She looked up, darkness coating the land and, in the distance, the trees of Kosel seemed to be breathing with movement. She clutched her amulet and prepared to draw its magic, not even willing to consider that it might fail her.

DUSK FELL, smoothing the harsh edges of the land with its shadows. The brown shades of the trees were replaced by gray ones, the dying grass more black than green.

Jayden kicked a rock as he walked, having abandoned the guards, who were all fast asleep. The Eloms would be ready soon, and they would continue their journey to Edoline. He could see Kosel clearly now, its pine guards standing tall. They would reach Edoline shortly after sunset, faster than anticipated.

He kicked the rock again and watched it roll. He would see Altessa soon, could visit the grave of his father, and he would rule as king. Jayden took a deep breath and watched it mist and vanish as he exhaled.

Once more, he kicked the rock, but this time it stopped abruptly. Jayden squinted in the darkness. An Elom had stepped on it, or rather a Pack member, wearing some of the armor of Elihor.

"Are we ready?"

The Elom didn't answer. Not that it could with words, but it could at least nod.

"I'll head back to camp," Jayden said tentatively. The half-Elom was breathing hard, its dirty armor heaving up and down in a broken tempo.

Jayden was turning around just as the Pack soldier leapt towards him. Shocked, he stood there, rooted in place, staring at the sharp teeth angling for his neck, the claws extending to reach him…

Someone knocked into him, throwing him to the

ground. There was a brief struggle and the sound of something snapping.

The second Pack member stood up, towering over its slain companion. Jayden recognized Pack Nacker.

"Thank you," he whispered. Pack nodded and pointed for him to head back to camp. Jayden did so immediately, not needing any convincing.

He didn't look back, sensing Pack's eyes burrowing into his back until well after he was out of sight.

Shala was not ready to let this dark magic touch her as well. She was trapped, she knew, by the Crimson Circle, and her friends would be lost too if they allowed the magic to change them.

She looked around her wildly. What could she do? The Crimson Circle would not allow her to escape, and that would end her time in the Circle, she was certain. She wasn't ready to give up her dreams just yet.

Stay or go. Shirina had told her she could stay or go. She had offered them a choice. Shala had seen the faces of the adepts when they had been offered that choice. So many wanted to go, some of her friends included. She had wanted to rob them of choice, just as these Crimson Circles were about to do to her friends.

No.

She couldn't let that happen. A weakened Circle was

one thing, but one ruled by Siabala was unacceptable. She needed to stop them.

She needed to stand for what she believed in, and die if necessary. She smiled.

It's what Shirina would do.

***

TREVON SKIRTED THE DUNES, a silent killer. He could see the other Westland warriors gliding along the sands towards the Crimson Circles. They'd waited all day for them to separate. To be vulnerable.

Breck had been clear. Kill them before they could utter a word.

Only the Crimson Circles, though.

Trevon pulled his bow free and targeted the heart of the witch. He was about to fire when the Orange Circle behind her jumped onto her back, screaming like a mad woman as she pulled on the Crimson Circle's hair.

Swearing, he dropped his bow, pulled his long knife free and ran towards the fight.

***

ELDER MOTT HEARD the commotion and kept his cool, signaling for the rest of the adepts to remain seated. He scouted with his magic. Five of the Crimson Circles were dead, and one was incapacitated.

They had failed. Siabala would find no more followers in Ravenhold. Except perhaps in these sproutlings.

"Let us lower our heads and concentrate on keeping our thoughts heavy," the Elder instructed them. They did as they were told, concentrating on the few teachings of magic they knew.

He allowed himself a smile as he invoked Siabala's magic.

KALE LINGERED in the shadows with Dayshon and some Westland warriors. The Crimson Circles were probably dead by now, leaving only the deadliest viper. Kale feared the sproutlings would be injured.

Grasky, Keeper of the Lisal Gardens, suddenly stepped out of the shadows and walked joyfully towards the Circle. Kale wished he could warn him, but to do so would only seal all of their fates.

"Elder Mott!" Grasky exclaimed, spreading his arms apart in greeting, as though he intended to pick the old man up in a bear hug.

"Keeper Grasky," the Elder politely responded. His voice dripped with venom. "We are in a private ritual," he added.

Grasky's arms lowered and he looked around at the youth, his eyes growing wide. "Oh, I understand," he said, holding a finger to his lips as the youth eyed him suspiciously. They were too young to know the Keeper of the Lisal Gardens yet.

"I have a matter of importance to bring to your attention, however." Grasky regained his composure. "From a mutual friend."

Mott's eyes narrowed with suspicion. Grasky whispered loudly enough for the hidden warriors to hear.

"My family has been the Keepers of the biggest Circle outpost in most of recorded history, Elder Mott. We are well-connected."

Dayshon shot Kale a look, and the old man pointed towards the back. Grasky was leading him away from the youth, giving them the chance to kill the Elder without endangering the sproutlings.

Dayshon nodded and motioned for his men to follow them into the darkness.

Kale watched the Elder go. He doubted the man was fool enough to fall for Grasky's act.

SHALA PULLED on the Crimson Circle's hair, bit her hand, elbowed her in the face, and did whatever was necessary to stop her from casting a spell. She had to knock her out somehow. She used to brawl with her brothers, but she had never managed to knock one of them out.

The two tumbled down the dune, Shala blinded by sand as she struggled to get her bearings. The Crimson Circle was already standing, so Shala just threw herself full force into her legs, knocking her down again, eliciting a cascade of swearing.

So she is human after all. She sat on her back and held her down, pushing her face into the sand, but the Crimson Circle was older and stronger. She pushed Shala off.

Shala stumbled to the side, landing on some rocks. She bit back her screams as the furious Elite began chanting. Shala grabbed a rock and threw herself at Crimson Circle again, but this time she was ready, slamming a wind spell into the disheveled Orange Circle. Shala crashed into the sand. She couldn't tell what was up or down anymore, her feet tumbling over her head, her arms flying everywhere, her face scratched by rocks and her robes filled with sand.

When the world finally stopped spinning, she stayed down for a just a moment before pushing herself back up again. She would *not* go down this easily!

But the Elite had disappeared from her sight. Glancing wildly around, she spotted a flash of white on the ground. The Crimson Circle lay motionless, a knife protruding from her chest.

A Westland warrior walked towards her, his hair red and wild in the moonlight.

She seemed to recall his name was Trevon.

He grinned at her. "You can throw a punch, girl, but you need to learn where to throw it!"

She stood straighter and dusted her robes. She was a mess and dared not think what the Circle would think. She caught herself. *Did it matter?*

"My friends!" she exclaimed, looking around her to see any sign of them.

"The rest of the Crimson Circles should be dead too. They'll be fine." Shala took a deep breath and offered him a smile, feeling like a weight had been lifted. She took one step before the alarms rang below.

"Let's go," Trevon said as he started running down the hill. She followed as best she could, stumbling on her robes in very un-Circle like behavior.

But she didn't care. Battle was afoot, and she didn't intend to stay out of it, even if her magic was of no use to her. The Circle was still worth fighting for, and Shala had no intention of giving it up.

The blood of the Elder had barely dried on Avarielle's tunic when Cassara cried out in warning and all three threw themselves to the side as a srock flew down the middle of the corridor.

It turned around and Cassara fired an arrow, piercing its eye, sending it careening to the ground.

"Been practicing?" Avarielle grinned at her as they stood back up and began running.

"Fear does wonders for my aim."

The walls around them flared to life, Siabala unleashing his magic. Cassara summoned her defenses and protected them from the onslaught, the red and black flames hungrily licking her white magic.

"Cassara," Shirina said as she looked at the princess. "Be careful, you're starting to open your floodgates too much. You'll drown in all of this magic." Cassara nodded and managed to close them a bit, or at least as much as she could while still maintaining her spell. How was she supposed to fight if she couldn't use her magic to its full potential?

"Can we keep moving?" Avarielle asked.

"Stay close, but yes."

The warrior nodded and the three moved slowly down the corridor, the flames turning blue around them as Siabala heightened his spell.

Avarielle swore as they reached a dead end.

"I can't navigate in this! We can't see where we're going, and it's getting hot!"

Cassara was drenched in sweat, her hair plastered to the back of her neck. She could stop the flames from burning them and keep some of the heat at bay, but they would still be cooked at this rate.

I guess we finally got Siabala's attention, Cassara thought as she concentrated on weaving her spell while not letting too much magic into her.

"Cassara, I'm going to cast a counter spell," Shirina said. "Siabala isn't here, so I should be able to stop this spell. But don't lower your shields until I say so."

Cassara nodded and the sorceress closed her eyes, put both hands on her staff and began chanting. The flames turned back to red and black and the heat began to lessen.

Shirina continued chanting, increasing her tempo, never stopping for breath. The flames withdrew completely and Shirina fell silent. Cassara waited, maintaining her spell.

"You can let go," Shirina whispered. Coughs wracked her body as she held herself up with her staff.

Cassara could see blood spatters on the ground. She moved towards the sorceress as she dropped her spell. Avarielle stopped her. Cassara turned to protest, but the warrior simply shook her head.

"She'll tell us if she needs us."

Cassara wasn't convinced. She looked Avarielle straight in the eye.

"Would you?" She looked down towards the warrior's belly, showing her she knew about the growing child. Cassara wondered how she could have missed it. Avarielle's face was slightly swollen, her body rounder under her armor. Still, she hid it well.

Avarielle's eyes narrowed. "If you're about to suggest that I stay behind…" Cassara held up a hand to quiet her.

"Do what you will. But if you need us, tell us."

Avarielle examined her for a moment before nodding. Cassara was relieved until it dawned on her that, between Shirina's sickness and Avarielle's pregnancy, she was currently the most battle-ready amongst them.

The thought terrified her more than Siabala's attacks.

SHIRINA LEANED HEAVILY on the staff, her throat raw and her breath ragged. The foul magic was making its way into her lungs. The staff shielded her from getting additional infections, but it couldn't stop the current dark magic from doing further damage.

She coughed again and forced herself to keep up. They couldn't afford to slow down.

Avarielle brought them to a large elaborate stone staircase leading to two large broken doors.

"These lead to Stormhold," she said as she started climbing two stairs at a time, Graysword before her as she scouted ahead. Cassara remained close to the sorceress.

Stormhold. The central keep, which Shirina had not even believed still existed. She would never have dreamed of one day setting foot inside its walls. Avarielle came back and motioned to them that the way was clear. Shirina examined the doors. They had been broken in from the side of Stormhold, not from Siabala's Rage. It looked like Siabala had received Circle assistance in escaping his realm.

She walked through the large doors and her breath was taken away by what she saw. Huge marble columns jutted up to the dark, high arched ceiling. Shadowed depictions ran the length of them, carefully chiseled within the soft stone. No magic illuminated their path. Shirina guessed that Siabala had drained the keep of its powers already. Another large stone staircase brought them higher still, tall windows lining each side of the room. It was as though the keep had been built for giants.

Large enough to be impressive even to creatures like Siabala and Samala.

The three moved quietly, Avarielle continuing to scout ahead.

"Seems deserted," she whispered. The moonlight illuminated the Bloody Mountains, peaks jutting and falling like silent sentinels. They couldn't see the land beyond that.

"We might as well stop to eat. This might be the last chance we get," the princess suggested, sitting on a windowsill and pulling out what remained of their rations. The warrior looked ready to protest, but then seemed to change her mind, keeping an eye out as she ate.

The sorceress looked at the food, knowing it would be impossible for her to swallow anything solid. It would just serve to re-open the scabs in her throat.

She settled for some water and sat down, wondering if Stormhold still retained its knowledge, and whether it could be hers to capture.

For Ravenhold.

Swallowing the cold water mixed with her blood, Shirina doubted she would live to see to her Covenant's revival. And if Elder Tally had spoken truth, she doubted any adepts would remain to train, anyhow.

"What's the best way to fight Siabala?" Avarielle whispered as they resumed walking the length of Stormhold, all silent stone. The warrior's eyes darted around the room, her hand on Graysword's pommel, her steps relaxed but deliberate.

"We need to keep the two magics separated when we find him. That should impede him from using his magic.

I can cast a ward to separate the magic near him from the endless well of the world, limiting Siabala's powers, and then you need to purify what remains within my ward."

"Sounds great," the warrior mumbled. "What does any of that even mean?"

"Cassara, you can filter the pure magic of Graydon by summoning what's near Siabala. I'll make sure no other magic gets in by casting a ward around us. Avarielle, you should be able to filter Elihor's magic, though how might be tricky."

"What do you mean?" Cassara asked. The warrior set her jaw. Shirina was not about to answer for her. But the princess was quick to figure out the unspoken words.

"The baby," she said flatly. "The baby can filter the magic. That's why your energy has changed. The baby is from Elihor."

"A descendant of Elihor, actually," Avarielle whispered.

It took a few moments for Cassara to fully grasp the warrior's meaning.

"If filtering Graydon's magic is dangerous for me, won't it be worse for the child?" She couldn't believe this was their plan. "How will we even get it to filter the magic?"

Avarielle looked annoyed. "We'll figure it out when we get there. There's going to be a way, that's why she's here." She pointed at Shirina, who kept her steady gaze on Cassara.

"That's your plan?" the princess asked incredulously.

"All of it? We came all of this way to face an enemy with a plan dependent on figuring things out as we go along?"

"Cassara, we're going to find a way. We have everything we need to succeed. We're just going to have to trust each other."

Cassara looked from the warrior's crossed arms to the sorceress' straight back. They seemed terrifyingly accepting. Then it dawned on her.

"You're not planning on coming back, are you?"

Their silence was answer enough.

43

The alarms resonated throughout the camp, Eastland trumpets and Westland shouts flaring to life. Breck stood at the front of the camp, watching the large many-legged monsters move towards them. *Like a cross between spiders, centipedes and blades.*

He briefly wondered if they would simply pass through the West on their way to the cities of the East.

He grunted. That would be a comfort if he didn't respect Prince Dayshon and Princess Cassara so much. What a bother. Things had been easier before, when the East had simply been the enemy. He couldn't risk it either way. To the north and south, his people's settlements could also be in danger.

"Eloms!" He heard the shout. More monsters unleashed into this night. Siabala was either growing in power, or he'd grown weary of their little game. Maybe he was trying to save his Circle Elder before he, too, got himself killed. Breck shouted orders to his men, to get them mobilized to fight back the monsters while Dayshon dealt with the Circle Elder.

At least Breck still had the Circle. He could always find reason to hate the Circle, which was small comfort in a quickly changing world.

THE ELDER FOLLOWED the Keeper of Lisal, whom he had always believed to be a useless man. *Let him think that he was saving the sproutlings,* thought Mott. *They're Circle property, just as he is. As all of Graydon is.*

Mott could feel the soldiers tracking them, including the heir of Rashim, one of his targets. He had hoped to first turn the sproutlings and then order them to deal the heir the death blow, proving their loyalty to the Circle and Siabala. He would find another way, he supposed. Taking down the prince had to be his priority. If the Keeper of Lisal wanted to oblige, so be it.

Of course, Siabala might expect him to prove his loyalty as well. Mott had been dragged into allegiance with the monster mostly through Delora's treachery. Too entangled to escape safely, he had chosen the safest route to power. Then the blasted Delora had been killed, leaving him as Siabala's next puppet.

He would find a way to make the best of that, as well. He always found a way.

Grasky stopped and turned, deciding he was far enough from the adepts. Mott looked towards the Bloody Mountains and smiled, letting the spell dissipate from his robes, willing Siabala's mark to return to his garments. Grasky turned pale as Mott's snow-white robes of Ravenhold reverted to their blood-soaked color.

"What…" the Keeper asked as the soldiers appeared, swords drawn, arrows at the ready.

"The new Covenant, Grasky," Elder Mott said. The soldiers let their arrows fly, but with a single motion of his hand, the Elder stopped them in mid-air. The Keeper of the Lisal Gardens looked wide-eyed from the dangling shafts to the red-robed man. "The Circle will not be requiring your services any further."

He summoned his power and let it engulf the air around him.

He was stopping arrows in mid-air!

Dayshon drew his sword and was about to attack when the air turned pure white, like a star shining right in front of them. He covered his eyes as a pair of strong arms threw him to the ground, something heavy landing on top of him as the world burst into flames.

Dayshon's boots cooked on his feet and he screamed as his exposed skin was singed, crackling until numb. Stars exploded before his eyes, mixing with the magical fires that surrounded them. He retched and fought to remain conscious, darkness collapsing his vision.

The light vanished and he was left gasping for breath. He opened his eyes and it took a few moments before they re-adjusted to the darkness. He felt lightheaded and numb.

The alarms sounded again, followed by the sounds of battle.

What was happening? Were they under attack elsewhere as well? Dayshon needed all of his strength to push the unmoving lump from on top of him. The man rolled off and landed beside him.

Jiles. The captain was dead, eyes wide and unblinking. *Jiles!*

He needed to move. He couldn't let him die in vain, protecting him. He had to kill the Elder Mott now. Grabbing his sword, he tried to stand, but fell back screaming. His feet had taken the brunt of the attack, the skin black, cracked and peeling. He thought some of his toes were missing, but couldn't tell in the misshapen lumps.

The smell of his own burnt flesh turned his stomach.

"You should be pleased," Elder Mott said as he walked towards him. "Your army has proved enough of an annoyance to draw the attention of Siabala himself. It's with his regards that I kill you today."

The Elder opened his palm towards Dayshon, staying out of the sword's reach.

Not like this!

He gritted his teeth and pushed himself up, screaming again as he launched himself forward, sword extended. The Elder easily countered the move and threw him sideways. Dayshon writhed. He had never felt such pain, and wished someone would just cut off his feet.

He grabbed his sword again and tried to catch his breath, to push himself up, to at least face death standing, but pain impeded every movement, and every action took forever to execute.

With one deep breath he attempted to clear his mind, and struck out, only to collapse on his knees.

"Tsk," the Elder said, a pause in his spell. "A king dying on his knees."

Dayshon gritted his teeth. "Better than an Elder living on his."

Mott's face twisted with anger and Dayshon struck up with his blade, reaching forward, the blade making contact. Dayshon caught himself on all fours and wretched, then pushed himself back to his knees. He could not stand for the death blow, perhaps, but he intended to face it nonetheless.

Blood dribbled down the Elder's side where his blade had struck. A painful but hardly deadly blow.

He resumed chanting, not even acknowledging Dayshon. The heir of Rashim kept his eyes fixed on the man's, red light growing around the irises as the spell progressed.

Dayshon forced himself to keep looking at those eyes, waiting for the spell to be set. The Elder paused as his eyes grew wider, and he stopped chanting. He slowly fell to his knees before Dayshon, and for a moment, the prince thought the Elder meant to embrace him as he died. But then he noticed a darker red stain appearing on the red robes, and a blade swung down, cutting his head clear off as he collapsed to the side, some of his blood splattering the kneeling prince.

Trevon pulled his sword free as he stepped over the Elder, a look of disgust on his features.

"I'm starting to make a habit of this," he said, cleaning his blade on the Circle's robe. "Trick is you have to make sure to kill them in one shot."

Dayshon found his breath again and looked up to the warrior, unable to form words of thanks.

"You're welcome," Trevon said with a grin, then looked at the prince with concern. "Maybe we'll get you to a healer, your Highness." The use of his title made Dayshon wonder how badly hurt he looked, but before he could process his own pain, the sounds of battle reached him. He turned sideways to see it. The giant silver-legged creatures from a few nights ago were back. Except this time, their forces had no magic with which to protect themselves.

"Trevon, we have to get down there and help."

"I'll go get a healer, wait here," Trevon said, ignoring Dayshon's order.

"Trevon! Get me down there! Our men will be slaughtered!"

"I'll be back," the Westlander said as he took off down the slope. Dayshon turned on his side, white lights exploding before his eyes as he dragged himself forward, towards the battlefield, knowing full well he would not reach them in time to make a difference.

44

Cassara glanced sideways at her companions. Shirina and Avarielle were both quiet and introspective.

She forced herself to stop looking at them and concentrate on what lay ahead. She would probably do well to get ready for battle herself. Siabala had sent no further attacks, which Shirina had surmised might mean Stormhold still benefited from some of its magical wards.

A small comfort.

Cassara cast another glance at Avarielle and sighed in annoyance. *It was her choice,* she repeated over and over again.

It had not bothered Avarielle terribly to know she was heading into battle pregnant. There were no guarantees a world would still exist for her to raise a child in, so fighting seemed a logical alternative, especially since she was the only one who could wield Graysword. And they needed all the magic they could get.

What bothered Cassara now was that the plan to destroy Siabala apparently meant using the child. And Avarielle seemed not to care.

It's just a child! Just a baby. No say, no hope, no knowledge of what was happening. They should protect children, not use them as sacrificial victims to powerful beings.

She felt sick to her stomach. But what choice did they have? How else could they stop Siabala if not by using the heir of Elihor? Even if that heir hadn't even been born yet?

And none of us will probably live to bring the child back to safety.

Avarielle would never become a mother. Shirina would never revive the Circle. And Cassara would never see Edoline again.

This was it. Her last moments in this land, before fighting a battle they could only win by sacrificing a child…

She stopped walking.

"What now?" Avarielle asked, annoyed.

Cassara looked down, unable to face the warrior as she spoke, her voice a whisper in the giant hall. "I don't want to live in a world that sacrifices children for the greater good. Isn't that how the Circle justified its Harvests?"

She forced herself to look up. Avarielle didn't meet her eyes, and Shirina looked off into the distance.

Cassara pleaded. "Is there no other way to defeat Siabala?"

Shirina sighed. "None that I know of, Cassara. And unless we split the magic again, a lot of people will die. Not just adepts, but anyone with magical affinity."

Cassara looked up at her. "Can I do it myself? Can I just take in the light and break it from the darkness?"

Shirina pondered for a moment. "I don't know. It might work. Unless Elihor's magic also needs to be filtered. Siabala may be able just to use one strand to his advantage."

Cassara nodded. "It doesn't matter. We'll try that first."

"If you fail, Cassara," Shirina warned, "we'll have lost our chance to filter both magics at once."

The princess could hear the sorceress' unspoken words: *Because you'll be dead.*

Cassara nodded. "Maybe. But we have no guarantee the baby will be able to filter the magic, either."

Avarielle and Shirina exchanged a quick glance.

"Now listen," Cassara said, stepping forward. "I don't care if you both think it's unnecessary to live to make Siabala's end worthwhile. We're all getting out of here if we can." She turned to the warrior. Cassara's heart was racing and she knew her skin was flushed, but she didn't care. She needed to get her point across. She lowered her voice as she faced Avarielle. "Getting yourself killed won't salve the pain of his death, Avarielle, and neither will killing the child."

She turned to Shirina to avoid seeing the pain and fury

on the warrior's face. "And your death will absolve you of making difficult decisions, yes, but don't you want to take a chance at making them, Shirina? The Circle can live or die, it doesn't matter, but you at least can live. Maybe start something new."

She forced a shaky breath into her lungs. "I'm terrified that you've both decided the outcome of this battle before it's even begun. Siabala probably has his ideas on how this is going to end, too, so maybe we should keep an open mind."

She met both of their gazes. Avarielle looked ready to hit her and Shirina looked pensive.

"I want to go back home, that's all," Cassara whispered, no longer certain how to reach her friends. "I want all of us to go back home. If I'm better at protective magic, then let me do what I do best. Let me protect you. Let me protect *all* of us." She let the moments of silence slide by awkwardly.

Avarielle took a deep breath and grinned weakly. "I don't care if you figure out a way to get us all out of here alive, Cassara. I'm still not naming this child after you."

Cassara smiled and the three resumed walking. This time, Cassara didn't feel suffocated by the fear of death.

"Up there," Avarielle whispered to her two companions. One last staircase led to the top of the Keep. Siabala waited there, she was certain. He was bound to the mountains, and by killing them, by killing Cassara, he was destroying the chances of the magic ever being separated again.

He would not be able to resist the lust for her blood. The battle call that throbbed in Avarielle's veins was the same as the one that throbbed in his veins, shared by generations of oaths sealed by spilled blood.

He wanted her dead, too, she could sense it. She had angered him, displeased him by refusing his gift. Kryde's dead red eyes, his soul shattered by Siabala's flames, flashed in her mind. She held the vision. Revenge would soothe the pain of his loss.

Now that they exited Stormhold's wards, she could sense Siabala's magic again. The link they shared was strong and undeniable.

And she would sever it with the key that had forged it: Graysword. She clutched her blade, the magic coursing through her body and attacking the child. Shirina stepped forward and placed her hand on the warrior's belly. Avarielle needed all of her self-control not to hit her. Soon the magic of Graysword no longer stung.

"It will buy him time," the sorceress whispered. Avarielle choked on the word.

"Him?"

Shirina nodded and said nothing of the tears filling Avarielle's eyes. The warrior took a deep breath and buried the emotions deep within her, both the love for the child and for his father.

She would grieve later. If she was granted the time.

She couldn't let the speed of her feet or her hands be hampered by the heaviness of her heart.

Not now, as she was finally about to claim her revenge.

They stepped out onto the roof, a gentle snow drifting down. The clouds only partly covered the moon, providing them with some light. Just enough to see they were alone.

"Where is he?" Cassara asked as she looked at the mountaintops surrounding them.

"He'll come soon enough," Avarielle said, slowing her heartbeat and deepening her breath, Graysword pulsing with eagerness.

She could finally wash Kryde's blood from her blade by bathing it in Siabala's.

45

The attack on Edoline came just as a light snow began to fall. They almost missed the first line, the darkness was so thick. At first, it looked like all of Kosel moved towards them, a quickly approaching monster. Then one of the guards caught sight of moving red in the field, bathed in the moonlight. He screamed and started firing arrows, the monsters gaining ground fast.

The incoming army fire a volley of powerful arrows, thick-shafted projectiles embedding deeply in the wall and wounding those directly behind it. Some archers fell dead. Others scrambled to take their place.

Altessa's heart accelerated but she was careful to hide it. Captain Emran looked ready to pass out.

Useless! She missed the old captain of the guards more than ever. Klar had mounted a defense against Eloms, with no warning or time to prepare. It had failed, but still, he had faced death standing.

"All archers to the wall!" Altessa screamed. More men scrambled forward, firing arrow after arrow. She could hear grunting. The enemy was closing in. She peered through the orchard wall and saw them in the moonlight, running at breakneck speed, some felled by arrows, most rising again.

"Aim for their necks or heads!" she called, noticing the weakness in their armor. The archers tried, or so Altessa assumed. But their aim proved poor and the creatures were too fast.

Altessa clutched the amulet. She could feel it grow warm and warmer still.

It began to glow.

The first creature jumped into the ditch and the archers managed to kill it, but it had diverted too many of the archers' attention from the tide of incoming monsters. More and more began to clear the open field and the ditch proved to be only a slight inconvenience, the creatures jumping across or falling in and leaping back out of it. When they had mounted the defenses, they had not anticipated that the monsters would be such powerful jumpers.

The first few creatures reached the wall, grabbing men through the holes with their long claws, spearing them and pulling them through, sprays of blood darkening the fresh snow fall.

Altessa took a step back. Captain Emran seemed to snap out of it. "Spears! Spear them through!"

The men scrambled to obey the captain's orders, but it

was too late. The creatures were pulling the wall apart, tearing it to pieces, the trees tumbling into the ditch, dragging down most of the archers and some of the monsters.

The rest jumped across the now-filled ditch.

Altessa held the amulet up with a trembling hand. She could smell the monsters, and they were coming so fast…

Please protect Edoline.

She opened the floodgates of magic, gasping as the powers of Graydon greedily entered the amulet and burst back out, guided by Altessa's desire to save her home.

The sky above Edoline exploded in brilliant white light.

"WHAT'S THAT?" Cassara asked as light covered the Eastland horizon. She already knew the answer, feeling it as deeply as she had felt Avarielle's need for the magic while she carried the amulet.

Someone was using the amulet! Cassara wondered if the air of Graydon was being sucked towards the East, before realizing she was witnessing a furious rush of power unlike anything she had ever seen. The magic was wild and torrential, now freed from Samala's anchor. And Elihor's magic answered the call of the amulet as well, dancing with the strands of light, united but still separate entities. Whoever wielded her amulet would be pummeled by an onslaught of magic.

Altessa!

"That's Edoline!" she gasped. "That's my sister, my amulet!"

"Incoming!" Avarielle screamed as she threw herself into Cassara, knocking the princess down. The roof shook, and for a moment Cassara believed the whole keep would collapse.

"Focus, Cassara," Avarielle said as she stood at the ready.

The blood drained from the princess' face. Red eyes glowed in the darkness, showing the towering giant that was Siabala, his gray skin shining even in shadows, his long red hair like flames around his head. He towered over them all, as tall as his brothers had been, yet seeming more human. He smiled with sharp, white teeth.

Avarielle stepped in front of her, and Siabala focused on her.

"You've come back." He looked pleased. "I'd invite you to join me, but I know you're too stubborn. I'll just enjoy killing you."

He held up his hand and a wind slammed into the three of them, forcing them to clutch the stones of the roof to avoid being blown off. Cassara clung to the stone with frozen fingers and waited for the wind to stop, trying desperately to catch her breath as the world swirled around them.

She tried not to think of Edoline.

THE WIND WAS AN UNEXPECTED BLESSING, the silver legs lifted out from underneath the monsters, knocking them to their sides and giving the troops momentary respite. Breck knew a losing battle when he saw one, and this was a spectacularly losing battle.

"Pull back!" he screamed as the Eastland forces struggled to keep the Eloms under control. But his screams were ripped away by the wind.

Even if he could figure out how to retreat from this battleground, he knew he wouldn't do it. Not with the Eastlanders and Circle adepts as witnesses.

He might be an old Westland fool, but he still had his pride.

ALTESSA WAS LOST. The magic ripped through her and broke her over and over again, robbing her of her identity, her emotions, her hopes and fears. Her dreams vanished one by one, like stars exploding in the sky.

She couldn't recall her name. The light was everywhere and everything and it coated her and soothed her and kept her warm.

She let it, knowing no better, remembering no time before this one.

The magic fires abated only when her strength ran out and she crumpled to the floor. Blood rushed in her ears.

She could see her hand unfurl before her eyes, the amulet resting in it, the metal dull as snow slowly covered it. She stared at the snow, unable to summon enough warmth to melt it.

She could no longer move her fingers and her vision blurred, yet she could still make out the field of burned and burning corpses, some friends, some foes.

And in the distance, monsters still coming for Edoline and the final seal.

46

The moment the wind died down, Avarielle stood and leapt, screaming as she brought Graysword down on Siabala's head. He raised a giant hand and struck her, tossing her aside. She clung to Graysword as she landed in a crouch, ready to pounce again. Shirina stepped up as she finished chanting her first spell of warding.

He growled and turned to her, but the warrior moved with more speed than the sorceress had ever seen, slicing Siabala's thigh before shifting away and barely avoiding a blow.

Shirina completed her spell, unfurling it on the monster before her. The spell of warding fell on him and took effect, his magic severed from him, at least temporarily. Now, she needed to trap the magic here, too. To form a bubble around Siabala.

Avarielle attacked again, this time managing to inflict a

cut on Siabala's arm. He growled, and Avarielle lunged out of his reach to avoid two great, angry fists. Cassara stood frozen nearby, wide-eyed and terrified.

Just one more spell...

Shirina began casting the second ward, so that Cassara could split the magic here and hopefully render Siabala mortal enough to kill.

This will work! She pushed all of her hopes into her magic, not caring if that wasn't the Circle's way. All of Graydon and Elihor, both their broken lands, were at stake. She pushed the words out of her lips as quickly as possible while clearly uttering them, willing her strength into each syllable, hands clutching her staff like it was her last remaining lifeline.

Just as she was about to cast the ward, Siabala leapt and landed right in front of her, grabbing her by the robe and tossing her like a rag doll, clear over the roof edge. Shirina tumbled into the darkness below, chanting as she fell.

***

THE LIGHT HAD VANISHED up ahead, which was a blessing for Pack Nacker and his men. Time was running out for them. It had to end now.

He could see the monsters running towards the manor, a great field of them dead and burned. And whatever powers the daughter of Edoline had managed to unleash, it was now spent.

Pack leapt to the front, reached the manor and practically threw the boy off. He wanted to be away from him. He needed to be away from the scent of blood, could barely resist its allure. The guards were also dropped and the Pack ran to meet the incoming monsters, pitting Siabala's creations against each other.

He met the first beast and tore it to shreds, his troops meeting the others. There were many, but he and his men had been lusting for blood, and this would do. Pack wished he could scream in victory, but settled for the next kill.

At the end of it all, he had managed to remain human long enough to die remembering that his own name was Pack Nacker.

***

KALE KOLDER STOOD at the sidelines, watching the beasts rise again. The troops could handle the Eloms well enough, but the tall creatures had too many legs and too much speed to be easily downed. They speared the men through before they could even hope to target the creatures' heads.

He watched, wishing he could help. He heard men scream, could smell rot and death, and wept at the sight of the fall of Graydon, imagining the fall of Elihor had been similar.

He sensed someone beside him. It was an Orange Circle from Graydon's Covenant, who looked like she'd taken a sand bath. *Shala*. He remembered her name. Her eyes shone with determination.

"I saw what you did," she said.

He looked at her, waiting for her to continue. "With the adepts a few days ago. You pulled some of Elihor's magic away from them. You bought them time to cast their spells."

Kale looked intently at her. "I bought them time. But I couldn't save them."

She held her chin up and curled her fists.

"Do you think you could do it again?"

CASSARA SUMMONED HER MAGIC, more out of terror than a deliberate attack. She reached out wildly, towards Shirina, Avarielle, Siabala…she sent her fires madly around them, trying to fulfill multiple desires.

The warrior jumped up and engaged Siabala again, her strength and speed almost matching the giant creature's. Avarielle screamed. Siabala bellowed.

Save Shirina. Protect Avarielle. Kill Siabala.

The magic responded in strength. Suddenly, Cassara was filled with power and knowledge, reaching out for the falling sorceress first. She could see Shirina tumble headfirst, a flurry of crimson and white fabric and raven hair, the sorceress' eyes closed as she continued chanting, either uncaring or unafraid of death. Cassara reached out to her and snatched her in a teleportation spell. Shirina appeared back on the rooftop just as her chanting completed, her eyes snapping back open. The sky surrounding them turned bright white. Cassara drew her fires back in.

"Now, Cassara!" Shirina hissed.

Cassara closed her eyes, placed her hands where her amulet had once been, and summoned all of the magic of Graydon trapped in the warded space.

JAYDEN RAN FOR THE MANOR. He wasn't sure what to look for, or what to do, but he would do what was necessary to stop Siabala and save Edoline. He ran over bodies, ignoring the putrid smell, the destroyed courtyard, the fires still flickering on the cut trees.

He ran through the first cedar hedge, into the Courtyard of Travelers, jumped through the second hedge and stopped in the Courtyard of Stars. Carsyn and Kaden were close behind, Gragor nowhere to be seen.

The Courtyard of Stars had been the main feature of this manor, created to admire the constellations above. Jayden's blood pounded in his ears and all he could hear was his ragged breath. The roots of his hair stood on end as he gazed up at the main porthole, showing the constellation of the Lost Lovers. The stars that were said to symbolize Graydon and Elihor, who had sealed Siabala and erected the Wall of Loss.

The young king of Edoline walked through the fine

snow, kicking it up as he went, until he found the stone which indicated where to stand to perfectly view the constellation.

He fell to his knees and brushed away the snow until he could make out the finer details of the stone, from Elihor's face to Graydon's eyes. The two were in an embrace, although separated by fog or light. *Or a Wall.* He ignored his frozen fingers as he cleared away the surrounding snow. The stone was firmly placed within the ground, and he doubted he could lift it. It was as though it had always been here, a part of this land, of the earth where Graydon was said to have thrown himself into the sea.

The easternmost point of the land that now bore his name. That would be Edoline. The same place where a seal had been forged.

The snow cleared, Jayden stood up and looked at the uncovered stone, as though truly seeing it for the first time.

Carsyn swore as he looked down.

The round stone very much resembled a seal.

47

Shala stood atop a dune and looked down at the field. From her vantage point, she could see the energies of the beasts perfectly. She knew how to strike them and spare the men, if they moved out of the path of the falling corpses.

Beside her stood her friends. They were ready to follow her lead, faces drawn and determined, taking her word on what the Sight revealed to her.

She took a deep breath, the snow fresh and gathering on her orange cloak. She imagined a crimson cloak on her shoulders instead, having mastered the Sight already at her level. She let herself believe it was crimson for a moment before the wind billowed the orange fabric before her.

She sighed. She didn't want to leave the Circle, and she never would. She just wished she could have proved herself before dying.

Old man Kolder stood beside them. She saw that he had begun to withdraw the magic of his ancestor. The time for daydreams was over.

The air suddenly became lighter, easier to breathe. Shala smiled as she drew in pure, white magic and unleashed it onto the great beasts below.

It wasn't the Circle's bidding, but it was her will.

CASSARA COULD SEE the magic dancing around her in a frenzy, trapped within Shirina's wards. So very much, yet so little. Compared to the vastness of Graydon, this was nothing. She was certain she could pull all of it within herself.

She summoned all of Graydon's power, ripping apart the threads of shadow to claim the light and leave the darkness writhing in its wake. Graydon's magic snaked around and within her, warming her entire body. A vortex of magic danced around her as Elihor's magic tried to reclaim some of it, but Cassara forced Graydon's powers to remain within her, out of reach. The dark strands lashed at her, catching garment and hair in its outburst.

Cassara felt vast and endless, a fertile ground of possibilities and hope, warm and suffocated by all of the power she held.

She closed her eyes and counted, intent on keeping it all within her until someone told her to release it, or death claimed her.

CASSARA'S FACE was pale and drawn and she was surrounded by a halo of light, her blond hair billowing about her even though no wind remained. Her right hand clutched her chest, her other was wide open at her side, every finger flexed.

Shirina could see that she had drawn all of Graydon's magic back inside her. If she released it, the shadows would form again, and Siabala would regain some of his powers.

They needed to end it now.

Siabala screamed and ran towards the princess, shards of rocks flying as he crushed them. His eyes glowed red now, but he could summon no magic, the shadows beyond her wards out of his reach. But he could still crush them all with physical strength alone.

Shirina stepped in front of Cassara. She went to summon a protective spell to stop Siabala's attack, before realizing that Cassara had drawn all of the magic within her. She was as powerless as Siabala.

Shirina held up her staff and planted her feet firmly, with no intention of moving,

AVARIELLE'S BATTLE scream rang in the night. The time of her revenge had come.

Graysword glowed red and black, the energies from

the child mixing with hers, becoming one instead of fighting each other. Graysword wanted it to end, too. For the curse to stop. For the chance to be free.

Free of blood.

She screamed and jumped, slashing down and planting the blade through Siabala, this time summoning all of her powers.

He stumbled before he reached Shirina. Avarielle pulled her blade free and he turned, collapsing to his knees.

"Most impressive," he said. She gritted her teeth, wanting to end it, now. Before he took anything else from her. To avenge Kryde. But also to reclaim her life, and the life of her son.

She screamed again and swung the blade down, pulsating with raw power, cutting through Siabala's neck like butter.

His head toppled, falling to the ground in a pool of his own black blood. He remained on his knees for a moment before crashing onto the stones, Avarielle sidestepping him to avoid being crushed.

She caught her breath and waited, each passing moment crushing her with disappointment as she looked at Siabala's corpse.

"Is that it?" Avarielle asked.

She felt no different. No release. No change in Graysword.

No freedom from this curse.

Shirina watched Siabala die, and caught the warrior's look of disappointment and disgust. She touched Cassara lightly on the arm. "You can let go now, Cassara."

The princess released the magic, her head tilting forward as though a great burden had been removed from her shoulders. The light shone so brightly that Shirina had to look away. The strands of Graydon's magic bounced around in the sorceress' wards, cut off from the rest of the world. Shirina watched the light and reached out to touch it.

Maybe the magic will be safe now. Maybe I can let go of this staff.

She watched as the brilliant light danced with the velvety darkness, a soft sensual mix before they blended to become shadows once more.

Shadows that would kill her and what remained of the Circle.

"I'm so sorry, Shirina," Cassara whispered beside her.

Shirina lowered her wards and watched the shadows of magic dance, harbingers of the Circle's demise and her own failure.

48

Siabala felt his powers torn from his body, deserting him after he had just reconnected with them. No. Not deserting. *Stolen.* Ripped away from him, leaving him less than he could be, less than he had ever been.

All because of Graydon's cursed descendant.

He screamed and charged her, intent on ripping off her head, the blond hair whipping around her. So intent was he on his goal that he didn't see the Grayloft coming.

A stupid mistake.

Then he felt the scalding touch of Graysword, like an angry dog biting its master. A bite powerful enough to down his still very mortal shell. He saw his own body collapse to its knees, admired the strength that emanated from it, even in death, and felt the power of it as it crashed on the ground.

His mind ceased working slowly as well, cut off from the life-giving organs of his torso. Siabala did not fear death.

His body was not his soul. His soul was more, so much more than his body could ever be. And without having to worry about his mortal shell, perhaps he could become even more.

***

GRAGOR FOUND Altessa lying amidst burnt corpses, covered by a fine layer of snow. He knelt beside her.

"My queen," he said with trembling lips.

She was pale and he doubted she still drew breath. He was too late.

He had failed to garner help for her when she had needed it. He had failed in his mission, caught up by the needs of the rest of the world and forgetting his first goal.

Altessa. She had shown him kindness when there had been none in this world.

She had asked for little in return, only help.

He held her as the sounds of battle changed. He looked back. The Pack was losing, almost none of them remaining. The red-armored creatures were breaking free, slick in dark blood as they clawed the ground and threw themselves forward.

Towards the manor and Altessa.

"I'll protect you," he whispered, unsheathing his sword. He would stand guard for a final time over his queen.

JAYDEN STOOD BY THE SEAL, watching the snow accumulate on it, flexing his fingers nervously. Kaden watched him, wishing he could offer his king sound advice. They couldn't move the seal, that much was evident. It was so tightly ensnared by the ground it proved as immovable as a mountain.

"We have to protect it," Jayden said.

"We can't, Jayden. They're too powerful." Kaden could hear the monsters running towards them. Where was Gragor? It didn't matter now, they needed to protect Jayden.

"If we don't protect the seal, then all is lost." The young king stomped his feet down decisively. "We *will* protect this seal."

"They're coming," Carsyn said, and Kaden looked up. They were jumping the first hedge, red armor glowing in the growing daylight.

"Behind us, young king," Kaden ordered, standing before Jayden. He nodded to Carsyn. The old guard nodded back, eyes coming into sharp focus.

"No lies about what an honor it was serving with you," Carsyn mumbled. "It was a pain and made me lose sleep."

Kaden chuckled. The first monster jumped over the hedge and the guards summoned the green fires of the Circle.

Don't let them fail now! He could feel the magic slither within him, unnatural and forced, like snake venom coursing through his thin veins. Still, he grabbed it, forced it to flow, and flung it into the incoming beasts, Carsyn joining in.

He felt young again, as young as he had been the first time he had used the magic, after Circle Elders had forced it within him.

The light of their magic flickered all around them, amplified by the white carpet of snow. He remembered first gaining the magic, and then using it on the enemy during the Westland Wars. Except the enemy had turned out to be innocents, and he had yet to understand that the price of power would be a lifetime of regret.

The beasts were strong, but the guards were determined to win. Theirs was a magic that defied that of Graydon and Elihor, sparing them the disease of shadows.

They sent the fires ripping through the beasts, annihilating the hedge separating the Courtyard of Stars and the Courtyard of Travelers, the bush crackling as it burned, the cedar overpowering the stench of burnt flesh.

But the beasts kept coming, until Kaden could no longer count how many he had slain. Carsyn fell backwards, towards Jayden, and Kaden stepped before them to keep them safe.

"Jayden," Kaden said calmly. "Pull Carsyn back." Kaden saw Carsyn's feet sliding away, the old, withered guard light enough for young Jayden to drag. Kaden was careful to keep the green flames burning, but he backed away too, checking his footing with each step so as not to slip on the fresh snow.

Must protect Jayden. If nothing else mattered, it was to give Edoline a fighting chance. He didn't know about Graydon, whether or not it would find a way to survive. But he knew a losing battle when he fought in one, and he didn't intend to die fighting for a world that had abandoned him.

He moved back, so intent on protecting his king as the monsters stormed ever closer, that he realized too late he'd gone past the seal. And the monsters crouched over it, just on the edge of the dying green flames.

"They're getting the seal!" Jayden screamed, running toward it. Kaden turned and grabbed the young prince, dropping his magical guards at the same time as he pulled him back, away from the fading green fires, the monsters and the seal.

He gasped as he forced Jayden back, trying to summon his magic back, but knowing he had exhausted his body's limited reserves.

He quickly realized that it didn't matter. The beasts weren't paying attention to them, raising clawed hands and striking down with all of their considerable strength. The seal broke.

A spray of magic flew from it, killing the nearby monsters and sending Kaden flying backwards as he tried to protect Jayden from the shards of rock. The magic escaped like a chain, long kept taut, breaking and snapping back towards its other extremity.

Kaden watched it fly towards the Bloody Mountains,

and was glad King Alexavier had not lived to see his kingdom so destroyed.

4 9

The chain whipped towards them, made of magic so potent it forced the sorceress, the warrior and the princess to their knees. Lightning coursed through the air, making the roots of their hair stand on end, their eyes aching from the light.

"The third seal!" Shirina screamed over the symphony of the heavens. The skies broke open and pulsated with red light. She looked back at her companions and added, "It's Siabala."

"I thought we just killed him!" Avarielle screamed.

"His body, not his soul." The sorceress looked up, thunder booming against Stormhold, the keep glowing with the red light.

"What do we do?" Cassara asked over the din.

Shirina looked to the sky, the shadows of magic all drawn within it. He was absorbing the very magic of Graydon and Elihor, all of it, undoubtedly to become even more powerful and deny magic and life to the inhabitants below.

Red lightning struck the few still separate strands of light and darkness, fusing then into deep shadows. He was taking all of the magic. And he would unleash it onto their world.

"We have to separate the magic," Shirina said. "We have to do the same thing, just on a grander scale."

Cassara clenched her jaw and nodded, blue eyes fierce with determination. "Tell me what to do."

Shirina wished there was another way. One that involved only her, and not the young princess of Edoline. *No.* The future queen of Rashim.

Her friend.

"You have to go in there and tear the magic apart." She looked towards the red glow.

"In the sky?"

"It's not the sky. It's an illusion. I mean, there's something else up there. Siabala's soul was trapped there long ago. Maybe that was the purpose of the Wall of Loss. To keep the magics separate and to serve as a pillar for Siabala. I don't know, Cassara, but can't you see he's up there?"

The sorceress looked with the princess, at all of the magic gathering there. She couldn't do what needed to be done from here anymore. And she would need to do it to all of the magic, not just that which had been contained here. It was suicide on a grand scale.

"If we don't stop Siabala now," Shirina said, hoping the

princess heard her over the whipping winds, "he'll grow too strong for us to defeat. We must destroy his soul before it is fully reformed."

"How will you come back?" Avarielle asked, standing by Cassara protectively.

"You were willing to sacrifice yourself," Cassara answered.

"But not you!" Avarielle shouted back. Cassara locked eyes with Shirina, and the sorceress kept her gaze locked with hers, though she wanted to close her eyes.

"There must be another way!" Avarielle screamed. "We can't just sacrifice you!"

Cassara smiled at her. "Thank you for giving me the courage to fight."

And with those words she vanished in a flash of light, casting a teleportation spell as easily as she would open a door.

"Where did she go?" Avarielle asked, looking up at the red light in the sky.

"Avarielle," Shirina hissed. The warrior turned around, Graysword unsheathed. Monsters poured out of the keep, scrambling up the stairs toward them. Jaws slack, dragging limbs, eyes glossed over, gray robes with double circles above their hearts.

"The adepts of Stormhold," Shirina said, clutching her staff as she summoned her fires.

Avarielle stood back, disgusted, when a srock landed right beside her. She uttered a curse of surprise and struck out as the beast hit her in the stomach. Bones snapped as she was thrown back like a rag doll.

Shirina unleashed her flames and struck the creature hard, burning off its wings as she sent it plummeting over the edge of the keep.

"Are you all right?" Shirina cried as she cast more fires into the adepts of Stormhold. They tumbled back, robes ablaze, knocking the next wave back down the stairs. The choke point of the stairs would prove their only advantage in this battle.

When the warrior failed to answer, Shirina turned around and knelt beside her. Avarielle was on both knees, clutching her midsection.

"Is he all right?" she asked.

Shirina placed her hand on Avarielle's back and let a healing spell infuse her.

"You took more damage than he did," she said gently, pouring healing spells into the Grayloft, relieved that her immunity to Graydon's magic did not include healing spells. Fractured bones never properly healed were tended too as she saw to her newly fractured ribs. Her arm had been terribly injured recently, multiple fractures barely healed along the bone. A lifetime of battles had not been kind to the warrior, nor had her time in Siabala's Rage, and Shirina repaired what she could with what little time she had.

"If you made more friends than enemies, you wouldn't be such a mess," Shirina mumbled.

"You're one to talk, staff girl," Avarielle replied, the

words weakened by her forced breath. The warrior gave a slight chuckle, and the sorceress allowed herself a smile. She stood up and offered her hand to the warrior. Avarielle hesitated for a moment but then took it, the two clasping hands and locking eyes for a few moments before letting go. The sorceress clutched her staff, the warrior her sword, as they stood side by side.

Shirina could hear the scraping of adepts coming back up the steps. She looked up at the sky, where shadows still gathered.

CASSARA FLOATED IN THE SKY. She didn't think she was fully herself anymore, but a spirit of the girl she had once been, playing music in Edoline, dreaming of nothing more than to continue doing so. The Traveler's Song rang all around her, music from a time she longed for more than ever. She wanted to play her flute. Where was it? She reached into her bag, ethereal and corporeal all at once, and grasped the comforting wood of the flute.

The shadows stroked her skin, snapping her back to herself. What was she doing? She needed to stop Siabala, before the shadows reformed his soul. She could see a faint outline of him far away. If he was reborn now, they would never stop him.

She brought both of her hands to her chest and closed her eyes.

Graydon, Samala, whoever's magic I now wield, please help

me gather it all within myself and keep it safe and filtered, away from Siabala.

She uttered the words over and over again as she took in the magic, strand after strand, breaking it from the dark magic, leaving clouds of darkness behind. She took the magic in, as much as she believed possible, and then she uttered the words again, and took in more. And more.

Until she didn't even know who she was anymore, and why she even lived. Gathering the magic within her was all that mattered.

———

"HOW IS SHE DOING?" Avarielle asked, wincing as she shifted Graysword. Shirina had done what she could for the warrior. She hoped it would be enough for the upcoming battle.

Shirina threw some flames into the next wave of adepts, trying to ignore the trembling of her hands.

She looked up. Cassara's presence was obvious. Like a lighthouse on a dark ocean, she glowed with the intensity of a thousand fires. But Shirina could see that the magic couldn't all be contained. Cassara would absorb some, and then it would escape, only to reform with the shadows immediately.

And the princess only grew weaker.

"Not well," Shirina said. "She can't do it, Avarielle. Not alone."

"What does she need?" Avarielle asked, looking at the

sorceress. Shirina simply stared at her and didn't answer. The warrior already knew.

In order to truly separate the magic, they needed someone to absorb the darkness as well.

"Take it...I mean him. Take him," Avarielle said, looking to the top of the stairway, where more adepts appeared. Annoyed, Shirina threw a wide blanket of fire on them.

"Take him?" Shirina asked, knowing full well what the warrior meant.

"He's not that old," Avarielle ignored the question. "Is he even viable?"

Shirina nodded. "He's very strong, and with a few spells, his breathing will be healthy, but…"

Avarielle faced the sorceress. "Shirina, there is nothing left for us unless we stop Siabala, and that means no future for this child either. Take him and bring him to Cassara." She clutched Graysword and added in a whisper, "make sure he gets a shot at life."

Shirina nodded. Avarielle angrily wiped some tears away. "What do you need me to do?" she barked.

"Just lie down. I can teleport the child out. It'll be the fastest means, and I know his location with the recent healing spell I cast." Shirina hesitated. "It will feel exactly like what it is, Avarielle. Like someone is ripping out a piece of you."

Avarielle lay down and nodded. She could hear more adepts coming up the stairs. They seemed only empty husks, devoid of powers. But their numbers were great enough to overwhelm them, given the chance.

"Eli, your kind is annoying!" Avarielle said as she cast a quick glance at the red sky. The adepts were moving faster. The sorceress knelt by her and Avarielle locked eyes with Shirina.

"Can you do it while I'm fighting?"

"I might hurt you more," Shirina said honestly, knowing full well the adepts would reach them before she could finish her spell.

Avarielle's eyes blazed as she pushed herself up. "Do what you have to do," she said, "and so will I." She jumped up and screamed, Graysword freed from its scabbard and easily downing two adepts.

"Take him out now," Avarielle said through gritted teeth, the warrior determined to hold her ground while asking Shirina to rip a piece out of her.

Shirina hesitated and stood up, watching the graceful movements of Avarielle as she poured all of her grief into slaying the next monster. The sorceress relented, wishing she could come up with a better plan.

"Don't use your magic," she said. "It'll interfere with my spell."

Avarielle looked at Shirina as though she were insane, but still the warrior jumped back and sheathed Graysword, pulling out two long knives instead. Where she hid all those weapons, the sorceress couldn't even begin to guess.

The warrior moved back in and attacked swiftly,

having to strike the adepts several times before ending them. She would lose ground faster, but was still intent on keeping them off the sorceress while she chanted her magic to life. The adepts moved slowly, as though their limbs were weighed down by death, but enough crowded Avarielle to prove dangerous.

Shirina began to weave her spell, hoping she would prove precise enough not to kill Avarielle as well.

She finally had her chance to kill her, and found that she now lacked the desire to do so.

AVARIELLE MOVED QUICKLY, trying to ignore the warm tingling sensation spreading across her abdomen. She concentrated on the enemy instead and on not getting her head cleaved in. The adepts were little more than rotting corpses, but from the few hits she had received, she knew they possessed inhuman strength.

Shirina chanted in the back, Avarielle trying to ignore the growing sensation. And the fact that she'd given her permission to rip the child from her body.

She struck down another monster as the pain intensified, cutting off her breath as she stumbled, fighting to retain her footing and avoid a blow.

"Just take him out!" Avarielle screamed, the agony spreading down her legs and up her back, even her eyeballs throbbing. She could barely breathe and struck out wildly, almost blinded by the pain.

"Now! Take him out now!"

She would need Graysword. Blood washed up her throat and she spat it out.

Shirina was completing her spell, and could easily leave Avarielle for dead.

Bloody stupid way to die! Agony ripped like fire through her belly.

She buckled and fell to her knees, failing to avoid a blow that sent her reeling onto her back.

NOW! she screamed in her mind as she fought to grab a hold of Graysword, spitting blood as she pushed herself back up. One of her knives had vanished. She kicked out and knocked an adept down, slicing its throat before it hit the ground.

"Shirina!" She screamed as her body exploded in pain, blood rushing out of her mouth.

She spat twice, and the pain lessened. She could see somewhat, though her heart was all that she could hear.

The child was gone. She knew it as surely as she knew that if she didn't move, she would die.

Ignoring the wound within her and the empty sound of her single heartbeat, Avarielle jumped up and pulled Graysword free, summoning her fires as she waited for the first cries of her son, wishing she could see his face, wishing Kryde was here to watch her back.

SHIRINA LOWERED the blood-covered sack to the ground and opened it, coaxing air into the boy, casting a slight spell to encourage his breath. His blue lips parted and he cried out.

Graysword's magical fires danced around Avarielle, but she had lost a lot of ground, and the adepts were surrounding her and moving past her towards where the sorceress knelt.

Shirina wrapped the child in her crimson cloak and, ignoring the biting cold, she began to summon her fires.

She was tired and slow. She opened her eyes to finish her spell, jumping as an adept stood directly in front of her. Shirina struck out with her staff, knocking the adept down, only to have it reach up again and grab Shirina's staff.

The sorceress pulled back, trying to break free, but its grip was deadly. Another adept joined the first, its long brown hair still dangling from the half-removed scalp.

The adepts pulled on the staff. Shirina fought to keep it, holding the child close to her body with one arm. If she lost her staff, she would lose her connection to Graydon. It was the only way she could get the child to Cassara and fight against Siabala.

Shirina flushed with anger, realizing she couldn't fight them alone. She screamed over the sounds of the crying child: "Avarielle!"

The warrior responded immediately, the magical fires moving closer to the sorceress, hacking down the line of adepts. But the adept facing Shirina kept holding the staff, looking up at the sorceress. The Crimson Circle thought she saw intelligence flicker for a moment before the eyes grew blank again.

The adept twisted her arm at an unnatural angle and then struck down over her own leg. The staff shattered in two and Shirina felt as though her own bone had been broken. She screamed and fell to the ground, Graysword's fires dancing above her.

Stunned, Shirina stared at the two halves of the staff. She put the child down near her and tried to reforge it as Graysword flashed again and again, Avarielle grunting from the effort.

It was useless. The staff of Graydon was broken, and no power she possessed would make it whole again.

She had lost her magic.

CASSARA CRIED. She could feel the tears streaming from her eyes, tears of magic and light, mixing immediately with the darkness. Shadows surrounded her, and before her Siabala's frame continued forming, his features now visible.

He observed her as his voice grumbled.

"Your ancestor couldn't kill me. Neither can you. You are the ones who must die. You are the scourge of my land."

She looked back in his eyes and continued crying, grief

unlike any other gripping her soul. For Siabala's brothers, for her land, for Avarielle's unborn child.

She cried and the heavens cried with her.

Satisfied the creatures were stopped for now even though she could hear more shuffling downstairs, Avarielle turned back to Shirina. The sorceress knelt on the ground, cradling the two halves of the staff.

But it was her screaming child that drew her attention.

She picked him up gently, cradling his head in her hand as she kept him swaddled in Shirina's cloak.

He was so small. She hoped she hadn't done wrong, couldn't believe she had ever wanted him gone.

His eyes were closed and would probably remain that way for quite some time. She wondered if he would have her eyes or Kryde's. She hoped for Kryde's.

The skies rumbled and the snowflakes turned to small balls of light, drifting on the winds around them.

"What are those?" Avarielle asked as she looked at them and stood, holding the child close. He was so very small, and she held him gently, afraid her callused hands, covered in blood, would break him.

"The light," Shirina said, finally looking up from her broken staff. "Cassara is losing the battle."

Avarielle looked down and swallowed hard. She looked at the broken staff and whispered, "Can you still get him to her?"

Shirina pulled at the leather strap that ensured she would not lose the staff. She tugged on it and broke it off, letting it fall to be buried in the snow of light. Her skin kept the impression of the binding, blistered and raw from its long wear.

"I can," Shirina said. Avarielle looked at her and knew the teleportation spell would be the last spell she would ever cast.

Avarielle nodded and gazed at her son, too young to open his eyes.

"Cassara will bring him back," Shirina said, her voice lacking its usual bite.

"I know." The princess would give her own life before the life of the child, of that Avarielle was certain.

Still, handing the child over to the sorceress felt like cutting her own heart strings.

"Shirina," Avarielle whispered, looking the sorceress in the eye. "Thank you."

The sorceress deadpanned. "Don't worry, Avarielle. I don't expect you to name him after me."

Avarielle gave a short laugh. "That's good. I don't think Blight-of-my-Existence is a good name."

The sorceress gave a slight smile and looked down gently at the child she now held. Avarielle placed her hand on the sorceress' arm and squeezed, lending her what strength Shirina was willing to accept. The sorceress met her eyes, nodded once, and began to chant. Avarielle swallowed hard and stepped back, not breaking eyes with the sorceress as she vanished within a soft halo of light, her song haunting the air after her departure.

They were gone. She'd given Shirina her son, and she'd left, to die by magic.

Avarielle looked up towards the red sky, where her son would soon fight his first battle, wishing she could fight it in his stead.

But this was not her battle. She unsheathed Graysword, the blade warm and comforting in her hand, and turned to face the next wave of adepts as they arrived at the top of the stairs.

"Eli's blood, I've had enough of all of you adepts!" Avarielle said as she struck down the next monster, and the next, losing herself in the waves of death while waiting for life to return to her.

The shadows crept into her throat, then her chest, her legs, her arms, her mind...they tangled within her, squeezing veins and blocking airflow.

She ignored them, keeping the child close, concentrating on keeping him safe.

She didn't matter anymore. Crimson Circle Elite Shirina. Marguerite Monlie. No part of her, no incarnation of her name mattered anymore. There was no more Circle, no more land, no more family and no more home.

Except for the one she could give this child.

She spotted Siabala, the beast almost fully formed, creating a new body from the shadow magics which had forged his soul. Shadows lashed against the skies, and Siabala's eyes were open, staring directly at the light. Shirina headed for the light. For Cassara. The princess was more ethereal than physical now, her hair turned to light, her blue eyes open and shining.

Shirina approached her, certain that the princess was losing. The magic formed so many shadows around her that even with the child, she would still lose.

They were doing something wrong.

Shirina stayed in the realm of teleportation a moment longer, analyzing the predicament, her mind focused and clear as she made peace with her death.

Maybe Cassara wasn't going about it the right way. Maybe she needed to shepherd the magic, and not cage it.

Negotiate with it and not force it. The magics were born from the souls of two powerful beings, Siabala's brothers. They were strong, independent, and would hate being trapped. Cassara needed to win them over.

Shirina allowed herself a slight smile. The princess was good at negotiations.

"Cassara," she called, as ethereal as the princess. "Cassara, I bring you Avarielle's child. Release the light, Cassara. Release it and encourage it to remain separate." Tears streamed down Cassara's face and continued to fall to the world as a rain of light. "You're a princess, don't you know how to negotiate?"

Cassara focused on Shirina, as though truly seeing her now.

"Well?" Shirina asked. "Can you negotiate this, or can't you?"

Cassara smiled, blinked, and then began unleashing the magic. Her eyes grew less clouded. Siabala hollered.

He was coming to life again, the magic of Graydon quickly reuniting with that of Elihor. The shadow that would become Siabala feasted on the shadow magic.

As they would feast on her, shortly.

Shirina ended her teleportation spell and appeared before the princess, handing her the child. Without hesitation, just as Cassara gently took the child, the shadows of magic bore into Shirina and consumed her.

The sorceress longed for the light.

***

Cassara cradled the child in her arms. He was so small. Dirty. And wrinkly. And she loved him right away, wanting to keep him safe. To protect his mother, too. And Shirina.

She looked back to Shirina, the sorceress' eyes accepting and unafraid as shadows engulfed her.

"Shirina!" Cassara screamed, the sound repeated mockingly by Siabala's almost fully formed soul. The child began crying and screaming, the sound echoed by the surrounding magic.

The strands of magic frayed at the sound. Cassara stared at the magic and stopped trying to comfort the child. He cried louder and louder, Elihor's magic separating momentarily from Graydon's at every wail.

The magic was responding to his needs!

She cradled him and watched the magic break. She

needed to force Graydon's magic to stop wanting to bond. But how? She wasn't about to start crying like a child.

Herd the magic. Shirina had told her to herd it. Cassara reached into her bag and pulled out her flute. She looked at the poorly oiled wood, the flute painstakingly carved with her own two hands and the guidance of her mother. Except for the pattern. She had never been able to choose a design for her flute, complaining instead that she wanted a finer instrument.

She remembered her mother's words. Cassara had wanted to play the harp, at first. *A flute is a simple instrument. Good enough for a shepherd, good enough for a princess.*

She formed a basket of light and put the child down in it before her, the child crying more intensely now that he no longer felt her warmth.

"Soon you'll have reason to rejoice," she whispered to him, bringing the flute to her lips. She took a deep breath and played the first note of the Traveler's Song.

The music bounced playfully in the sky around her, Graydon's magic dancing around it, answering the call of Samala's Song of Awakening as it broke free of Elihor, who danced to the tune of someone else.

Cassara played and played, losing herself in the music, the child's cries becoming timed with the cascade of music.

AVARIELLE WAS GROWING TIRED. Only fear and worry fed her limbs as she hacked another adept. She had no way off this roof, no means of escape, and no greater magic to plow through them. Their bodies were stacking up and still they kept coming, their stench and her own loss of blood making Avarielle dizzy.

Graysword flashed once again, the snow of light ending. Dark red blood covered the fresh snow. She knew that a lot of the blood was hers, but couldn't afford to examine her wounds. Her body was numb and frozen, her movements slow as she struck the next adept. She missed the warm sands of her home. Blood still splashed up in her throat, due to whatever damage the sorceress had inflicted when she'd ripped out her child.

But, for once, Avarielle didn't blame the sorceress. They had all made choices that had led them here. She took a step back to risk looking up. The red glow was dissipating.

She swore she could hear her child cry, and the sweet notes of Cassara's flute dancing in the air above.

Avarielle's heart hammered. She wished she could dance, but settled for cutting down the next adept instead.

DAYSHON CHEERED as the monsters were felled by Circle magic, the warriors shouting from the battlefield as they destroyed the remaining Eloms. Trevon stood up and looked at the sky, the red glow in the distance growing.

"Do you hear that?" he asked.

Dayshon strained to see, ignoring the healer's handling of his feet, the salves potent and efficient at cutting the pain of his burnt flesh.

Then he heard it. From the sky a distant flute sounded, so soft it could be mistaken for a summer's breeze. But he knew it to be his wife's, and he feared it was little more than their funeral dirge.

KALE KNELT by the Orange Circles, feeling useless. He had managed to buy them some time, but they now lay dying, having destroyed the creatures by forfeiting their own lives.

He cradled Shala in his arms. She looked peaceful, and it hurt him even more. She was so young, too young to lie dying in an old man's arms. He should be the one passing away quietly here, not her.

The wind shifted around him and he looked up. He could breathe again. Not just take in air, but truly *breathe.* Like a great weight had been lifted from his chest. Like he was back home, in Elihor, infused solely by her magic.

He looked up and allowed his eyes to really see the world and focus on the magic, invoking the Sight. Dancing above him lazily were both Graydon's and Elihor's magics, and none of the smothering shadows.

He looked down.

Shala's throat was clearing, the magic of Graydon surrounding its child, keeping its adept safe.

She opened her eyes, her light so bright Kale's eyes teared up. The Covenant of Graydon would live for another day.

———

THE CREATURES HAD VANISHED the second the seal had broken. The guards and Jayden had remained silent in the darkness as the snow accumulated around them.

The sky sometimes danced red, at other times it wept light. The three of them stood motionless in the Courtyard of the Stars, unable to tear their eyes away from the symphony of the sky. Jayden wanted to look for Altessa, but he already knew she was dead. Aside from them, he doubted anyone else in the manor still lived.

Kaden grunted beside him, and Jayden drew in his breath and held it captive as the two old guards fell to their knees, clutching their chests.

Don't leave me too! He was frozen by fear and grief as they gasped, their labored breaths misting upwards.

"Don't leave me," he managed to whisper. Kaden stopped moving for a moment, green mist joining his breath and then vanishing into the heavens. The same happened to Carsyn, before he fell over on his side, unmoving.

Kaden looked over at him quickly.

"Any excuse for a nap," he grumbled as he stood back up.

"Are you all right?" Jayden asked, ashamed he had frozen, yet so relieved that the guards still lived that he didn't care.

Kaden looked pensive. "Our magic is gone. Whatever the Circle had done to the magic of Graydon to inject it in us, it was purified."

Jayden's pulse accelerated. "What if more monsters come?"

Kaden placed a hand on the young king's shoulder. Carsyn began to rise while mumbling. "I think our battle is over, at least for now."

He looked up, snowflakes falling from the dark well that was the sky, save for far on the Westland horizon, which seemed stained with blood.

Jayden spoke to no one in particular as he looked up. "Cassara said she'd come back."

Neither Kaden nor Carsyn answered.

51

Shirina was lost, a child of light made of shadows. She was wrapped in the magic, warm and comfortable, like a child in the womb. But not her mother's, rather Ravenhold's.

She envisioned everything she could have done to change the course of the Circle's history. Not out of a desire to, but rather out of a deep need. She let the thoughts drift into her mind before vanishing again, hopes for a life that was no longer hers to claim.

Ravenhold was gone.

Crumbled to dust, taking its knowledge with it, and she had failed to acquire more, to gain all that she should know. *All that I must know.*

She would change things. No more Harvests. No more Marguerites turned into Shirinas. No more hiding from the world. No more trying to control it. *Just...learning.* Just teaching.

The Circle was gone.

Maybe now the remaining adepts would have a clean slate. Peace with the West, dependence on Graydon. The inability to hide. They could make a difference still. With or without magic, they had a knowledge of history and legends unrivaled in all of Graydon.

And if the magic returned, they could really make a difference. They could save Graydon by re-sowing the seeds of life into its earth.

Shirina was gone.

Shirina had been gone for a long time. Shirina had vanished during her last moments in Ravenhold, just as Marguerite had vanished during her first moments in the Keep. The sorceress didn't think it mattered that she was gone.

She was not necessary for Graydon and accepted her fate, a cool logical thought overshadowing the desires in her heart.

"We're not coming back, are we?" she heard a woman's voice ring around her. "We're never going to see each other again?"

Shirina was snapped out of her reverie, her mind forced to focus. The voice seemed so familiar.

A man's voice answered. "Not if we're going to stop Siabala. Not if we're going to save our people."

Graydon. Shirina knew the voices because they were still part of the magic she had wielded for so long. An imprint left on the very fabric of her soul.

"A wall of magic is the only way to stop him," the man said.

The woman echoed his words. "The only way."

Someone caressed her cheek, a warm inviting touch.

Samala had told them to create dams and barrels to stop Siabala. A Wall was an effective dam.

A wall was the only way to stop him. The goodbye swelled in her heart. Without hearing or seeing anything, she could feel the farewell, and the magic released by their deaths to form the seals to hold down Siabala's body. While the Wall kept his soul broken, unable to form without the shadows of magic.

Now there was no more body to seal. So only one magic user would be enough to ensure his soul would never reform.

And it could not be her.

In the land of no lands, Shirina closed her eyes and wished death would allow her peace.

———

Siabala felt the memories stir to life, felt the Crimson Circle's wish for death. He would grant it to her, if he could, but his soul was being torn apart by Graydon and Elihor.

Once again.

Their voices rang around him, imprinted on a magic he had helped create with his brothers.

Elihor and Graydon had betrayed him, trying to keep

it all for themselves, and none for his people. A part of them survived yet, in the ancient magic of the Wall, in the land of no lands where they had abandoned his soul.

He wanted to kill them all. To avenge his people's blood with the humans' blood. If only his soul could form again.

If only he could have destroyed Graydon as quickly as Elihor.

If he had craved only revenge, and not life, he could have killed them all.

SIABALA JERKED AWAKE. He was trying to move, but Cassara did not stop playing her flute, nor did the child stop crying. His face was splotched red and wet with tears, his small arms flung back beside his head. The princess wanted nothing more than to soothe his tears, but she needed them for now.

Soon it would be over.

The world around them glowed, parts with light, parts with darkness, in a breathtaking dance. The strands were separated, but Cassara didn't know what to do now. Siabala's soul was fading, the strands broken apart and the creature that he had once been vanishing before her eyes.

But his outline lingered in mist, waiting for the magic to mingle so that he could be reborn.

Cassara kept playing, but fatigue slowed her fingers. She had to do something, to keep the magics separate, to ensure they would never reunite and reform the soul of Siabala.

How do I stop him?

She was growing exhausted, and the child's cries were waning. They were running out of time!

"The Wall of Loss." Cassara recognized Shirina's voice. She looked around, wanting to answer, but unable to stop playing. She could feel the sorceress' breath on her ear.

"You must summon the Wall of Loss once more to stop his soul from forming. It's the only way." A pause. A hesitation. Without seeing her, Cassara knew the sorceress hated the next words.

"You're the only one who can do it, Cassara. I'm so sorry. I would do it if I could, but I'm simply not powerful enough." There was no bitterness in her voice.

Just grief.

Cassara had meant to come back home. She had never wanted to leave Edoline, and certainly had never meant to leave it forever. She closed her eyes and imagined the sound of the surf against the cliffs, the swaying of the orchard in the breeze, the blooms dancing in the moonlight. She could smell her land, the freshly plowed fields, the apples of autumn, the crisp winter air.

You can go back whenever you like.

Dayshon had promised. Dayshon had promised, but it wasn't up to him. He would remarry. He would find another.

And he would take care of Jayden and Altessa.

She opened her eyes, the child's cries weakening. The

flute seemed so small in her hands. Cherry wood from her land. She should have carved cherry blossoms on it. It was a decision she had never been able to make, and now it seemed so obvious.

She stopped playing and picked up the child, placing the flute in the cloak beside him.

"Will you take him?" Cassara whispered.

Shirina appeared before her, filled with a strand of light, the magics not mixing right away. The sorceress nodded.

Cassara grabbed her arm, almost surprised when she connected with flesh. "Shirina, the Circle must live. Think what you will, but I know it must. Otherwise, this too will be lost. Don't let it be lost, Shirina."

The sorceress' harsh features softened as she nodded, and then vanished in a halo of light, Cassara willing only Graydon's magic within her. To heal her. To keep her whole. And to bring her safely back down.

Once satisfied only the purest magic would enter Shirina, she turned toward her enemy, to the outline of Siabala. She had beheld what damage he could inflict with limited resources and magic. Were he allowed to return, he would destroy everything and everyone she loved.

Cassara had meant to go back home. To see Edoline bloom again in spring.

She kept her eyes on Siabala as she imagined the Wall returning, forced the image to become reality, and witnessed the magic being separated and the seed of Siabala's soul remaining trapped within it. She clung to the image of everything and everyone she loved, creating a defensive spell.

It's your strength, Shirina had said, and she had been right. She was good at keeping others safe.

In the flickers of light around her, she saw the falling blooms of Edoline.

A RUSH of wind and magic knocked Avarielle down. She jumped back up as snow whipped her face, but the adepts had stopped coming, Stormhold's roof a cemetery for its fallen.

Gone was the red glow of Siabala. Instead, flickers of light danced all around her, buzzing with energy. She recognized the Wall of Loss.

"It can't be," she whispered. She looked down at Graysword. The magic wasn't changed at all. It remained the same. The curse was unbroken.

"It can't be," she repeated. Why was the Wall back? Was Siabala not dead?

She felt watched and whipped around, sword at the ready. Shirina stood there, holding the red cloak that had cradled her child.

Avarielle sheathed Graysword and quickly bridged the gap, gently taking the child from the sorceress' arms.

"He is weary, but he will live," Shirina said, her voice flat and tired. So many questions pounded Avarielle's weary mind as she coddled her son, careful not to get blood on him. The sorceress spared her trying to choose one.

"Siabala was too powerful," Shirina sounded exhausted. "We can only make sure his soul can't be reborn. With his body dead, he doesn't really exist now, unless the shadow magic reforms."

Which meant the Grayloft curse wasn't broken. Maybe couldn't be broken.

I'm sorry, Avarielle looked at her child, at the innocent features as he slept, lips parted. She cradled him in one arm and pulled the cloak gently around him, to make sure he wouldn't catch cold. And noticed the flute nestled beside him.

She whispered the question. "Cassara?"

Shirina didn't answer, though Avarielle could see the grief in her eyes.

"Is she dead?"

The sorceress shook her head. "She's gone. The Wall of Loss is needed to keep the magics apart. And it requires her in order to exist."

Avarielle practically spat the words at Shirina. "That's a pile of Circle crap and you know it. Cassara is not her magic. Cassara is much more than her magic." She wanted to shake sense into the sorceress, and only the swaddled baby stopped her from doing so. She wasn't ready to lose anyone else. Not to Siabala.

"Bring her back, Shirina," she whispered, holding back the threat that wanted to escape her. "Bring her back."

Shirina's gaze was unflinching. Her eyes began to

narrow. Avarielle drew in breath. She'd seen that look on the sorceress before.

"What? What is it?" Avarielle demanded to know.

"When Cassara helped you and Pack Nacker's men in the ancient city, when the Circle adepts attacked..."

"You mean the kealers."

She nodded slowly. "Yes. She was far from you and yet she obviously managed to cast a direct spell to you."

She stopped and looked up, frustrated. "I don't know, Avarielle. There might be the possibility to save her body, but she might lose part of her soul. She's split the two before, her body and her soul. It's something Elders and Elites can do to some degree, astrally project, but they can't cast magic at the same time."

The Wall of Loss shimmered more strongly, a steady hum of magic dancing around them. "But," the sorceress said, meeting Avarielle's eyes, "when Graydon and Elihor formed the Wall, they had to sacrifice themselves to maintain it."

"Did they?" Avarielle asked. "I've heard different stories in Elihor. Some say their armies killed them for separating the worlds."

Shirina shook her head. "I heard them, Avarielle. Graydon and Elihor. They knew they weren't coming back."

"Great, now you're hearing things," Avarielle mumbled. "Did they say they had to die? Or just that they'd be separated?" She paused and looked down at the child as she whispered. "For lovers, separation is a form of death."

Shirina sighed. "Fine, say I'm wrong in my interpretation. There is the possibility, then, if we do split Cassara's magic from her body, that her magic will die with her. That the Wall won't be as stable, or as strong without a full seal that includes body and soul. If that's the case, the Wall of Loss would fall again, and Siabala would rise. Even if it holds, when Cassara dies, the Wall vanishes."

Avarielle looked down at the infant she cradled. He was so small in her arms, too covered for her to see. She could feel his tiny breath fill his body, in and out. He was quiet, sleeping from his ordeal.

She gave Shirina a sad smile.

"He's already fought Siabala once, and he's not even an hour old," Avarielle whispered. "Do you think you and your Circle can figure out a way to keep the magic apart, or stop Siabala from reforming? You'll have years, Shirina. Look at what we accomplished without warning in such a short time. We killed part of him, at least."

Shirina looked down, her fists clenched by her side, her white robe billowing in the slight wind.

"And," Avarielle added softly, "do you believe you'll be able to revive the Circle without Cassara's help? What if Jayden and Altessa are also dead, and there is no more heir of Graydon. What then? Is defeating Siabala even a possibility?"

The warrior stopped. She didn't know how else to convince Shirina. Graysword's magic lingered within her, the battle lust still strong. If her son had to one day fight

Siabala, she would make sure he was ready. And never take up the blood oath to Siabala. If the blood of Elihor even allowed him to wield Graysword.

She turned and looked over her land, ravaged and eaten by the ancient cities. Her people would have to move further east. If Cassara lived, she would never need to worry about an Eastland attack.

She sighed. "Shirina, our choice here could be stated in grandiose fashion. Choosing our battlefield. Ensure a descendant of Graydon lives. Eli, we can even say we're trying to fully reunite the lands, why not? But, in the end, it boils down to this: Do we save our friend, or don't we?"

Shirina looked at her and nodded slowly.

"What can I do?" Avarielle asked.

"Make sure I don't get killed," the sorceress said with a slight smile before closing her eyes, her magical chant lingering in the air around her.

Avarielle held the child and watched Shirina stand perfectly still, her eyes closed and her features strained. She had no idea what the sorceress was up to, but knew it would prove Cassara's best chance. She scowled at her own sense of comfort at having the sorceress near.

She stepped back and looked up towards the endless sky, hoping to see more than the tears of magic that surrounded her.

SHIRINA RETURNED to the magical realm, now filled with Cassara's magic. The sky sang and welcomed her home. None of the shadows lingered, nor any dark strand, and Shirina wanted to weep at the pureness of Graydon's magic. Coins of light danced and flashed around her, vanishing and re-appearing lazily, sounding like drops of water in a lake.

The sorceress was not convinced that saving Cassara was the wisest course of action. The Grayloft had made interesting points, but in the end, they were still giving a time limit to the Wall, which could be severely cut short should the princess fall in an accident while still in her prime.

The Circle's knowledge was so limited now it made her heart ache. But perhaps there would be libraries in the ancient cities below. She would have to go look. And with little time and few resources, it would give her a more powerful foothold in reforging the Circle. They would be needed, and all of Graydon would support them.

No Harvest would take place, but that didn't matter. Children and even adults would come of their own accord. And the three Circles could work together. She would make sure of that, as soon as she found all of their survivors.

Stopping Siabala would be one goal, yes, but making sure the magics could safely co-exist was also important. Not the shadow strands that would reform his soul, but the two strands co-existing side-by-side without merging.

The Circle had to live beyond the next battle.

She spotted Cassara, more light than substance, her eyes closed as though she could not bear to look at what she had done.

She reached the princess. Shirina was just an astral projection, a piece of her soul riding the magic, too tired to teleport safely.

"Cassara," she said, "you have to come back with me. We need you. Leave your magic here and come with me. You can do it, just as you did when you saved Avarielle and the Pack in the ancient city."

The princess did not respond. "Trust me, Cassara. Come back with me, to Edoline."

The princess' eyes opened slowly, blue depths void of human emotion. Was she already too far gone? Was her soul too mingled in the creation of the Wall of Loss to leave a piece of it within her body?

She needed to reach her. Shirina tried again. "Cassara, come back to your husband, your brother and your sister. To Edoline. Come back and live your life and watch them live theirs."

Shirina wished the warrior was here. Avarielle was stubborn and a fool, but she could appeal to the princess' emotional side much more effectively. Shirina's strength, really, lay in pissing people off.

That'll have to do.

Shirina stood directly in Cassara's line of sight and looked down at the princess. "Well, since you're stuck here, you might as well know that it turns out the Circle was responsible for your family's death." The princess blinked. Shirina continued. "They allowed the Eloms to continue streaming into Graydon. We could have stopped them long ago, but chose not to."

Two more blinks, and she thought she could see the head tilt slightly to focus on her. As Shirina continued speaking, she felt the bitter words choke her too. "This could all have been avoided. But, in the end, the Circle's survival is what matters. I'll make sure it's stronger than ever."

She whispered the final words, certain the princess now focused on her. "Stay here then. Be weak and satisfied with your simple death." She scoffed. "At least with you out of the way I don't have to worry about playing nice. I think I'll start by repaying that blasted warrior for my jaw."

Cassara could see her now, she was certain. But she still wasn't getting through. Shirina leaned in and whispered in the princess' ear, the blond hair, more light than substance, caressing her face. "Your mother's death was orchestrated by the Circle too. Your aunt was just a pawn, first of the Circle, then of Siabala."

Shirina had barely uttered the words when she was slammed into and something began squeezing her middle. She could *feel* the pain, regardless of the fact that she was just a projection. She tasted blood and could barely breathe.

She kept her gaze cool as she looked at Cassara, though she wanted to plead with her to let her go. Instead, she whispered, "Don't you want to make sure your family never suffers at our hands again? You're the only one who can."

The princess looked at her, her head cocked sideways, her face replaced by stars as Shirina began to lose consciousness. She wasn't certain what would happen to her if she passed out while out of her body, but she imagined the consequences would prove unpleasant.

The pressure released and she gasped. Cassara stood before her, more substantial. More human.

"You're trying to make me angry," she stated, her soft voice resonating in the light around them.

Shirina faced her and gave her a weak smile. "I'd say I succeeded, too." The anger melted from the princess' face and she looked younger again, like in the first days they had met. Shirina was reminded the princess was still so young to have borne so much responsibility.

Shirina stepped up to her and took her in her arms, the princess not fighting back, letting herself be held. The sorceress closed her eyes and remembered suddenly what it had felt like, being held by her own mother. She could feel the tender kiss on her forehead as a child, before the Circle had ripped her away.

"Let's go home, Cassara," she whispered in the princess' ear, and held on tightly to her as the light consumed them both.

AVARIELLE WISHED she knew what was happening. The sorceress still stood, but blood trickled down her chin and splattered on her white robe. Her lips turned a sickly blue shade and her eyes were squeezed in pain.

The warrior looked up and then back at the sorceress.

"I'd keep you safe if you had told me how to bloody help you, you stubborn witch."

The lights flickered in the Wall, the buzz of the magic changing, becoming more like a song. Avarielle held her breath. The sorceress buckled and fell, Avarielle barely catching her with her free arm. She still hit the ground roughly, but at least she didn't bang her head. The world exploded in light around her and she crouched over Shirina and the baby. She hoped no battle was coming.

She had no clue how she would manage to save them both.

The light dissipated and the sorceress' eyes flew open. Avarielle kept a steadying hand on her.

"You're safe," she said. Shirina blinked, met the warrior's eyes, and nodded, taking her at her word.

"Well?" Avarielle asked. The sorceress sat up and looked around, dazed. Avarielle stood and offered her hand, which Shirina accepted. She pulled her up.

"It's beautiful," she heard Cassara say, and the warrior whirled around. The princess stood near, looking up at the Wall, the lights shimmering and singing around them like snowflakes.

Tears welled in her eyes.

This motherhood thing is making me soft.

"It's your magic," Shirina offered. "You'll never be able to use it again."

Cassara barely nodded. She tore her eyes away from the Wall and looked at her two companions, her eyes small and tired.

"Thank you," she said, looking ready to collapse. Avarielle closed the gap between them and held her son in one arm, and the princess in the other. Shirina rose and took the princess' other side, and Cassara smiled at each in turn.

"Let's go home."

EPILOGUE

The blooms were a few days shy of opening, their white tips betraying their imminence, the spring air soft and soothing. Cassara watched her shadow stretch before her as she walked towards the village, the surf rolling in below, striking the cliffs.

She paused and took a deep breath. There was no one else following her this night. Kaden and Carsyn were back at the manor, Emala would be joining her in Massir, and anyone else who might have followed her was now long gone.

Except for Jayden. She took in a deep breath of sea air, letting its coarseness refresh her. He would rebuild with the help of the villagers. The front orchard had been reseeded already, the courtyards manicured, and her sister's grave filled with beautiful blooms.

Jayden locked himself up every night, in their father's study, having already adopted the tired shuffle. He was afraid. And nothing she had managed to say or do would make him come with her on a nighttime walk. Not even if Orliys, now Colonel of Edoline's new army, offered to follow closely.

Cassara stopped at the midpoint between the village and the manor, where she could see both. She reached up and unfastened her amulet, taking it into her palm. The silver and gold always seemed to glow with their own light, ever since it had channeled both the light and the darkness. She imagined Altessa's hand clutching it instead of her own, and she wanted to hurl it into the sea, so that it would never take another life.

She sighed and fastened it back around her neck, trying to ignore its cool presence. Avarielle and Shirina were both insistent she should always keep it with her, so that it would be passed down to her descendants. She understood the necessity, but wished she could have buried it with her sister.

She felt a chill and closed her eyes. She let the sound of the waves wash away Siabala's laughter, allowed the spring warmth to remove the chill of winter still clinging to her bones, and took a deep breath filled with the promise of life, cleansing her of the stench of death she had not yet managed to shed, even though months had already passed.

Tomorrow she would return to Massir, to help her husband rebuild his kingdom. Their kingdom.

She heard a movement beside her and jumped, opening her eyes as she reached for her knife.

"It's me, Cass," Jayden said as he held up his hands. He gave her a little smile. "I thought that since you're leaving tomorrow, I'd join you tonight."

Cassara smiled at him. Their shadows mixed in with those of the orchard, the leaves dancing in the wind, playing an eerie symphony in the night air. Jayden swallowed hard, his hands turning to fists at his side.

She took his arm in hers and they walked towards the village in silence. It would have been an adventure, a year ago. Jayden would have been excited then, whereas now he was afraid of shadows in his own kingdom, no matter how often she told him the enemy had been defeated.

They reached the village and headed for the small inn, Jayden keeping close. He stopped and she turned to look at him. He looked embarrassed.

"I'm not sure it's proper for a king to be doing this," he mumbled. Cassara gave a quick laugh.

"Well, I'm queen of a bigger kingdom, Jayden, and I'm doing it, so brace yourself, we're going in!" She grabbed his arm and practically dragged him into the inn.

The villagers shouted in welcome, and although it was obvious to Cassara that some of their joy was forced, she still appreciated it. Barlos placed a small chair on the stage, and Jayden sat near her. Orliys stepped into the inn and nodded to her from the back. Cassara returned the gesture with her eyes and grasped her freshly oiled flute, the wood smooth and welcoming, carved with the blooms of Edoline.

She brought the flute to her lips and began playing an

old Edoline air, filled with hope of a long summer and a strong harvest. Jayden grinned from where he sat, letting himself be carried by the music. He chatted with some of the villagers and shared laughter with them. Cassara's notes bloomed in the air above them.

Tomorrow, she would be returning to Massir, and she didn't mind. She had her future there, and she missed Dayshon dearly.

Her past would always remain here, in Edoline, and she would return when she needed to. Looking at her brother's light-filled eyes and at the hopeful villagers around him, she knew beyond a doubt that her little kingdom by the sea would bloom even more beautifully than ever before.

SHE COULD SEE the bonfires and dancers in her dream, could hear the singing of her people, could feel their pride and joy. Then the fires went out and the guttural cries of the Eloms could be heard throughout the camp, and she couldn't find her family...Avarielle woke up with a start, sending her covers flying as she shot up.

Disoriented, it took her a few moments to remember where she was. She sat back down on her bed, gulped down some air and allowed herself a low chuckle. She was covered in sweat from the nightmare, and missed the feel of her weapons beside her. She stood up and checked in the crib. Rojon was fast asleep, his little fist clutching his blanket. He looked healthy and was growing up fast, now that they were back in Elihor and he was safe from Graydon's magic.

Avarielle peered out the window. It was dark, and dawn wouldn't come for some time yet.

Perfect.

She threw on some clothes, tied her hair back, and slipped out of the room, leaving Rojon to sleep. Kale was in the room next door, and he would tend to him if he cried, which he rarely did. Navigating the corridor in the dark, she quietly entered the foyer and felt the tug on her heartstrings at the sight of Graysword. The blade stood on display, untarnished, its golden hilt and silver blade glistening in the moonlight. She took a deep breath and stepped forward, grabbing hold of the hilt.

She could feel the magic course through it still, could feel its need to be used, to fight another demon, to protect the heirs of Graydon. Except that there were no more monsters, and the heirs of Graydon were currently too far away for her to help.

She sheathed the blade and walked outside in the cool night air. She smiled, feeling free despite the shackles of her family's curse. She still had a choice, at least for now. Eventually she would need to go back to protect Cassara from anything that might harm her. To keep her safe so that the Wall of Loss would also remain.

But for now, she needed to tend to Rojon, who could not safely remain in the land of Graydon. When he was older, he could withstand the powers of Graydon, as his grandfather had done for so long. But until that time, she didn't want to think about what it meant for their future. She was certain most of her nightmares stemmed from the upcoming necessary separation, her worry taking on the face of old fears and foes.

The warrior reached a quiet hill, beyond the small village. Survivors were popping up from all over, and Elihor was slowly rebuilding. Kale was relishing helping out, which was nice. He was proving a great friend.

She planted her feet firmly, closed her eyes, and took a deep breath. She lowered her head and waited for her heart to beat at the desired pace. Then she reached back, grabbed hold of Graysword and unsheathed it, letting herself feel the strength and magic of the blade. She struck down and turned, opening her eyes and striking out again at an imaginary foe, forcing her muscles to maintain their strength.

She whipped around and struck once more, the blade like an extension of her as she let her feet take over and danced in the night air, guided by a melody of dreams and memories. Her muscles were warmed up, her skin glistened with effort, and the rest of her dream had vanished as her mind had emptied, focused only on the graceful movements of her body.

She stopped and glanced sideways, seeing an unfamiliar shadow by a tree. She wasn't frightened. She doubted she had many foes left in this world who would offer her a true battle challenge.

"Show yourself," she ordered.

The shadow broke from the tree, and she broke into a grin at the sight of Trevon. She quickly closed the gap and embraced him.

"Trevon! I thought you'd be in the West helping rebuild!"

He gave her a quick grin. "Too dull without you, and besides, Breck has it all under control." He shrugged. "I thought I'd come see how you and Little Rojon were doing." He paused. "I crossed Siabala's Rage."

It was Avarielle's turn to shrug. "Not much left in that place."

He glanced at her sideways, as though he intended to ask about her time imprisoned there, but wisely kept his peace. Avarielle was glad. She didn't want to think about it. Nor about the fact that Siabala still had a hold on her. She sheathed Graysword, suddenly not wanting to feel the blade's magic, dormant or otherwise.

"How long are you staying?" Avarielle asked as she began walking back towards the village, intent on changing the subject.

"As long as you'll have me, I guess!"

Avarielle stopped again and turned to face him. "You're welcome as long as you want to stay. But, I may have to ask a favor of you."

Trevon lowered his head respectfully. "Anything, of course."

Avarielle felt tired. She didn't want to impose on her friend any further. He had already done so much. But she still held Siabala's powers, and she understood more than anyone else that he still lived, soul formed or not, and that were he to return, his wrath would be even worse.

"You may not agree once you hear what I have to say," she whispered. He waited patiently.

She looked into the distance, toward the East, where the Wall glittered in the night, its blue and white energy reminding her on her sleepless nights of Cassara and her powers. And of the oath she had taken to protect her, even if it was only to fight off a much older, deeper blood oath.

"I need to make sure Cassara is kept safe." She ran her hand through her hair. "It's something I intend to do myself, at some point, but for now, with Rojon…"

Trevon placed his hands on her upper arms, quieting her. She forced herself to meet his eyes. "I understand," was all that he said.

Avarielle swallowed hard and looked down. Trevon didn't understand, really. They had never told the whole story and never would, for fear it might endanger Cassara's life. But he was loyal to a fault, giving up his own hopes and dreams for those of the Graylofts.

Avarielle smiled at him. "Do you want to see Rojon?"

He smiled back and nodded, letting his arms drop. They resumed walking back towards the village, Avarielle's heart lifted at the peacefulness of Elihor and at Trevon's presence. And then breaking again as she realized it was all just transitory. Trevon would leave again soon, and in a few years, at most, she would follow to stay with Cassara. In case any demons should return.

But tonight, she would go and hold her son, and watch

the sunrise with her oldest friend, and she would allow it to soothe the darkness in her own soul, at least until the next sunset.

SHE DUG into the dirt with her fingers, found the roots of the last plant and cupped it, unearthing it, careful not to wound the plant more than necessary. Once the plant was freed, she stood and walked to the new flower bed, the small holes waiting for their new prize. The earth was rich, and the plants would fare well.

Her work on that flower bed complete, Shirina stood up and stretched her back, looking towards the midday sun. She would work continuously if it were possible, but her body required rest. She had never regained her full strength, following the battle with Siabala.

It didn't matter. What she needed now was more than magic. It was hard work, finding the right allies, and followers as devoted as herself to the knowledge.

The first two were no problem. She was used to difficult labor, and the magical calluses on her hands had been reinforced by the gardening calluses. She had a powerful ally in Cassara, who was beginning her trek back to Massir today. She would join her, soon, and offer her help in rebuilding Graydon. Cassara understood the importance of the Circle, perhaps even better than Shirina herself did, so she would accept the help, knowing that doing so would support Shirina's cause.

She looked around the gardens, the flowers blooming or on the cusp of blooming. She had moved flowerbeds to rebuild a new teleportation circle. Not one that would be used to spread messages or stir political turmoil, but rather one that would serve to bring back knowledge and history. Next, she would build one in Massir, and the Southern Coalition. And the West, if she could convince them she could do good there. That might take some time, especially with Avarielle choosing to remain in Elihor, for now.

She turned and walked back towards the large stone home that had once been Grasky's. She felt her heart ache at the memory of the groundskeeper, killed trying to save Circle sproutlings. He would agree with her basing the new Circle of Graydon in the Lisal Gardens. It was more accessible than Ravenhold had ever been, and would keep them closer to the land. If another attack struck their land again, they would know sooner.

She paused and looked towards the stump of the tree that Graydon had planted, where her own staff had sprouted. It was dead now, petrified. Either the magic of Elihor, Siabala, or the lack of Grasky's care, had seen to its downfall. Regardless, she intended to keep its petrified remains as a reminder of their past and of the fragility of their future.

Someone entered the gardens. Shirina felt her heart swell, surprised at the feel of Circle adepts. It had been months since she had dismissed them all, sending them back home to find their families and help them. To return afterwards if they so chose.

She felt them now, walking the gardens. There were few of them, ten at most, but it was a start. She watched them walk up the path towards her, dressed in Circle robes or plain clothing. She knew she wasn't much of a sight, her own robes dirty from gardening, but the Crimson Circle had been proudly embroidered on them.

Shala stood before her, still proud but less haughty. She was growing up quickly, much to Shirina's pleasure. She had high hopes for the Orange Circle.

"We went home, Crimson Circle Elite, and now we return. The Circle is our home, now."

Shirina nodded slowly, allowing a smile to grace her lips. This would be a different Circle, a real family.

"I'm glad you've decided to come," she said, meeting each adept's gaze. They all looked back with various degrees of fear or joy. She would need to show them, still, that this was different.

"There are rooms in the home for you, in the East Wing. Please choose ones to your liking, and we shall gather after for lunch in the main hall." She paused and met Shala's unflinching gaze. "We have much to discuss and decide. Together."

The Orange Circle nodded and gave her a slight smile, which reached her eyes. It was genuine. Shirina watched them head to the house, energy picking up their steps. They had not known what to expect. Shirina hadn't been certain herself. Once they had all vanished into the house, she followed, letting her eyes adjust for a few moments to the dimness inside. She could hear some whispers down the hall as they chose rooms. She left them to it and turned into the kitchen to pour herself a hot cup of tea, using a bit of magic to keep the water warm. It was a small spell that made all the difference in her day.

She walked to the study, wood floors creaking as she passed a large staircase with a banister. The home was small for the entire Circle, but they could expand it. It was a beautiful start. And in Grasky's study, Shirina had found more books than she could have hoped for. None of the deep secrets of Ravenhold, but enough old tomes on history and science that she knew they had a good foundation on which to rebuild.

She headed for the desk. The two halves of her staff hung on the wall behind it, another reminder of magic's unreliable nature.

Shirina pulled out a pen and ink, and started a fresh sheet of paper. With careful script she jotted down her memories of Circle secrets. All of the secrets, those that were shameful, dark, embarrassing and corrupt, as well as those that would inspire and help rebuild. They could not learn from their mistakes unless they shared them all, and Shirina intended to ensure that none of the knowledge would be lost.

The only thing she would not write down was the weakness of the Wall of Loss. That should Cassara fall, so might its magic. That was knowledge she would pass down only when she was certain of her allies and inheritors.

She wrote carefully, the dirt of her hands mixing with ink. She would rebuild Ravenhold's libraries, first with her memories, then with current history and knowledge from throughout the land.

And then she would help rebuild Graydon, one stone at a time. Until the next battle call sounded.

But by then, the Circle, her Circle, would be ready to answer that call.

The end...for now

www.ingramcontent.com/pod-product-compliance
Lightning Source LLC
Chambersburg PA
CBHW061342190726
48288CB00005B/1569